Regency RAKES

2 Glittering
Regency Romances

AN UNSUITABLE MATCH
by Claire Thornton

THE LOVE CHILD
by Meg Alexander

THE Regency RAKES

THE Regency RAKES

by

Claire Thornton & Meg Alexander

MILLS & BOON

First published in Great Britain 2003 by
Harlequin Mills & Boon Limited,
Eton House, 18-24 Paradise Road,
Richmond, Surrey TW9 1SR

THE REGENCY RAKES © Harlequin Books S.A. 2003

The publisher acknowledges the copyright holders of the individual works as follows:

An Unsuitable Match © Alice Thornton 1995
Originally published under the name Alice Thornton
The Love Child © Meg Alexander 1998

ISBN 0 263 83665 7

138-0103

Printed and bound in Spain
by Litografía Rosés S.A., Barcelona

AN UNSUITABLE MATCH
by
Claire Thornton

Claire Thornton grew up in Sussex. It is a family legend that her ancestors in the county were involved in smuggling. She was a shy little girl, and she was fascinated by the idea that she might be distantly related to bold and daring adventurers of the past – who were probably not shy! When she grew up she studied history at York University, and discovered that smugglers were often brutal men whose main ambition was to make money. This was disappointing, but she still feels justified in believing in – and writing about – the romantic and noble heroes of earlier ages. Claire has also written under the name of Alice Thornton.

Also by Claire Thornton
in Mills & Boon Historical Romance™

RAVEN'S HONOUR
GIFFORD'S LADY

PROLOGUE
1819

'WHAT did he say?' Mary demanded tensely.

'He said, "Tell Mary it's over,"' Donald replied. '"She was right, it would be a very unsuitable match, and. . ."'

'And what?' Mary prompted sharply as the large Scotsman's voice trailed away.

'"And a scandalous marriage,"' he finished unhappily.

Mary stared at him. Her grey eyes were wide and stormy with distress, but she didn't weep. Donald had never seen her weep, no matter how cruel life became – and life had been very cruel to Mary Drayton.

She bent her head abruptly, pressing tightly clenched fists against her mouth as if she was trying to hold back a cry of agony.

She was nineteen years old. A slight girl, slender-boned and apparently fragile. Her soft, tawny-brown hair should have ringed her face in a halo of curls, but it was currently dressed in a severe style which emphasised her slim neck and natural poise.

Her voice, which had sounded so harsh when she'd prompted Donald's reluctant revelation, was normally low and melodious. A testament to the

5

fact that she had been reared as a gentlewoman. But her clothes were cheap and ill-fitting, uncompromising evidence of the hardship and impoverishment she had suffered for the last five years.

Yet, despite everything that had happened to her, her skin was still beautiful and unblemished, and so naturally fair that sometimes it seemed almost translucent.

But now all the colour had been bleached out of her face. She was as white as alabaster, and her eyes were huge and very dark as she struggled to come to terms with the grievous loss she had just suffered.

Donald watched as she rocked silently back and forth, her hands still pressed against her mouth. He was powerless to comfort her.

'They say like always returns to like in the end,' he said heavily.

'Did you give him my letter?' Mary asked, her voice husky with unshed tears.

'Aye.'

'Did he read it? Does he know where I am? Why didn't he come and tell me himself that he'd changed his mind?' With each question she sounded more and more overwrought.

'I don't know.' Donald shrugged helplessly. 'Maybe he didn't have the courage.'

'Of course he has the courage!' she snapped. 'I dare say he wanted to save me pain. After all, he's only told me what I've been telling him for the past four months. It *would* have been a scandalous marriage!'

Her voice cracked on the last few words and she turned away to stare blindly across the room.

'What are you going to do now, lass?' Donald asked awkwardly.

'I don't know.'

'Maybe you should——'

'*Not now*!' Suddenly Mary's composure broke.

She fled out of the parlour and up to her chamber, closed the door and turned the key in the lock. Old habits died hard, and she'd slept behind a locked door for the best part of five years.

Then her strength gave way and she fell on the floor, desolately sobbing out her grief and loss.

Outside there was a gale blowing, and it rattled the window-panes in their shrunken, rotting frames, but Mary didn't hear it. Nor did she hear the missel-thrush in the wind-tossed branches of the cherry tree, singing its heart out in the teeth of the winter storm.

She sat in a chair by the window, and listened to the inn sign creaking in the wind. It was past midnight. No doubt everyone else was asleep, but Mary was still awake. She was calmer now. The storm of tears had passed.

Though she had little energy for the task, she knew it was time to plan for her future. There was no one else to do it for her. Donald had been her loyal defender ever since he'd first entered her life nearly three years ago, but he always relied on her to make the decisions. He had provided the

muscle and she had supplied the wits that had
enabled them both to survive in St Giles. And St
Giles was one of the most notorious thieves'
kitchens in London.

Mary hadn't always lived in St Giles. Her father
had been a rector and, as a child, she had lived a
sheltered, happy life in a quiet rural parish in
Sussex.

But her mother had died when she was twelve.
And then, when she was fourteen, her father had
also died – and she'd discovered that he had made
no adequate provision for her. For nearly a week
she'd thought that she would have to go and live
with the squire, Sir Richard Moorcock, and his
family – to be a poor companion to Sir Richard's
daughters and an unpaid skivvy to his wife.

Then Mary's uncle, Alf, had appeared. Alf was
her mother's brother. But, until his arrival, Mary
had only been dimly aware of his existence. He
had been disowned by his family over twenty years
before, and she had disliked him from the first
moment she met him.

But Sir Richard had been too grateful to be
absolved of responsibility for her to ask any
searching questions, and Alf had taken her. Mary
had sometimes wondered whether, if Sir Richard
had known *where* Alf was taking her, he would
have been less sanguine about his decision.

Because Alf had kept a flash-house – a den of
thieves, murderers and whores – in Church Lane
in St Giles. He had also been a notorious fence,

buying and selling stolen goods from all over London.

The shock of being thrown into such earthly purgatory had nearly killed Mary, but then she'd begun to wonder what Alf wanted with her. She'd soon discovered that he hoped to turn her innocence and quick intelligence to his advantage. A battle of wits and wills had ensued between them, which had ultimately ended in an uneasy truce.

Then, quite by chance, Mary had met Justin and they'd fallen in love. Despite all her protests that she wasn't a suitable match for him, he'd been determined to marry her.

The last time she had seen him, he had been about to visit an old friend in the north, but he had insisted on taking her into a jeweller's shop and having a wedding-ring engraved for her.

Then, only four days previously, while Justin was still away, Alf had been killed in a drunken brawl. Mary had seized her chance. With Donald's help, she had sold her uncle's alehouse to one of his competitors before the news of his death was widely known. Then she'd got out of Church Lane before anyone could retaliate.

She'd known that Justin would have no idea where she'd gone, so she'd sent Donald to tell him while she'd waited at a little inn several miles north of London. For three days she had been happy, not only because she'd escaped Church Lane, but because at last she had something more to offer Justin than her love. A dowry in the form of the profit she'd made selling the alehouse. Only now he wasn't coming. . .

She was abruptly recalled to her surroundings by a crash. She jumped, startled by the unexpected noise, then relaxed as she realised what had happened. The creaking from the inn sign had become increasingly distressed and at last the pole had broken and the sign had smashed to the ground.

Mary wasn't particularly surprised. The innkeeper was so lackadaisical about his responsibilities that he was bound to have ignored the rotten pole. She suspected his negligence was prompted by ill-health rather than sloth. Nevertheless, for three days her fingers had itched to do properly the tasks which he did carelessly and incompletely.

The sound of voices floated up from below as doors opened and people gathered around the fallen sign, but Mary paid no attention to them. She was sitting bolt upright, staring into space, as she suddenly realised how best she could invest her capital and preserve her independence.

'I'm buying the inn,' said Mary to Donald next morning. 'I've already settled the bargain with the landlord. I hope you'll be willing to stay and help me.'

'Aye,' Donald agreed stolidly, without further comment.

The Scotsman had survived twelve years in Wellington's army, but he only thought quickly in a fight – the rest of the time he was quite content to let Mary do his thinking for him. Indeed, there were times when it almost seemed as if he would be lost without her. Certainly she had provided him with both his conscience and his purpose in life for the past three years.

'And in the meantime,' Mary continued, 'I'd like you to go up to London and collect the wedding-ring Justin ordered for me before he went away.'

'*What*?' Donald exclaimed, startled. 'Why? I told you what he said.'

'I know. But I'm very young to be a landlady,' Mary replied calmly. 'And a widow is much more respectable than a spinster.'

Donald stared at her, chewing his lip uncertainly. 'Surely it would be better not to have a constant reminder of what's happened?' he protested.

'Perhaps, but I want that ring,' said Mary. She spoke quietly, but Donald had heard that tone in her voice before, and it was clear that she would brook no argument. 'I don't imagine Justin will have any use for it,' she continued. 'And if I'm going to be anyone's widow, I might as well be his. I'll never marry anyone else.'

CHAPTER ONE
1826

THE November sun had already set when the carriage drew up outside the posting-house.

'We'll spend the night here,' Mr Penrose decided.

'Yes, sir.' Mary climbed down from the coach and cast a quick, professional glance over her surroundings. She had nothing to complain of in the speed with which the ostlers had responded to their arrival, but she would reserve final judgement until she had seen the state of the linen and tasted the supper that was laid before them.

'We'll eat in an hour when we've had time to recover from the journey,' said Mr Penrose.

'Yes, sir,' Mary agreed, and stood back to let him precede her into the inn.

Fifty-five minutes later she finished doing her hair, cast a shawl around her shoulders to protect her from the winter draughts, and went down to supper. But when she reached the foot of the stairs she hesitated. She had no idea which of the private parlours had been assigned to Mr Penrose.

She looked around for someone to ask but, although she could hear a mumur of voices coming from the taproom, there was no one in sight. She shrugged, and knocked lightly on the first door she came to. If it was't Mr Penrose who answered, she could always apologise and withdraw.

A familiar voice called for her to come in. She did so before she'd had time to think. Then she stopped short, as if she'd been hit with a mallet, staring in disbelieving shock at the man in front of her.

It hadn't been Mr Penrose's voice and it wasn't Mr Penrose pouring himself a glass of brandy, his back half turned to the door.

'What is it?' he asked, without troubling to look at her.

He was a tall, dark-haired man, dressed in the clothes of a gentleman. But, despite the elegance of his appearance, there was no disguising the innate power in his muscular body.

Although it was a cold evening he had discarded his coat, and his well-cut silk waistcoat emphasised the broad set of his shoulders and his lean waist. Even when he was performing the simple task of pouring brandy he moved with the contained, controlled power of a lazy tiger. And Mary knew that he was a fearless horseman and an excellent athlete.

He still had his back half turned towards her. But she knew that when he looked at her he would have strong, unforgettable features. A square jaw, slightly aquiline nose, and penetrating hazel eyes which were sometimes humorous, sometimes grave – and always capable of seeing more in two seconds than most men could see in a lifetime.

It was Justin!

The crazy beating of her heart seemed to thunder in her ears. She felt dizzy with shock. Unable to move or utter a single sound in response to his question.

'Well?' he demanded, swinging round impatiently when she didn't reply.

He stopped abruptly, the words dying on his lips, and she saw his eyes widen in surprise.

In the hallway behind her the shadows were dark but, though she didn't know it, she was standing in a circle of warm candlelight. Her fair skin was like porcelain, and her brown hair shone softly in the glowing light. She looked hardly older than when he'd last seen her.

She stared at him, her gaze locked on his face, her lips still slightly parted with surprise. He had changed, but at first she thought the differences were only superficial – then she met his eyes.

His gaze was hard and cynical. She could see no remains of affection, let alone love for her – only dawning anger in the fierce hazel eyes.

'Dear me,' he drawled, his calm voice at variance with the barely concealed hostility in his expression. 'What an unexpected pleasure. How did you find me?'

'I didn't.' Mary was too shaken to feel any surprise at his question. She only knew that he was furious at their unexpected meeting. It hurt her almost more than she could bear. 'I wasn't looking for you. It was an accident.' She felt her hands begin to tremble and hid them in the folds of her skirt.

Justin Hawkridge smiled sardonically. 'A very convenient accident,' he observed.

He strolled past her and closed the door. She felt her throat constrict as he brushed against her. She didn't know why he was so angry, but she knew him well enough to be acutely aware of the power in his large, lean body, and the effort it was costing him to appear calm.

She pressed her arms more closely against her sides, trying to make herself as small as possible. She was struggling desperately to maintain her own composure, but it didn't occur to her to leave. She had never walked out on Justin before, and somehow she couldn't bring herself to do so now.

He returned to the sideboard and poured out a second glass of brandy. 'How much do you want?' he asked harshly.

'What?' she repeated stupidly, staring at the brandy he was offering her in bewilderment. Nothing he said seemed to be making any sense.

'Let's not be coy about this, sweetheart,' he advised curtly. 'We're not children, and there's nothing more sordid than wrapping up a straight-forward bargain in mealy-mouthed euphemisms.'

Mary took the brandy automatically since that was clearly what he expected her to do. She still didn't know what he was talking about. If he had shown pleasure, or even indifference, at meeting her again she would have been better able to cope with the situation. But his undisguised hostility was undermining her confidence and her wits.

Only pride enabled her to keep her confusion and distress under any measure of control.

She struggled to understand what Justin meant while he watched her sardonically.

'You think I've come to ask you for money,' she said at last. 'Because I . . .because we. . . You think I've come to beg – or maybe even to black-mail you!'

Her voice rose in shocked realisation, and she stared at him in horror, seeing confirmation of her suspicion in his unyielding expression.

'Oh, you can't blackmail me, sweetheart,' he replied mockingly. 'It would be your reputation – or what's left of it – that would suffer, not mine. But I might be amenable to a little, no doubt charming persuasion.' His gaze flicked over her suggestively.

Mary closed her eyes, sickened and appalled by what he was insinuating. Yet she knew that, from his point of view, it was a reasonable assumption. There was an unmistakable aura of wealth about him, and she thought it likely that his intermittent differences with his family had been reconciled. It wasn't surprising if he thought she wanted to trade on her past association with him.

Nevertheless, now that the first shock of seeing him had passed, she was bitterly hurt and angry that he could accuse her of such a dreadful thing. She had done nothing to deserve it.

She met his gaze boldly, fierce, unconquerable pride in her stormy grey eyes.

'No, sir,' she said, her voice as cold and unyielding as his had been. 'I didn't know you were staying here until I opened the door and saw you. It was an honest mistake. I won't trouble you any further.'

She put down the brandy glass with an angry click and turned towards the door.

'*Mary*!'

She glanced back at him, startled by the urgency in his voice. But, before he had a chance to say anything else, there was an ingratiating knock at the door, and the landlord came in.

'Your dinner is nearly ready, my lord; I wondered if you——?' He broke off, staring at Mary in surprise.

'Ma'am! I didn't expect. . .'

'I came into the wrong room by mistake,' she explained. 'I couldn't remember which parlour you had assigned us. I was just leaving.'

'I do beg your pardon! Please, allow me to escort you. Your uncle is waiting for you in the rear parlour. My lord, please excuse me; I will be with you shortly.' The landlord divided an anxious bow between them.

Mary allowed herself to be ushered out of Justin's presence in a state of disquietude. She was deeply disturbed by their unexpected encounter but, even though she told herself that they had nothing more to say to each other, she was almost equally distressed that they had been interrupted. It was hateful to part with him on these terms.

She wondered why he had called her back, and then thought bitterly that it was probably to heap further accusations on her head. She wished she'd never met him again. She'd understood why he hadn't felt able to marry her, but it was agonisingly painful to be confronted with his cruel assumptions about her.

My lord, she thought, remembering what the landlord had said. That meant Justin's father was dead. He had finally acceded to his inheritance. No wonder he had such an air of prosperity. Donald had been right – like returned to like – and a baron's son would never completely forget what was due to his position.

It was very difficult to join Mr Penrose and talk calmly to him as if nothing untoward had happened. But Mary had had a great deal of practice at doing difficult things, and Mr Penrose was too preoccupied by his own troubles to notice if she seemed distracted.

'Uncle?' she asked, raising her eyebrows enquiringly, when the waiter had left them alone.

Mr Penrose flushed uncomfortably. He was a thin, rather stooped man in his late fifties, who seemed older because his manner was inclined to be both fussy and anxious. He had been a regular customer at Mary's inn for several years, and she was fond of him, but she couldn't help wondering what his reaction would be if he ever found out about her life before she'd become landlady of the Lazy Cat.

'I thought it would save you embarrassment,' he explained hurriedly. 'It's most unusual that we should be travelling alone together like this – and after what happened this morning...'

Mary suppressed a smile. That morning an impudent ostler had made a suggestive remark about old men and young women travelling together, and Mr Penrose had been brooding about it all day.

'Thank you,' she replied. 'But please don't feel badly on my account.'

'But I do,' he said earnestly. 'You have put yourself to so much trouble on my behalf, and I am involving you in a situation which promises to be most unpleasant – most unpleasant indeed.' He dabbed anxiously at his mouth with his napkin.

'I involved myself,' said Mary calmly. 'It may be that I'm mistaken. I hope I am.'

'Tell me again what you heard,' Mr Penrose begged. 'Perhaps there has been some mistake.'

'It was late one evening,' Mary began patiently, although she had told the story to Mr Penrose many times before. 'Your nephew Samuel was staying at the Lazy Cat on his way back to Bath after visiting you. He'd had half a bottle of brandy, and he was talking to his manservant, Phelps, when I overheard him. He said that you'd flatly refused to cover his debts, or allow him to draw on his own inheritance to do so.'

'It's true.' Mr Penrose nodded energetically. 'I thought if I forced him to face up to the consequences of his imprudence he would be more responsible in future. It was a most unpleasant interview. He used very violent language.'

Mary looked sympathetic, but she didn't comment directly on what Mr Penrose had said.

'Then he said that if he failed to repay his debt to one particular money-lender he might as well blow his brains out there and then because the man wouldn't wait another two years to get his money,' she continued.

'I always said it was foolish for my brother to leave his fortune in such a constrained way,' Mr Penrose remarked. 'I am to have control of it until Samuel is twenty-five – or until I feel he is sufficiently responsible to manage it himself.'

'I know, you told me,' said Mary drily. 'You also told me that if you died before Samuel was twenty-one another trustee would be appointed, but if you die after that time he can claim control of his fortune immediately. I think your brother must have had a very unusual way of managing his affairs.'

'He did,' said Mr Penrose unhappily. 'I suppose he thought that because I was so much younger than him the possibility of my death wouldn't arise – and he wouldn't have wanted to insult Samuel by appointing a trustee from outside the family.'

Once again Mary refrained from comment. She had never met the elder Mr Penrose, but she knew his son. If Mr Penrose senior had been anything like Samuel, it didn't seem impossible that he had deliberately engineered a situation which would lead to conflict among his surviving relatives.

'Please go on – I've been interrupting you,' said Mr Penrose.

'Well, then he talked about ways of getting hold of the money he needed,' Mary continued. 'He seemed to think he had two options. The first was to continue pursuing Miss Burleigh in Bath. . .'

'I believe she's a very considerable heiress,' said Mr Penrose. 'In normal circumstances I would say it was a highly suitable match——'

'The second possibility. . .'

'Yes, I know. He threatened to. . .to arrange a fatal accident for me.' Mr Penrose twisted his napkin nervously between his fingers. 'Perhaps you were right and I should have brought my lawyer with me – or my agent. But the *scandal* if anyone else found out about this. . .and perhaps it's all a mistake. . . Oh, my dear Mrs Drayton,' he added anxiously. 'I didn't mean to question your integrity – but perhaps he was only talking in his cups and didn't mean anything by it.'

'I hope that's all it is,' Mary said quietly.

'And I shouldn't have brought you,' Mr Penrose asserted, returning to his original theme. 'Exposing you to——'

'I made the charge against him,' said Mary firmly. 'It's only fair that I should be willing to attest to it when you confront him and, if necessary, apologise for my mistake.'

She also felt very strongly that, since it was her warning which had prompted Mr Penrose to confront his nephew, she had an obligation to ensure that no harm came to him as a result of doing so.

She would have felt happier if Mr Penrose had brought his lawyer or man-of-business with them, but despite her misgivings she was reasonably confident of her ability to handle the situation.

Besides, she was honest enough to admit to herself that, after seven years of respectable inn-keeping, she was beginning to feel bored and restless. She might wish she were going to Bath in less fraught circumstances, but she couldn't deny she was looking forward to the visit – or at least, she had been.

But that was before she'd met Justin. It was hard to concentrate on Mr Penrose's problems when Justin was only on the other side of the wall. His accusations had wounded her to the heart. But she didn't understand why he'd been so angry, and she kept wondering what he'd been going to say when the landlord had interrupted them.

'I beg your pardon?' She realised Mr Penrose had said something to her and she hadn't been paying attention.

'I was suggesting that we retire,' he said. 'We've travelled a long way today and you look tired. I am sorry to have caused you so much incon-venience. I shouldn't have brought you, but I really am grateful for your company.'

Mary summoned up a smile. 'I only hope that my presence can be of more practical benefit to you when we meet Samuel,' she said sincerely.

She didn't sleep at all that night. Her mind was full of Justin. Seeing him had vividly reminded her

of the time when they had been lovers. Unlike
many young noblemen, he hadn't ventured into St
Giles on a wild spree, but because he was genuinely curious about all aspects of London.

The first time she'd seen him, he'd been sitting
quietly in the corner of her uncle's alehouse. His
clothes had been shabby, and he'd clearly had
nothing of value on his person – a prudent precaution – but Mary had known immediately that
he was in a different class from Alf's normal
clientele. Even if his voice and manner hadn't
betrayed him, his clean-limbed, active grace would
have done so.

It had surprised Mary that no one bothered
him. But both Alf and his customers had left
Justin alone. She'd discovered later that his relative immunity to harm was caused by a combination of two things – his enviable ability to fade
into the background when he wished to do so, and
his equally notable ability to defend himself if
anyone decided to dispute his right to remain
unobtrusive. Since he wasn't doing any harm, and
he wasn't an informer, it was easier to leave him
alone.

And after his first visit Alf had even become
quite proud of his noble customer, and let it be
known that he would be extremely displeased if
any harm came to Justin.

But Mary still hadn't been able to understand
what he was doing in the flash-house until she'd
seen his sketchbook. Many of the sketches had
been done from memory – even Justin was wary

of getting out his sketchbook in the Blue Boar –
but all had been equally effective in capturing the
squalor and indignity of life in St Giles.

Despite his own privileged position Justin had
seemed to have an insight into the lives of those
less fortunate which was neither patronising nor
sentimental. After nearly five years among the
coarse, wretched, or dangerous inhabitants of
Church Lane, Mary had responded instinctively to
his pictures – and to the man who'd had the sensitivity to produce them. They'd fallen in love with
the sketchbook open beside them.

But that had been seven years ago. And when
Mary remembered the way he had spoken to her
last night, and the rich elegance of his fine clothes,
she began to wonder whether Justin Hawkridge
was the same man.

She got up early, and went out into the cold,
pallid morning light. A walk might clear her mind
and she strode briskly along the highway for over
a mile.

The sun was rising, illuminating half the sky
with a brilliant pink and silver sunrise, when she
retraced her steps. She paused to admire it, resting
her hands on top of a gate to look out across a
silver-turquoise meadow and the dark line of trees
beyond.

The wind caught a stray tendril of tawny hair
and whipped it into her face. She tucked it back
inside her bonnet with slender fingers, and shivered. She'd never been extragavant, and very few
of the clothes that were practical for her life at the

Lazy Cat were also suitable for a visit to Bath. She was wearing her best pelisse, which looked reasonably elegant but was nowhere near as warm as her everyday overcoat.

She rubbed her hands together to bring some warmth into them, and carried on walking. But when she returned to the inn, instead of going straight inside, she went to visit the stables. It was something she did every morning at the Lazy Cat and she was naturally curious to make comparisons.

A couple of stable-lads looked at her curiously, but no one approached her. She paused in front of a stall where a handsome chestnut snorted, tossing his head and eyeing her warily. She spoke to him softly and eventually he deigned to let her pat him.

She heard footsteps behind her, but she didn't look round.

A quiet voice said, 'Careful ma'am, 'e don't always take to strangers. Sometimes 'e can snap. Mind you,' the groom added, ''e seems to 'ave taken to you.'

Mary glanced at the man and smiled. 'Is he a high-stickler, or just bad tempered?' she asked, stroking the chestnut's nose. He snorted and nudged her hand.

'Just bad tempered, I reckon,' the groom replied.

Mary laughed, and the horse tossed his head at the unexpected sound. 'I'll bear that in mind,' she said.

The groom looked perplexed, and then embarrassed. 'I'm sorry, ma'am, I didn't mean you weren't...'

'I know,' she reassured him.

He was about twenty, she guessed, though his thin face looked older. He was short and slightly built, with narrow, stooping shoulders. He had probably been underfed for most of his childhood, but his eyes lit up when he looked at the horse. He wore the costume of a tiger – a gentleman's personal groom.

'What's his name?' Mary asked, nodding towards the chesnut.

'Barabbas,' the groom replied, always willing to talk about his charges.

'And that one?' Mary gestured to the next stall, where a perfectly matched chesnut mare stamped her forefoot in the straw.

'Mary...'

'A name with many associations,' said another, deeper voice behind her. 'So often it conjures up an image of saintliness – but it could just as easily describe a whore.'

Mary caught her breath. She hadn't heard Justin approach. She started to tremble, so she gripped the top of the wooden panel to hide it. Another hand appeared and lightly gripped the panel a few inches away from hers. He must be standing right behind her. She felt trapped.

'You startled me, sir,' she said, without turning round.

'My apologies.' But there was no apology in Lord Hawkridge's voice.

The tiger faded discreetly away and Mary was left alone with Justin. She knew she ought to turn and face him, but he was too close behind her – and she couldn't bear the possibility that he might still have that cold, hostile look in his eyes.

'Does this uncle treat you any better than the last one?' Justin asked mockingly in her ear.

'He's not. . .' she began instinctively, then bit her lip as she realised what Justin would inevitably think if she denied any relationship with Mr Penrose.

'I didn't think he was,' Justin murmured provocatively. 'I am reasonably well-acquainted with your family tree, sweetheart. Alf was your only surviving relative.'

She felt a light touch on her hair, then his fingers gently stroked the nape of her neck. She froze, startled by his caress. But as he continued to play with a tendril of her hair she was overwhelmed by a flood of sensations and remembered emotions. Her heart began to race and she was rooted to the spot, no longer capable of rational thought. He was very close behind her and she longed to turn towards him, to feel him take her in his arms, but she was afraid to move in case it broke the spell. This was only an interlude, it couldn't be real.

'I'll admit Penrose is wealthy,' said Justin softly, his breath ruffling Mary's hair, 'but couldn't you do better for yourself than a wizened old man?

There are plenty of younger, more exciting lovers to choose from.'

'He is *not* my lover!' Mary swung round indignantly, heedless of the consequences, and found herself almost breast to breast with Justin.

'Not a very satisfactory one if my lightest touch can hold you so mazed!' Justin taunted her. His face was in shadow; she couldn't see his expression.

She heaved in a deep, outraged breath, but before she could say anything his arms locked about her and his mouth closed on hers. She struggled to free herself, bracing her hands against his shoulders and pushing him away, but he was far too strong.

She wasn't afraid, but she'd seen too much violence to find any pleasure in an embrace that was forced upon her. She was on the point of kicking him – which would have been painful, since she was wearing wooden pattens – when his hold on her relaxed and, instead of being demanding, his lips became coaxing on hers.

All she had to do now was step back and she would be free – but she couldn't do it. He knew her too well and he was taking advantage of his knowledge.

It was cold in the stables, but his body was warm against hers. She could feel the power in his large frame, and now that his strength was no longer being used against her it excited her. She didn't remember if he'd made her feel like this in St Giles, but a flood of unfamiliar, stimulating sensations were washing over her. He teased her lips gently, persuasively, until they parted to allow him to explore her mouth more fully.

Mary couldn't resist. She had needed him and wanted him for so long that now she felt like a starving woman who'd been offered food. She had to take it, even though she knew the bread was poisoned. There was no future in this. They would never meet again. And, like all his kind, Justin Hawkridge was taking what he wanted, when he wanted it.

His kiss became more urgent, stirring dormant passions within Mary. Hardly knowing what she was doing, she pressed herself against him more closely, her hands beginning to slide up around his neck. . .

Then Barabbas snorted, his head only inches from theirs, and they were both startled. Mary sudenly realised what she was doing, and shoved Justin away from her, the violence of her reaction revealing how much his kiss had affected her.

'Dammit, Justin! You may be a lord but I'm not a common whore!' she insisted furiously, her churning emotions finding release in anger.

'There never was anything common about you,' he agreed sardonically. He was breathing rather rapidly, but otherwise he seemed completely in control of himself – and the situation. 'But I still say you could do better for yourself. Or is Penrose an indulgent companion? Does he allow you to see other men as well?'

Mary slapped Justin hard across the mouth. He

seized her wrist and held it in a vice-like grip. For a moment he loomed over her, but she was too angry to be afraid.

'You harpy!' he snarled. 'I ought to beat you for that!'

'The mark of a true gentleman!' Mary mocked, wrenching her arm out of his grasp. 'First you make unfounded, unspeakable accusations about me, then you want your revenge when I retaliate. You used to have more integrity.'

'*Integrity*. . .!' Justin exclaimed.

'Mr Penrose is not my lover,' Mary said through clenched teeth.

'He's not your uncle either.'

'He's my husband's uncle.'

They stared at each other in silence. A mail-coach pulled up in the courtyard outside, and the yard and stables were suddenly full of ostlers. Mary stepped aside to allow a string of glossy brown horses to be led past her, but apart from that neither she nor Justin paid any further attention to the activity all around them.

Justin caught her left hand in his, looking down at the ring on her third finger. 'I see,' he said, his voice suddenly expressionless. 'Have you been married long?'

'Four years.' Mary drew her hand away, hoping he couldn't hear the pounding of her heart. It was a lie, but it didn't matter. The only thing that mattered was that she couldn't let Justin outface her.

'Then it seems I must offer my belated congratulations.' He bowed ironically. 'Does he know about your life in the Blue Boar?'

Mary lifted her head proudly. 'Do you think I would marry anyone who didn't?' she asked coldly. 'Good day, sir.'

CHAPTER TWO

'I'VE made enquiries,' said Mr Penrose. 'Samuel has gone out of town on a visit for several days.'

'Do you know where he has gone? Is he expected to return?' Mary asked briskly.

'No. He doesn't seem to have been very informative about his destination,' Mr Penrose said, answering the first of her questions. 'But they certainly seem to expect him to come back,' he continued, 'and Miss Burleigh is still here. Do you think we should try to find him?'

'No,' said Mary firmly. 'It would be most uncomfortable to confront him with our suspicions under someone else's roof. We'll wait for him to return.'

'But I am keeping you away from your business for so long,' Mr Penrose protested.

'Donald will be able to manage things for a few days,' Mary said. 'And I have never been to Bath before. I assure you, sir, if you would do me the kindness of escorting me to the Pump Room tomorrow, I will feel well-repaid for the delay.'

'My dear Mrs Drayton, I would be honoured,' he said.

'The story of how Bath was founded always reminds me of the story of the Prodigal Son,' said

Mr Penrose as they made their way to the Pump Room next morning. 'The way Bladud became a swineherd when he was turned out of his father's household. But of course he had to leave because he had leprosy, not because he was greedy for material pleasures.'

Mr Penrose paused, a brooding look in his eyes. He was obviously thinking about another young man who was all too greedy for material pleasure.

'Tell me more about Bladud,' Mary prompted.

'Well, then the pigs began to develop sores on their skins!' Mr Penrose exclaimed. 'Think how dreadful the poor fellow must have felt – that even pigs weren't safe in his company. But then one day the swine plunged into a muddy quagmire after some acorns – and when they came out their skin had been cured! Then Bladud was able to go home, and later he returned and built a city on the site of his cure.'

'And people still drink the waters to this day,' Mary murmured. 'I wonder if anyone has tried it on pigs recently?'

'Mrs Drayton!' Mr Penrose looked shocked, then unexpectedly mischievous. 'Perhaps we won't enquire too deeply into that,' he suggested.

The Bath season was already underway, and the Pump Room was full of people. Some of them were there to take the waters, but most of them were more intent on seeing and being seen. They promenaded up and down under the watchful eye of Nash's statue, accompanied by discreet music from a small chamber orchestra.

Mary was fascinated. Since her childhood she had never had a chance to mix on equal terms with the gentry, let alone the aristocracy. Bath was no longer as fashionable as it had once been, but it still had its adherents. She watched them with interest.

'I think perhaps I'll take a glass of water,' said Mr Penrose. 'The last few days have been very trying; it would be a sensible precaution – don't you think?'

'It would indeed,' Mary agreed. She noticed that Mr Penrose seemed to be increasingly prone to ask her opinion, but he had good reason to feel anxious and in need of reassurance.

'Good gracious!' he exclaimed suddenly. 'I do believe that's my old friend Benjamin Knightley with his wife. I haven't seen him for years!'

Mr Penrose began to thread his way eagerly through the throng, leaving Mary with no choice but to follow.

'Penrose!' Mr Knightley shook his hand vigorously. 'You've been buried in Hertfordshire for so long I thought you were dead!'

'No, no!' Mr Penrose assured him, wincing slightly at the suggestion. 'How do you do, ma'am?' He shook Mrs Knightley's hand, then turned towards Mary. 'Allow me to introduce my niece, Mary Drayton. Mary, these are my old friends Benjamin and Isabella Knightley.'

'I'm very pleased to meet you,' Mary said courteously, although she couldn't help wondering about the wisdom of the introduction.

'Delighted, I'm sure,' Mr Knightley replied gruffly. 'You must be Abigail's girl. I must say, you don't look much like her. Didn't she marry a Campbell?'

'That's right,' said Mr Penrose quickly. 'I'm afraid Mary is a widow.'

'Oh, you poor thing!' Isabella exclaimed sympathetically. 'So young, too. Do join us.'

'You're very kind,' said Mary. She sat down, glancing briefly at Mr Penrose who was nodding and beaming in a most uncharacteristic fashion. It had never occurred to her that he would entangle her quite so deeply in his family matters, but he seemed happy with the result.

The next fifteen minutes provided Mary with equal parts amusements and bewilderment. She managed to field a number of questions about people she'd never heard of, before encouraging Mrs Knightley to expatiate on her own family. The subject which Mrs Knightley most enjoyed discussing was her grandchildren, and Mary was listening to a convoluted description of an incident in the nursery, when she glanced up and saw Justin approaching them.

He moved with the same powerful, easy grace which Mary remembered so well. The room was crowded, but he had no need to force a passage through the people. He smiled and exchanged greetings with the few acquaintances he had in the Pump Room, while strangers stepped instinctively out of his path, as if acknowledging that he had the right of way. Mary wondered confusedly how she could ever have imagined that he had a talent for fading into the background.

Mrs Knightley became aware that she no longer had Mary's full attention, and looked up to see what had distracted her.

'Good heavens!' she exclaimed. 'He seems to be heading straight for us. Benjamin! Do you know that man?'

Mr Knightley looked round, and almost goggled at the sight of Justin. 'It's Lord Hawkridge! He was pointed out to me in London, but I've never spoken to him. Penrose. . .?'

'No!' said Mr Penrose in a strangulated voice.

If Mary hadn't been so agitated, she would have found their reaction amusing, but as it was she could only stare at Justin with a considerable amount of apprehension. He was every inch the aristocrat in his bearing, but he had a dangerous gleam in his eyes.

He came to a halt in front of them, and bowed to Mary. 'Mrs Drayton,' he said suavely, 'I do hope you've recovered from the discomforts of your journey?'

'Yes, thank you, my lord,' she replied sedately. 'Please allow me to introduce you to my uncle, Mr Penrose, and his old friends, Mr and Mrs Knightley. Lord Hawkridge.'

She carried out the introductions without faltering, though inwardly she was seething with speculation about Justin's presence, and anxious about what he might say. She didn't miss the cold expression in his eyes as he acknowledged Mr Penrose with a brief nod.

'I had no idea you were acquainted with his lordship, my dear,' said Mr Penrose nervously.

'It was only a very fleeting meeting,' Mary explained hastily, her quick glance daring Justin to contradict her. 'I accidentally went into the wrong parlour by mistake, one night at an inn when we were on our way to Bath. It hardly seemed worth mentioning.'

'Not worth mentioning!' Mr Knightley croaked. 'My lord, it's an honour to meet you! I'm a great admirer of yours.'

'You flatter me, sir,' Justin replied drily. 'Mrs Drayton, perhaps you would care to take a stroll around the room with me – unless you have any objection – sir?' The last few words were directed at Mr Penrose, and there was a cold, almost contemptuous expression in Justin's eyes as he said them.

'No – oh, no,' said Mr Penrose. 'No, indeed.'

'Are you here for the sake of your health, my lord?' Mary asked, accepting the support of Justin's arm without obvious enthusiasm. 'My uncle was telling me only this morning how efficacious the water once proved in the curing of swine.'

Justin's cold, haughty expression relaxed slightly.

'You've just shocked your fish-faced companion out of what little wits he appears to have,' he said sardonically as they walked away. 'Don't you have any understanding of the respect due to my position?'

'No,' said Mary flatly. 'Do you have any understanding of how much you've just embarrassed me?'

'Oh, I think I have a very fine appreciation of that – Mrs Drayton,' Justin retorted. 'Your paramour is very keen to show you off to his friends, is he not?'

'He is *not*——' Mary began through gritted teeth, then broke off as another couple came too close.

'But he isn't your husband's uncle – because you don't have a husband,' Justin pointed out. 'And this——' he laid his hand over hers, his fingers lightly touching her wedding-ring ' – is a prop to provide you with added respectability.'

Mary tried to draw her hand away, but his grasp tightened and she desisted. She was beginning to feel extremely disturbed. It was bad enough to have to walk side by side with Justin, pretending that they were no more than chance acquaintances, without the added distraction of his hand on hers. His touch filled her with conflict, because her heart and body still remembered when they had been lovers, even though she was currently furious with him – and confused by his angry response to her.

'I should have used another name,' she said bitterly. 'But it never occurred to me I'd need to. As I keep telling you, there's a perfectly innocent explanation for the whole thing, though why I should have to explain anything to you I can't imagine.'

'You have very flexible principles,' said Justin savagely. 'I expect you find them useful in your profession. But you really ought to change your name for your father's sake.'

'My *father*!' Mary exclaimed.

'I dare say that, as a man of God, he would be most disappointed in the path your life has taken.'

Mary jerked her hand away from him. 'As a man of God he should have made more provision——' She broke off, catching her lower lip between her teeth. Her face was rigidly expressionless, but her grey eyes were stormy.

'You're drawing attention to us, sweetheart,' Justin murmured, and drew her hand through his arm again.

Mary saw that they were indeed the centre of attention, and forced herself to appear composed, 'You are a bastard, Justin,' she muttered through grimly smiling lips.

'You may be right,' he conceded.

'What?' Mary's eyes flew to his face.

'That last comment was below the belt. Strike it from the record – but I don't retract anything else I've said.'

Mary caught her breath, more shaken by his oblique apology than she had been by his accusations. It was almost frightening to realise how well he knew her – all the weak spots in the armour she had built around herself. No one else could have wounded her so unerringly – and no

one else could have recognised so quickly what
they'd done.

'Is that Nash?' she asked, speaking at random,
looking up at the statue in an alcove at one end of
the room.

'Yes.'

'Well, now I've seen the Pump Room,' she said.
'It's turned out to be far less remarkable than I'd
supposed. I'd like to return to the others.'

'As you wish.' Justin inclined his head ironically. 'I'm sure you'll find their company less
stimulating than mine.'

'I certainly hope so,' Mary retorted. 'Are you
staying in Bath long, my lord?'

'That depends.'

'On what?'

Justin smiled blandly.

'Ah, allow me to return your niece to you,' he
said as they rejoined Mr Penrose and the
Knightleys. 'I'm afraid she's not impressed by the
unfortunate Beau, but then I understand that he
himself often had a rather cavalier way with visitors to his domain. Good day to you all.'

He nodded briefly and strode away.

'Well, what a very unusual man,' said Mrs
Knightley in the silence that followed his
departure.

'He's a very rude man,' said Mary forthrightly.
'He seems to delight in setting people's backs up.'

'My dear! What did he say to you?' Mrs
Knightley breathed.

'Nothing of consequence,' said Mary crisply.

'But the tone of his conversation showed neither kindness nor consideration for others. I cannot abide a man who shows no charitable feelings towards those less fortunate than himself.'

She caught herself up as she saw that the Knightleys were staring at her in open-mouthed astonishment, while Mr Penrose was listening almost proudly to her outburst.

'Well, never mind Lord Hawkridge,' she said more temperately. 'Mrs Knightley, you were telling me about what happened to Jemima the day the squirrel got into the nursery.'

It was late afternoon when Mary slipped out, unaccompanied, to make her way to Barton Fields. She had no idea if Justin would respond to her hastily scribbled message, but she wasn't prepared to risk another meeting in front of other people. And when she'd made discreet enquiries about possible meeting-places, the open space of the common-land had seemed ideal.

It was a bleak November day. Grey clouds scudded overhead, threatening rain, and a bitter wind cut through Mary's clothes. She shivered, but she was grateful for the weather. No one was likely to be out on such a day unless they had business of their own to attend to – and that made it much less likely that they would pay attention to her business.

Mary reached the Fields and looked around. She had a moment of panic that Justin wouldn't come, or that if he did come they wouldn't be able to find each other – and then she saw him.

He was striding towards her, apparently indifferent to the knife-like wind. But since he was wearing a heavy, caped greatcoat he had good reason to be warmer than Mary. She was still wearing her Sunday-best pelisse, and she was very cold.

'You summoned me?' said Justin ironically, by way of greeting.

'I asked you to meet me,' Mary corrected him. She hesitated. Now that he was here, in front of her, she didn't quite know how to begin.

'Why?' Justin raised his dark eyebrows. 'Are you looking for a new protector?'

'No, I'm not!' she retorted forcefully. She might have known he'd put the worst possible interpretation on her actions.

'You mean you're satisfied with the one you've got?' Justin asked disbelievingly. 'But sweetheart, he doesn't even dress you very well.' His sharp eyes had seen the way she hunched against the cold in her thin pelisse.

'He doesn't dress me at all!' Mary snapped.

'Ah, you mean he's more interested in *undressing* you,' Justin said. 'Well, I can understand that ambition – although I don't imagine he achieves it with any style.'

'For God's sake, Justin!' Mary exploded. 'I've told you I'm not his mistress. Why can't you believe me?'

'Because I know you,' he replied tautly, his

expression both mocking and angry. 'I can remember how you told me once you'd do anything to survive – even if it meant sharing the bed of a cracksman. I don't suppose you shed one tear when he was transported, did you?'

For a moment Mary stood very still. It was true that she'd once been forced to become a thief's mistress in return for his protection, but she'd never hidden the fact from Justin. She'd never had any secrets from him. She could hardly believe how brutally he'd flung her degradation in her face.

Her fair skin was as pale as porcelain as she met his scornful gaze, and she looked nearly as fragile. It was almost possible to imagine that the November wind would blow her slender body away like last summer's dried flowers – except for the fierce, proud expression in her stormy grey eyes.

'I didn't weep for Bill. Why should I?' She lifted her chin defiantly. 'He protected me before Donald came, during that brief time when Alf turned completely against me – but he didn't do badly out of the bargain. And I will not bow my head in shame before you or anyone else. I did not steal. I did not lie. And I did not trangress any law made by man.'

She was breathing quickly when she finished speaking, but her gaze was locked with steadfast intensity on Justin's face, heedless of the freezing wind tugging at her clothes.

Justin looked down at her. His expression was

no longer mocking. She couldn't quite tell what he was thinking. He lifted his hand and touched her cold cheek with his warm fingers.

'I wonder what the righteous would say if they knew what the lilies of the field have to sacrifice to be arrayed in cheap broadcloth?' he said quietly.

Mary bent her head. She could deal with Justin's anger, but his kindness nearly destroyed her defences. She could feel tears threatening, but she was determined not to give way to them in front of him.

She took a step backwards.

'That's all in the past,' she said, trying to sound brisk and practical. 'I'm more interested in the present. I can understand why you were suspicious of my motives the first time we met – but I told you it was an accident. And I *don't* understand why you've continued to be so hostile – or why you tried to embarrass me today. I came to ask you to leave me alone.' Her voice faltered slightly on the last few words, but she managed not to look away.

'Very good, sweetheart,' he said sardonically. The momentary tenderness in his manner had disappeared. 'You must have been practising. Your technique is excellent. If I didn't know better I might truly believe you're an innocent wronged.'

'*Stop it*!' Mary cried, pushed almost beyond endurance by his continued antagonism. She pressed her hands against her cheeks, heedless of the way the wind whipped her skirts against her legs. 'Justin, you were the one who decided we weren't a suitable match. *Of course* you were right, but you don't have to go on and on demonstrating how very unsuitable I was.'

'*What*?' For a moment Justin stared at her, disbelief and doubt in his eyes, then he seized her shoulders. 'What the devil are you talking about? You *disappeared*!'

He shook her roughly, and her bonnet fell back from her head, hanging by its ribbons around her neck. Mary gazed at him, stunned by the violence of his reaction to her words.

'I had to disappear. Alf was dead,' she said jerkily. 'But I sent you a letter.'

'What letter? I never received a letter.' Justin's fingers dug into her shoulders. A few drops of rain had started to fall, but neither of them noticed.

Mary stared at him, trying to understand what was happening. It would be easy to accuse him of lying, but Justin was too proud and confident to hide behind deception. If he said he hadn't seen her letter, then he hadn't seen it – and that didn't make sense.

Her eyes lost their focus as she looked back over seven years to the moment Donald had stood in front of her and told her Justin didn't want her. Donald had never liked or trusted the young nobleman. Perhaps he'd been jealous of what Justin meant to Mary. With slow, horrifying certainty, she realised that Donald had lied.

She felt cold then, in a way which had nothing to do with the November wind. Until that moment she had trusted the Scotsman, but now it seemed that even he had betrayed her. It wasn't safe to depend on anyone.

'Tell me!' Justin demanded insistently.

Mary focused on his face: hard, suspicious, questioning.

'I gave the letter to Donald,' she said simply. 'He came back and told me you'd decided we weren't suited after all.'

'And you believed him!' Justin exclaimed incredulously.

'Why not? He was right,' Mary replied bleakly.

'That wasn't his decision to make,' Justin said harshly. 'What happened to you? How did you survive? Who looked after you?'

'No one! I didn't need anyone to look after me!' Mary snapped furiously, insulted by his ready assumption that she couldn't manage on her own.

'How?' Justin demanded. 'Those years in Church Lane only left you fit for one thing. You could hardly have found genteel employment as a governess or a lady's maid after that.'

Mary wrenched herself out of his grip, staring at him in appalled understanding.

'That's how you think of me, isn't it?' she cried. 'That's why you flung Bill Crawford in my face just now. Is that how you've always thought of me? Fit only to be a common whore?'

Justin opened his mouth to say something, but she swept on, paying no attention to him.

'Did you pretend you wanted to marry me so that I'd agree to be your mistress? Well, you needn't have put yourself to the trouble. I would have been your mistress then, willingly – but not now. I wouldn't be any man's mistress now!'

She turned to go, but he seized her arm and swung her round to face him.

'What about Penrose?'

'I've told you!' she spat at him. 'There's a perfectly innocent explanation for why we travelled together.'

'Then tell me what it is.'

'*No!*' She was too angry to explain anything to Justin, and too hurt that he still didn't trust her word. Besides, Mr Penrose wouldn't like it if his family business was discussed with anyone else.

It was raining harder now, slanting icy spears of water into her face. She shivered, and pulled her bonnet back on to her head. Somehow the rain seemed to have doused the heat of their argument. There was nothing left to say, yet Mary couldn't quite bring herself to walk away.

She held out her hand to him.

'I'm sorry you thought I'd run away,' she said steadily. 'I'm sorry that you never received my letter. But it's over now, and it ended for the best for both of us. Please, let's leave it there.'

He took her hand in his, and she felt his virile warmth encircle her cold, slender fingers.

'You should buy a muff,' he said. 'Shall I escort you back to your hotel?'

'No, thank you.' Mary wasn't going back to the hotel, but she had no intention of telling Justin that. 'If we meet again, please don't continue to snipe at me, my lord. It doesn't do justice to either of us.'

She turned and walked away, knowing that he was watching her, almost disappointed that he'd let her go so easily. But there wasn't anything left to say. If she was honest she knew that their love had never really had a chance. The only possible role she could ever play in Justin's life was as his mistress – and she was never again going to gamble her security and independence on someone else's good intentions.

The icy wind nearly blinded her, but it was only when she reached up to brush a hand across her eyes that she realised hot tears were mingling with the rain on her cheeks.

'My dear, are you sure you don't mind that we are no longer staying at the hotel?' Mr Penrose asked anxiously after dinner that evening.

'Of course not,' Mary assured him. 'This is a beautiful house. I've never stayed anywhere so elegant.'

'I suppose it is rather pleasant,' said Mr Penrose, looking around as though that particular aspect of the situation had hitherto escaped him. 'But when Knightley told me of the possibility of hiring it I immediately thought of the greater privacy it would afford us – I mean for our interview with Samuel,' he added hastily, in case Mary had mistaken his meaning.

'I quite understand,' said Mary.

'Also, I can never feel entirely at home in a

public hotel. One can never be sure that the linen is properly aired, or that things will be done exactly to one's taste,' Mr Penrose continued. 'Not that I mean to imply that things aren't done handsomely at the Lazy Cat, of course.'

Mary smiled. 'I know that,' she said. 'I'm not unhappy with the situation. I know we're in Bath in rather distressing circumstances. All the same, you are providing me with an opportunity to do several things I've never done before. I'm very grateful to you, sir.'

Mr Penrose flushed. 'You're too kind, too kind,' he muttered. 'Um, did you never have a chance to visit here with your husband? I suppose you could never leave the inn?'

'My husband died before I bought the Lazy Cat,' said Mary. She twisted her wedding-ring absent-mindedly. It wasn't an uncommon gesture for her.

'It must have been dreadful to be left alone so young,' said Mr Penrose sympathetically. 'But I dare say Donald was a great support and comfort to you. He has always seemed a most loyal servant.'

'Yes.' For a moment a rather cold look crept into Mary's eyes. 'Yes, he's devoted to me. Mr Penrose...' she roused herself '...it occurs to me that while we're waiting for your nephew to return it might be worthwhile making Miss Burleigh's acquaintance.'

'Miss Burleigh?'

'To see if we can discover how advanced their courtship is,' Mary explained.

'Oh, I see. But I don't know the Burleighs,' Mr Penrose protested, looking worried. 'I wonder if the Knightleys do? Perhaps they would be able to provide us with an introduction.'

'Even if they don't, I don't foresee any problem,' Mary replied. 'Miss Burleigh and her mother were at the Pump Room today; I enquired. All we need to do is approach them, tell them how highly Samuel has spoken of Miss Burleigh, and presume upon our relationship with him to introduce ourselves to them. It should be quite easy. Would you like another cup of tea, sir?'

Mr Penrose regarded her with something like awe.

'Are you never at a loss, ma'am?' he asked.

Mary smiled. To tell the truth, after all the years of being deferential to her customers, she was feeling slightly nervous about introducing herself so brashly to the heiress. But she had no intention of letting Mr Penrose know that.

'Very frequently,' she replied. 'But I've discovered that, to be a successful landlady, it pays never to let your guests know when they've disconcerted you.'

CHAPTER THREE

'THERE has been a delivery for you, ma'am,' said the butler austerely. 'From Madam Eustacia, the dressmaker.'

'For me!' Mary exclaimed. 'Are you sure there hasn't been any mistake?'

'No, ma'am. The direction on the attached note is most clear.' He offered her the letter on a silver tray.

Mary glanced down at it and recognised Justin's handwriting. Her heart immediately began to beat faster, but she gave no outward sign of her agitation.

'Thank you, Grigson,' she said calmly, picking up the letter. 'Would you have it taken up to my chamber, please?'

'Certainly, ma'am.' He bowed and went out of the drawing-room.

Mr Penrose had hired the servants with the house while the owner, a retired merchant who'd fallen on hard times, was away. Mary was sure the household was already seething with gossip about its temporary tenants. This incident wasn't going to do anything to discourage speculation, but there was nothing she could do about it.

She broke open the seal with a trembling hand

and read the note. It was very brief. 'Armour comes in many guises.'

It was signed with a single, unadorned H. Mary had seen the same initial on Justin's finished sketches. She let her hand fall into her lap, tears of relief pricking at the back of her eyes. Her first thought was that their friendship wasn't going to end on a note of bitterness after all. She glanced at the clock. She was due to go to the Pump Room with Mr Penrose very shortly, but she still had a few minutes in hand.

She ran upstairs and opened the package from the dressmaker. She wasn't surprised to discover that it contained a pelisse, beautiful, fashionable – and warm. There was also a cosy muff. She touched the rich cloth gently, caught in a rush of conflicting emotions.

She could hardly accept the gift when she was trying so hard to distance herself from Justin – and when he had accused her of such dreadful things. But it was typical of him that he should have responded to a practical need. He had never been content simply to sketch the pinched and hungry faces in St Giles, though Mary doubted if anyone else knew of his philanthropy.

She could have been insulted by the implicit suggestion that she could be seduced by a warm coat. But she was far more moved by the fact that he'd noticed she was cold. No one else ever noticed when she was cold or uncomfortable. Even Mr Penrose, who'd spent three days travelling with her, hadn't noticed how cold she'd been in her thin pelisse. Justin might think of her as little better than a common street-walker, but at least he cared enough about her not to let her go cold.

Perhaps the gift was a sign that he believed her explanation of what had happened. Perhaps he'd forgiven her for disappearing without telling him where she was. It didn't fully assuage her hurt at the way he'd flung her dishonourable past in her face, but it softened her grief.

She heard a sound from the doorway and looked up. A maid was standing there, a milliner's box in her hands.

'This just came for you, ma'am,' she said eagerly.

'Thank you.' Mary opened it.

'It's beautiful!' the maid exclaimed. She touched the pleated silk which lined the bonnet almost reverently. The merchant was a widower, and very little female finery ever came into the house. 'Look how it brings out the colour of your eyes,' she continued. 'You must wear it to the Pump Room this morning. Did you order it when you went out yesterday afternoon?'

Mary alllowed the assumption to go by without correcting it. Almost without realising she'd done so, she'd decided to accept the pelisse. If Justin intended it to be the first step in her seduction she would correct his misapprehension. But if it was intended as an olive-branch she could do no less than accept it.

*   *   *

'My dear, you look splendid this morning,' said Mr Penrose as they made their way to the Pump Room. 'You see what a difference even one glass of the water can make. Oh, but you didn't take any.' He paused, looking puzzled.

'It must be the Bath air,' said Mary calmly. 'It's very invigorating, is it not?'

'That must be it.' Mr Penrose's expression cleared. 'Oh, dear, I do hope that the Knightleys know Miss Burleigh – and that they're here.'

'Never mind,' said Mary. 'If they aren't, I shall impersonate the kind of gushing, impulsive female who simply *cannot* wait for a formal invitation to meet someone she's heard such fine things of. After all, sir, Miss Burleigh may be an heiress, but you're hardly lacking in consequence yourself.'

Mr Penrose puffed up slightly at her praise, then deflated equally quickly.

'My father made his fortune in India,' he said. 'We didn't exactly come over with the conqueror. Of course, Martlesham House is one of the most elegant residences in Wiltshire, but even so. . .'

'How is it you come to live in Hertfordshire when your family home is in Wiltshire?' Mary asked.

Mr Penrose flushed.

'My brother resented the fact that, apart from the house, my father divided his fortune equally between us,' he replied. 'He was most unpleasant to me. I found it more comfortable to move away – and my late wife came from St Albans.'

'I hadn't realised you were a widower!' Mary exclaimed.

'Oh, yes,' said Mr Penrose sadly. 'She died giving birth to our first child. It was stillborn.'

'I'm so sorry,' Mary said gently. 'How dreadful for you.'

Mr Penrose glanced at her.

'It was nearly thirty years ago,' he said. 'If it wasn't for her portrait in the drawing-room I think I might almost believe it never happened. She was such a beautiful, loving creature,' he added wistfully. 'You see, we are alike in having lost our partners young.'

Mary looked down, unable to think of anything to say.

The Pump Room was crowded as ever, but the Knightleys were nowhere to be seen, and Mr Penrose did not number any of the other people present among his acquaintances. It was a long time since he'd been to Bath.

'Never mind,' said Mary. 'There's Miss Burleigh and her mama over there. All you need to do is remember that you're a man of consequence, and that in introducing ourselves to them it is we who are doing them the favour.'

'I'll do my best,' said Mr Penrose meekly. 'I surely believe that they should be honoured to meet you, my dear.'

Mary glanced at him, rather startled by the warmth in his tone, but by then they'd reached the Burleighs.

It wasn't, in fact, very difficult to ingratiate

themselves with them. As far as Bath was concerned, Samuel Penrose was a very personable young man who was also heir to a considerable fortune. The terms of his father's will – and his own profligacy – were not generally known.

'This is my daughter, Lucinda. And this is my cousin, Miss Emma Lewisham,' Mrs Burleigh concluded the introductions. 'Unfortunately, my husband died several years ago, but Miss Lewisham has been a great support to me.'

Miss Lewisham produced a smile which managed to convey both her gratification at Mrs Burleigh's compliment and her humble belief in her unfitness to receive them. It set Mary's teeth on edge, but nothing in her demeanour revealed her true feelings.

'I'm very glad to meet you all,' she said warmly, but without any hint of unbecoming boldness. The charming manners she'd learnt so long ago at the rectory still stood her in good stead. No one could have guessed how unusual such a situation was for her. 'It's my first visit to Bath, and we don't have many acquaintances here,' she continued, 'but it's so pleasant to meet new people, isn't it?'

Mrs Burleigh smiled. 'I'm sure you'll soon have many friends here,' she said. 'Won't you join us for a while?'

'Thank you.' Mary's smile lit up her eyes and she sat down beside Lucinda, hoping that Mr Penrose would have the good sense to entertain the two older ladies.

'I believe you reside in Bath permanently,' she said to Lucinda. 'You must know it very well.'

'I suppose I do,' Lucinda replied hesitantly.

She was by no means an unattractive girl, but she was shy and a little awkward in her manner. And at the moment she was also nervous because she didn't know Mary and she didn't know what to talk about. Mary could easily see how she might have been dazzled by the attentions of a dashing young man – if that was what had happened.

'I must admit, I still feel a little strange and out of place here,' Mary confessed. 'We only arrived two days ago. And I've led a very retired life for the past few years. Perhaps you could point out some of the Bath notables to me?'

'I'd be delighted to,' Lucinda said, much more sure of herself now that Mary had given her an opening.

The next few minutes were occupied by an increasingly lively and confidential conversation between the two young ladies which left Mary with a mischievous sparkle in her grey eyes and Lucinda giggling behind her fan.

Despite the fact that Mary had an ulterior motive for gaining Lucinda's confidence, there was nothing contrived about the way in which she drew the younger woman out. She liked people, she enjoyed meeting new acquaintances, and she easily found herself warming to Lucinda. It was a long time since she herself had looked at the world with such innocent yet hopeful eyes.

'You must be very fond of your cousin,' Lucinda

said at last, blushing slightly. 'He is a very fine young man, isn't he?'

'I'm afraid I don't know him very well,' Mary replied apologetically.

'Oh, but surely——?'

'I grew up in Scotland, and my marriage kept me in the north,' Mary explained. She found it very difficult to lie to Lucinda, but she didn't have much choice. 'It's only recently I've come south. Samuel spoke very highly of you, but I must rely on *you* to learn more about *him*.'

Lucinda blushed even rosier. 'He's very charming,' she said, stammering slightly. 'He waltzed with me at Mrs Carling's ball. I'm not very good at dancing,' she added naïvely, 'but he assured me I would improve with practice.'

Mary didn't feel the slightest desire to smile. She could recall all too clearly the contempt with which Samuel had spoken about Lucinda Burleigh. His threats about terminating Mr Penrose's life might or might not have substance to them, but he represented a very real danger to Lucinda's future happiness.

'Forgive me, Miss Burleigh, but how old are you?' she asked quietly.

'I will be twenty-one next May,' Lucinda replied, almost as if she were confessing to a crime. 'Papa died just before I was due to come out,' she added in an undertone. 'And since then Mama hasn't felt up to the rigours of a London season.'

'No, I see.' Mary glanced at Mrs Burleigh, who

was busily chatting to Mr Penrose, and quite complacent about the growing friendship between her daughter and his putative niece.

At twenty-six – although of course Mrs Burleigh didn't know her precise age – Mary was too old to be considered competition for Lucinda. She was also Samuel Penrose's cousin – Samuel had made a very good impression on Mrs Burleigh – and Mr Penrose's niece. Almost as importantly, she was very prettily behaved, charming and warm-hearted. All in all, just the kind of friend Mrs Burleigh would have chosen for her daughter.

'I've never had a London season myself,' said Mary, who would have been quite startled by the trend of Mrs Burleigh's thoughts if she'd known them. 'I've often thought that, once the first excitement wears off, it must become very tiring. And if you don't have many acquaintances you always have the worry that there won't be anyone you can talk to.'

'Oh, yes!' said Lucinda eagerly. 'You understand perfectly. There's nothing worse than sitting out every dance with Mama or Cousin Emma.'

'But surely here in Bath you have acquaintances?' Mary protested.

'But they don't want to dance with me,' said Lucinda simply. 'Besides, we've only lived here since Papa died. It's not quite the same as people you've grown up with. And Mama says I must be very careful not to be taken in by people who are more interested in my fortune than in me,' she concluded, with the air of one who was quoting a much repeated warning.

'Do you have a fortune?' Mary asked delicately.

'I will have.' Lucinda sighed. 'That's what makes it so difficult,' she confided. 'I know I'm not very elegant or...or lively. So it does seem much more likely that people would be interested in me for my money rather than myself, don't you think?'

'No!' said Mary emphatically. 'Miss Burleigh, if you give them the chance I am sure you will find many people who will like you for yourself.'

'But how am I to distinguish them?' Lucinda asked. 'That's why I was pleased when Mr Penrose... That is, Mama says he is very wealthy too. So he cannot be interested in my fortune, can he?' There was a measure of doubt in her voice. She wasn't as foolish as she first appeared, or perhaps she just wasn't used to the notion that anyone could find her attractive.

It was a tricky question for Mary to answer. She didn't want to tell Lucinda of her suspicions about Samuel, but nor did she want to encourage her friendship with him.

'I don't believe anyone could fail to enjoy your company,' she said, choosing her words very carefully. 'But rich men, as well as poor men, can sometimes have a distressingly material view of life.'

Lucinda stared at Mary, a question forming in her eyes, but before she had a chance to voice it Mr Penrose interrupted them.

'My dear Mary, isn't that Lord Hawkridge approaching us?' he said suddenly.

Mary looked around. 'Yes, it is,' she said. Her heart skipped a beat. She wasn't sure whether she was pleased to see him or not; she only wished she didn't have to confront him before so many curious eyes.

'Good gracious! Are you acquainted with him?' Miss Lewisham gasped. 'My sister lives in South Audley Street, and she sends me all the society gossip. Apparently he's a dreadful rake! He keeps mistresses on all the main post roads the way some men keep horses!'

'*Emma*!' Mrs Burleigh exclaimed, outraged.

'Good heavens!' Lucinda stared at Justin wide-eyed, while Mr Penrose gave him another, far more penetrating glance.

'I'm very sure he doesn't,' said Mary drily, just as he reached them.

Justin gave no indication that he'd heard her comment, but acknowledged her and Mr Penrose with a somewhat curt greeting. Mary's temper began to rise. He had no business to single her out, then treat her in such a cavalier manner. But she kept her face expressionless as, once again, she was forced to introduce him to her companions.

Once she'd finished her introductions, she withdrew from the conversation, and waited to see what would happen next. It was a curious situation. The Burleighs, like Mr Penrose's father, had made their money in trade, and they showed a distressing tendency to be overawed by Justin's title – not to mention his rather formidable presence.

'I don't believe we've seen you in Bath before, my lord,' said Miss Lewisham breathlessly, before anyone else could speak. 'I hope you'll find the city to your liking.'

'Thank you, ma'am. It has already provided me with a great deal of entertainment,' Justin replied rather coldly. 'I had forgotten how quickly scandal spreads here. Perhaps it's carried in the water which everyone drinks so assiduously.'

Miss Lewisham went a dull red and deflated into her unbecoming purple gown. Justin raised his eyebrows very slightly, then turned his attention to Lucinda.

'I went for a stroll this morning,' he said to her, smiling with far more warmth than before, 'and I confess, I was impressed. I'd forgotten how fine some of the architecture is here. But it must seem commonplace to you, since you see it every day.'

'Y-yes – I mean no,' she stammered. 'The view from Beechen Cliff is very nice.'

'I must make a point of going there before I leave,' said Justin, without a hint of condescension in his voice. 'Mrs Drayton, may I persuade you to take a brief promenade with me? Please excuse us.'

'What are you trying to do? Destroy all my credibility?' Mary demanded when they were out of earshot. It wasn't what she'd meant to say, and as soon as the words left her mouth she caught herself up, miserably aware of what his probable response would be.

'No,' Justin replied mildly.

'Oh,' she said.

She was disturbingly aware that, despite all their bitter words, there was still a strong emotional bond between them. More than that, she could feel the undisciplined spark of excitement that flared in her every time he came near her – and every time he touched her. Even now, in the crowded Pump Room, she was acutely conscious of the warmth and strength of his arm beneath her hand.

'Why did you send me the pelisse?' she asked abruptly.

'Because you were cold,' he replied.

'Is that the only reason?' she challenged him, turning to face him.

He smiled. 'You may interpret it as an invitation to share my bed if you wish,' he said softly. 'But there's no obligation.'

'And which post road did you intend I should adorn?' Mary flashed before she could stop herself.

His smile broadened, and she saw a gleam of amusement in his hazel eyes.

'I'm afraid the stories of my amorous adventures have been greatly exaggerated,' he murmured, so low that only she could hear. 'Even if they were only half true I doubt if I'd have the energy to crawl out of bed in the morning – let alone walk across this room to procure you a glass of water.'

'I don't want any water,' Mary protested. What she wanted to do was find out exactly how much truth there was in the rumours about his mistresses, but she couldn't quite bring herself to ask him. She told herself it didn't matter.

'My dear girl, of course you do,' he corrected her solemnly, guiding her through the throng of people. 'You can't come to Bath without tasting the water. I trust my small gift didn't cause you any embarrassment with Penrose?' he added.

'He didn't notice,' said Mary. 'Besides, despite your repeated insinuations, it's none of his business. I came to Bath to help him out of a fix, and I'd hate to cause him distress – but I'm no more answerable to him for my behaviour than I am to you, my lord!'

'What fix?' Justin asked a few minutes later as she was sipping her water.

'That's none of your business, Justin.' She lifted her head and met his gaze squarely, a determined, almost steely look in her grey eyes. 'The only reason I accepted the pelisse was to save myself embarrassment,' she said steadily. 'It will make no difference to my relations with you.'

Justin looked down at her. Mary couldn't read the expression in his eyes, yet there was something strangely intimate about the moment.

'How did such an indomitable spirit come to be housed in such a fragile vessel?' Justin asked at last, very softly. 'I never thought of you as a common whore. I know you did what you did out of grim, uncompromising necessity.'

His words warmed Mary more than she could ever have believed possible. But then she saw his hand start to lift towards her, and she was jerked horribly back to the reality of her surroundings.

'Don't touch me!' she snapped, stepping back.

'Ah, of course, I'm not supposed to do anything which will provide fuel for Miss Lewisham and all her soul-mates here today,' Justin remarked in his normal voice, although there was a slight flush on his swarthy cheek. 'I shall endeavour to live up to your exacting requirements. May I take that glass from you? What fix?'

'I told you, that's none of your business,' said Mary, still shaken by what had just nearly happened. 'And how did you know where to have the pelisse and bonnet sent? Did you follow me last night?'

'Hardly. Since you'd picked such an out-of-the-way spot for our assignation I was more or less forced to follow the same route back into town that you did,' Justin said drily. 'You can't blame me for being curious when you turned off at Queen Square. You must admit, it's a rather irregular arrangement.'

Mary bit her lip as she heard the sardonic tone creep back into Justin's voice. 'Mr Penrose doesn't trust the linen in public hotels,' she explained, aware that it sounded a rather lame excuse.

Justin raised his eyebrows. 'That must cause him considerable inconvenience,' he said blandly. 'Why are you cultivating the gauche Miss Burleigh?'

Mary blinked. She'd expected him to reiterate his earlier suspicions about Mr Penrose, but instead he'd completely changed the subject.

'She's not gauche, she's just a little unsure of herself,' she said, adjusting to the new turn that the conversation had taken. 'Don't alarm her, Justin. It's not fair.'

'I didn't alarm her,' he pointed out calmly. 'I made an innocuous, not to say boring remark about the architecture of Bath. You can't get much less alarming than that!'

'You seem to have an ability to alarm people just by saying good morning,' said Mary roundly. 'I can't think why they're all so in awe of you!'

'It's certainly not a trait you share,' Justin replied drily. 'How did you care for the water?'

'I've tasted worse,' she said. 'I'd like to go back to the others now, please.'

'Surely you use the word "like" inappropriately?' Justin murmured provocatively, but he did escort her back to Mrs Burleigh's party.

'You've been trying our water,' said Miss Lewisham, leaving Mary in no doubt that she and Justin had been under observation for the whole time they'd been away. 'I'm sure that's a wise precaution. Did you not wish to try some, my lord?'

'My doctor informs me that water in all its guises is poison to my system,' Justin replied austerely. 'It's a great inconvenience to me, but one must abide by expert advice.'

'Indeed one must.' Miss Lewisham nodded

energetically. 'I drink very little water myself. Do you care for tea, my lord?'

'Unfortunately not. It's made with boiling water, you see.'

'Oh, dear me. Yes. Of course. So it is,' Miss Lewisham agreed. 'But surely——' she looked perplexed ' – you cannot be confined to drinking nothing but *intoxicating* liquids?'

'No. Vinegar,' said Justin heavily.

'Vinegar!' Miss Lewisham exclaimed. 'Oh, yes, yes, I quite see that that would be an *excellent* solution to the problem!'

There was a muffled gasp from Lucinda, and then she hid her face behind her fan. Mrs Burleigh looked slightly uncomfortable, and Mr Penrose disapproving.

'Mary, my dear,' he said, pointedly ignoring Lord Hawkridge, 'Mrs Burleigh has been kind enough to invite us to a small party she is having tonight for Miss Lucinda. I said that we would be pleased to accept.'

'Of course we would,' said Mary warmly, although her first thought was that she hadn't got anything suitable to wear. But she could deal with that problem later.

'Lord Hawkridge,' said Mrs Burleigh diffidently, 'would you care to join us? It won't be anything grand, I'm afraid, but we'd be honoured by your presence.'

'Thank you, ma'am, I would be delighted to accept.' Justin bowed slightly and took his leave of them.

'He certainly is a very handsome figure of a man,' said Miss Lewisham as he walked away. 'And one has to forgive the aristocracy a certain laxity of moral standards.'

'Emma!' said Mrs Burleigh despairingly.

'My dear, I can't help noticing... That is to say... Oh, dear...' Mr Penrose's voice trailed away unhappily.

They were sitting in the drawing-room of the house in Queen Square.

'What is it, sir?' Mary asked courteously, although she thought she knew what Mr Penrose wanted to say.

'Please forgive me, Mrs Drayton,' he assured her earnestly. 'I don't mean to be in any way impertinent, and I am deeply aware of how much you are putting yourself out for me...'

'You are concerned about the attention Lord Hawkridge seems to be paying me,' said Mary equably, when once again Mr Penrose proved unable to complete his sentence.

'I know it's not my concern, and I'd never wish to be thought interfering,' said Mr Penrose anxiously. 'But a man of his ilk really isn't to be trusted.'

'I think he is amusing himself,' said Mary calmly. 'Please don't disturb yourself, sir. I am very well able to take care of myself.'

Mr Penrose looked at her uncertainly, his thin face even more creased with anxiety than usual.

'It wouldn't do, you know, even if you were my

niece,' he said. 'And if his lordship ever found out that you're really an innkeeper——' He broke off, dabbing his lips with his handkerchief. 'Forgive me, my dear, I did not mean to imply... That is to say, I often feel you were more truly born a lady than I was born a gentleman.'

Mary smiled. 'My father was rector of a large Sussex parish,' she said. 'I used to play with the squire's daughters. But that was a very long time ago.'

'The hurly-burly of life in a public house must have come as a great shock to you after such a childhood,' said Mr Penrose tentatively. He was clearly dying to know the whole story, but was too polite, or timid, to ask.

'It did take me a little while to get used to the change in my circumstances,' Mary acknowledged. She stood up. 'Excuse me, sir. I must go out.'

'Why?' Mr Penrose demanded, with uncharacteristic bluntness. Then he flushed uncomfortably.

Mary felt a flicker of annoyance. She was getting tired of having her every action questioned, first by Justin and now by Mr Penrose. But she knew Mr Penrose had her best interests at heart – that he was probably anxious in case she had an assignation with Lord Hawkridge – so she bit back a sharp retort.

'I must buy a new dress,' she said. 'I have nothing to wear to Miss Burleigh's party.'

Mr Penrose stared at her in consternation. 'Oh, my dear Mrs Drayton, I had no idea that in accepting Mrs Burleigh's invitation I would be putting you to such expense. How thoughtless of me. Please, you must let me reimburse you.'

'That's quite unnecessary,' Mary replied stiffly.

'No, I insist,' he said. 'I cannot allow you to be out of pocket on my behalf. It's unthinkable!'

Mary hesitated. But she was a practical woman, and it seemed to her that, in the circumstances, Mr Penrose's offer was quite fair.

'Thank you, sir,' she said, accepting it.

CHAPTER FOUR

MARY was hesitating outside a dressmaker's establishment on Milsom Street when she heard a light footstep behind her. Her breath caught in her throat, and she didn't need to turn round to know who it was.

'I found Madam Eustacia very helpful this morning,' said Justin in her ear.

'Which is a very good reason for me not to visit her this afternoon!' Mary retorted, swinging round to face him. 'Especially dressed like this!'

'Your ineffectual cavalier set you a problem when he accepted Mrs Burleigh's invitation, didn't he?' said Justin, amusement in his voice. 'I saw it in your expression at the time. The everlasting cry of womanhood: "But I haven't got a thing to wear!"'

'I haven't, but I will have,' said Mary through gritted teeth. 'Go away, Justin. People are looking at us.'

'You will be the envy of other, less favoured damsels,' he assured her infuriatingly.

Her eyes flashed dangerously. 'I doubt it,' she said curtly.

He raised his eyebrows.

'Perhaps I should come in with you?' he suggested. 'I could offer my advice – I have an excellent eye for colour – and then I could carry your purchases home for you afterwards.'

Mary took a step backwards.

'No,' she said. 'Definitely not.'

'Why? Would Penrose object?'

'*I* would object,' said Mary, but a faint colour stained her fair cheeks at his question. It followed so pat upon Mr Penrose's warning.

'He's cautioned you against me!' Justin exclaimed. 'For what reason?' The humour had vanished from his face and now there was a dangerous gleam in his hazel eyes.

'Because men of your ilk are not to be trusted!' Mary flashed. 'He suspects you of harbouring improper thoughts towards me!'

'Something he would know nothing about?' Justin said derisively.

'No, he doesn't!' Mary exclaimed indignantly, as much offended on Mr Penrose's behalf as she was on her own. 'He's never treated me with anything other than respect.'

'Then he has water in his veins, not blood,' said Justin harshly. 'You should look elsewhere for company, sweetheart. You have too much fire to be satisfied by such an arrangement.'

'Are you suggesting I become *your* mistress?' Mary demanded, too angry to be circumspect. 'You must be out of your mind!'

There was a moment's silence. Justin looked at her, his mouth set in a hard, unyielding line, an angry flame in his eyes.

'At least the dressmaker would come to your

door,' he drawled cuttingly. 'And I would do my best to ensure that your other needs were adequately catered for.'

His gaze flickered over her, the hard yet intimate gleam in his eyes leaving her in no doubt as to his meaning.

Mary caught her breath in horror. She felt as naked and wounded as if he had stripped her clothes from her back. Whatever his protestations that he didn't see her as a common whore, he had made his opinion of her plain enough.

'No,' she said in a low, throbbing voice. 'No, never!'

She turned and went into the dressmaker's.

'Oh, ma'am, you do look lovely,' said Hetty, the maid who was helping her dress.

'Thank you.' Mary glanced at herself in the mirror.

It seemed to her that the beauty of her clothes was not matched by the woman wearing them. She felt tired and plain. But perhaps her superficial finery would be enough to deceive others as effectively as it seemed to have done Hetty.

She had spent far more on the dress than she had intended to, and certainly more than Mr Penrose had given her. But, even though she knew that her extravagance had been inspired by the desire to show Justin that she didn't need him, she didn't regret it.

Besides, this was probably the only fashionable

party she would ever go to, and she meant to make the most of it.

She had chosen a simple yet elegant dress, in a deep rich blue, which complemented the delicate translucence of her skin and the changing lights in her grey eyes. It had a wide skirt adorned only by a single trim, large puffed sleeves which reached to her elbows, and a low neckline, cut straight across from slightly dropped shoulders, which emphasised her slender neck and excellent carriage.

Her hair was arranged in loose curls, dressed with a ribbon. To complete the ensemble she wore long white gloves, silk pumps, and a simple gold locket which was the only ornament she had to remind her of her mother. Somehow she had managed to preserve the trinket through all the vicissitudes of her life in St Giles.

'You really do look beautiful,' said Hetty, almost reverentially.

She was so sincere in her flattery that Mary started to feel better. A hint of pretty colour crept into her pale cheeks, and the merest suggestion of a sparkle illuminated her eyes.

'You must be looking forward to tonight,' Hetty added.

'Yes, I am,' Mary admitted.

It was true. She was feeling nervous and on edge, but she had never been to such a party before, she would never have the opportunity to do so again, and she was determined to enjoy it.

And more than anything she wanted Justin to

see her in her beautiful gown and know that she needed neither him nor his charity.

'You'll be the belle of the ball,' said the maid enthusiastically. 'You'll dazzle all the gentlemen, ma'am.'

'I'm hardly in the first blush of youth,' Mary protested, smiling ruefully.

'You don't look a day over twenty, ma'am,' said Hetty stoutly.

Mary shook her head in laughing disbelief, flattered but not convinced, though Hetty's championship had done a great deal for her morale.

But when she caught a glimpse of herself in the mirror she thought that perhaps there was some truth in what Hetty said. Despite the hardships she had endured, the years had been kind to her. Her eyes still had the capacity to sparkle with mischief when she was amused, her tawny-brown hair shone warmly in the candlelight and her fair skin remained as pure and unblemished as it had been the day she'd left the rectory for the last time.

In fact, apart from the depth of experience in her fine grey eyes, she really might have been a débutante about to attend her first party.

For tonight she would pretend that it was so.

'Perhaps you'll catch the eye of Lord Hawkridge,' said the maid, innocently throwing Mary's emotions into turmoil.

'What do you mean?' she asked carefully.

'He'll be there too, won't he?' Hetty prattled on, unaware of Mary's reaction to her comment.

'A very fine gentleman by all accounts, though a bit odd.'

'In what way?' Mary asked curiously, relaxing slightly as she realised that the girl was only repeating gossip.

'Well, my cousin Annie works up at the hotel,' the maid began confidentially, 'and she was busy cleaning out the hearth in the coffee-room yesterday morning, ready to make up the new fire, when she heard someone behind her. So naturally she turned round to see who it was, and there was his lordship, bold as brass, *drawing* her!'

The maid paused dramatically, her eyes sparkling with excitement.

'Good gracious!' said Mary encouragingly, since a response seemed to be called for. 'What did she do then?'

'Well, she's got a bit of a temper, has Annie,' the maid continued. 'So she asked, sharp, like, what he thought he was doing, and he showed her. She said there were little pictures all over the page, all higgledy-piggledy, without any rhyme or reason to them. Little pictures of her cleaning the hearth, and a chairman outside the Pump Room rubbing his hands to keep them warm, and a skinny lady drinking the waters like she thought they were poison. . .' Hetty ran out of breath.

'I see,' said Mary. 'Did she find that reassuring?'

'She said he was a proper gentleman,' the maid replied. 'He told her he'd been in the coffee-room since before she'd come in – he must have been up early, or perhaps he never went to bed – and she was such a picture of diligence he couldn't help drawing her. He said he was sorry he'd startled her, and hoped he hadn't put her out – and then he gave her half a crown. She said he was a proper gentleman, not at all stand-offish, but not familiar either, if you take my meaning.'

'Yes, I do,' said Mary, smiling faintly. She could just imagine the scene.

She wondered what the awestruck Knightleys, or even Miss Lewisham, would say if they heard the story. It seemed that, for all the occasional grandeur of his manner, Justin still retained the ability to see everyone he met as an individual. In fact, he'd probably liked Annie better than Miss Lewisham. He'd never been able to abide humbug.

Her eyes fell and she gripped her hands tightly in her lap. If only things could have been different. But even if the years in St Giles had never happened it wouldn't have made any difference. The rector's daughter could never be a suitable match for the baron.

'It must be nice to have your picture drawn,' said the maid wistfully. 'Not when you're cleaning out the hearth, of course – but in your best dress and bonnet.' She caught sight of Mary in the mirror and smiled excitedly. 'Perhaps he'll draw you, ma'am,' she suggested. 'That would be something, wouldn't it?'

'I'm not sure I want my likeness taken,' said Mary sharply, then she saw the maid's crestfallen expression and relented. 'Yes,' she said, 'it would be something.'

'My dear!' Mr Penrose stood up as she came into the drawing-room, staring at her as though he'd never seen her before. 'You look exquisite!'

'Thank you, sir,' Mary replied.

Then, as he continued to stare at her, she began to feel slightly uncomfortable. She had denied to Justin that Mr Penrose had any romantic interest in her, but she was no longer entirely sure. Not that she suspected he was going to invite her to become his mistress! But she could sense that his regard for her was growing warmer. She hoped it would never become any more than that.

'Would you care for a glass of sherry before we leave?' Mr Penrose asked after a moment.

'Yes, thank you,' Mary said. She smiled ruefully. 'I confess, I am a little nervous.'

'But you have no reason to be,' he assured her. 'I will be the envy of every other gentleman present – at having such a lovely niece, I mean.'

'You are very kind, sir.' She sipped her sherry, very conscious of the anxious tension in her companion, and the steady ticking of the clock on the mantelpiece.

She put her glass down. 'Shall we go? We wouldn't want to be late.'

To her own surprise, Mary turned out to be a great success at Lucinda's party. For this, three things were partially responsible. Firstly, she was new to Bath. Secondly, she was believed to be the niece of a wealthy man. And thirdly, gossip about the way Lord Hawkridge had twice singled her out in the Pump Room had already reached nearly every guest present. Naturally everyone was curious about her.

But the main reason why she was a success owed nothing to such vulgar factors. She had come to the party determined to enjoy herself, and her pleasure in her surroundings was infectious. She had charm and warmth and, although she would never have believed it, an air of innate good breeding.

To some extent, of course, she was acting a role. She was certainly aware of the irony when she heard herself described as a 'pretty-mannered, modest young woman' by old Mrs Melville. But on another level she was only being herself, for this genteel society – or something like it – was where she had begun, and where she might have ended if her father had made better provision for her.

'I'm so glad you could come, Mrs Drayton,' said Lucinda eagerly, when all the introductions were over and she had time to speak confidentially to Mary.

'It was very kind of you to invite us at such short notice,' Mary replied warmly, 'especially as we are little more than strangers.'

'It doesn't seem so,' Lucinda assured her. 'How easily you make friends,' she added almost enviously. 'I never know what to say to people

– apart from the most mundane remarks that nobody could be interested in.'

'I think you underestimate yourself,' Mary said, smiling. 'And overestimate the wit and intellect of everyone else! Most conversation is pretty mundane if you ever really listen to it.'

'I suppose so,' said Lucinda doubtfully. 'I dare say you've had a lot of experience of meeting people,' she added, diffidently anxious to learn more about her new friend.

'I've travelled quite a bit,' Mary replied. It wasn't exactly true, but she'd met a lot of travellers, which, in the present context, seemed to come to the same thing. 'You soon discover that most people are too busy working out what they're going to say when it's their turn to pay full attention to what you're saying.'

Lucinda gasped. 'I thought I was the only one who did that!' she exclaimed.

'Don't you believe it!' Mary said mischievously, smiling at the girl.

But despite her calm exterior Mary was still feeling very edgy. So far Justin hadn't appeared. It was possible that he'd decided to cut the party, or that he'd deliberately chosen to be late in order to make a grand entrance. Mary knew it would be better if he didn't come, but she desperately wanted him to do so.

She wanted him to see her in her beautiful gown and know that she didn't need him to survive. She wanted him to see her mixing with these people, to see how well-liked she was and how comfortable she was in this setting. And most of all she wanted him to see that there was more to her than the wretched, frightened girl who had once purchased crude protection for herself by becoming a thief's moll.

She caught herself up as she realised that she'd just glanced nervously at the doorway for a third time, and tried to concentrate on what her companion was saying.

'It's Lord Hawkridge!' Lucinda exclaimed.

Mary looked up, and there he was, bowing to his hostess.

'Oh, dear, he's coming over here,' said Lucinda.

A pulse began to beat in Mary's throat. 'Of course he is,' she said in a voice she didn't quite recognise as her own. 'It's your party.'

He acknowledged both ladies courteously, his gaze resting briefly on Mary before he turned his attention back to Lucinda.

'Miss Burleigh, I would apologise for my tardiness, except that the blame rests entirely with you,' he said, a twinkle in his hazel eyes.

'With me?' Lucinda squeaked, staring at him in agitated alarm.

'You advised me to see the view from Beechen Cliff, did you not?' Justin reminded her, sitting down beside her. 'You were quite right – it is very impressive.'

'Oh, I see,' said Lucinda, understanding dawning in her expression. 'But I had no idea. . . That is, I did not mean for you. . . It was so windy today.'

'It was a trifle draughty,' Justin acknowledged. 'But I turned my collar up, and I was able to make several sketches before the light failed.'

Apart from that first, quick glance, he hadn't paid any further attention to Mary.

She gripped her fan tightly in her hands. Was he ignoring her to punish her for refusing to be his mistress? Or did he simply think there was nothing left to say between them? A great weight settled on her chest. She could not believe how agonising his indifference was. His anger had been preferable.

'Sketches? Of course!' Lucinda exclaimed, a combination of awe and nervous eagerness in her eyes. 'Cousin Emma says you are famous for your paintings, my lord.'

'Miss Lewisham exaggerates,' said Justin, smiling. 'If I have a talent at all, it is for pen-and-ink sketches, not for great, sweeping landscapes – or even for formal portraits.'

'You must have visited many exhibitions,' said Lucinda wistfully. 'I have often wished... But Mama has no liking for London, and I could never persuade her to go to Rome.'

'Perhaps you will have an opportunity to do so one day,' Justin said. 'Do you paint yourself?'

'I did a water-colour from Beechen Cliff,' Lucinda admitted shyly. 'Mama liked it and showed it to all her friends, but I didn't think it was very good. It was too dark, and some of the washes were muddy. Sometimes I think there is not enough colour in the world!'

'You would appreciate Turner, I think,' said Justin.

Mary listened, making no effort to take part in the conversation. Why should she? Lucinda had clearly forgotten her new friend in her natural excitement at discovering that she shared an interest with Lord Hawkridge. And Justin...well, Mary had always known she wasn't fit to be anything but his whore.

All around her people were talking, laughing and flirting, while beside her Justin and Lucinda talked about old masters, but Mary sat as poised and unmoving as a marble statue. Mrs Burleigh's well-appointed drawing-room faded away, and she saw the horror and filth of St Giles as vividly as if it were there in front of her. She could smell the stench of Church Lane, and feel the disgust that had overwhelmed her when her uncle's leering customers had reached out with groping hands to touch her.

She'd spent a year resisting Alf's determined efforts to turn her into a genteel thief. Her uncle had had so many plans for her – but she'd thwarted them all. She'd been proud of herself. But then he'd withdrawn his protection from her, in the hope that desperation would finally break her spirit.

So, in anger and fear, she'd struck her bargain with Bill Crawford. She'd agreed to be the crack-man's mistress in the hope that he'd protect her from others even worse than he was. And he had. Until he'd been caught cracking a house in

Berkeley Square and been rewarded with transportation for his bad luck.

She'd never made the same bargain again. Donald's arrival in Church Lane, and his instant, unquestioning, unswerving loyalty, had ensured that.

But once was enough. Nothing would ever change the fact that she'd knowingly sacrifice everything she'd been taught to hold dear. Nothing would ever wash away the stains of that bargain. No honest man could ever be expected to marry her.

She had told Justin so, seven years ago, and he had refused to accept it. No one could blame him if he had finally come to see the truth of her words.

'Mrs Drayton!'

Mary jumped. Mrs Burleigh's crowded drawing-room once more slid into view, and she saw Lucinda staring at her anxiously.

'Is something wrong?' Lucinda asked, forgetting to be diffident in her concern.

'No. Oh, no,' Mary said uncertainly. She tried to smile, but the attempt faltered. The horrors she'd seen still lurked at the back of her grey eyes. For a moment the crowded, brightly lit room seemed less real than her memories of St Giles.

'It is very warm in here,' said Justin quietly. 'It wouldn't be surprising if Mrs Drayton felt faint. Perhaps you could procure her a glass of lemonade, Miss Burleigh?'

'Of course.' Lucinda got up immediately, not at all put out by the request.

'I am not faint,' Mary protested, struggling to regain her self-possession.

'I know,' said Justin gently. 'But it was better than telling her that for a few minutes you weren't at her party at all – she might have asked where you'd gone.'

'How did you know?' Mary whispered, shaken anew by the understanding in his eyes. Sh'd been so sure that he no longer had any interest in her.

'It wasn't difficult,' he said softly. 'Whatever's happened to you in the last seven years, I doubt if anything has hurt you more than that.'

Mary caught her lip between her teeth, trying not to give way to tears. Just when she was feeling most lonely and abandoned, he had reached out to her with kindness. She should have known that he would at least show her that courtesy.

He laid his hand on her gloved forearm, just above her wrist. She felt the warmth and reassurance in his touch, and suddenly all she wanted to do was throw herself into his comforting embrace. She wanted to feel his strong arms soothing her and his deep voice telling her that everything was all right – that he'd forgiven her the sins she'd been forced to commit to save herself.

But that was a dream that could never come true. Oh, yes! If she weakened she might one day lie in his arms. She might even hear him tell her that she'd only done what she'd had to do. But there would never be true forgiveness for what had happened in St Giles. How could there be?

She looked at him, her eyes sparkling with

unshed tears, and her lips twisted into a crooked smile.

'Let us call a truce, sweetheart,' he said very quietly. 'At least for tonight. I won't ask questions you cannot – or will not – answer. And you can stop treating me as if I'm a cross between Casanova and Bluebeard.'

He stood up before Mary could reply, and she felt bereft as he took his hand away from her arm. Then she saw that Lucinda was approaching with a glass of lemonade.

'Perhaps you will do me the honour of allowing me to take you down to supper later, Mrs Drayton?' he said. 'Miss Burleigh.' He acknowledged Lucinda courteously and strolled away.

'Do you feel better?' Lucinda asked solicitously.

'Very much, thank you.' Mary smiled at her. 'I'm so sorry to have made such a spectacle of myself. I'm not normally vapourish.'

'I don't think anyone else noticed,' Lucinda reassured her. 'I didn't myself at first, but then Lord Hawkridge saw that you were unwell and he indicated that I should speak to you. I think he was afraid that you might be startled if he did so.'

'That was very – considerate – of him,' said Mary. Her throat was choked with unshed tears, but she took a small sip of lemonade, forcing herself to swallow it.

'I think he is a nice man,' said Lucinda. 'He did not seem at all bored to be talking to me about art. He told me all about the great pictures he's seen in Italy, and. . .'

She prattled on, repeating almost verbatim much of what Justin had said to her, offering no cues signalling the need of a reply. Such loquacity was so uncharacteristic that Mary was sure that Lucinda was merely trying to provide her with an opportunity to recover her composure. She was very grateful for the girl's tact and kindness. And by the time Mr Penrose approached them she was more determined than ever that Lucinda shouldn't be hurt by Samuel.

'My dear, you look a little pale. Are you quite well?' Mr Penrose asked anxiously.

'Oh, yes,' Mary replied brightly. 'I did feel a trifle faint a few minutes ago, but Miss Burleigh kindly brought me some lemonade and now I'm quite refreshed.'

'I saw Lord Hawkridge conversing with you,' said Mr Penrose, looking put out. 'What can he possibly have had to say at such length?'

'He was talking to me,' said Lucinda, surprisingly. 'He was telling me about a tour he made of Italy.'

'I see.' Mr Penrose gave the appearance of a man who had a great deal to say, but who had unfortunately just had a gag shoved in his mouth.

Lucinda glanced from Mr Penrose to Mary. 'Excuse me,' she said. 'I think Mama is beckoning to me.'

'What a very thoughtful girl she is,' Mary said warmly. 'Have you had any private conversation with Mrs Burleigh, sir? Does it seem to you that there is any substance to the idea that Samuel is trying to fix his interest with Lucinda?'

Mr Penrose had been about to make a further comment on Lord Hawkridge, but instead he frowned, looking even more anxious and wizened than normal.

'I fear so,' he said heavily. 'Apparently Mrs Burleigh was in daily expectation of receiving a formal visit from him before he suddenly went out of town. But perhaps——' he brightened '– that means he has thought better of the scheme.'

'Or perhaps he was simply trying to pique Miss Burleigh's interest. Or perhaps he had some other business that he urgently had to attend to,' said Mary drily. 'Mr Penrose, don't you think it might be advisable to give Mrs Burleigh some hint that he won't have control of his inheritance for another two years?'

'No!' Mr Penrose exclaimed emphatically.

'But if Lucinda is truly considering marrying him, that is something they have a right to know,' said Mary reasonably. 'I'm not suggesting that you should mention our other suspicions. But when the marriage settlements are drawn up the constraints on his inheritance will become common knowledge. They might as well know sooner rather than later.'

Mr Penrose shook his head obstinately. 'It may not be necessary for them to ever know,' he said. 'And I cannot feel comfortable discussing Samuel's affairs with strangers before I have first discussed them with Samuel.'

Mary pressed her lips together, but she didn't pursue her point. Around them, couples were beginning to go down to supper, and she saw Justin walking towards them. So did Mr Penrose. She heard him give a muffled exclamation of annoyance, then Justin was bowing before her.

'Mrs Drayton,' he said, 'may I escort you down to supper?'

'Thank you, my lord,' Mr Penrose intervened stiffly before Mary could speak, 'but that will not be necessary. I will escort my niece myself.'

Justin raised his eyebrows haughtily. 'I believe Mrs Drayton is already promised to me, sir,' he said coldly. 'Is that not so, ma'am?'

'Mary!' Mr Penrose exclaimed, too put out to show his normal, anxious awe of Lord Hawkridge. 'Is that true?'

Mary hesitated, glancing from Justin's arrogant, unyielding expression to Mr Penrose's unbecomingly flushed and indignant face. She had no doubt of what the outcome would be if Mr Penrose refused to back down, and she had no desire to be the centre of an unpleasant scene. She laid her hand lightly on his arm.

'Forgive me, Uncle,' she said, 'but I believe I did promise Lord Hawkridge I would go down with him. I'm sure Miss Lewisham would be delighted to go down with you.'

For a moment Mr Penrose looked obstinate. Then she saw the acquiescence in his eyes, and felt a flicker of relief. She stood up and allowed Justin to escort her out of the room.

CHAPTER FIVE

'How can you tolerate him?' Justin demanded as they walked downstairs.

'He is a *little* trying,' Mary conceded. 'But he's very worried at the moment.'

She was on tenterhooks as to what Justin might say to her, yet at the same time she felt almost exhilarated. Whatever happened in the future, she was with Justin now. And he had spoken kindly to her. If this was to be the last time they met, at least they could part on friendly terms, without bitterness. She knew that was the best she could ever hope for.

There was a cold supper laid out in the dining-room. Justin went to fetch Mary something to eat and a glass of champagne. The moment she was alone she found herself the centre of a small group of young people. She had enjoyed a lively conversation with them earlier in the evening, but now she felt almost frustrated by their friendliness. She wanted to be with Justin.

'Mrs Drayton, do you care for riding?' asked a young but extremely dashing young man in a heavily embroidered waistcoat.

'Very much,' Mary replied, trying hard not to follow Justin with her eyes.

'I was sure you must!' he exclaimed. 'Caroline

and I——' he nodded towards his sister '—are planning to set up an expedition to ride over to Norton St Philip tomorrow. We're going to have luncheon at the George. Would you care to make up one of our party?'

A quick smile lit up Mary's eyes. Riding had been her one extravagance during her years at the Lazy Cat, though she'd always been careful to do nothing to draw undesirable attention to herself. Her love of speed had been indulged only very early in the morning, when there was no one to see her galloping flat out across the fields behind the inn.

'I'd love to do so,' she said. 'Unfortunately, I can foresee at least two problems. I haven't got a horse and, since I didn't expect to be riding when I came to Bath, I didn't bring a riding habit.'

'Oh, that's easily solved,' Caroline said quickly. 'You can borrow a habit from me, and Peter will arrange to hire a hack for you. Do say you'll come.'

'Well. . .' Mary hesitated.

She had no doubt that she would enjoy the expedition, but she'd never intended to become so caught up in the social whirl of Bath. Besides, although it was flattering to be included so generously in the activities of her new acquaintances, she couldn't help wondering how they'd react if they found out she wasn't Mr Penrose's niece.

'I did promise my uncle I'd go to the Pump Room with him tomorrow morning,' she said, glancing across to where Mr Penrose was staring darkly at his fellow guests. 'Thank you, my lord,' she added as she accepted the champagne and the plate of elegant patties that Justin offered her.

A slight constraint fell upon the group at Justin's presence. The young people were somewhat in awe of him, and not quite sure what to say to him. It was Caroline who broke the silence. She was too ebullient to remain overawed for long.

'Lord Hawkridge, don't you think a ride would be better for Mrs Drayton than a glass of water in the stuffy Pump Room?' she demanded.

He smiled. 'You sound like a woman after my own heart, Miss. . .?' He paused, raising his eyebrows enquiringly.

'King,' she supplied. 'Caroline King. This is my brother, Peter. And this is Adam Hastings.'

'How do you do?'

There was a round of mutual acknowledgements, then Peter King said shyly, 'Would you like to accompany us, my lord? Of course, if you have another engagement. . .' His voice trailed away as if he was amazed at his own presumption.

'I'd be delighted to do so,' Justin replied immediately. 'And I'm sure, between us, we can persuade Mrs Drayton that a ride in the fresh air is just what she needs.'

'I'll have my best habit sent round to you first thing,' said Caroline eagerly. 'And we'll call for you at ten o'clock. And Peter will hire a horse for you.'

'Let me take care of that,' said Justin smoothly.

'I will have to procure a mount for myself, and I can just as easily do so for Mrs Drayton as well.'

'It seems that all my objections have been overruled,' said Mary, smiling.

Her frustration at having her brief interlude with Justin interrupted had been ameliorated by the prospect of riding with him. They wouldn't be alone together, of course, but that was probably a good thing. She wanted the solace of his company, but she knew that for both their sakes she had to continue to keep him at a distance.

Then she glanced across the room towards Lucinda. Despite the fact that the party was in Lucinda's honour, she was sitting talking to her mother and Mrs Knightley. She looked both sad and uncomfortable. Mary didn't say anything, but her lips pressed together in a firm line. A faint smile illuminated Justin's eyes as he followed the direction of her glance, but he didn't say anything either.

'But she probably won't want to come,' Caroline protested, quickly divining Mary's thoughts. 'Mrs Burleigh will say it's too hazardous, and Lucinda never does anything even remotely adventurous. Besides, she hasn't got a horse either.'

'Not an insurmountable problem,' Justin said. 'I would be happy to deal with it.'

'It is her party, Caroline,' her brother pointed out. 'My lord,' he appealed to Justin, 'perhaps if *you* asked Mrs Burleigh would be more willing to agree.'

'Miss King?' said Justin quietly.

Caroline pouted for a moment, then she smiled ruefully.

'I didn't mean to be ungracious,' she said. 'It's just that I've never really felt I know Lucinda. Perhaps if she comes for a ride with us it will be different.'

'In that case I will execute my commission without delay,' Justin declared.

Mary watched Lucinda's face light up as Justin spoke to Mrs Burleigh. Then she glanced across the room to where Mr Penrose was virtually ignoring Miss Lewisham in his efforts to keep an eye on Lord Hawkridge. She wondered what he would say when she told him about the riding trip – but it really wasn't any of his business.

After supper there was an impromptu dance. Mary looked on, outwardly calm, but inwardly apprehensive, as the preparations were made. She had learnt to waltz over a decade ago with Sir Richard's daughters, romping round the nursery at the manor-house while her father played chess with Sir Richard, but since then she had never had an opportunity to practise.

She had just decided that she wouldn't dance, when Justin appeared at her side, pre-empting Peter King by seconds.

'Dance with me?' he asked.

'I don't think so,' said Mary, although suddenly the prospect of waltzing had become extremely enticing. 'I haven't danced since I was fourteen,' she explained. 'I'm not sure I remember how.'

'In that case it's essential that you dance with me first,' said Justin reasonably. 'You can practise on me, and I'll promise not to tell anyone how many times you step on me.'

Mary was surprised into laughter.

'What a gallant offer!' she exclaimed.

'It is, isn't it?' he agreed.

He took her hand, and even through her gloves she felt the warm, compelling pressure of his fingers. As he drew her on to the dance-floor, and circled her waist with his other hand, she suddenly wondered if this was a good idea. He was too close to her, and she was too intimately aware of his every move. She could feel the warmth of his hand through the thin fabric of her dress, and her heart began to race.

She knew she was blushing, and she didn't dare look up at him. She couldn't remember ever feeling this fierce excitement in his presence when she'd first known him. But in those days she had almost deliberately closed her mind to the physical attraction between them.

Seven years ago, the sordid bargain she had struck with Bill Crawford – when she had sold herself to the thief in return for his protection – had still been a very recent memory. And it had severely numbed her capacity to experience sensual pleasure. She had loved Justin deeply. But it had been for his compassion, his humour and his insight – not for the burning desire that his touch aroused in her.

But in the years since they'd last met something

had changed. Now she was acutely aware of every aspect of his physical presence. She was almost shamefully conscious of the latent power within his large frame, and the confident assurance with which he guided her around the floor.

She remembered the way he'd swept her into his arms in the stables three days ago, and how difficult it had been for her to resist. If he kissed her again she would be even less able to withstand the aching yearning that he ignited in her.

But she had to resist him because otherwise she was doomed to become his mistress – and that would destroy her.

'I could keep the time for you,' Justin murmured in her ear. 'One, two, three, one, two, three. . .'

'Be quiet!' Mary whispered fiercely. 'I've got to concentrate!'

'I'd noticed!'

Mary gasped indignantly, and put all her effort into minding her feet. In fact she concentrated so hard that she almost forgot it was Justin she was dancing with, and it was only later that she wondered if that was what he'd intended. Had he realised how disturbed she was becoming and deliberately tried to distract her?

For a brief instant she almost panicked, but then she reassured herself that he couldn't possibly have known the cause of her agitation. He was simply being kind to her because he knew she was feeling unsure of herself in unfamiliar surroundings.

The music was beguiling and the room was full of colour and light. Almost in spite of herself Mary began to relax, giving herself up to the enjoyment of the dance. It was an innocent pleasure, and her joy in it was as pure and untarnished as a soap bubble, floating up in the sunlight.

But her happiness was as fragile as the bubble – and inevitably the music came to an end.

She danced the next waltz with Peter King.

'How excellently you dance!' he exclaimed. 'But I dare say you've had a great deal of practice. Lucinda Burleigh was telling me earlier that you've travelled. I expect Bath seems very tame in comparison to some of the places you've seen!'

'Not at all!' Mary replied quickly. 'In fact, I can hardly remember when I last had such an entertaining time. Everyone has made me feel so welcome!'

'You make it very easy for us to do so,' Peter complimented her.

'Thank you, sir,' she said, more gratified by his flattery than she cared to admit to herself. After so many years of providing unobtrusive service to her customers, it was unbelievably comforting to be noticed as a woman in her own right. When this adventure was over, she would go back to her old life at the Lazy Cat, but at least she would take some happy memories with her – as well as painful ones.

She sat out one dance with Lucinda.

'It's your doing that I've been invited tomorrow, isn't it?' the younger girl asked.

'Oh, no – Mr and Miss King arranged everything,' Mary replied lightly.

'But I'm sure Caroline wouldn't have asked me if you hadn't suggested it,' said Lucinda. 'I know she thinks I'm dull. I once heard her describe me as a mouse without a squeak!'

'She's certainly a very outspoken young lady,' Mary said drily. 'No doubt she'll learn to be more circumspect in time. Are you happy to come with us?'

'You mean, do I feel offended because I've only been invited at your prompting? And by someone who has such a...a *diminishing* opinion of me?' Lucinda asked quietly.

Mary glanced at her, a quick, almost rueful smile in her grey eyes.

'Yes, that's what I meant,' she said.

'No.' Lucinda sighed. 'I don't blame them for thinking I'm boring,' she added. 'But I would like Caroline to like me. Does that sound stupid?'

'No,' said Mary gently. 'I can remember times when I've felt the same way.'

'Peter King danced with me earlier,' Lucinda continued, more brightly. 'He does so sometimes; I think he feels sorry for me.'

'Perhaps he likes you,' Mary suggested.

'I don't know.' Lucinda began to pleat her handkerchief nervously. 'Excuse me, ma'am, but does Mr Penrose disapprove of Lord Hawkridge paying attention to you?' she asked in a rush.

'I'm not sure that he is paying any special attention to me,' Mary replied calmly, although her heart began to beat a little faster.

'I didn't mean to be impertinent; it's just – it's just that I think you should know that Cousin Emma often speaks a great deal of foolishness!' Lucinda blurted, her words tumbling over each other in her haste to say them. 'I think Lord Hawkridge is a very kind man, even if he did make fun of her this morning – which she quite deserved for being so toadying to him.'

'Thank you,' said Mary. She smiled at Lucinda. 'You are very considerate.'

'Then you aren't offended?' Lucinda asked, relieved.

'Of course not.' Mary looked away, watching the dancers twirl around the floor. Candlelight reflected from the softly shining silk dresses. She knew it was a sight she would remember for a long time.

'In return for your kindness, may I also risk being impertinent?' she asked abruptly, turning back to Lucinda.

The girl nodded, although she looked slightly apprehensive.

'Are you very attached to Samuel?' Mary asked bluntly.

Lucinda began to pleat her handkerchief again, not meeting Mary's eyes.

'I think he is a very handsome and charming gentleman,' she said in a low voice. 'I was so thrilled when he singled me out – and he was kind to me. . . Do I sound very foolish?' She looked up suddenly.

'No.'

'But I think. . .' Lucinda took a deep breath, as if she was trying to keep up her courage '. . .I think you were warning me against him this morning in the Pump Room, and now I'm not sure. I think. . .perhaps it was too good to be true that anyone could be interested in me for myself. After all, even a rich man who wanted to improve his estate might think it was worthwhile marrying me to do so, mightn't he?'

She tried to smile bravely, but she had to catch her lower lip between her teeth to stop it trembling.

'My dear, it wasn't your desirability I was calling into question,' said Mary quietly. 'I'm sure that somewhere in the world, possibly even in this room, there is a man who would marry you even if you didn't have a penny to your name.'

'I did wonder why Samuel went away so suddenly,' Lucinda told her. 'If he'd truly cared about me he would have told me why – or perhaps he wouldn't have gone. Or maybe he saw that I was getting too attached to him and he thought it was better to leave.'

It seemed to Mary that Lucinda was taking her own inadequacy for granted. According to Lucinda's interpretation, either Samuel was only interested in her for her fortune, or he wasn't interested in her at all, and had left her to prove it.

It was very difficult to think of anything to say

which might help. It certainly wasn't going to do much for Lucinda's self-esteem to discover that Samuel's only motive for courting her was to pay off his debts.

'Can I be very odious and give you some unsolicited advice?' Mary asked, trying to find a way out of the dilemma.

Lucinda nodded.

'Supposing we forget about Samuel for a moment and imagine that a hypothetical Prince Charming is just about to walk through the drawing-room door,' said Mary. 'And he is an honourable, noble and worthy man. And suppose he sees you, and you see him, and you both fall instantly in love – the rest of us would be green with envy.'

Lucinda smiled wanly at the fantasy.

'But if at that moment he carried you away across his saddlebow to live the rest of your life in an enchanted kingdom, you would never learn any more about the world you left behind than you know right now,' Mary continued. 'You might never get to see for yourself the paintings and statues in Rome – or even get another chance to paint the view from Beechen Cliff without muddying the washes.'

Lucinda acknowledged the last few words with a distracted smile, but for the most part she watched Mary's face intently.

'Are you telling me I shouldn't fall in love with Samuel?' she asked, still painfully absorbed by her immediate anxieties.

'I'm telling you that when you gamble with

something as important as the rest of your life you should be very clear of what you stand to win or lose,' said Mary. 'Believe me, I know what I'm talking about!'

'You do look dashing, ma'am,' said Hetty approvingly, next morning.

Mary laughed, taking one last glance at herself in the mirror.

The riding habit Caroline King had sent round was a vibrant cherry-red, with a neat bodice and huge flowing skirts. It was trimmed with braid almost up to the elbows, and there was more braid on the bodice and skirt. The costume was completed by a tall hat, which had a filmy veil attached to its crown. Mary knew the veil would flutter provocatively at the slightest breeze, and it amused her to think how much Caroline must enjoy wearing it.

'I think Miss King is the dashing one,' she said to Hetty. 'It was kind of her to lend it to me.'

'I'm sure you'll have a wonderful time, ma'am,' said Hetty. 'It's a beautiful, fine morning, and there isn't much wind either.'

'Thank you.' Mary smiled at her, and then went down to face Mr Penrose.

He looked up disapprovingly as she entered the drawing-room.

'A most unsuitable costume,' he grumbled. 'I cannot think how you came to agree to such an expedition. Have you forgotten why we came to Bath?'

'No, I haven't,' said Mary calmly, laying her hat down on the table. 'You came to Bath to confront Samuel with your suspicions, and I came to support you. But I have always been as concerned for Miss Burleigh's sake as I am for yours.'

'That's no reason to go riding with Lord Hawkridge!' Mr Penrose protested.

'I'm not – or only incidentally,' Mary retorted. 'I'm going riding with Lucinda Burleigh and her friends. Mr Penrose,' she continued blandly, 'you won't allow me to mention our suspicions to Mrs Burleigh, and it may be that you are right to do so. But it cannot do any harm to encourage Lucinda to take a more active part in Bath life. If she has more friends, it may be that she won't be so susceptible to the flattery of your nephew and we won't need to take any further steps on her behalf.'

Mr Penrose stared at her, chewing his lips nervously. Then his expression cleared a little.

'I'm sorry, my dear,' he said heavily. 'I did not mean to seem critical. I dare say you may be right about Miss Burleigh. But I cannot help being concerned about you. Miss Lewisham was telling me such things about Lord Hawkridge last night. . .'

'I expect she was,' said Mary briskly. 'Scandal appears to be her only interest. *Our* concern should be Samuel. From what Lucinda tells me, he seems to have left Bath only the day before he came to demand money from you. Something must have prompted his hurried departure – a communication from the money-lender perhaps. But he hasn't been back to Bath since, though that was certainly his intention when I overheard him talking to Phelps.'

'Perhaps he's thought better of his wild words,' said Mr Penrose hopefully. 'Or perhaps he's hiding from the money-lender.'

'That could be possible,' said Mary thoughtfully, tapping her gloves against her hand. 'From the sound of him, he employs extremely violent collection methods. But I'm not convinced. What do you intend to say to Samuel when we do see him?'

'I don't know,' Mr Penrose admitted anxiously. 'I suppose I must let him have enough money to pay off this debt – and then warn him against such behaviour in future.'

'I think you should give him complete control of his fortune immediately – if that's possible,' said Mary frankly. 'And also make it clear to him that he is not – and never will be – a beneficiary under your own will.'

'But I am supposed to hold his inheritance in trust for him until he can deal with it responsibly!' Mr Penrose protested. 'It is not responsible to hand it over to money-lenders, or fritter it away on wild living. And as to my will – he is my only close relative.'

'I know,' said Mary drily. 'That's precisely my point, sir. There is nothing you can do about his extravagance. He will undoubtedly dissipate his fortune as soon as he gains control of it. It makes no difference if he does so now or in two years' time.

'And as far as your own property is concerned,' she continued after a pause, 'leave it to your old school, the local foundling home, the Royal Society, the Church. . .it doesn't matter. But make sure Samuel knows your death will never be of any benefit to him. Then we can all sleep more comfortably at night.'

Mr Penrose stared at her, horror dawning in his face at the forcefulness of her advice, and the deadly serious manner in which she spoke.

'You really do think I'm in danger,' he said, the depth of his shock audible in his voice. 'I didn't know. . . I thought it was just that he was talking wildly in his cups. I thought. . .just scandal. Perhaps he would try to take advantage of Miss Burleigh, but. . .' He gazed at her, kneading his hands together in distress. 'Oh, dear! Oh, dear! Whatever am I going to do?'

Mary crossed quickly to his side, sitting down beside him.

'There is no reason to be so alarmed, sir,' she reassured him. 'If you do as I suggest, he will have no motive to hurt you. Can you break the terms of your brother's will?'

'Yes. Once Samuel had reached twenty-one, it was left at my discretion as to when I gave control to him,' said Mr Penrose miserably. 'That's why he is so angry with me. Are you really sure?'

'I have heard men make threats before,' said Mary quietly. 'It may be that he was speaking idly, but I don't believe he was.'

'Why didn't you tell me what you feared

before?' Mr Penrose asked fretfully, but then he answered for her, before she could speak. 'You did, I just didn't understand how seriously you meant it. I will do as you suggest. This very morning I shall go into Bath and have a new will drawn up. And I shall set in train the arrangements for handing over control of his inheritance to Samuel. Oh, I do hope these precautions aren't necessary.'

'So do I,' said Mary. 'But they cannot hurt. And when you've done that I think we should perhaps make further enquiries about Samuel's whereabouts. We cannot let this matter drift forever.'

'No,' said Mr Penrose. He looked at her with something that was almost a smile on his thin, nervous face. 'You seem to be far less daunted by all this than I am, my dear.'

'That's because I'm not directly involved,' Mary replied. 'It's always easier to give advice when it's not your problem.'

She glanced round as the door opened, and stood up as the butler came into the room.

'Lord Hawkridge and his friends have arrived, ma'am,' he announced.

'Thank you. I will be with them directly.' She caught up the long train of her skirt in her hand and went to pick up her hat. Then she looked at Mr Penrose and smiled. 'I'll see you later, sir. Please don't worry too much. I'm sure we can sort things out satisfactorily.'

CHAPTER SIX

'You ride very well,' Justin said. There was genuine appreciation in his voice, and Mary blushed rosily at the compliment. Praise from Justin meant so much more to her than from any other man.

'Thank you!' she replied, a sparkle of pleasure in her eyes.

Their party had separated quite naturally into three couples, with Caroline King and Adam Hastings leading, Lucinda and Peter King next, and Justin and Mary bringing up the rear. Occasionally Mary would hear a ripple of laughter carried back on the wind from Caroline, and she knew that the ebullient Miss King was enjoying a lively flirtation with her companion.

Lucinda was more subdued, both because she was shy and because she was far less at home in the saddle than Caroline. But Mary noticed that Peter was taking good care that nothing should alarm either Lucinda or her horse.

'I should have guessed you'd be an excellent horsewoman,' said Justin. 'But we've never had an opportunity to ride together before. Did your father teach you?'

'No. One of Sir Richard's grooms.' Mary smiled reminiscently, looking back over the years to her childhood. She glanced at Justin, a mischievous twinkle in her grey eyes. 'We used to gallop over the Downs as if the devil himself were after us,' she confessed. 'Thomas used to say, "Now, Miss Mary, now, Miss Liz, remember you're *ladies*," but it never used to stop us.'

'I don't suppose it did!' said Justin, grinning. I can't think of a better incitement to go faster. I dare say you got into all sorts of scrapes.'

'Oh, yes!' Mary laughed. 'Elizabeth was always slightly more restrained than I was. I always wanted to go farther and faster. I came off in a ditch once, when Thomas had already warned me not to tackle it. I was very young then. I let go of the reins and Daphne cantered off home. Thomas made me walk back through the village in my muddy habit to punish me for my wilfulness – I was so humiliated!'

Justin laughed. 'I wish I'd seen that,' he said.

'If you'd seen it my folly would have been immortalised on the pages of your sketchbook and I'd never have lived it down!' Mary retorted.

'Possibly.' He grinned. 'On the other hand, I'm only four years older than you, so if you were very young at the time. . .'

'I was ten,' said Mary.

'Ah, well, in that case I would certainly have sketched you,' said Justin. 'I was quite a competent draughtsman by the time I was fourteen – and even more inclined to sketch everything I saw in those days than I am now.'

'Lucky for me you didn't see me, then,' said Mary.

'Perhaps. Have you had much opportunity to ride recently?' He asked the question casually, as if it were of no importance, but Mary suddenly realised that he was waiting alertly for her answer.

She caught her breath. She had been enjoying her memories of the uncomplicated happiness she had known as a child, but now she had to deal once more with the difficulties and uncertainties of the present.

'I do ride,' she said cautiously, 'but not often on such a fine mare as this one.' She leant forward and patted the grey appreciatively on the neck. The mare tossed her head, snorting, demonstrating her quality, and Mary laughed. 'I was expecting a tired hack. Where did you get her?'

'I borrowed her from a friend of mine,' Justin replied. From the gleam in his eyes, Mary knew he was aware that she'd evaded his question, but for the moment it seemed he wasn't going to press it. 'For a price,' he added.

'What price?' Mary asked, intrigued by the amusement in his voice.

'He wants me to paint a portrait for him,' Justin explained.

'Oh.' Mary looked at him suspiciously. His expression was grave, as befitted a man who had undertaken a serious commission from a friend, but Mary knew him too well to be deceived. 'Whose portrait?' she demanded.

'Fanny Matilda's.'

'And who——?'

'His prize sow.'

Mary was startled into a choke of laughter. The mare's ears twitched responsively to the unexpected sound, and Justin grinned.

The winter sunlight was clear and bright, and a warm glow of happiness had brought pretty colour to Mary's cheeks. The soft tawny curls which peeped out beneath her tall hat shone in the light and her veil fluttered in the breeze.

'You'll enjoy that!' she exclaimed, glancing instinctively towards Justin, expecting to see an answering gleam of humour in his expression.

Instead she found herself gazing straight into his eyes. He was no longer laughing. He was looking at her with an intensity which made her pulse race. Both horses came to a standstill, as if they were aware of their riders' preoccupation.

Justin's neat chestnut crowded the mare. The grey flicked her ears irritably, but she made no other protest. Then Justin slipped an arm around Mary's shoulders and leant over to kiss her.

His lips were warm and persuasive on hers. She felt his tongue, gently probing and coaxing her still closed mouth, and her lips parted instinctively.

The world spun away. She had no power to protest. She turned towards him, leaning into the kiss, one hand loosely holding the reins. Her other hand, still grasping her riding crop, lifted to clutch at his collar.

The kiss deepened as he began to explore her mouth, taking his time, slowly and insistently arousing her, matching his actions to her responses. Last night she had nearly lost herself in his arms when they'd danced together and he had gently reminded her of their surroundings. Today he made it impossible for her to be aware of anything but his caresses.

Excitement and pleasure coursed through her. She forgot her good intentions to keep him at a distance, and clung to his collar like a drowning man clinging to a rope. Last time he had kissed her she had been angry and insulted by his unfounded accusations. This time she had already been in sympathy with him and it was easy to surrender herself to his kiss.

He could sense her willingness, and her desire, and his arm tightened around her shoulders. She was leaning far over into his embrace, supported partly by his arms and partly by the side-saddle. It was a precarious cradle, yet she felt quite secure.

At last he lifted his head. She opened her eyes, a soft, instinctive sound of protest in her throat. He was breathing quickly, his hazel eyes – only inches from hers – dark with passion, but he smiled crookedly.

'If we pursue this much further we may both end up in an indignified heap on the grass,' he murmured.

Mary gasped, suddenly remembering where they were – and what had happened. She straightened up hurriedly, feeling the cool breeze on her burning cheeks. She glanced ahead; Lucinda and Peter were almost out of sight. She could only hope that neither of them had looked behind. She gathered up the reins.

'We must catch up,' she said hurriedly, feeling confused and embarrassed and unsure of herself.

'Not yet.' Justin caught her arm before she could urge the mare forward.

Mary looked at him, her bewilderment and uncertainty evident in her eyes. She had been trying to convince herself that a few hours in Justin's company would be enough to compensate her for all the lonely years ahead. But now he had confronted her not only with his desire for her but also her desire for him.

She was afraid. It would be so easy to give in to him. And then she would lose everything. Her self-respect, her independence, her security. She couldn't let Justin, of all men, do that to her.

'What are you afraid of?' he asked softly.

'*Nothing*!' Mary denied, more vehemently than she'd intended.

'Then why won't you talk to me?' he demanded. 'You used to talk to me, for God's sake! You used to tell me whatever you were thinking.'

'That was a long time ago,' said Mary tautly.

'I know that!' He bit off the hastily uttered words, staring at her in exasperation. 'What have you been doing these last seven years?' he asked more temperately.

'Managing,' Mary replied, her eyes briefly losing their focus as she remembered the loneliness that lay behind her.

'*How*?'

Mary glanced back at him. It hurt her that he couldn't let that question rest. That he couldn't trust her when she'd told him that she'd lived a respectable life.

'How do you think?' she asked bitterly. 'I've done very well. I don't need your help, or anyone else's, my lord.'

'You never did,' said Justin, an icy note creeping into his voice.

Mary heard the coldness and a wave of despair swept over her. She stretched one hand impulsively towards him.

'Please don't!' she begged, her pain visible in her eyes. 'I'll be leaving Bath soon. I couldn't bear it if we parted on terms of bitterness after we've already——' She broke off, no longer trusting her voice to remain steady.

'After we've already what?' Justin asked, taking her hand. His eyes were hard and searching on her face, but he held her hand in a warm and comforting clasp. Mary wanted to cry, but she swallowed back her tears and smiled bravely.

'All this time you've thought I deserted you and I've believed you no longer wanted me,' she said. 'Isn't it enough to know that neither of us betrayed the other? We've moved on since then. You've come into your inheritance, I've...made a new life for myself. We can't go back.'

'If you're trying to tell me you no longer feel anything for me, I don't believe you,' said Justin harshly. 'We don't have to go back, we can go forward – if only you would allow us to do so.'

'No!' Mary dragged her hand out of his grasp. Any minute now he would renew his offer to make her his mistress and she didn't want to hear it. She didn't want to be reminded of the only role she was fit to play in his life – and she was afraid she wouldn't have the strength to refuse him.

She put her heel to the mare's side. The grey bounded forward, eager to stretch her legs, and the chestnut matched her instantly. Mary leant forward, urging the grey into a gallop. The wind whipped at her skirts and tugged at her hat. Normally she would have gloried in the power of the mare's smooth stride, but today she was simply trying to escape. She wanted to gallop through the fresh winter morning forever, until her past was left so far behind that she could no longer see it or remember it.

The horses' hooves drummed on the ground, echoing the pounding of her heart. Trees flashed past her, blurred and indistinguishable from each other. Faces of men long dead or gone from her life flashed upon her inner eye with far more clarity. Her father, her uncle, Bill Crawford, even Donald. She had trusted them all once, and they had all betrayed her. She wished she could forget them, erase them from her memory – but she couldn't. They would be part of her forever.

Ahead of them she could see Lucinda and Peter. They had turned to look back. Beside her she could see Justin out of the corner of her eye.

'Mary!' he shouted over the thunder of hoofbeats.

She ignored him. She wondered if he would try to grab her reins. She was so overwrought that if he had done so she would have slashed at him with her crop.

But he didn't. The chestnut dropped back to a canter as they approached the others, and the grey slowed instinctively. A bitter smile twisted Mary's lips. It happened every time. At the very moment when she thought Justin was going to impose his will on her – force her to accede to his wishes – he drew back, and left her free to make her own decision.

It was one of the reasons why she loved him. She had never thought his forbearance sprang from weakness. It was a measure of his confidence in himself that he was prepared to give her so much room. But it made it so much harder to walk away from him.

For a brief instant she wondered what it would be like to be his mistress. Would he accord her the same freedom of choice in those circumstances? Perhaps there could be a future for them. Perhaps he would understand her need to preserve her independence. She could keep the Lazy Cat, maybe get someone in to help Donald run it when she was away. . .

The vision of a life which included Justin floated tantalisingly before her eyes. Then it faded. It was a compromise which could only bring unhappiness. She could not bear to live a life of such subterfuge – and she couldn't tolerate the fact that any children she bore would have no right to their father's name. She had sacrificed her own good name, but she could not inflict a similar shame on any innocent soul she brought into the world.

'I wish I could ride like you,' said Lucinda enviously, breaking into Mary's thoughts.

'It's only practice,' Mary replied, speaking with a lightness she didn't feel. 'I try to ride most mornings.'

She saw Justin glance at her sharply, and realised she'd inadvertently partially answered his earlier question, while at the same time arousing his curiosity.

'I hope you live somewhere you can indulge your taste for speed,' he said humorously, but with an intent expression in his eyes. 'It would never do to gallop like that down the Row.'

Despite herself, Mary smiled.

'It would certainly cause a stir,' she agreed. 'Perhaps I should try it one day when I'm feeling bored.'

'I'd like to be there to see you do it,' he said, an answering gleam in his eyes. 'With my sketchbook close to hand – to catch all the startled reactions.'

Peter laughed, but Lucinda turned eagerly towards Justin.

'Is it true you agreed to paint a pig in exchange for borrowing these horses?' she asked.

'Yes, Miss Burleigh.' He bowed slightly in her direction.

She stared at him incredulously.

'I thought Pete – Mr King – was teasing me!' she exclaimed. 'Are you sure you want to? A *pig*!'

'Not just any pig,' Justin said gravely. 'Fanny Matilda is a matriarch of substance – with several prizes to prove it. She also has a countenance full of character and dignity. I will enjoy the commission.'

Mary glanced at him, hearing the sincerity in his voice. She knew he was speaking the truth. Justin could find beauty and interest in the most unlikely subjects.

'You've already met the *grande dame*, then?' she said teasingly.

'Oh, yes. Henderson was very anxious for me to make her acquaintance.'

'But how will you set about it?' Lucinda asked, genuinely interested.

In a few moments a lively discussion ensued on the merits of oil or water-colour for the commission, the need for preliminary sketches, and exactly how the model was going to be posed.

Mary dropped back, and found Peter riding beside her.

'I hope Miss Burleigh is enjoying herself,' he said.

'She certainly seems to be doing so,' Mary replied, smiling.

She was grateful for the distraction of conversation. It would have been so easy to lose herself in contemplation of Justin and her own problems, but she was conscious that she still had to present an unexceptional manner to her other companions.

'Perhaps we should have made more of an effort

to include her in our diversions before,' Peter conceded contritely. 'But she has always been so retiring, and I was. . .that is, we were anxious not to seem as if we were only pursuing her friendship because she's an heiress.'

'Your sensitivity does you credit,' said Mary drily.

He flushed. 'You think I should have made more of an effort, ma'am?' he asked awkwardly. 'But Caroline——' He broke off, obviously not wishing to repeat his sister's opinions on the subject.

'You were in a difficult situation,' Mary said more kindly.

'I did start to pay more attention to her,' Peter insisted eagerly. 'But then Penrose appeared and she seemed so taken with him. Of course, he's rich. I could hardly compete——' He broke off again, looking vexed with himself for his indiscretion.

'Do you really think Miss Burleigh is more interested in a man's possessions than in his character?' Mary asked quietly.

'Of course not!' he exclaimed indignantly.

'Well, then.'

'But my prospects are in no way comparable to Penrose's. Though there is something about him I cannot quite like. . .' He caught himself up, his eyes flying to Mary's face in consternation. 'I'm sorry,' he said stiffly. 'I had forgotten he was your cousin.'

'Please don't apologise,' said Mary calmly. 'If

we are to be entirely honest, I must confess that I also find there is something about him that I cannot quite like – but I beg you will never repeat that to anyone.'

He met her eyes steadily for a moment. She was increasingly coming to the opinion that there was more to him than his flamboyant waistcoats suggested, and she wasn't disappointed.

'You have my word,' he said seriously but without over-emphasis. 'Thank you, ma'am.' He urged his horse forward to overtake Lucinda and Lord Hawkridge, and a moment later Justin fell back beside Mary.

'*Where* do you manage to ride most mornings?' he asked immediately.

'Justin——'

'No,' he interrupted her without apology. 'If you think I'm going to let you disappear without any idea of your whereabouts, you are much mistaken. You did it once – you're not doing it again.'

'I *didn't*——' Mary broke off, biting her lip. She looked up and met Justin's eyes.

'So you say,' he said drily. 'Does Penrose have some kind of hold over you? Is that why you're so reluctant to trust me?'

'No!' Mary insisted.

'It does seem unlikely,' Justin conceded, a faint smile on his lips as he saw her outraged expression. 'You have a far stronger personality than he has. But you might be using him to protect you from someone else – the way you once used Bill Crawford.'

'*No!*' This time anger throbbed in Mary's voice. 'I don't need his protection or anyone else's. I can look after myself.'

'Then what is so terrible about your life these past seven years that you can't tell me about it?' Justin demanded fiercely. 'Do you have so little faith in my ability to understand?'

'I don't want you to understand!' Mary retorted wildly. 'I want you to leave me alone! Why can't you believe me when I tell you I managed by myself? I have done nothing to be ashamed of – nothing.'

'I didn't say you had any reason to be ashamed,' said Justin tightly. 'But it's hard to believe your life is entirely – to your choosing, shall we say? – when you're so adamant in refusing to tell me about it. Don't you think I have any right to know what's become of you?'

'Right?' Mary spat furiously.

Too much had been said already, and she was still wound up from Justin's kiss. She was far too upset to realise that she was making him the target for all the accumulated anger and pain of her life.

'I don't think anyone has any rights left in me, my lord – not even you!' She lifted her chin proudly; her veil fluttered defiantly in the breeze. 'Hasn't it occurred to you that I might not have told you where I live simply because I don't want you to follow me?' she demanded.

Justin stared at her, tight-lipped. Once again

the horses had come to a halt, but this time the gulf that had widened between them seemed almost unbridgeable.

'Why?' he demanded.

'Because I never want to see you again,' she flung at him.

There was a moment's silence. The mare tossed her head restlessly, and Mary shortened the reins instinctively.

'I don't believe you,' said Justin harshly, a muscle twitching in his rigid cheek.

'Of course you don't!' Mary exclaimed recklessly. 'You don't believe anything I say! But if I'd told you I was Mr Penrose's mistress, or that I'd been living in a brothel all these years, you'd have believed that!'

'*Mary!*'

'Don't touch me!' The grey mare danced uneasily aside as she saw Justin reach out towards her. 'I was happy!' she said bitterly. 'My life was ordered and comfortable. Then you just appear and think you can turn it all upside-down – but I'm not going to let you. No one's ever going to do that to me again.'

She swung the mare round and cantered after the others.

They ate a hearty luncheon at the George. It was an inn which, Peter cheerfully informed Mary, was famous for, among other things, providing shelter for the Duke of Monmouth during his ill-fated rebellion against James II.

'Apparently someone took a shot at him through the window. Missed him, of course, otherwise there'd have been no battle of Sedgemoor.'

'You know a great deal about local history,' said Lucinda shyly.

'I've lived in Bath all my life,' Peter replied gruffly, but he looked gratified.

Mary might have been pleased at the tentative friendship which was building between them, but she felt too disturbed to show more than a superficial interest in her companions. She needed time alone and she needed time to think, to come to terms with what had just happened – but she didn't have either. She wondered painfully if perhaps it was impossible for her to reach a comfortable understanding with Justin. Their feelings ran too deep and too strong. They must be lovers – or forever be at war with each other.

'Don't you think, Mrs Drayton?' said Lucinda, and Mary suddenly realised that she hadn't been paying any attention to the conversation.

'I beg your pardon?' She summoned up a smile and from then on forced herself to show an interest in her companions. Though she couldn't bring herself to look at Justin.

They lingered over the meal, and it was only towards the end that Mary discovered that Justin had been as remote from the others as she had.

'My lord! You've been sketching us!' Lucinda exclaimed suddenly.

Mary glanced round quickly. He wasn't even sitting at the table. He'd withdrawn slightly, just as he had used to do in the Blue Boar, when he'd wanted to observe without himself being observed. And they had all been so engrossed in their conversation that they hadn't noticed.

'Please, may I see?' Lucinda asked eagerly.

He hesitated fractionally, then handed her the sketchbook. They were seated informally, with Mary on Lucinda's right and Peter on her left, Caroline and Adam on the opposite side of the table with Justin.

Lucinda looked down at the picture, then she held it silently for Mary to see. On her other side, Peter craned his neck to get a better view.

The sketch had originally been intended to show all three of them, but Lucinda and Peter had been blocked in only roughly. All the artist's attention had been devoted to Mary. He had depicted her with her head turned towards Lucinda and Peter, apparently listening to her companions, yet she was clearly isolated from them.

Her pride, her pain and her loneliness were there for all to see, unrelentingly pinned to the cruel white page – but so was Justin's response. If he hadn't spared her, he hadn't spared himself either. And she saw more clearly than if he had spoken that he was as wounded as she was by everything that had happened between them.

She turned her head away, unable to look at the image any longer.

'May I see?' Caroline reached out imperatively to take the sketchbook. Then, when Lucinda did not immediately give it to her, she stood up, clearly intending to go and look over Lucinda's shoulder.

Lucinda turned the page quickly.

'I don't think you've flattered me, my lord,' she said, sounding almost vexed. 'I'm sure my nose isn't so long – and I'm positive you've made my eyes too small.'

'I didn't notice. . .but why don't you take your revenge, Miss Burleigh?' Peter said eagerly.

He reached over and picked up Justin's travelling ink-well, putting it down beside Lucinda.

'Oh, I couldn't!' she protested instinctively.

A warm smile dawned in Justin's eyes.

'Of course you can, Miss Burleigh,' he said. 'See, I will even sharpen your weapon for you.' And he picked up his knife and reshaped the pen nib for her.

'Well, if you're sure,' she said doubtfully.

'Go on, Lucinda!' Caroline urged her. 'I've never seen anything you've drawn. It will be fun.'

Lucinda glanced at Caroline, possibly recognising that she was being treated rather like a sideshow. Then she looked back at Justin. For a long moment she did nothing but study him, and Caroline stirred restlessly. Then Lucinda dipped the pen in the ink and began to draw with far more confidence than might have been expected in the circumstances.

Adam went to stand beside Caroline. They were all engrossed in what Lucinda was doing. Mary stood up and went quietly out of the room.

* * *

'Mrs Drayton.'

Peter found Mary standing in the churchyard. She was looking towards the church. Her veil was blowing jauntily behind her, but her expression was bleak and unfocused, and he didn't think she was aware of her surroundings.

'Mrs Drayton?' he said again.

She turned towards him. For a moment her eyes remained blank, then her familiar smile illuminated them.

'You shouldn't let considerations of wealth stand in the way of what you want,' she said, as if they were continuing a conversation. 'There are so many other, far more insurmountable barriers. Are we ready to go now?'

'Yes, ma'am.' He offered her his arm. 'We promised Mrs Burleigh we would bring Lucinda back in good time. She drew a very nice picture of Lord Hawkridge,' he added with satisfaction. 'I think it surprised Caroline.'

'I'm so glad,' said Mary warmly.

CHAPTER SEVEN

'MARY?' said Justin.

She glanced at him but she didn't answer. Once again they were riding in couples, in the same pairings and order that they had ridden out.

'Unless you want to break up what appear to be two extremely satisfactory flirtations – at least, from the point of view of those enjoying them – you have to ride with me,' he went on, an edge of humorous resignation in his voice. 'You might as well talk to me.'

'There isn't... I don't think there is anything left to say,' Mary replied almost wearily.

'Don't you?' said Justin. 'I think there will always be something left to say between us.'

There was a note of deep sincerity beneath his light tones, and Mary glanced at him swiftly. Her grey eyes were wide and hurt. It was almost as if she was looking to him for reassurance.

He swore softly under his breath.

'Every time I try to talk to you, we end up fighting,' he said. 'All I want——' He broke off. 'Why are you so afraid I'm going to turn your life upside-down?' he asked gently.

Unexpected tears filled Mary's eyes and she turned her head away. She didn't want Justin to be kind to her – not now. It wasn't fair.

'Mary?'

'Because you're a lord. And I am...what I am,' she said painfully, without looking at him. 'I won't be your mistress, Justin. And if you won't be my friend there isn't much left, is there?'

He didn't immediately reply, and the bitter core of despair within her began to grow till it threatened to engulf her. It seemed to her that his silence was answer enough. She listened to the muffled thud of hooves on the turf and wondered if he would ever speak again.

'There was once,' he said at last.

'But we were a lot younger and far more foolish then,' Mary retorted, dashing a tear from her cheek and finding relief in brisk practicality. 'Besides, I don't suppose your father would have permitted the match.'

'I didn't always do what my father wished,' said Justin mildly. 'Very rarely, in fact. It was one of the main reasons why we couldn't spend more than half an hour in the same room without coming to cuffs.'

'On trivial matters,' Mary persisted impatiently. 'But marriage is important. You couldn't marry to bring disgrace and scandal into your family.'

'I've heard you say so many times,' he said slowly. 'Is that still what you think?'

'Of course it is!' she exclaimed. She glanced at him quickly, then equally quickly turned away again. 'How could I think anything else? But I'm not prepared to be your mistress. Not now. I...' Her voice faltered and she didn't try to continue.

It was colder than it had been in the morning. The wind cut more chillingly through her riding habit, and clouds were appearing on the horizon. If they didn't make haste it would rain before they reached Bath.

'We must catch up with the others,' she said. 'Mrs Burleigh won't like it if Lucinda gets soaked through. I don't think Mr King would like it either – although I suppose if she catches a chill it will at least make it more difficult for Samuel to pursue her – though of course I'd never wish her to be ill. . .' She was talking for the sake of it, hardly aware of what she was saying. She simply wanted to bring the conversation back to less immediately painful topics.

'I don't know what you're talking about,' said Justin, interrupting her without ceremony. 'And at the moment I don't particularly care. Look at me. Just. . .look at me.'

She turned her head reluctantly, unwilling to meet his eyes, but unable to resist the deep tone in his voice.

'You've told me several times you won't be my mistress,' he said steadily. 'Now I'm telling you that I will never again make you such an offer.' His lips twisted in an unamused, almost self-mocking smile. 'You may trust me on this,' he added. 'Even my father never doubted my word.'

Mary looked down, her heart pounding. Her first feeling was not one of relief, but of loss. Yet he'd only given her what she'd asked for. How could she be so fickle? Because she wanted so much more. But at least she could be as gracious in accepting his promise as he had been in making it.

She lifted her eyes to meet his steady gaze. She knew his features so well. His hazel eyes which always saw more than she expected. His firm yet sensitive mouth. His strong jawline, and that air of casual authority he wore, as if he had no need to raise his voice to be heard.

Was she saying goodbye to him now? Would she ever see him again?

'Thank you, my lord,' she said formally. 'Will you. . .can we still be friends?'

A smile illuminated his face, flecks of gold dancing warmly in his hazel eyes. It was a smile of affection – if not love.

There was a time when he'd always looked at Mary like that, before all the misunderstandings and bitterness had come between them. It reminded her of the past so forcefully that she could hardly believe this might be the last time they met.

Surely she would wake up and find it was all a dream? That her uncle and Bill Crawford were only figments of her imagination – no greater impediment to her happiness than pantomime demons?

But if there had been no Alf she would never have been to St Giles – and she would never have met Justin. She could not change the past. Only live with it.

'Is that what you want?' Justin asked. 'To be friends?'

'Yes.' Mary did not trust herself to say anything more than the single word.

Justin drew the chestnut to a halt and stretched out his right hand to her.

'Then we will be friends,' he said.

She hesitated, then put her right hand in his, feeling the firm pressure of his fingers as they shook on their agreement. She would never again know the touch of his hands – except, perhaps, in the formal gestures of greeting and parting. There was a bitter taste in her mouth and her throat was full, as if it was choked with all the tears she had struggled not to shed.

'Now we really must catch up with the others,' she said, taking up her reins again and trying to sound businesslike, though she felt as if she'd been mortally wounded.

'But not so quickly that you don't have time to tell me why we've been cultivating Miss Burleigh so assiduously over the past two days,' said Justin as they urged their horses into a gentle trot. 'And also, now I come to think of it, where Samuel fits in. Who *is* Samuel?'

Mary glanced at him doubtfully. He sounded so normal it was hard to believe everything that had gone before.

'Mr Penrose's nephew,' she revealed cautiously. 'And I didn't know we were cultivating Miss Burleigh.'

'Well, you certainly are,' said Justin judiciously.

'I'm just along for the ride – so to speak. But I haven't been backward in drawing her out – in so far as Peter King has given me an opportunity to do so. I just wish I knew what all this effort was in aid of. Friends do talk to each other,' he added as she hesitated.

'Yes, I know. But it's not my secret. And Mr Penrose is *so* anxious to avoid scandal,' Mary replied uncertainly.

She could think of nothing better than to confide her worries about Samuel to Justin, but she knew that Mr Penrose would hate it.

'I don't claim to be Penrose's friend,' Justin said drily, 'but as *your* friend I will engage not to create a scandal.'

'I know that.' Mary threw him a quick smile.

It was becoming easier to speak naturally to him by the second. All that was left of what she had lost was a dull ache beneath her breast. But she told herself that it was better to hold the comforting light of a candle in her hand than cry forever after the unattainable moon.

'It's a trifle complicated,' she said slowly.

'I'm moderately intelligent.'

'To explain, I meant,' she retorted. 'I think the best place to begin is with the fact that Mr Penrose's brother – whose name escapes me at the moment – left his fortune to his son, Samuel, in a particularly contentious way.'

She went on to describe the threats she'd overheard Samuel make, and her instinctive decision to warn Mr Penrose.

'Where did you hear these drunken ravings?' Justin asked, frowning.

'In perfectly unexceptional circumstances,' Mary replied quickly, a challenge in her eyes.

Justin glanced at her shrewdly, but he didn't pursue the matter. 'And then you went to warn Penrose,' he said. 'Why did he believe you? Did he know you? Did he already have doubts about the nephew?'

'I've been distantly acquainted with him for years. But as to whether he believed me, I'm not entirely sure that he did,' said Mary frankly. 'At least, not until this morning, when I told him he should change his will.'

'Why did you do that?' Justin asked sharply.

'Because I don't think there's any action we can take against Samuel unless, God forbid, he does something to warrant it,' Mary explained thoughtfully, unaware of the frown in Justin's eyes. 'The best protection for Mr Penrose is to hand over control of Samuel's fortune immediately, and make sure he can never get his hands on Mr Penrose's. And the best protection for Lucinda. . .'

'Is Peter King,' Justin said.

'Not necessarily,' Mary replied quickly. 'I was going to say friends. If she doesn't feel lonely and excluded, she's less likely to be susceptible to a fortune-hunter's charm.'

'Is Samuel charming?' Justin asked, a curious expression in his eyes.

'He has never seemed so to me,' Mary said

honestly. 'Arrogant, rude and potentially cruel, I would have said. But they seem to like him well enough in Bath.'

'And how have you been in a position to make such an assessment of his character?' Justin asked conversationally.

Mary looked up and met his eyes.

'I know,' he replied for her. 'In perfectly unexceptional circumstances. Are you aware that friends often reveal more to each other than simply their names and their immediate concerns?'

'But we can only be friends while I'm in Bath,' said Mary flatly. 'We hardly inhabit the same social circle, my lord.'

'I have many friends,' Justin replied equably. 'They don't all frequent Almack's. My friend Henderson, for example, is a large-hearted farmer with three sturdy sons and a prize pig he is extremely fond of. He doesn't seem to have any inflated notion of my consequence. He was quite adamant that I couldn't borrow that mare unless I agreed to paint Fanny Matilda.'

'But he doesn't have. . .' Mary caught herself up, biting her lip.

'It's true he doesn't have such a dubious past,' Justin agreed cheerfully. 'At least not to my knowledge. But who knows what skeletons might not come bouncing out of his cupboards if we rattled the doors long enough? Do you really think Samuel meant his threats?' he added more seriously.

'Yes,' said Mary simply. The colour which had

flamed in her cheeks at Justin's casual mention of her past slowly cooled. How could he be so light-hearted about something which had wounded her so badly?

'Then why did Penrose make you come to Bath with him?' Justin demanded. 'Surely he knew he was exposing you to an unpleasant scene at best – and personal risk at worst?'

'He didn't make me come – I chose to do so,' Mary said quickly. 'I'd made the accusation; it seemed to me I had a duty to stand by it. And I was worried about Mr Penrose. I wasn't sure if he'd be able to handle Samuel. Besides. . .'

'Besides what?'

'I was getting bored,' she admitted, almost defiantly. 'Perhaps I wasn't born to lead an entirely respectable life after all.'

Justin smiled, but his expression was distracted.

'There are degrees of excitement,' he said. 'Go home, Mary. I think you've already provided Miss Burleigh with all the protection she needs – and I will undertake to provide whatever help Penrose needs. There's no reason for you to be involved in this business any longer.'

'You'll look after Mr Penrose?' Mary said, staring at him in astonishment. 'But you don't even like him!'

'No, I don't,' Justin agreed. 'But friends often perform unpleasant tasks for each other – so I'm told. And I don't like the idea of you having anything more to do with a man like Samuel Penrose.'

'I can take care of myself,' Mary protested, torn
between gratification at his concern for her welfare
and irritation that he should so readily assume
that he needed her help.

'I dare say you can,' said Justin austerely. 'But
that doesn't mean you have to put yourself at risk
to take care of every ineffectual nincompoop you
meet!'

'Mr Penrose is not a nincompoop! He's. . .he's. . .'
Mary's sense of humour got the better of
her and she started to giggle as she remembered
some of Mr Penrose's more exasperating
characteristics.

Justin's expression relaxed. There was a hint of
relief in his eyes, although Mary didn't see it.

'Oh, it's not fair to make fun of him,' she gasped
after a moment. 'It's not his fault he's inclined to
be a little. . .a little over-concerned about things.
And he has good reason to be anxious at the
moment.'

'I might feel warmer towards him if he'd shown
more concern for *your* safety,' Justin retorted.
'And if he hadn't been so keen to adopt you as his
niece.'

'Oh, that was for my sake,' Mary assured him,
a humorous light in her eyes. 'The first night on
the way to Bath he was particularly fussy. The
kind of guest you want to throttle. First he sent
the supper back twice, then he complained about
his sheets – and there was nothing wrong with
either. I was quite surprised. He'd never been so
difficult when he came. . . But of course he was

very agitated. The next morning one of the ostlers made a lewd remark about us – and then it was Mr Penrose's turn to be embarrassed.'

'And that accounts for transforming you into his niece?' said Justin, raising his eyebrows. 'But why did he persist with it when you came to Bath and met people he already knew?'

'I don't know,' said Mary honestly. 'I mean, obviously the same basic situation still applied, but I was never so surprised as when he introduced me to the Knightleys as his niece. I've been on tenterhooks ever since that someone who actually knows his sister and her family will appear. That *would* create a scandal.'

'If he's so concerned with appearances, why the house in Queen Square?' Justin asked, a not entirely friendly expression in his eyes.

'I told you,' Mary replied calmly, although she was aware of the chill in Justin's question. 'He doesn't trust the linen in hotels – and he was very ill at ease in those surroundings. He's very nervous about confronting Samuel. He wants it to be in private.'

'More fool him,' said Justin drily.

'That's what I thought,' Mary agreed. She sighed. 'Perhaps I should have made more of an effort before to impress upon him the possible danger, but... Oh, Justin, he's old enough to be my father, but he seems to have no more genuine understanding of the evil that can exist in the world than ——'

'I've always wished I could have met your father,' said Justin quietly as she broke off.

'You would have liked him,' said Mary, unsurprised that he had followed the trend of her thoughts so easily. 'He had no affectations. He was always himself. And he was so friendly and kind and – good.'

Justin didn't say anything, and when she glanced at him she saw that his lips were pressed together and the line of his jaw was very pronounced in the pale afternoon light.

'I would favour a little less virtue and a little more foresight – wouldn't you?' he demanded bluntly, meeting her gaze.

'You know I would,' she replied, sighing. 'But he's still my father and it's better if I remember the good things—— Oh, what's the point of talking about it? It's all in the past now, anyway.'

'Will you go home and leave me to deal with Penrose?' Justin asked after a moment.

'No, I won't,' said Mary flatly. 'Mr Penrose would hate it if he knew I'd been discussing his affairs with you. And Samuel isn't even in Bath. I don't know what we'll do if he doesn't turn up soon. I can't stay here indefinitely.'

'Of course not, you have a business to run,' said Justin smoothly. 'I expect Donald's been a great help to you. Is he still with you?'

'Yes, he——' Mary broke off, staring at Justin.

'Too many clues, sweetheart,' he murmured provocatively, just as they were about to catch up with Lucinda and Peter. 'In what – unexceptional – circumstances could you overhear Samuel make such threats? Have experience of the kind of guest you want to throttle? And be surprised that Mr Penrose could prove such a difficult guest? Besides, I've just remembered a rumour I didn't pay much attention to when I first heard it – that you stung Seb Collins for a very fair price for the Blue Boar before you left Church Lane. If that rumour was right, you'd have had all the capital you needed.'

Mary drew in her breath indignantly.

'If you've always known I sold the Blue Boar, why the devil did you accuse me of selling myself to a richer man?' she demanded in a furious undertone.

'Because it was only one of many rumours,' Justin replied. 'And I knew Seb Collins. I couldn't imagine anyone pulling such a trick on him. Not even Alf. You must have been very lucky.'

'I wasn't lucky,' said Mary categorically, her eyes blazing. 'I held my own against Alf for five years! Did you really think I wasn't a match for Seb?'

She was outraged by his easy assumption that it was more likely that she would have become another man's mistress than that she could have outwitted one of the most notorious bosses in St Giles. Justin had known the truth all these years and he hadn't been able to credit it! Even he had preferred to think the worst of her!

By this time they were riding alongside Lucinda

and Peter King and Mary quite deliberately turned her back on Justin and smiled at the others.

It seemed, in any case, that Peter wanted to talk to her, because he allowed his horse to fall back, leaving Lucinda to ride on with Justin. Mary observed the manoeuvre with a certain amount of amusement.

'Your friendship with Miss Burleigh seems to be flourishing,' she said blandly. 'As does your sister's with Mr Hastings,' she added, glancing ahead to where Caroline rode with Adam, their conversation apparently still as lively now as it had been several hours ago.

Peter looked at her, but he refrained from comment.

'Quite,' Mary said, a rueful expression in her grey eyes. 'You're very tactful, sir.'

'You look happier, ma'am,' he ventured. 'I was afraid, earlier... Have you known Lord Hawkridge long?'

'We met on the road to Bath, a few days ago,' Mary replied. She sighed. 'Yes, I knew him several years ago,' she admitted, 'but that isn't——'

'I'm not prone to gossip,' he assured her quickly. 'Was that before——?' He broke off, flushing. 'I'm sorry, I didn't mean to pry,' he said awkwardly.

'It was before I was married,' said Mary quietly. 'A long time ago. Now, what can I do for you, sir?' she added more briskly. 'And does it have anything to do with Miss Lewisham?'

Peter stared at her in blank amazement. 'Are you a witch, ma'am?' he demanded.

Mary laughed. 'No,' she said. 'But if I were you the problem of Miss Lewisham would be looming quite large in my mind. If you call on Miss Burleigh at Lansdown Crescent, Miss Lewisham will undoubtedly hang on your every word, and then comment *sotto voce* on your handsome figure and elegant waistcoats as soon as she thinks you're out of earshot. And if you try to arrange an assignation with Lucinda anywhere else, Miss Lewisham will probably chaperon her – and a similar situation will ensue. Yes, if I were you I would certainly be giving some thought to the problem of Miss Lewisham.'

Peter grinned uncomfortably.

'I wasn't expecting you to sum up the situation so. . .so. . .'

'Bluntly?' Mary supplied helpfully. 'Or tactlessly? I would be very concerned if I thought you were trying to take advantage of Miss Burleigh's innocence, or her good nature——'

'I assure you——' Peter began.

'But I don't think that is the case,' Mary continued, ignoring his interruption. 'Have you mentioned your reservations about Miss Lewisham to Lucinda?'

'I didn't quite like to,' he admitted. 'It seemed so calculating, and not quite. . .' He paused, clearly unable to find the words to express his unease with the situation.

'Calculating is only another term for foresight,'

said Mary, 'and I'm all for exercising that. How would it be if I asked Lucinda to come shopping with me tomorrow morning? I'm sure I could do with another bonnet, or a new pair of gloves. And no one could fault you if you met us by chance on Milsom Street?'

'Thank you, ma'am,' he said gratefully.

'Don't thank me until we see if she'll accept my invitation,' said Mary.

'Miss Lewisham,' said Justin a few minutes later as they once more fell back behind the others.

'Did Lucinda say anything about her to you?' Mary asked curiously. She was still very angry with him, but she was holding her irritation at bay. She'd had enough of recriminations and arguments for one day.

'Not exactly,' said Justin. 'We had a very round-about conversation in which she managed to make it plain to me that she didn't think the worse of me for making fun of the old trout in the Pump Room yesterday morning. She also expressed the view that it was a pity elderly people so often feel it necessary to usurp the conversation of their younger relations. She didn't phrase it quite like that.'

'I don't suppose she did,' said Mary. 'But Miss Lewisham is an awful cross for anyone to bear. She terrifies the life out of me.'

'Why?'

'Justin! Think what would happen if she ever found out the truth about me!' she exclaimed.

'But you won't be staying in Bath,' said Justin

reasonably. 'And why should you care what a vicious-minded tattle-tale thinks about you?'

'I don't,' said Mary. 'But I care what other people think about me.' She looked ahead towards Lucinda and Peter.

'She won't find out,' said Justin calmly. 'The worse thing she can discover is that you're not really Penrose's niece.'

'That's bad enough!' Mary protested.

'Not necessarily,' he said. 'As far as I can tell, there are only two people in Bath whose opinion you really care about. And I doubt if either of them would think the worse of you if they knew the reason for your unintentional masquerade.' He smiled crookedly. 'Judging by the way Lucinda covered up your picture at the George, she has your best interests at heart,' he added. 'And Peter King seems to think highly of your opinion.'

Mary closed her eyes briefly, remembering the distress she had suffered earlier in the day, and grateful that Lucinda had so effectively hidden the sketch from the others.

'I'm sorry,' Justin said quietly. 'I didn't mean to do that to you. It started off as a sketch of all three of you. But...you were the subject I was interested in. Not that I think Caroline or Hastings would have seen anything in it. They don't strike me as having that kind of insight.'

'They do say the pen is mightier than the sword,' said Mary shakily, trying to smile. 'It's not easy to be confronted with yourself in such circumstances.

Much worse than unexpectedly catching sight of yourself in a mirror.'

'I know.' Justin brought the chestnut to a halt, reached into a large pocket and pulled out his sketchbook. He tore out the page with her picture on it and offered it to her. 'Keep it or destroy it,' he said. 'It's yours.'

Mary took it, hardly able to bring herself to look at it, but unbelievably moved by his action. Now she need never fear the strangers who might one day look through his sketchbooks – as she had once done – asking questions and possibly even commenting on her picture. And wondering what she meant to the artist.

'May I see the sketch Lucinda did of you?' she asked on impulse.

'Of course.' He handed her the sketchbook.

She looked down at it and smiled. Lucinda's style was less polished than Justin's. The proportions were not quite right, and she lacked his minute powers of observation and insight into his subject. But the likeness was very good. It had amused him to be sketched, and Lucinda had captured his quizzical expression beautifully. Mary had seen him wear just that look many times.

'Do you want it?' she asked abruptly.

Justin leant over without comment and took the sketchbook out of her hand. Then he tore out that page also and gave it to her.

'I'm sure Miss Burleigh would be flattered that you like it,' he said, almost flippantly.

Mary glanced at him, startled, but she couldn't read his expression.

'Thank you,' she said. She folded the two sketches neatly together and tucked them carefully inside the bodice of her habit. 'I think we'll beat the rain back,' she said. 'I hope so, or Mrs Burleigh may not allow Lucinda to come shopping with me tomorrow morning!'

CHAPTER EIGHT

'GOOD morning, Mrs Drayton, I am so pleased to see you again,' said Mrs Burleigh warmly. 'Please sit down. Lucinda's just getting ready. She hasn't been able to stop talking about her outing yesterday.'

'Thank you.' Mary smiled. 'I'm glad she enjoyed it,' she said. 'I think we all did. It was a beautiful day for a ride.'

'Riding over to Norton St Philip must have seemed very slow to Lord Hawkridge after his London entertainments,' said Miss Lewisham. She spoke with a little tinkling laugh, her sharp eyes on Mary's face. 'But I dare say Bath seems very dull to you also, Mrs Drayton – since you have seen so much of the world.'

'Oh, no,' Mary replied serenely, although Miss Lewisham's manner set her teeth on edge. 'I have received such a warm welcome from everybody that I could not possibly find Bath dull.'

'It was kind of you to ask Lucinda to go shopping with you,' said Mrs Burleigh with dignity. 'I find I get very weary on such expeditions, but I'm sure Lucinda should go out more.'

'On the contrary, it's I who am grateful,' said Mary. 'Lucinda has a very good eye for colour; I shall be glad of her advice.'

'Mrs Knightley has often said I have excellent taste,' said Miss Lewisham. 'I would be happy to come with you, Mrs Drayton. Lucinda is rather young to be entirely depended upon not to make a mistake.'

'I'm sure Mrs Drayton appreciates your offer, Emma,' said Mrs Burleigh before Mary could speak, 'but I would like you to come to the Pump Room with me this morning.'

She glanced up and smiled as her daughter came into the drawing-room.

'I'm so sorry to have kept you waiting, ma'am,' Lucinda exclaimed, looking flustered.

'That's quite all right,' said Mary, smiling. 'I have no urgent commissions to execute.' She stood up and turned to Mrs Burleigh. 'Good morning, ma'am. Thank you for letting Lucinda come out with me.'

'I was in terror that Cousin Emma would insist on joining us,' Lucinda confided a few minutes later when they were safely out of the house. 'She's been hinting that she wanted to do so ever since she found out you'd invited me.'

'I don't think your mother would have agreed to that,' Mary said, glancing curiously at Lucinda. She wasn't sure whether her young friend knew that Peter King intended to meet them later, or whether it was just that Lucinda didn't particularly like her cousin.

'She will say things that make me blush for her,' said Lucinda, unaware of Mary's scrutiny. 'And for me! Oh, Mrs Drayton, it was a lovely day yesterday, wasn't it?'

'I was afraid you might find it rather tiring,' Mary said mildly. 'Since you aren't used to riding so far.'

'Oh, no!' Lucinda protested vehemently. 'Well, actually,' she admitted, with a rueful gleam in her eye, 'I am a little stiff this morning, but I wouldn't tell Mama for anything! Did...did *you* enjoy yourself, ma'am?'

'Yes, I did, thank you,' Mary replied. 'I'm used to taking my rides alone. It was very pleasant to have company for a change.'

For a moment Lucinda looked as if she wanted to pursue the subject. But, if she did, she thought better of it. They walked a few paces in silence, then Lucinda asked brightly, 'What kind of bonnet did you have in mind, ma'am?'

'Good gracious! Isn't...isn't that Mr King coming towards us – with Lord Hawkridge?' Lucinda exclaimed as they were walking along Milsom Street. She was clearly trying to appear unconcerned, but the rosy colour tinging her cheeks gave her away.

'I do believe it is,' said Mary gravely. 'What a coincidence.'

Lucinda threw her a startled glance, not unmixed with suspicion, but she didn't have time to say anything before the gentlemen greeted them.

'Good morning, ladies,' said Justin courteously.

'I hope you're none the worse for your ride,' Peter said eagerly to Lucinda.

'Oh, no!' she exclaimed. 'I enjoyed it immensely.' Then she blushed, clearly wondering if she'd shown too much unbecoming enthusiasm.

There was a few seconds' silence as the young people gazed at each other, neither quite sure what to say next.

Mary felt a considerable amount of sympathy for Lucinda. She herself hadn't expected Justin to be with Peter, and she was feeling foolishly nervous and tongue-tied. She never wanted him to know how long she had sat looking at the picture Lucinda had drawn of him, hours after she should have been asleep.

'Perhaps, ladies, if you're not in a hurry, you might care for a stroll in Sydney Gardens?' said Justin eventually, only the faintest gleam in his eyes indicating that he found the situation amusing.

'By Jove, yes, sir! What a good idea!' Peter exclaimed. 'Miss Burleigh, do say yes. It's far too beautiful a morning to waste shopping.'

There was no doubt what Lucinda wanted to reply. Nevertheless, she glanced questioningly at Mary.

'I'll have many opportunities to purchase a new bonnet,' Mary said instantly. 'But I haven't been to Sydney Gardens yet – and I really ought to do so before I leave Bath.'

'What an accommodating chaperon you are,' Justin said softly a few minutes later, when Lucinda and Peter were walking a few paces ahead of them.

'It is all right, isn't it?' Mary asked, suddenly anxious. 'I mean. . .'

'You were so clearly determined to throw them

together yesterday, I thought I'd better make some enquiries,' said Justin, an edge of laughter in his voice. 'Respectable family. Not wealthy, but completely acceptable. Caroline's generally regarded as a bit fast, and Peter's waistcoats inspired a few derogatory comments – but they're the worst thing I discovered about him. Do you think Lucinda will be able to exercise a restraining influence over him?'

Mary stifled a choke of laughter. She felt strangely light-headed, not herself at all. She told herself it was simply the bright sunlight in her face, and the crisp, fresh air in her lungs, but she was afraid it was the feel of Justin's arm beneath her hand. And the new harmony which seemed to exist between them.

Something had changed since yesterday. She was still annoyed that he hadn't believed she'd sold the Blue Boar. But she was overwhelmingly relieved that he finally knew she'd lived a respectable life all the years they'd been apart. And he'd worked it out for himself – she hadn't had to tell him.

She no longer had any secrets from him. He knew her for what she was, and she could once again be herself with him. That freedom was worth a great deal to her. And so, she told herself, was his assurance that he would never again ask her to be his mistress. She could walk beside him, take pleasure in the brief, formalised contact that social convention permitted them, without fearing the consuming passion which threatened her resolve – and her integrity.

'I also made some enquiries about Samuel,' said Justin.

'And?' Mary looked up at him sharply.

'You're right, he is generally well thought of in Bath, but I got Henry——'

'Henry?' Mary interrupted, frowning.

'My tiger,' Justin explained.

'I remember!' she exclaimed after a puzzled moment, as she thought back to that morning on the Bath road when the tiger had introduced her to Barabbas and Mary, the two high-spirited chestnuts who pulled Justin's curricle. 'I'm sorry, go on.'

'It's easier for him to make enquiries among people who wouldn't dream of gossiping about Penrose to me,' Justin said. 'Penrose's servant, Phelps, is not well-liked. He's regarded as a bully who's not afraid to use his fists to get what he wants. Does that tally with what you know of him?'

'It doesn't surprise me,' Mary replied. 'But he didn't try anything at the Lazy Cat. No one picks a fight with Donald unless they have a good reason. Or they want to prove themselves – like cocks on a dunghill,' she aded acidly.

'How *is* Donald these days?' Justin asked. He spoke politely, but Mary heard the undercurrent of hostility in his tone and wasn't deceived.

'He did what he thought was best for me,' she said, meeting Justin's eyes squarely.

'He acted out of jealousy and possessiveness,' Justin contradicted her harshly. 'I'm looking forward to my next meeting with him.'

'No!' Mary suddenly had a dreadful vision of Justin confronting the huge Scotsman.

Justin was fifteen years younger than Donald. Strong, athletic, and quite capable of taking care of himself. But Donald was four inches taller, he carried more weight, and he was a vicious fighter. Mary hated to think what the outcome would be if they came to blows. And, whatever happened, someone she cared about would be hurt.

Donald might have lied to her, but without him it would have been much harder to survive in Church Lane, and she might never have succeeded in selling the Blue Boar to Seb Collins. He had badly damaged her trust in him, but she would never forget how much she owed the Scotsman. And she loved Justin.

'Justin! Let it be!' She clutched convulsively at his arm, turning to face him in the winter sunlight. 'Nothing you say to Donald is going to change anything. Please!'

He looked down into her wide, urgent eyes. For a moment she could see nothing but his face – and the searching, yet quizzical, expression in his eyes.

'Please, Justin!' She shook his arm insistently. 'Don't pursue it.'

He smiled, flecks of gold appearing in his hazel eyes, and her heart turned over at the thought of him being hurt.

'Are you so sure your Scottish Goliath would be a match for me?' he asked, almost chidingly.

'No.' She shook her head, although that was certainly her fear. 'But. . .'

'And what makes you think the situation would come to blows?' he asked quizzically.

'You're angry. . .'

'I'm very angry,' he corrected her. 'But I'm not necessarily going to try to relieve my feelings by trying to pound your over-zealous protector to a pulp.' He smiled crookedly. 'Don't keep looking at me like that, sweetheart, or I may forget where we are.'

Colour flooded Mary's cheeks, and she pulled away from him.

'You *promised*!' she exclaimed.

'I promised not to ask you to be my mistress,' Justin replied calmly. He took her hand and drew it back through his arm. Mary tried to pull away, but his free hand closed over hers.

'Let me go!' she said fiercely.

'No.'

'Justin!'

His fingers encircled her slender wrist, holding her too tightly to allow her to escape, but not tight enough to hurt her. He wasn't wearing gloves, and her hands had been tucked snugly inside her muff before she'd met him. There were no barriers between them. Mary couldn't deny the current of excitement which pulsed between their joined hands, or the fire which leapt within her at his touch. After a moment his grip relaxed, and she felt his fingers softly caress the palm of her hand.

She caught her breath.

'Please don't!' she begged in a whisper. 'It's not fair.'

'Nothing ever is.' He kept his hand over hers, but he began to stroll once more after Lucinda and Peter, compelling her to do likewise. 'Don't keep fighting me, Mary.'

'What are you trying to do?' she demanded in a shaken undertone. 'Get me to plead with you to renew your offer? How could you?'

'No.' He glanced around at their surroundings with an air of barely controlled exasperation. 'Dammit, I'm sick of trying to talk to you in public places. Where's Penrose. . .?'

'I don't——'

'Senior.'

'The Pump Room. No. . .he was going to see his lawyer. . .I think.' Mary struggled to think clearly.

'But he's not at Queen Square?' Justin queried impatiently.

'I don't think so,' she said uncertainly.

'It doesn't matter if he is,' Justin asserted decisively. 'I'm sure he can spare us one room to hold a conversation in.'

'But I don't want. . .'

'You may not want to talk to me, but I have every intention of talking to you,' Justin said grimly. 'I'm sure King will be glad of the opportunity to escort Lucinda back to her mama.'

'But I can't just abandon her,' Mary protested, hurrying to keep up as he lengthened his stride.

'You aren't abandoning her. You're leaving her in the unexceptional care of a very respectable young man,' said Justin. 'No one could blame you for doing so when you've just become the victim of a painful migraine.'

'But. . .' It was too late to protest. They'd already caught up with Lucinda and Peter, and Justin was making their excuses, his manner towards Mary half humorous and half solicitous.

Despite her confusion and agitation, Mary had to grit her teeth at his subtle suggestion that she was fatigued by her recent exertions. For her apparent fragility belied an excellent constitution, and she was rarely ill.

'Dammit, why did you have to make me sound like a wilting violet?' she demanded, as soon as she was free to do so. 'And if I am such a poor thing, why are we striding along as if the hounds of hell are on our heels?'

Justin slowed his pace, a reluctant grin lightening his rather set expression.

'I'm sorry. I didn't mean to overtax your strength,' he said solicitously.

'I've a good mind to kick you in the shins and then cry for help,' said Mary crossly. 'You've got no right to abduct me like this.'

'I'm not abducting you,' Justin retorted. 'I'm escorting you to a place where we can have an uninterrupted – and unobserved – conversation. And don't tell me there isn't anything left to say.'

'I wasn't going to.'

'My God! What an admission!' Justin exclaimed. 'Perhaps all this fresh air is going to your head. We'd better get you within the stuffy security of four walls immediately.'

Mary turned her head away, trying not to give way to the rather hysterical laughter that was bubbling up inside her. She didn't honestly think that Justin was going to renew his offer to be his mistress – nor did she think he'd been callously playing with her feelings in Sydney Gardens.

In fact, she wasn't quite sure what to think. But, strangely enough, she felt closer to him as they walked decorously through Bath – occasionally pausing to exchange greetings with acquaintances – than she had done for seven years.

She was aware of his seething impatience as he replied courteously to Mrs Melville's polite enquiry about his mother. And she had to look down to hide the dancing amusement in her eyes when he was waylaid by a retired captain he had sketched only two days before.

'I showed the picture to my sister, and she said it was a most speaking likeness,' said the grey-haired old soldier. 'You have a rare talent, my lord.'

'Thank you, sir. And please convey my compliments to your sister,' said Justin, controlling his exasperation admirably. 'I'm afraid we cannot delay. Poor Mrs Drayton is feeling unwell, and I promised to escort her home.'

'Of course, of course. I do hope you recover

quickly, ma'am.' The old captain lifted his hat to Mary.

'My father always warned me that I shouldn't treat the whole world as my brother,' said Justin darkly as they continued on their way. 'Now I can see I should have paid more attention to him.'

Mary started to laugh. Justin glanced at her, then his lips quirked in a self-deprecating smile.

'You think I'm being ridiculous?'

'No,' she gasped, catching her breath. 'Justin, how come there are people like the poor captain who treat you as if you were a long-lost friend, yet I've seen you walk across the Pump Room as if you expected the seas to part for you? You cannot behave like that most of the time.'

He slowed his pace, looking down at her, a rueful expression in his eyes.

'I was angry both times I met you in the Pump Room,' he said. 'When I'm angry I have a tendency to become arrogant. And the Lewisham woman didn't help. Here we are. Let's hope Penrose is out – or I may become arrogant again!'

Grigson opened the door. His expression when he saw Justin was a nicely judged mixture of curiosity and disapproval, but Mary ignored it.

'Is Mr Penrose in?' she asked briskly.

'No, ma'am.'

'I see.' She glanced back at Justin. 'I'm afraid you may have had a journey in vain, my lord. But if you would care for some tea, we could wait for my uncle to return.'

'I would be glad to do so – if it won't put you to

too much inconvenience,' Justin replied, smoothly falling in with the mild deception.

'By no means,' said Mary. 'Please have some tea sent up to the drawing-room, Grigson.'

'Yes, ma'am.' The butler bowed and departed in his stateliest manner. Mary caught Justin's eye and a flicker of shared amusement passed between them. Then she turned and led the way upstairs.

Justin glanced around the drawing-room, then went straight over to the window. Mary had a sense that he was impatiently waiting for the tea to be brought before he spoke to her.

Now that she was no longer caught up in his urgency to get to the house in Queen Square, nervousness rose up within her. They'd had many difficult conversations over the past few days, but none quite like this. Her mouth felt dry and it was hard to swallow. She wanted to say something to break the tension, but she couldn't think of anything. And she wasn't sure if she could trust her voice anyway.

He was so close. Just on the other side of the room, looking out across the Square. She could sense the tension in him, and the barely contained energy. She knew it was only rigid self-control that was keeping him silent until they could be reasonably safe from interruption.

What was he going to say? And how would she respond? A wild hope was beating in her heart, nearly choking her with its intensity.

There were footsteps outside the door and Justin moved away from the window.

'You have an excellent view of the Square,' he said as the butler came in with the tea-tray.

'I expect the garden looks particularly charming in summer,' Mary replied, hardly recognising the sound of her own voice. 'But I've never visited Bath before, so I have to use my imagination. Thank you, Grigson.'

The butler went out, closing the door softly behind him. The moment he had done so, Justin came towards her. She stood up instinctively, lifting her eyes to meet his. He caught her hand in his, and she felt the same thrill of excitement which had affected her so powerfully in Sydney Gardens.

'Mary...' he began. Then, as she continued to look mutely up at him, she saw his eyes blaze with sudden fire, and he pulled her roughly into his arms.

She gave a soft cry, partly of surprise, partly of protest, and he stifled it with his mouth. She tried to push him away, but her arms felt weak and her efforts were half-hearted at best. He was holding her so tightly, she could feel the urgent warmth of his body through the many layers of cloth that separated them.

Yesterday his lips had been gentle and persuasive on hers; today they were demanding and insistent. An answering flame of passion flared up from deep within her. She had been excited and stimulated by his touch earlier, and now she was almost instantly aroused by his lovemaking. She slipped her arms around his neck, clinging to him eagerly. Her lips were already swollen and throbbing from his fiercely irresistible kisses. But when he drew back slightly, and ran his tongue delicately across her burning lower lip, another, deeper wave of pleasure swept through her.

She trembled responsively in his arms and he pressed her more closely against him. Beneath his urgent, questing hands her dress was creased and rumpled, but she didn't care. And when he lifted his head to look down at her he saw that her eyes were dilated with desire. He groaned softly, and bent to kiss her neck. She felt his lips teasing her tender skin, and she let her head fall back as golden fire coursed through her veins. Her hands clutched convulsively at his shoulders.

Nothing had prepared her for the fierce, uncontrollable passion which filled her. She only knew she wanted more of him – much more. A soft sound of almost desperate longing escaped her, and she twined her fingers in his hair, surrendering herself to him completely, abandoning responsibility for whatever followed to him.

She seemed to dissolve in his arms as the world whirled about her in a dizzying kaleidoscope of lights and colour and fire.

And then the world steadied, and she found herself standing quietly within the circle of his embrace. Her face was pressed against his shoulder. His head was bent over hers, his breath ruffling her hair, but he was no longer trying to rouse her to new heights of passion.

She could hear his heart pounding, and the rasp

of his breathing, but his hand was gentle as he stroked her hair. She felt confused and disorientated, unsatisfied desire still raging through her body. But gradually her trembling lessened and she became more fully aware of her surroundings.

She could hear the clock, its measured mechanical ticking in sharp contrast to the wildly human beating of her heart and Justin's. Then she became aware of the sound of muffled voices from the Square. And the rich yet subdued colour of Justin's coat so close to her eyes.

And then she realised what had happened – and exactly where she was.

Never in her life had she so completely lost control of herself. It was no thanks to her restraint that they were not now lying in a tangle of petticoats and disarranged clothes on the drawing-room floor.

She closed her eyes, shame and embarrassment consuming her. After this she had no one but herself to blame if Justin thought she was a loose woman. How could he fail to see her as a suitable candidate to be his mistress when she had so little propriety?

She wanted to wrench herself out of his arms, but the moment she did that she would have to face him – and see the condemnation in his eyes. She tensed instinctively, and his hand ceased in its gentle stroking.

'Mary?' he said quietly.

She spun out of his arms, turning her back on

him and pressing her hands against her fiery cheeks.

'Don't look at me!' she begged in a strangled voice.

'But I like looking at you,' he replied mildly. 'I cannot imagine an occasion when it will not give me pleasure to look at you.' He touched the back of her neck very softly, but she flinched away from his hand.

'Turn around,' he said, gently insistent.

Mary didn't answer. Her face was buried in her hands, and her shoulders were hunched protectively. She had made a shocking discovery about herself, and she could not bear to meet anyone's eyes – least of all Justin's.

She had known she loved him. And she had known she would find pleasure and comfort in his arms. But she had never before suspected how completely uncontrollable and all-consuming her desire for him was.

He had slept with her once when they'd first met, before he'd asked her to marry him. But she had been much younger then, and still encased in the emotional armour which had protected her from the horrors all around her in St Giles. Now she was older, and paradoxically more vulnerable, and she'd burnt her fingers in the fire he'd ignited. Or had she always had this capacity within her? Was that why she'd struck her disgraceful, unholy bargain with Bill Crawford? The bargain that damned her forever in the eyes of the respectable, pious world. What kind of woman was she?

Her eyes were blank with distress as she remembered every text she'd ever heard or read against the sins of the flesh – and the condemnation reserved for an adulterous woman. And she heard again the pinched voice of Lady Moorcock, Sir Richard's wife, delicately but distastefully alluding to a wife's duties.

In her own mind, Mary had always justified her bargain with Bill on similar grounds. He had, after all, given her the protection she so desperately needed – and which should have been provided by a husband. But she had experienced no pleasure in his bed, and little comfort. It had been easy to imagine she was performing no more than a duty – something which was essential for her survival.

But this was different. In Justin's arms she had been confronted by her true ardent nature. It was impossible to justify what had happened on the grounds of necessity – her own wanton spirit had betrayed her. She had proved she wasn't fit to be anything more than his mistress.

She heard her father's voice, echoing across the years. 'God's dispositions for us cannot be questioned. He must always know what is best for us.'

Was that why He had sent her into the hell of St Giles? Because that was where her unruly, sensual flesh belonged?

CHAPTER NINE

'MARY, turn round,' said Justin. 'Very well,' he added after a moment. 'As long as you don't decide to imitate a spinning top, I should be able to resolve this impasse.'

She heard the undercurrent of amusement in his voice and burned with fresh embarrassment.

In a moment she knew he was standing in front of her. She was staring at his feet, but she couldn't bring herself to lift her head and meet his eyes.

He sighed. 'And which ghostly voice are you listening to now?' he asked, almost conversationally. 'There are so many to choose from, aren't there? Your father, Alf, Sir Richard – I've never understood how he could let Alf walk off with you without making any enquiries about his suitability to take care of you.'

She did look up then, staring into his face with huge, desolate grey eyes, because he had so accurately divined the direction of her thoughts. His mouth twisted as if he was in pain, and he reached out to touch her cheek.

'My love, if I could line them all up in front of a firing squad I would do so,' he said, his voice not quite steady. 'But if you don't *tell* me I can't help.'

'I *can't*!' She pulled away from him.

Perhaps he hadn't noticed how wildly she'd

responded to his caresses. How she hoped that was the case. And if he hadn't noticed she could never admit to him the vision she'd just had of herself. She could never admit that to anyone, as long as she lived.

Then she caught sight of herself in the mirror, and a moan of distress escaped her lips as she saw the marks of passion still vivid on her face. She made a sudden movement as if she was about to run from the room, and Justin caught her arm.

'Don't touch. . .' The words stuck in her throat. After what she had just discovered about herself, it seemed almost hypocritical to order him to leave her alone.

'Let's have a cup of tea,' he said, guiding her back to a chair. 'It should be nicely stewed by now. We must hope no one in Bath ever discovers I've drunk any. My reputation would be completely destroyed.'

Mary stared at him numbly, unable to make any sense of what he'd just said.

'If you remember, I assured Miss Lewisham I couldn't drink anything with water in it,' he reminded her, pouring out a cup of tea. 'Perhaps we ought to get the butler to send up some vinegar later, just to add verisimilitude to my claim.'

Mary's lips curved into a faint smile, and she took a sip of tea. Justin watched her for a moment, then stood up and went to lean against the mantelpiece, staring down at the fire burning low in the hearth.

'Have you had any news about Samuel's whereabouts?' he asked abruptly, over his shoulder.

'No.' Some dim sense of normality was returning to Mary. She was no longer blind to everything around her, and she saw Justin's hand close into a fist at her reply. But his voice was quite calm when he next spoke.

'Has Penrose changed his will?'

'So he tells me.'

'Good. I can't see any reason for you to stay in Bath. Lucinda's well on the way to falling in love with Peter King, and Penrose can take care of his own affairs. I'll take you home.'

'Home?' Mary repeated. She seemed to have grown unbelievably dull-witted over the past hour. She had no idea what he was talking about.

'To your inn,' Justin said impatiently. 'That's where you want to go, isn't it?' He came back to her side, and once again she was aware of the barely contained energy seething within him. 'Perhaps when you are in familiar surroundings you will feel more comfortable and we'll do better,' he continued.

Mary stared at him blankly, and he suddenly dropped on his knees beside her, taking one of her hands in his.

'I didn't mean to frighten you,' he said roughly. 'My God, Mary! I know how many people have used you and hurt you in the past. It was just. . .it's been such a long time – I couldn't help myself. You have so much courage I forget. . . I'm sorry.'

The saucer tilted unnoticed in Mary's other

hand. It seemed so unbelievable that he should be apologising to her – and yet he was. She smiled tremulously and saw the golden flecks appear in his eyes as he brushed a tendril of her hair back from her face.

Suddenly things didn't seem so bad. It was hard to believe that where there was so much care and tenderness there could also be sin. Justin saw her eyes lose focus as she tried to make sense of her feelings.

Then half a cup of tea landed in her lap and she was jerked back to reality.

Justin helped her mop it up. Neither of them had any inclination to ring for help.

'I hope you aren't particularly fond of this gown,' he remarked after a while. 'I don't think it's ever going to be the same again.'

'It doesn't matter,' said Mary. 'Oh, dear, I'd better go and change it.' She stood up, and then looked at him doubtfully.

'I'm not going anywhere,' he said, a half-smile on his lips. 'Not until we've settled a few things. Do you want to go home, Mary?'

He meant to the Lazy Cat. But Mary suddenly realised that the Lazy Cat was no more her home than the Blue Boar had been. Her business provided her with security and independence – but it wasn't her home. She had left the inn soon enough when the opportunity arose. And going back there after everything that had happened would be very difficult.

'I cannot desert Mr Penrose now,' she said, evading the question.

'In that case, when you've changed your dress we must decide what can be done to expedite this business,' said Justin grimly.

Mary poured water from the jug into the basin and washed her face. The cold water was both refreshing and soothing. Then she looked at herself in the mirror.

Her hair was dishevelled, her gown was stained, and her eyes were haunted by her secret fears. No sly serpent had ever tempted her with the apple of knowledge. When she was fourteen she'd had it shoved in her mouth so forcefully that she'd nearly choked. She'd been choking on it ever since.

She had always been too angry and too obstinate to give up the fight for survival, but she'd sacrificed so much in the process. And for twelve years she'd been torn between defiance and shame.

On a day-by-day level she had become a pragmatist, responding to the demands of each situation as it arose, without questioning the impact of such accommodations on her fundamental beliefs. Of course, she had been forced to modify many of her childhood assumptions, but she had done so piecemeal, without creating any new, coherent code of values. There had never been time – and perhaps she had lacked the inclination.

Now she felt like a rudderless, anchorless boat,

tossed helplessly before the storms of half a lifetime of fierce, painful, bewildering emotions.

She had told Justin only three days ago that she had never broken the laws of men – leaving it open as to whether she had transgressed against heaven's commandments. But the second greatest commandment, the one which transcended all others except the commandment to love God, was to love one another – one's neighbour as oneself.

Despite everything that had happened to her, she had always dealt as fairly as she could with other people. And surely the overwhelming pleasure she had experienced in Justin's arms had been born of love – not simply of lust? So how could it be evil?

She gazed at herself in the mirror, hope dawning in her eyes. Justin must have known how passionately she'd clung to him, but he had not condemned her. He had been afraid that he'd frightened her. She frowned, trying to discover the significance of this new idea. She valued his opinion, and his insight.

But he came from a different social station. As Miss Lewisham had pointed out, a certain laxity of morals was forgiven the aristocracy. Could she really rely on his judgement on this matter?

Then she remembered that he'd dragged her back to Queen Square to talk to her – but he hadn't said anything. He'd simply kissed her. Had that been his intention all along? Or had he really meant to say something? And, if so, what?

For a few glorious moments while they'd been

waiting for Grigson to bring the tea she'd wondered if he was going to ask her to marry him. But that was before he'd kissed her. Now she found the possibility that he might do so almost alarming. Her heart and soul were too confused. She had been ruthlessly confronted with the realisation that she no longer knew what she believed. And, until she found out, she could not deal honestly with Justin.

She suddenly noticed that nearly twenty minutes had elapsed since she'd left the drawing-room. She stood up hurriedly and began to change her dress. There was no time now to think. For the moment she would have to do what she'd always done – face each problem as it arose, and hope there would be time for reflection later.

When Mary went downstairs, she found Mrs Knightley in the drawing-room with Justin. He was sketching her. The sight was so unexpected that Mary stopped short in the doorway. Then she noticed the innocent self-importance with which Mrs Knightley was posing, and a flicker of a smile illuminated her eyes.

'Mrs Drayton!' Mrs Knightley exclaimed. 'Oh. . .'

'Please don't get up,' Mary said hastily. 'I'm sorry, I hadn't realised you were here.'

'I came to call upon you,' said Mrs Knightley, careful not to open her mouth too much. 'Lord Hawkridge said you'd spilt some tea on your skirt and had to change your gown. But he said he was waiting for Mr Penrose, and we might as well wait together. And then he asked if he could draw me!'

'So I see,' said Mary, smiling, wondering why Grigson hadn't sent a maid to tell her of Mrs Knightley's arrival. Perhaps he'd hoped she'd be disconcerted to find Mrs Knightley ensconced with Lord Hawkridge. By now Bath gossip would have informed him that Justin was far more interested in her than he was in Mr Penrose. There was nothing she could do about it, and she didn't intend to worry about it.

She went to stand at Justin's shoulder. It was a good sketch, executed swiftly and cleanly in the small sketchbook that he carried everywhere in the large pockets which he always insisted his coats possessed. Mary wondered briefly and irrelevantly what his tailor had to say about that. Had he even carried a sketchbook when he'd gone to Lucinda's party?

But, despite the skill with which Justin had captured Mrs Knightley, Mary suspected that his suggestion had been motivated more by a wish to distract the lady than to flatter her. He could hardly have been in the mood for trivial conversation with a woman he barely knew.

'It's very good,' said Mary appreciatively. 'You are fortunate to possess such a talent, my lord.'

He glanced up briefly, a smile warming his hazel eyes.

'Thank you, ma'am,' he replied. 'I've never regretted it, although it has led me into some uncomfortable situations.'

'My lord?' Mrs Knightley exclaimed, fascinated.

Mary sat down and listened quietly while Justin related a couple of humorous incidents provoked by his habit of sketching anything that interested him. It seemed unlikely that they would have any further opportunities for private conversation in the immediate future and, on the whole, she was relieved. She had too much to think about.

When Justin had finished, and presented Mrs Knightley with her picture, Mary suggested that she might like another cup of tea to recover from the strain of posing.

'I'm afraid it doesn't look as if my uncle is going to return, my lord,' she said pleasantly to Justin. 'If you wish, I would be happy to give him a message for you.'

'Thank you, ma'am.' He stood up, accepting his dismissal, but she knew from the expression in his eyes that he would not leave quite so easily. 'He visits the Pump Room most mornings, does he not?' he said. 'Perhaps I may see him there tomorrow.'

'I will certainly tell him that you hope to do so,' Mary replied, ringing the bell as she tacitly agreed to Justin's suggestion. It would mean another public meeting but, in the circumstances, that might be a good thing. And by tomorrow she might have had a chance to bring some kind of order to her confused emotions.

'Please show Lord Hawkridge out,' she said when Grigson appeared. 'And then please bring us some more tea.'

*   *   *

'I've seen Samuel!' Mr Penrose burst into the drawing-room with far more haste than usual. He stood in front of Mary, almost wringing his hands in his agitation.

'Have you spoken to him?' she asked sharply. She had been sitting alone, her thoughts very far from the problem of Mr Penrose's nephew, but she responded immediately to his announcement.

'Only to ask him to call upon me here,' Mr Penrose replied. 'Oh, dear, oh, dear. . .'

'Is he coming?' Mary interrupted Mr Penrose's exclamations of distress without hesitation. 'When may we expect him?'

'Later this evening. He was most offhand with me. He said he had other appointments he could not break this afternoon. I didn't invite him to dinner. I couldn't tolerate the thought of sitting down to eat with him!'

'Of course not,' said Mary calmly. 'Well, it seems we have some time to prepare for him. Please don't feel so anxious, sir.'

He stared at her. His thin face seemed more lined than ever, and a nervous tick kept twitching at his right eyelid. He rubbed his eye distractedly. Mary stood up.

'Please, sir. Don't be so distressed.' She took his arm and urged him to sit down beside her on the sofa. 'I'm sure we're going to have an unpleasant interview with Samuel – but no more than that. You've changed your will, and done everything necessary to put him in control of his own affairs. As soon as we have informed him of both those facts you can safely wash your hands of him.'

'It's so hard to credit such villainy,' said Mr Penrose fretfully. 'I wish none of this had ever happened!'

'I'm sure you do,' Mary agreed. 'But, however unpleasant it makes life, surely it's better to know what he was planning than to continue in ignorance?'

'I suppose so,' said Mr Penrose miserably. 'Oh, why couldn't he be a gentlemanly, well-regulated youth? What a scandal there's going to be.'

'Don't think like that,' said Mary firmly. 'You have always done what is right and proper, and you have nothing to reproach yourself with. What Samuel does in the future is no concern of yours. You are not accountable for him.'

Mr Penrose looked at her, then his expression cleared slightly and he almost smiled.

'You are not at all daunted by the prospect of confronting him with our suspicions, are you?' he said wonderingly.

'I'm not looking forward to it,' said Mary frankly. 'But he is not my nephew, so I can consider the problem more objectively.' She laid her hand reassuringly on his arm. 'Soon it will all be over and you can go home, sir, I assure you.'

'You have been so kind to me,' said Mr Penrose distressfully. 'I don't know why you should put yourself to so much trouble for me. I cannot begin to——'

'I have only done what anyone would have done

in the same situation,' Mary interrupted briskly. She could see a certain warmth developing in Mr Penrose's eyes which she didn't want to encourage.

'I don't think so,' he replied sadly. 'I cannot be sure that I would have acted in the same way if our positions were reversed.' He sighed, and then took a deep breath, meeting her eyes almost reluctantly. 'I have not always been entirely courteous to you since we came to Bath,' he said with difficulty. 'I am sorry if I have ever seemed to criticise your behaviour.'

'You've been under great strain,' Mary replied. 'You've never been less than a generous host. And our visit here was hardly of your choosing.'

'Nevertheless. . .' He stood up abruptly, taking a turn around the room. 'Well, we must wait until we have spoken to Samuel,' he said at last.

'Yes, sir.'

Mary briefly wondered whether she should let Justin know what had happened. He would certainly be interested to know that Samuel had returned to Bath. But, on the other hand, there was little he could do to help. He could hardly be present at their interview with Samuel without giving rise to all kinds of questions which Mary was reluctant to answer.

Besides, it still rankled that he'd chosen to believe that she'd needed the protection of a rich man, rather than being able to fend for herself, when she'd left St Giles. She would not go running to him with this problem as if she were an empty-headed, panicky fool.

'Mr Samuel Penrose,' the butler announced.

'Thank you, Grigson, that will be all,' said Mary, when she realised that Mr Penrose was too perturbed to speak.

Samuel glanced sharply in her direction as the butler closed the door. A frown appeared in his eyes. Mary guessed that, although she seemed familiar to him, he couldn't quite place where he'd met her.

He was of average height, with a good figure and a handsome face. He dressed with elegance and propriety, and when it suited him he had a conciliatory manner. But Mary had seen him at his worst, his face flushed with brandy, his demeanour crude and disgusting.

There had been occasions, before seeing him again, when even she had doubted the seriousness of his threats. But when she looked at him now she knew she'd been right to worry. His eyes were hard and suspicious as they rested on her, and she could sense the potential for violence in him.

'Uncle,' he said, turning on Mr Penrose, 'I was not expecting you to have company.'

Mary found that hard to believe. Bath gossip would surely have informed him already that she had accompanied Mr Penrose. And Samuel of all people would know that he didn't have a cousin called Mary Drayton.

'Good evening, sir,' she said, when once again

it seemed that Mr Penrose wasn't going to speak. 'We've met before, althought I dare say you don't remember me. My name is Mary Drayton.'

Her hands were concealed in the shawl she was wearing to protect her from the winter draughts, and she didn't offer to shake his hand.

'My cousin Mary?' he asked, a hard, ugly note in his voice.

'No, sir.' Mary didn't offer an explanation for the deception. She didn't feel she owed Samuel anything. 'I'm the landlady of the Lazy Cat.'

She saw a hint of recognition in his hot eyes as that piece of information allowed him to place where he'd seen her before.

'Then you're a long way from home, wench,' he said jeeringly. 'What wiles have you played off on the old fool to persuade him to come jaunting so far from Hertfordshire – and with such a question-able companion?'

'How dare you speak so?' Mr Penrose burst out. He spoke with a kind of nervous indignation, as if his feelings of outrage had overcome his anxiety. 'Mrs Drayton is a respectable woman who has been put to great inconvenience by you! You and your dreadful, *dreadful* threats!'

Samuel threw his uncle a hard, contemptuous glance, but it was on Mary that his eyes came to rest. She could see him making a rapid assessment of her character and intentions, but when he spoke his tone was scornful.

'Hardly respectable, sir, if she is prepared to masquerade as your niece. What lies did she tell you about me to insinuate herself in your favour? She must know very well you're a rich man.'

'Are you denying you threatened to kill me to obtain control of your father's fortune?' Mr Penrose demanded excitedly.

'For God's sake!' Samuel's lip curled contemptuously. 'I may not appreciate your interference but in two years' time I'll be free to tell you to go to hell. Why should I risk the gallows to kill you now?'

'Because Smash Burke threatened to consign your corpse to the Thames if you didn't pay your debt to him,' said Mary coldly before Mr Penrose could speak. 'I don't suppose either your fine friends in London or even the brutish Phelps will be enough to protect you from Burke indefinitely.'

Samuel's eyes narrowed dangerously, then he swung round to confront Mr Penrose.

'You stupid old fool!' he snarled. 'Don't you see what she's trying to do? She knows you're too prudish and respectable to give her house-room in normal circumstances so she's invented the most outrageous lies she can think of to get close to you. Look at her!' He flung out a hand towards Mary. 'Standing there so demure and modest. She knows exactly how to twist you round her finger!'

Mr Penrose stared at his nephew.

'Are you denying that you threatened either to marry Miss Burleigh or to kill me to recoup your fortune?' he said. Two hectic spots of colour were burning on his parchment cheeks, and his hands were clenched convulsively by his sides, but his voice was steady.

'Of course I am,' Samuel declared impatiently. 'Dammit, I've never pretended to like you, but I'm not that base!'

Mr Penrose took a deep breath. Now that battle was well and truly joined, he seemed to have his nervousness under control.

'I don't believe you,' he said.

Samuel stared at his uncle, an ugly expression on his face.

'Don't you?' he said insultingly. 'And what do you intend to do about it, you stupid old buzzard? Do you think anyone would believe such an accusation – supported only by the word of an alehouse doxy?'

Mr Penrose's features were rigid with uncharacteristic anger. For a moment it was almost possible to see a likeness between uncle and nephew.

'You will speak courteously of Mrs Drayton,' he said bitingly. 'As to what I intend to do, I have already done it. It wants only two more signatures and you may have control of your fortune. Though you would have done better to wait another two years. Your father was nearly as big a wastrel as you, but I've done my best to recoup his losses these past five years.'

Mary glanced sharply at Mr Penrose, suddenly realising that there might be undercurrents here that she had not suspected.

'If that is the consequence of having false allegations laid against me, I can only be grateful for them,' said Samuel sarcastically. 'If you have nothing more to say, I will take my leave of you. But may I suggest you take a closer look at the credentials of your fair informant, uncle? I would hate to see her turn you into an even bigger fool than you already are.'

'There is one more thing to say,' said Mary as Samuel reached for the door-handle. 'In view of the circumstances, I advised your uncle to change his will to exclude you. He has done so. A copy rests with lawyers in Bath, and information to that effect has been transmitted to his lawyers in Hertfordshire. His death is no longer of any benefit to you at all.'

'You *bitch*!' Uncontrollable fury suddenly distorted Samuel's handsome features, and he lunged towards Mary. He had been angry before, but this was different. His temper had exploded beyond all reasonable levels. His lips were curled back in a terrifying snarl and his fist was raised to strike.

Mary heard Mr Penrose give an exclamation of pure horror, but she didn't pay any attention to him.

'Stand still!' The icy command in her voice cut through even Samuel's fury – but even more important was the small pistol she was pointing steadily at his heart.

He slammed to a halt.

'Harpy! You wouldn't *dare*!'

'If you make another move against me I will shoot you,' she said. Her voice was ruthless and inflexible, and her eyes as cold and penetrating as steel. There was no wavering in either her gaze or the hand which held the pistol. The concealing shawl had fallen, unheeded, to the floor. She stood straight and slender in the unexceptional surroundings of the drawing-room. But there was nothing commonplace or fragile about the way she confronted Samuel, and neither of her companions had any doubt that she would do exactly as she said.

Mr Penrose stared at her in shocked amazement. Though he didn't know it, she looked very much as she had done the day she forced Seb Collins to hand over a fair price for her uncle's alehouse. She had held the pistol in her hand that day also – but then she had had the added reassurance of Donald's presence. Today she knew she must deal with Samuel alone.

She held Samuel's savage glare with her own, diamond-hard gaze.

'You little bitch! Do you really think you can get away with threatening *me*?' he demanded harshly. The blind fury had been kicked out of him by the sight of the pistol, but his sullen rage was almost more frightening.

'Why not?' said Mary. 'If your response to Smash Burke is anything to go by, threats seem to work.' She lifted her hand slightly as he made a hasty movement, and he snarled in frustration.

'There are two points I'd like to draw to your attention,' she said coldly. 'Then you can go. As I've already mentioned, you no longer stand to gain any financial or other practical benefits from

Mr Penrose's death. Nor do I, incidentally – in case you were planning to overturn the will on the grounds that I've manipulated his affections. But it occurs to me that you might wish to take revenge, either upon your uncle or me – and that would be a very bad idea.'

'Why?' He stared at her offensively. 'Do you intend to stand guard over him with that insignificant little gun for the rest of his life?'

'No,' she replied. 'But a statement of what I overheard at the Lazy Cat is already lodged with the lawyers. And first thing tomorrow morning an account of this interview will join it. If anything untoward happens to either of us, you will immediately fall under suspicion. Just as important, from your point of view, is the fact that I have several powerful friends who won't wait for legal sanction to avenge me if any harm befalls me.'

'Really? Then why aren't they here now?' Samuel sneered.

Mary's smile was coldly unamused.

'Do we look as if we need them?' she asked. 'But I am handy with a pen, sir. And when I wrote my statement I also wrote to several friends – not least to Donald Campbell. What do you think Donald would do to you if you hurt me?'

She saw Samuel's expression change.

'The ugly Scotsman at the Lazy Cat?' he demanded.

Mary didn't answer, but she saw that her threat had gone home. She wasn't comfortable using Donald in such a way, but she didn't think she was putting him at any great risk. All she wanted to do was impress upon Samuel that the possible satisfaction of taking revenge upon either Mr Penrose or herself was far outweighed by the potential consequences to himself. To some extent she thought she'd done that, but it was hard to tell. Samuel was too sullen and angry for her to be sure that he would see things rationally.

'I don't think there's anything left to say,' she said. 'You have got what you most urgently wanted – control of your own fortune. And, as far as Mr Penrose and I am concerned, there should be no reason for us to discuss this meeting with anyone else in future. Nor for anyone to read the statement I've left with the lawyer – unless you give them cause to.'

'I could ruin you,' said Samuel viciously. 'Think of the scandal if it ever came out that you're not his niece! And after you've been living with him these many days! You'd never be able to show your face in respectable society again!'

Mary laughed, although the pistol remained steady in her hand. 'After tonight I have no further need to stay in Bath,' she pointed out. 'And if you raise a scandal about us we might just choose to be less discreet about your affairs. Besides, I'm sure it won't do any harm for my business to be known as the landlady in the notorious Penrose scandal! The curious will come from miles around to stay at the Lazy Cat!'

Samuel snarled impotently. Then he turned and slammed out of the room. Mary heard his feet on the stairs and the banging of the front door. She went to the window, too cautious to assume that Samuel had really left the house until she'd seen with her own eyes that he'd done so.

Looking down, she saw his shadowy figure striding away. Then she saw another, even more familiar figure loitering in the Square.

She leant her head briefly against the cold window-pane. How on earth had Justin known Samuel was there? She wondered what he would have done if she'd fired a shot.

He'd seen the movement of the curtains and came over to stand beneath the window, looking up at her. She was still holding the pistol, but her hand was by her side, half hidden by her skirts, and she kept it there. She waved with her other hand, in a gesture indicative that everything was all right. He hesitated, and she thought that maybe he intended to come in, but then he lifted his hat and swept her a magnificent bow. He would see her in the Pump Room tomorrow morning, and he was undoubtedly aware that Mr Penrose was with her.

He strolled away, in the same direction Samuel had taken, and Mary experienced a sudden, overwhelming desire to run down and call him back. Samuel had frightened her more than she'd anticipated and she wanted the reassurance of Justin's company. She wanted to tell him what had happened, hear his opinion and take comfort from his calm judgement.

But Mr Penrose was standing behind her, and

he was undoubtedly even more disturbed by Samuel than she was. And she had undertaken to deal with this business. She could not throw her hands up in dismay now.

CHAPTER TEN

MARY closed the curtains carefully, and turned back to look at Mr Penrose. His face was drained of colour, the bones beneath his face very prominent. He was clearly terribly disturbed and Mary couldn't blame him. She was feeling sick and shaken herself.

'I'm just going to check that the front door is secure, then I think we should both have some brandy,' she said quietly.

'I. . .' The word came out as little more than a croak. He swallowed convulsively and tried again. 'Mrs Drayton. . .'

'Why don't you pour out the brandy while I run downstairs?' she suggested.

If there was one thing she'd learnt in St Giles, it was never to take anything for granted. She wouldn't be able to rest completely easily until she'd seen the front door firmly bolted.

She ran lightly downstairs, shot the bolts, and went back up to Mr Penrose. He'd poured the brandy and taken a large gulp, but he didn't look much better for it. Mary laid the pistol down on the sideboard and picked up her own glass. Now that the crisis was over she could allow herself to feel the horror and disgust that Samuel had aroused in her, and her hand wasn't quite steady.

186

It had been an ugly interview, and she hadn't liked Samuel's response. Seb Collins had been a dangerous villain, but he had also been a practical businessman. Mary knew she'd gained a certain measure of respect, if not liking, from him. She'd never been afraid that he'd pursue her beyond St Giles.

Samuel was different, and neither she nor Mr Penrose could hide from him, even if they'd wanted to. She could only hope that she'd made the reasons for leaving them alone sufficiently compelling – but she wasn't convinced.

'My dear... Mrs Drayton... My God, ma'am!' Mr Penrose croaked helplessly.

Mary forced her bloodless lips into a smile.

'I hope I haven't shocked you too much, sir,' she said, trying to speak lightly. 'It was hardly ladylike of me to behave so forcefully.'

'You were...tremendous,' said Mr Penrose, finally managing to form a coherent sentence. 'I never guessed...' He coughed and cleared his throat, dabbing his lips with his handkerchief.

'That I was such a harridan?'

'That Samuel was so unspeakable.' He closed his eyes for a moment as if he couldn't bear to remember the horror that had just passed. 'My dear, I have been at fault throughout,' he said painfully. 'I have put you at risk, and I have given no proper thought to your safety. Tonight...if you hadn't been so capable of defending yourself...'

'But *I* knew what kind of man Samuel is,' said

Mary gently. 'I came to Bath with my eyes open – and prepared to deal with whatever arose.'

Mr Penrose stared at her. He was slowly recovering from his first shock, but he was far from being his normal self.

'I think you omitted a few important details when you were telling me your family circumstances, sir,' Mary said ruefully. 'I hadn't realised that Samuel's anger at being cut out of your will would outweigh his relief at getting control of his own fortune.'

Mr Penrose shook his head, as if trying to clear it.

'My brother was not provident,' he said distractedly. 'It was one of the ironies of the situation that he disposed of his property as he did. And one of the reasons why Samuel was so angry about the limitations on his inheritance. But there was still a substantial sum left when I took control of it, and I have done my best to build it up.'

'But your own fortune is considerably greater,' said Mary, stating a fact rather than asking a question.

Mr Penrose glanced at her, something almost approaching an apologetic smile in his eyes. 'I am much better at dealing with business matters than I am at dealing with people,' he said simply. 'Within certain limits I am prepared to take quite large risks on the movement of pieces of paper – and my judgement is usually sound. I have trebled the fortune my father left me.'

Mary took a deep breath.

'That might account for Samuel's irrational fury when he discovered you'd changed your will,' she said drily.

'I'm sorry. I should have told you,' said Mr Penrose contritely.

'I don't suppose it would have made any difference,' Mary replied. She took a sip of her brandy and then put the glass down. 'Except that I'm even more glad you changed your will. You don't live like a nabob,' she added, trying to lighten their mood.

'I'm not comfortable with ostentation,' Mr Penrose said. 'It's the challenge of the game I enjoy – not the fruits of my success.'

'Nevertheless,' said Mary, 'you must have considerable resources at your disposal. I think it's time you employed them against Samuel.'

'You don't think it's over?' Mr Penrose asked sharply.

'Do you?' Mary challenged him.

Mr Penrose stood up and took an agitated turn around the room. 'No.' He chewed his lip nervously. 'I didn't like the wild way he left here.'

'Nor did I.'

'What do you suggest I do?' Mr Penrose looked at her as if he was fully confident of her ability to advise him.

'In the first instance I think you should employ someone to make close enquiries about Samuel's activities,' said Mary. 'I'm not happy about relying on Donald's reputation to act as a brake on Samuel's worst instincts. You need another, more compelling method of bringing him to heel.' She tapped her fingers thoughtfully on the edge of the table.

'And then?' Mr Penrose prompted her, watching her with fascination tinged with admiration.

'If you can find a way to break him, do it,' said Mary bluntly.

'He's still my nephew!' Mr Penrose exclaimed. 'And you told him that as long as he behaved himself we wouldn't take any action against him.'

'I know, but he's dangerous,' said Mary. 'I had not realised until tonight how dangerous. And from what you've said it may be that his own fortune isn't going to be enough to pull him out of the hole he's in. We are not the only people who could suffer from his frustration.'

'Miss Burleigh!' Mr Penrose gasped.

'I think she's safe enough,' said Mary reassuringly. 'She was showing signs of being infatuated with him when we arrived in Bath, but I think her affections have taken a different turn since then. All the same, I think I may visit Mrs Burleigh tomorrow morning.'

'I'll come with you,' said Mr Penrose immediately.

'You won't find it an easy interview,' Mary warned him. 'But if you'd engage to distract Miss Lewisham's attention, that would be a great help.'

She looked up and found that Mr Penrose was steadily watching her, an odd expression on his face.

'Mrs Drayton...Mary, aren't you ever at a loss?' he asked her.

'Very often,' she said ruefully, as an image of her complete disintegration after Justin had kissed her flashed across her mind. 'But this is a practical problem, and I've always been able to deal with them.' She glanced at the pistol still lying on the table. 'Aren't you going to ask where I acquired such unladylike tendencies?' she asked curiously.

'I don't care,' said Mr Penrose surprisingly. 'It's enough to know that you are making such enormous efforts on my behalf – without asking anything in return.'

Mary flushed, disconcerted. 'I have only done...what seemed right,' she said uncomfortably. 'If we can bring this business to a satisfactory conclusion I will be happy.'

'Will you?' Mr Penrose's words seemed to fall like stones into the sudden silence. 'Forgive me, ma'am,' he continued hastily. 'I am not wise, and I often make mistakes in my dealings with other people, but I have known you for several days now, and I cannot believe that you are completely happy as the landlady of a coaching inn.'

'I assure you...' Mary began, startled by his uncharacteristic eloquence. She suspected that he was still being carried along on the tide of over-excitement that Samuel's visit had induced in him.

'You have done an excellent job,' he continued, unheeding of her interruption as the words seemed to flood out of him. 'And I am sure you are justly proud of the reputation the Lazy Cat has built up since you became its proprietor – but that's not the same thing, is it?'

'No.' Mary looked away. Too much had happened that day for her to be able to maintain any pretence about her contentment with her life.

'I'm a relatively old man,' Mr Penrose rushed on. 'There are many things which perhaps I cannot give you that you deserve to have. But I would be honoured... You would have security and comfort...and maybe even a chance to marry again – since I am so much older than you.' In the end his eloquence failed him, and he stared at her with painful hopefulness.

Mary looked at him. Her first response was astonishment, coupled with an instinctive rejection of his proposal. But that was quickly followed by an overwhelming sense of gratitude for his generosity.

'But you don't know anything about me!' she exclaimed.

'I don't need to know,' he replied. 'I know...I know I am only offering you a very poor bargain compared to what you deserve. But my dear... Mary, you know there can never be any future in your friendship with Lord Hawkridge. A man like that – he takes his amusement where he can find it, but he marries within his own station. I'm sorry,' he added as Mary stood up.

She moved away from him to stand looking down at the fire.

'I know that,' she said at last in a low voice, without looking round. 'I have no such expectations.' Then she lifted her head and met Mr Penrose's troubled, anxious gaze. 'Thank you, sir,' she said softly. 'I cannot tell you how much your offer means to me, but I can't accept it.'

'I know I'm a poor bargain, but please consider it – I beg you,' he urged her. 'It would mean. . .so much to me.'

Mary smiled tremulously.

'I think it is you who would have the poor bargain if I agreed,' she said. 'Come, sir, let us be friends.' She held out her hand to him. 'I would so much rather be a good friend to you than an unsatisfactory wife. And now,' she added as he took her hand, 'let us write an account of what happened here tonight to lodge with the lawyer tomorrow. I will feel much more comfortable if I know we've taken every possible precaution.'

When Mary and Mr Penrose arrived in Lansdown Crescent they'd already visited his lawyer, and they were making their morning call on Mrs Burleigh as early as they reasonably could.

'Wait a minute,' Mary said suddenly, just as they were approaching the Burleighs' front door. 'I've seen that fellow before somewhere.'

'Who?' Mr Penrose looked round anxiously. 'Where?'

'That thin, round-shouldered lad with a face like an underfed rat,' Mary said, indicating a nondescript personage hovering unobtrusively on the other side of the street.

'Do you think he's anything to do with Samuel?' Mr Penrose asked nervously.

'Well, it's not Phelps,' Mary replied. 'And why. . .? Dammit! I know who that is!'

She spun on her heel and strode straight over to the man, leaving Mr Penrose to tag anxiously behind.

At her approach, the thin man tried to look even more inconspicuous and started to sidle away down the street.

'Henry!' said Mary imperatively.

He turned towards her instinctively at the sound of his name, and then she saw the suspicion of a reluctant grin flit across his face.

'Who? Me, ma'am?' he asked innocently.

'What are you doing here?' she demanded. Her first thought was that Justin had sent his tiger to keep watch over her, but she dismissed that possibility immediately because Henry had been in Lansdown Crescent before they'd arrived. 'Is Samuel Penrose inside?' she asked sharply.

An admiring grin spread across Henry's face. ''Is Lordship said you were as sharp as a tack,' he said approvingly. 'No, ma'am.'

'Then why are you here?' Mary asked, ignoring Mr Penrose's exclamation of surprise.

''Is Lordship didn't trust the look of Master Samuel when 'e left Queen Square last night,' Henry explained. 'So 'e set me to keep watch over 'im. Which same I've bin doing——'

'Then where is he now?' Mary interrupted impatiently.

'I'm *telling* you, ma'am,' the tiger replied reprovingly. ''E went for a carriage ride this morning and picked up Miss Burleigh and the old biddy when they were out walking. I tried to follow, but I was on foot and I lost 'em, so I went back to tell 'is lordship. 'E said to come back 'ere and let 'im know as soon as they returned.'

'I see.' Inside her muff, Mary's hands closed into fists.

'Surely not a significant event,' Mr Penrose said anxiously. 'And Miss Lewisham——'

'Is coming down the street towards us,' said Mary tautly.

'I'll get 'is lordship.' Henry prepared to dash off.

'Wait!' Mary said sharply. 'The more information you can give him the better. Miss Lewisham! What has happened?' She went forward to take Mrs Burleigh's elderly companion by the arm.

'Mrs Drayton!' Miss Lewisham was too distressed to feel any surprise at meeting Mary. She was out of breath and flushed, and her skirts were muddy. 'He's taken her!' she cried, horror in her eyes.

'How?' Mary demanded.

'There was a coach!' Miss Lewisham's lip began to tremble and tears started in her eyes. At any moment she was going to give way to a fit of weeping.

'Where?' Mary's voice cracked like a whip, and

she seized Miss Lewisham by the shoulders, start-
ling her out of her incipient hysteria.

'On the London Road.' Miss Lewisham stared
at Mary in blank surprise. 'He threw me out on to
the side of the road and forced Lucinda into the
coa-coa-coa——'

Mary thrust the weeping woman into Mr
Penrose's appalled arms.

'Take her inside,' she commanded. 'Henry, go
and tell Lord Hawkridge what has happened, and
ask him to meet me at the house in Queen
Square.'

'Yes, ma'am!'

'And Henry. Make sure he does call for me.
Lucinda will need me.'

'Yes, ma'am.' The tiger sprinted away, leaving
Mr Penrose to stare at Mary over Miss Lewisham's
wilting body.

'I'm sorry, sir,' said Mary, a cold, grim
expression in her eyes. 'I don't have time to come
in and talk to Mrs Burleigh. But please assure her
that we will find Lucinda and bring her back. No
harm will come to her – and no scandal will touch
her. Be sure to tell her that. She will be in an
agony of worry and she is not strong. Don't let
her become too distressed.'

'But Lord Hawkridge. . .' Mr Penrose began.

'Has an aversion to innocent girls being hurt by
scoundrels.'

Mary picked up her skirts and began to walk as
fast as she could back to Queen Square. Once she
was well away from Lansdown Crescent and the

only reputation she had to worry about was her own, she ran.

She arrived in Queen Square just as the curricle with the glossy chestnuts drew up outside the house. 'Wait! I will be with you in two seconds,' she said breathlessly, giving Justin no time to speak.

She brushed past Grigson and ran up the stairs to her bedchamber. She paused only to collect her pistol and hide it in her muff and to take several coins out of her purse.

'Is there anything wrong, ma'am?' Grigson asked when she came back downstairs.

'No,' said Mary. 'My uncle has been called away, but I dare say he will be back by this evening. I am not sure when I will be returning. But if not today then I'm sure it will be tomorrow. In the meantime, please tell callers that we are not at home.' She put the coins into his hand, and went to climb swiftly into the curricle.

'Where's Henry?' she asked.

'He took a horse and went ahead to see if he could discover anything more,' said Justin, immediately setting the chestnuts in motion. 'What the devil happened last night?' His voice was harsh and his expression grim.

Mary leant back against the leather upholstery and tried to catch her breath. Now that, for the time being, she had done everything she could, she found that her hands were trembling. She gripped them together and took deep breaths, waiting for her heart to stop pounding so furiously.

Justin didn't repeat the question. He took one glance at her flushed, panting face and then concentrated on getting out of Bath as quickly as possible.

As soon as Mary had enough breath to speak coherently, she told him all about the meeting with Samuel Penrose.

'Dammit!' he swore when she'd finished. 'I knew I shouldn't have let you become involved in this business.'

'You didn't let me!' Mary snapped back. 'I was the one who initiated this. And even I didn't guess how unstable and vengeful Samuel is.'

'I should have come in last night,' Justin declared tensely.

'It wouldn't have prevented this. How could we have known what he intended to do?' Mary demanded. 'But I wish to God I'd warned the Burleighs against him when I first wanted to. If anything happens to Lucinda it will be my fault.'

'Don't be ridiculous! Besides, nothing's going to happen to her. We'll catch up with them first.'

'I hope so.' Mary let out her breath in a long, unsteady sigh, trying to ease the tension in her slight body. 'I was so determined to discourage him from taking his revenge on Mr Penrose or me that he is taking out his spite on Lucinda instead,' she said wretchedly.

'Or he may simply be trying to obtain a rich wife,' Justin pointed out. 'Judging by the route we're taking, Scotland is their destination. Lucinda's still a minor, isn't she? He may even be intending to hold her hostage in the expectation that Penrose will pay up to avoid a scandal. In which case he certainly won't hurt her.'

Mary didn't reply. She was remembering the expression in Samuel's eyes when he'd lunged towards her the previous night. A practical, cool-headed man might try to make good his losses by a scheme to blackmail Mr Penrose or the Burleighs, but she doubted if Samuel was capable of thinking so rationally.

She didn't voice her fears; there was no point. Nothing she said or thought would make any difference. All that counted was catching up with Samuel and rescuing Lucinda.

They travelled quickly, and Henry continued to range ahead of them, occasionally leaving small, badly scrawled messages for Justin at staging posts. It was lucky that he did so. For with his greater turn of speed he was twice able to back-track when Samuel's route became unclear, and leave messages which prevented Justin from taking a wrong turning. That he was riding his horses into the ground to do so was apparent from a comment made by one of the ostlers when Justin stopped to change horses.

'We're gaining on them,' said Justin as he set the curricle in motion again.

'Yes.' Mary flicked a stray lock of hair out of her face, and put her hand back inside the comfort of her muff. 'But Samuel's not wasting any time. He's changing his team at nearly every stage.'

'Better for Lucinda, perhaps,' Justin replied,

negotiating a tricky corner with consummate ease. 'The more his mind is concentrated on the need for speed, the less attention he may give to her.'

'Phelps is in the carriage with them,' said Mary. 'I dare say Lucinda's too frightened to cry for help even when they halt.'

'We will catch them,' said Justin grimly. 'Are you cold?' he added, glancing at her briefly as she shivered.

'No.' It was a damp, grey, miserable November day. The sun had barely appeared from behind the clouds, and even Mary's new pelisse and muff were no protection from the cutting wind. But she was hardly aware of her own discomfort. All her thoughts were with Lucinda.

'We will catch them,' said Justin again, this time more gently.

'I know we will.' It was true; Mary had no doubts on that score. She was with Justin, and Justin would catch Samuel. It was only what happened to Lucinda in the meantime that worried her.

She lapsed into silence, watching the horses as they ate up the miles. Justin was hiring the best, and Mary was dimly aware that both he and Henry were laying out money very freely on this venture.

It didn't surprise her. Whatever his relationship with her, Justin would have done his best for Lucinda Burleigh. He had a deep-rooted objection to cruelty and unkindness.

'How did you know Samuel was coming to Queen Square last night?' she asked suddenly.

'Henry was watching for his return to Bath,' Justin explained briefly.

'Of course he was,' said Mary, wondering how she had failed to realise that Justin would take such a precaution.

'It isn't you who should be rebuking yourself for not taking this matter seriously enough,' he said harshly, as if he was aware of what she was thinking. 'I had not fully grasped the nature of the man. When Henry came back and told me he'd taken up Lucinda in his carriage. . .'

Justin pressed his lips together grimly; his jaw was rigid.

'I think, my love, that we'd better make haste to resolve our differences,' he continued after a moment. 'We will then be in a position to give our combined attention to any problems which arise in future – and we might do better.'

Mary turned her head to look at him. His profile was stern and unyielding, his concentration fixed on the horses and the road. He was hardly in the mood for pretty speeches, but he seemed to take it for granted that they would have a future together. Her thoughts slipped back to their meeting yesterday. She had never yet had any opportunity to come to terms with the confusion she had experienced then.

She didn't question that she loved him. She had always loved him for his insight, his kindness and his humour. When she had met him in St Giles she had felt for the first time in her life that here was someone who could understand her, someone in whom she could place her trust.

She still felt that. But the lost years, his hurtful assumptions about her, and her own unruly emotions, had tarnished the first purity of their love.

And, even now, when her thoughts should have been entirely given over to Lucinda's plight, she was profoundly conscious of his powerful body so close beside her. She was aware of the tension in his arms as he held the reins and the forceful thrust of his legs as he braced himself to obtain every reasonable ounce of speed he could from his team. He was not a cruel or violent driver. The horses responded to his hands and his voice, not to the lash of his whip.

Mary was shamefully conscious of how much she longed to have him make love to her. To lie in his arms and surrender to the urgent desire he aroused in her. It was not a maidenly or a modest emotion – but then, ultimately, she wasn't a maidenly or modest woman. She could deny what she was, or she could accept it. But if she accepted it, did she scourge herself for her unruly passions – or did she embrace them willingly?

She did not know. But she was beginning to recognise that there might be other reasons for her uncertainty besides the strictures of her childhood.

When she had lost herself in Justin's arms, she had also lost all control of herself and the situation. And she had spent all her adult life struggling to achieve control and independence. She had been more self-assured when she'd been facing Samuel with a pistol than she had been when she'd tried to handle the emotions which Justin aroused in her. Was she simply afraid of what might become of her if she truly surrendered to him?

A few spots of rain fell, but she ignored them. She was thinking about the consequences of giving in to Justin – and how little she really knew about him. These past few days had been the only time she had ever come remotely close to inhabiting his world.

The aristocracy were different.

She remembered Miss Lewisham's scandalous story that Justin kept mistresses along the main post roads in the way that some men kept horses. He'd denied that – but there must have been some reason why the story had gained currency.

She glanced at him surreptitiously. The virile energy which created so much disturbing excitement in her must have found an outlet over the past seven years.

'What are you thinking?' he demanded suddenly.

'Have you had many mistresses?' she asked, her voice sounding harsh in her ears.

He didn't answer immediately.

'There have been several, over the years,' he replied at last in an unemotional voice.

'Do you have one now?'

'Yes.'

Mary's hand closed into a fist so tightly that her nails dug into the palm of her hand. She had known it must be so, but hearing it didn't make it any easier. Dear God! What was to become of her? She was in love with a man who could calmly tell her that he had another mistress. She was suddenly unbearably jealous of the woman – and furious with Justin.

'What's her name?' she grated.

'Bernadette. She claims her father was a French nobleman,' he said drily. 'I don't think she'll be disappointed to terminate our liaison. I don't spend enough time in London for her – and I don't pander sufficiently to her whims.'

'Terminate. . .?'

Justin checked the horses, and they dropped back to a walk. He turned to look at her.

'I would have done it the moment I first laid eyes on you,' he said quietly. 'But, as I said, she lives in London and I've been in Bath. Mary, I'm not going to lie to you about my virtue – or lack of it. But it doesn't make any difference to the way I feel about you. I was hurt and angry when I thought you'd deserted me. I wasn't looking for love from a woman.' He sighed, seeing the doubting, disturbed look in her eyes. 'Would you be more willing to marry me if I'd lived as a monk these past seven years?' he asked, half jokingly, half seriously.

'*Marry* you?'

'What did you think I meant to ask you yesterday?' he asked, whipping up the horses again.

Mary closed her eyes, a maelstrom of conflicting, overwhelming emotions flooding through her. Relief. Happiness. Doubt. Fear.

In the same moment Justin had admitted to having a mistress in keeping he had asked her to marry him. She had heard many times about the capacity of men to separate lust from love, but that didn't make it any easier to come to terms with the phenomenon in the man *she* loved.

Besides, just as she'd been coming to believe that her own fierce desire for him was acceptable, he had inadvertently raised the possibility that perhaps it was comparable to the feelings he'd had towards his mistresses.

CHAPTER ELEVEN

BEFORE Mary had time to respond to Justin's question she saw Henry coming towards them. His horse was lathered, but his face was flushed and bright with excitement.

'I've seen 'em, guv'nor!' he announced immediately. 'They're changing horses at the Red Lion. I went right past the coach and it's them all right. Only one way they can go now for the next ten miles!'

'Good!' said Justin with satisfaction. 'We can't be more than three or four miles behind them.'

'I'll have a fresh team ready for you at the Lion, guv'nor,' said Henry. 'This pair's blown. Leave the lady there?'

'You'll do no such thing!' Mary said fiercely.

Justin glanced at her, doubt in her eyes. She was sure he would have preferred to leave her in the safety of the inn, but she met his gaze with unswerving determination. After a moment a brief smile of reluctant acceptance curved his lips and he nodded imperceptibly.

'Mrs Drayton stays with me,' he said. 'Miss Burleigh may need her. Have the horses ready.'

Henry needed no second telling.

'He could have been a jockey,' said Mary, looking after the tiger's disappearing figure. Her mouth was suddenly dry, and her heart was thudding, but she still managed to sound calm.

'He finds it more interesting working for me,' said Justin. 'But I think we've exceeded all his expectations of excitement today.'

'I hope we don't exceed them any further!' Mary replied, her hand closing around the comforting handle of her pistol within her muff.

'So do I.'

Justin's profile was ruthlessly determined, and she was conscious of the coiled, fiercely contained energy within him.

'Do you know this part of the country?' she asked, suddenly remembering the familiarity with which the tiger had referred to the inn ahead.

'I've a house not far from here,' said Justin briefly.

After that, no further conversation passed between them. The curricle dashed into the inn yard and, at Henry's fiercely worded behest, the ostlers flew to their task.

With a fresh team, and the end of their quest in sight, Justin pushed the horses hard. Mary had to cling to the edge of the curricle to avoid being thrown out, but she made no complaint.

They rounded a bend and saw the coach. It was rumbling along on a straight, relatively good stretch of road. Justin gave a grunt of satisfaction, completely intent on his task. The horses sprang forward with even greater eagerness, and the gap between the two vehicles slowly closed. The curricle went past the coach at a clipping pace, barely inches between the wheels, and Mary saw the startled glance that the postilion threw at them.

In another few moments, Justin had turned the curricle and brought his horses to a quivering standstill. It was a display of driving skill which would have left a disinterested bystander open-mouthed with admiration, but Mary simply took it for granted.

Justin leapt from the curricle and ran towards the coach as the swearing postilion tried to control his plunging, snorting team. Henry grabbed Justin's whip and followed his master, still mounted. Mary wasn't far behind, her pistol in her hand.

'What the devil. . .?' Samuel's head appeared at the window of the coach.

Justin hauled open the door, seized him by the front of his coat and dragged him out of the carriage. Samuel struggled furiously, raising his fists, but he was taken by surprise and caught off balance. A crashing blow from Justin's right hand sent him sprawling on the muddy road, and Justin spun round in time to intercept a more calculated assault from Phelps. Mary heard Lucinda cry out in horror, but she paid no heed. Her attention was locked on Justin and the manservant.

As she had once said, Phelps was a swaggering bully, but he wasn't a coward. She knew immediately that he was a far more dangerous opponent than Samuel, and her pounding heart threatened to choke her when she saw how narrowly Justin evaded his first rushed attack. But Justin was aware of the danger too, and Henry was standing over Samuel's prone body with his master's whip. Mary took the time to look up at the postilion who was still struggling to calm his horses.

'For God's sake! What's going on?' he demanded frantically.

'Attend to your horses and don't interfere,' said Mary coldly. 'Did you know the lady wasn't a willing passenger?'

'It wasn't my place to know,' he said desperately. 'The servant hired the coach this morning. I didn't know what he had in mind.'

Mary's eyes flashed contemptuously, and she turned her attention back to Justin.

Phelps was down on one knee, half turned away from Justin as he struggled to get to his feet. Then he swung back towards Justin and she gasped as she saw the dull gleam of a knife in his hand.

She lifted her pistol, but she didn't fire. Justin was between her and the manservant, and he was moving too fast to give her a clear shot.

Henry's eyes were fixed on his master, but he didn't use the whip. If Mary had had any time to spare him a glance, she would have seen him watching the fight with grim satisfaction tinged with expectation.

Phelps lunged towards Justin. Justin side-stepped swiftly and seized the wrist of the manservant's knife-hand in a bone-crushing grip. In one continuous movement he yanked Phelps off balance and forward to receive a thundering blow in his stomach. Phelps doubled up and landed groaning beside Samuel.

Justin picked up the knife and tossed it into the field beside the road. Then he looked down at his victims, absent-mindedly rubbing his bruised knuckles as he did so. Both men were dazed, and Samuel was barely conscious. It wasn't in Justin to continue pounding them. He looked up at Henry, still mounted on his horse.

'Watch them,' he said curtly.

'Yes, guv'nor.' The tiger stared down at the two men with hot, angry eyes. He didn't hold with anyone attacking his master with a knife, and the whip was ready in his hand.

Justin glanced back at Mary, and smiled faintly as he saw the pistol she was holding. 'I should have guessed you would not be standing idle,' he said, a note of proud affection in his voice. 'If you will cover them for a few minutes, I'll reassure Lucinda and then find some cords to restrain them.'

'As long as it takes,' Mary told him grimly.

'Not long, I hope,' he said, and turned to the coach. 'Miss Burleigh?' he said gently, reaching out his hand to her.

She was shaking with shock and fear, hardly able to realise that she'd been rescued. Her muscles were too knotted with tension to allow her to move. She simply stared at Justin with huge, terrified eyes.

'Miss Burleigh. . .Lucinda, you're safe now,' Justin said quietly. 'Mary – Mrs Drayton – is with me. She'll look after you. But first I must tie up the two villains who abducted you.'

Phelps groaned and tried to push himself upright.

'Stay where you are!' Henry growled, and the whip cracked inches before the manservant's face.

Phelps subsided in the mud, the spirit knocked out of him.

Samuel stirred, his gaze still dazed and unfocused. He had no more fight left in him than his henchman.

Then he caught sight of Mary. His eyes focused and his expression changed. His face distorted in an ugly grimace of hate and he surged to his feet, taking Henry by surprise. The tiger's horse shied away and Justin spun round.

Henry had the horse under control in an instant, and Justin was already lunging after Samuel, but Samuel was in the grip of ungovernable rage. His lips were curled back in a hideous snarl and his eyes blazed with mad fury. He ignored both the lash of the whip across his face and the pistol levelled at him as he charged down on Mary.

She didn't waver. Her bullet hit him in the right shoulder at the very same instant that Justin seized him from behind and sent him crashing, unconscious, to the ground.

In the sudden silence, disturbed only by the sounds of uneasy, restless horses and the jingle of harness, Mary let out an unsteady breath.

'I do hate having to do that,' she said vaguely.

'Mary!' Justin reached her side and took the

pistol out of her numb hand. He slipped his arm around her waist and supported her against him. 'My God!'

For a moment she leant against his broad chest. She would have liked nothing better than to give way to her overwrought nerves within the protection of his arms. But she knew she couldn't allow herself the luxury of such self-indulgence. There was still Lucinda to think of – and Mary was desperately worried about what Samuel might have done to her.

'I'm all right,' she said, pushing herself away from Justin.

'Dear God! I'm sorry,' he said, and she knew he was as shaken as she was. 'I should have ——'

'I'm all right,' she repeated. 'No one could have anticipated such blind craziness, and I know you would have stopped him even if I hadn't shot him.' She lifted her head and managed to smile at him, and felt his arm tighten around her. 'I must take care of Lucinda,' she said. 'And God knows what we're going to do about. . .them.'

She slipped out of his embrace and went over to the couch, careful to leave a wide berth between herself and both Samuel and Phelps.

Behind her Justin looked up and met his tiger's shocked, admiring gaze. 'You won't find another lady like her in a million years, guv'nor,' Henry croaked.

'I know.'

Then Justin looked down at Samuel's unconscious body, black fury in his eyes.

'Today you made your last mistake,' he said, his voice quiet, cold and implacable. 'You'll never have an opportunity to make another one.'

Mary got into the coach and sat down beside its frightened occupant.

'Lucinda,' she said gently. 'It's all right. You're safe now.'

Lucinda gave a little choking gasp and started to cry, heart-wrenching sobs racking her whole body. Mary took the girl in her arms and stroked her hair, murmuring reassurances.

It took a long time for any vestige of self-control to return to Lucinda. But, despite her own agony of anxiety to know what had happened to the girl, Mary didn't hurry her. Outside she heard voices and the sounds of movement, but she ignored them. She had no idea what Justin intended to do next, but she was content to leave the decisions in his hands.

'Did he hurt you?' she asked at last, when Lucinda's storm of tears finally subsided.

'He di – didn't touch me,' Lucinda choked out. She scrubbed at her pale, tear-stained cheek with her sleeve. 'He ju – just talked to me. He s-said *such* things! About...about *you*, ma'am. He *hates* you.'

'I know.' Mary pushed Lucinda's damp, straggling hair out of her face. 'But he didn't hurt you?' She looked deeply into Lucinda's eyes.

Lucinda gulped back a sob and mutely shook her head.

'Thank God for that!' Mary said, heartfelt relief in her voice.

She looked up as Justin appeared beside the carriage. He had a hard, anxious question in his eyes, and she smiled reassuringly.

'She's just shaken,' she said softly. 'He didn't touch her.'

Justin's expression relaxed slightly.

'Miss Burleigh,' he said quietly, 'if you can bear to travel a short distance in my curricle, Henry will take you and Mary to a house of mine not far from here. It's about eight miles away, I'm afraid, but you'll be able to rest there – and Henry can ride post-haste to Bath to reassure your mother that you're safe.'

Lucinda nodded, still clinging to Mary, but she didn't say anything.

'What are *you* going to do?' Mary asked, keeping her voice subdued, but there was a sharp question in her eyes.

'I'm going to take this coach and the unholy pair outside to a friend of mine who's also a magistrate,' Justin replied evenly, but there was a cold, ruthless expression in his eyes. 'Between us we should be able to make sure that they never hurt anyone again – and without causing a scandal.'

Mary held his gaze for a moment, then she nodded, accepting his decision.

'Come on, Lucinda,' she said, helping the girl out of the coach.

The curricle had been turned to face the direction from which they'd come, and Henry was already holding the reins. He was looking mulish, and Mary suspected that he was reluctant to leave his master's side. She sympathised, but didn't say anything.

Justin's greatcoat was lying on the seat. He had taken it off when they'd stopped at the Red Lion, and now he put it around Lucinda's shoulders. He helped Mary up into the curricle, so that she was sitting beside Henry, and then gave Lucinda his hand.

Mary was sure he'd arranged the order of their seating deliberately, so that Lucinda did not have to sit next to a stranger.

'I will come as soon as I can,' he said. 'And Henry will take a message back to Bath.'

'Thank you, my lord,' said Mary.

'You watch that bas——' Henry snapped off what he'd been about to say and urged the horses into motion before Justin could reprimand him.

Mary looked back as they drove away, but she couldn't see either Samuel or Phelps. They were hidden from her by the coach. She wondered what Justin intended, but she wasted no time in speculation. She only wished she didn't have to ride away and leave him. Like Henry she would have been much happier to see the business through to its end – but they also had to think of Lucinda.

Even huddled in the greatcoat, the girl still shivered with cold and shock. Mary wondered if it would be better to take her the lesser distance to the Red Lion rather than to Justin's house – but then they would have to provide an explanation for their presence. There was no point in causing unnecessary gossip about what had happened.

'I've got some gin in me pocket,' said Henry suddenly. 'I know it ain't what she's used ter but it might 'elp.'

'Thank you.' Mary took the small flask from him and held it for Lucinda to take a sip.

Lucinda choked on the raw spirit, her eyes watering. 'That's horrible!' she gasped.

'I know.' Mary sniffed the cheap gin with reminiscent distaste, then screwed the lid back on. 'I've never acquired a liking for it either. But some people swear by it, don't they, Henry?'

'Me uncle, for one,' he agreed, picking up her light tone. 'Swore all the way down three flights of stairs one night when 'e'd taken a glass too much.'

'Oh, dear,' said Mary. 'I hope he didn't break anything.'

'Only 'is leg,' Henry replied. 'And 'e'd been meanin' to get a new one anyway, so it wasn't a problem.'

'A new leg?' Mary repeated encouragingly.

'Well, you see, ma'am, it was wooden,' Henry confided. 'And the woodworm had got into it. Riddled with holes, it was. Every time 'e stumped across the floor 'e left a trail of dust be'ind 'im. Made the devil of a lot of work for his old woman. She'd been on at 'im to change it for months. So getting drunk and fallin' downstairs was a blessing in disguise, really.'

'I can see how it must have been,' Mary agreed,

putting her arm comfortingly around Lucinda. 'I
had an uncle once who. . .'

She went on to make up a completely spurious
story about a non-existent uncle which Henry
topped with an even more outrageous anecdote
about an old aunt. She was grateful for the tiger's
help. She knew that nothing they said was of any
comfort to Lucinda, but it might provide her with
a distraction to hasten the journey – as long as the
stories didn't become too frivolous.

At last Lucinda stirred restlessly, and Mary
silenced Henry with a swift glance.

'I didn't want to get in the carriage with him,'
Lucinda said abruptly. 'When he stopped and
asked us to go for a drive with him, I didn't want
to go – but Cousin Emma made it so hard to
refuse. I really didn't want to go.'

'I know you didn't.' Mary hugged her
reassuringly.

'What's going to become of me?' Lucinda asked
helplessly. 'The scandal. . .'

'There won't be any scandal,' said Mary firmly.
'You're safe now. We'll take care of you.'

'I wanted someone to come. I wanted someone
to come. . .but since Papa died. . .' Lucinda
buried her face in her hands. 'I was so frightened,'
she whispered, her voice muffled. 'I was so fr –
fr – frightened.' She turned in Mary's arms, sobbing against her friend's shoulder.

'I know,' said Mary. Her eyes were bleak. She
was remembering the days when she had been as
afraid as Lucinda and there had been no one for

her to turn to. 'But you'll never be frightened like that again,' she continued gently. 'Because next time someone tries to persuade you to do something against your better judgement you'll refuse – won't you?'

Lucinda lifted her tear-stained face and looked at Mary.

'The only mistake you've ever made is to be too deferential to those who don't deserve your respect,' said Mary, smiling reassuringly. 'You had some doubts about Samuel from the first, didn't you? You should be proud of your insight. You have nothing to reproach yourself for.'

'I don't know,' said Lucinda uncertainly.

'And in future you will have more confidence in your opinions,' Mary continued. 'That's all you need, Lucinda. That's all you've ever needed.'

A very tremulous smile wavered on Lucinda's lips. Among all the other horrors that had assailed her that day was the fear that, somehow, she had been responsible for encouraging Samuel's behaviour. But Mary seemed to have no such concern, and she was doing her best to reinforce Lucinda's faith in herself.

'Did you really threaten to shoot him last night?' Lucinda asked wonderingly.

'She *did* shoot him today!' Henry exclaimed before Mary could reply.

'Ma'am?' The girl looked startled.

'I wounded him in the shoulder,' said Mary, glancing at Henry reprovingly. 'I'm afraid I made him angry yesterday. I told him Mr Penrose had cut him out of his will – and then I wouldn't let him throttle me to relieve his feelings.'

Lucinda shuddered.

'He hates you,' she said in a low voice. 'All he talked about was what he was going to do to you when he had the chance. But he was also afraid of someone called Burke – that's why he was taking me to Scotland. He said if Burke knew he was married to an heiress he'd hold off for a few more months. Then he was coming back for you. He said he knew where you lived. And something about a man called Donald. He said he was going to shoot Donald first. And then. . .' Her voice faltered. 'Oh, ma'am. I can't tell you what he said he was going to do to you.'

'It's all right, Lucinda, I can guess,' said Mary quietly. 'Don't think about it any more. He's not going to hurt you or me – or anyone else – ever again. We're quite safe now.'

'What's Lord Hawkridge going to do?' Lucinda asked anxiously.

'I don't know. But I know neither of us has any reason to worry about Samuel any more,' said Mary with absolute certainty. 'When Justin makes up his mind to do something, he does it. And I think he hates Samuel even more than we do.'

'Justin?' said Lucinda questioningly. 'Mrs Drayton, how did it come about that it was Lord Hawkridge who came with you to rescue me? How did either of you even know I needed rescuing?'

'It's a long story,' said Mary wryly, 'and Henry probably knows as much of it as I do by now. If

Samuel was ranting on about me in the coach you must have realised I'm not Mr Penrose's niece. . .'

'He said you were a dox – an innkeeper.' Lucinda hastily amended what she'd been about to say.

'I'm the landlady of a coaching inn called the Lazy Cat,' said Mary calmly. She was aware that Henry was also listening with interest but if he hadn't already known that fact he probably soon would have anyway.

'Several days ago I heard Samuel talking to Phelps at the inn,' she continued. 'He was making threats against his uncle, and he also mentioned the possibility of coaxing you to marry him. So I went to tell Mr Penrose what I'd overheard, and we came to Bath to confront Samuel. I'm sorry, Lucinda,' she added regretfully. 'If I'd taken you and your mother more fully into my confidence, today would never have happened. I feel very responsible.'

'It's not your fault, ma'am,' said Lucinda softly. 'I don't suppose Mr Penrose wanted you to tell me, did he? He seems a very anxious man. And you did warn me against Samuel. I knew that was what you were trying to do, and I understood. I should have been firmer with Cousin Emma.'

'That's the ticket,' said Henry admiringly. 'You're a lady after me own 'eart, miss. I'm proud to 'ave assisted in your rescue.'

'Thank you,' said Lucinda, looking both surprised and pleased.

* * *

' 'Ere we are, ladies,' Henry announced, bringing the curricle to a halt before a large, elegant house built in the classically grand style of the previous century. 'Allow me to welcome you to 'is lordship's Worcestershire residence. Famous for its helegant architecture and pictureskew surroundings. Mind you, it doesn't look its best at this time of year. You ought to come back in the summer.'

He jumped down from the curricle and went to knock on the front door, before coming back to help Mary and Lucinda down.

'Mr Dibley,' he said, when an elderly butler appeared at the door, 'we've got guests. This is Mrs Drayton and Miss Lucinda. They was involved in a carriage accident and 'is lordship said to bring them 'ere while 'e sorted everything out on the road.'

'Thank you, Henry,' said Mary with quiet dignity. She wondered whether Justin had told his tiger to provide them with an unexceptional reason for their presence or whether he'd made up the excuse on his own initiative. She smiled at the butler. Her manner was friendly, but neither over-familiar nor ingratiating. 'I hope we won't put you to too much inconvenience,' she told him, 'but we would be grateful to sit by the fire and perhaps have a cup of tea. Lord Hawkridge said he would come as soon as he had everything arranged, but I don't know how long that may take.'

'Of course, Mrs Drayton, please come in,' said Dibley. He spoke courteously, but she thought she detected a hint of disapproval in his bearing. 'I hope you are not hurt,' he added, stepping back to allow them into the house.

'Only a little shaken, thank goodness,' Mary replied. 'Oh, Lord Hawkridge did say we could send a message to our family to let them know we're safe.' She glanced towards Henry.

'I'll be back to take the message from you as soon as I've taken the curricle round to the stables,' he said instantly.

'This way, please, ladies,' said Dibley. He led them into a small sitting-room. 'I'll have the fire made up directly, and bring you some tea.'

'And some writing materials, also, if you please,' said Mary.

'Certainly.' He bowed and went out, and a few minutes later a maid came to make up the fire. Shortly after that a footman appeared with paper, pen and ink, and then the butler himself returned with a tea-tray loaded not only with tea but with a substantial cherry cake and several smaller savoury items too.

'Mrs Marlowe, the housekeeper, thought you might be hungry,' he explained. 'Please ring if you need anything else.'

'Thank you very much.' Mary's smile illuminated her eyes. 'And please thank Mrs Marlowe for her thoughtfulness. I think we will both be glad of something to eat.' She glanced at Lucinda who nodded.

'We will be serving dinner later,' said Dibley

rather austerely. 'Do you have any idea when his lordship will be returning, ma'am?'

'I'm afraid I don't,' Mary admitted.

'Henry says his lordship wishes you to have every comfort during your stay,' said the butler. 'I'm sure he would not want you to wait unduly for him. We will serve it at the normal hour.'

'Thank you.' Mary watched the butler leave the room, an odd smile on her lips. She was in Justin's house, talking to his servants. If Justin had meant what he'd said about marrying her, they might one day be her servants. It was a very strange notion.

She wondered what the stately Dibley would say if he knew about her relationship with his master. Would he approve? Or would he think she was completely unsuitable to be Lady Hawkridge?

She glanced around at her surroundings. Even this small sitting-room was imposing, and the glimpses she'd caught of the rest of the house had been similarly grand. *One* of Justin's houses, Henry had said.

Of course she'd know that Justin inhabited a world that was different from anything she'd ever known, but her vision of it had been vague and cloudy. The reality was rather daunting. Even Sir Richard had not lived in such a magnificent house. And, until now, the squire's house had been the most imposing country residence she had ever visited.

The houses she'd visited in Bath had somehow been different. Perhaps because she'd been aware that the Mr Penroses and Mrs Knightleys of the world were not so very much grander than she was. If they'd met her at the Lazy Cat they would undoubtedly have responded to her differently than they had when she was a guest at Mrs Burleigh's party. But her memories of her childhood had given her the confidence to treat them as equals.

She had no such memories to fall back on to tell her how to behave in a nobleman's house. She glanced at Lucinda and saw from her wide-eyed stare that she was feeling similarly overawed.

'Oh, ma'am,' Lucinda breathed. 'I had no idea Lord Hawkridge would live in a house like this. I hope he comes back before it's time for dinner. I shall be so nervous if we have to sit down to eat with all his servants watching us.'

'So shall I,' Mary admitted. 'But I'm sure we'll both rise to the occasion if we have to. In the meantime, we'd better write some messages for Henry to take back to Bath.'

CHAPTER TWELVE

JUSTIN didn't return in time for dinner, and they ate alone at one end of an imposing dining-table in an even more imposing dining-room.

There were several large oil-paintings on the wall, but none by Justin. Mary wasn't surprised. He wasn't the kind of man to make a vulgar, ostentatious show of his work in his own house.

It was an uncomfortable meal for the visitors. Both of them were preoccupied by the events of the day, but neither of them felt able to speak naturally in the presence of others. And their discomfort was increased by the fact that they were waited upon by expressionless servants in magnificent livery.

Mary felt particularly uneasy. Not only did she feel out of her depth in such surroundings, but she was desperately afraid that someone in the household might have recognised her. Justin had sketched her several times at the Blue Boar. There would inevitably be pictures of her in his old sketchbooks. All it needed was for someone to remember and put two and two together. . .

What made it worse was that if anyone did know anything about her they would also inevitably believe that she had run away to be the mistress of a richer man. That was what Justin had

225

believed until a few days ago, and there was no possible way that anyone in this household could know differently.

She glanced at the servants surreptitiously, but their faces were so expressionless that it was impossible to guess what they were thinking. She thought she detected a certain air of disapproval in Dibley's bearing, but that might simply be because he didn't like the unconventional way the guests had been foisted on the household.

There was nothing she could do to reassure herself; she just had to brazen it out. But she was becoming increasingly anxious not to stay in the house any longer than she had to. Justin had implied that he still wanted to marry her, but sitting in such stately splendour, painfully conscious of how out of place she was in such surroundings, Mary could hardly believe that he meant it.

She was glad when the meal was over, and they went back to wait in the small sitting-room. Lucinda had recovered her composure very well, but she was still extremely nervous, and both women jumped and looked startled when a servant came to build up the fire.

When they were alone again, Mary smiled ruefully at Lucinda.

'This will never do,' she said. 'We'll be as skittish as a pair of kittens on a windy day by the time Lord Hawkridge gets here if we're not careful.'

'What do you think he's doing?' Lucinda asked nervously.

'I don't know. He was taking them to a friend of his. But we don't even know how far he had to go.'

'Is he going. . .do you think he means it to come to court?' Lucinda asked, pleating the folds of her skirt convulsively.

'I don't think so.' Mary remembered the expression in his eyes as he'd looked at Samuel. Justin was a tolerant man, but he had an over-whelming hatred of the kind of vindictive cruelty which characterised young Penrose. He would not allow him to escape unpunished for his actions, but nor was he likely to do anything which would expose the innocent Lucinda to malicious, dam-aging gossip. 'Anyway, I dare say we will find out soon enough. In the meantime, perhaps we should find some way of distracting our thoughts from what's happened.' She glanced at a piano on one side of the room. 'Can you play?' she asked.

'Oh, yes,' said Lucinda eagerly, as if she was glad of the suggestion. 'Oh, ma'am, do you think anyone will mind?' she added doubtfully.

'Lord Hawkridge certainly won't mind,' said Mary firmly. 'And I would be grateful. I've always enjoyed music.'

'Do you not play yourself?' Lucinda asked, going to the instrument and opening the highly polished lid.

'I'm afraid not,' Mary replied. She had played once, but that had been over twelve years ago, and she had no confidence in her ability to do so now.

Lucinda touched the keys tentatively, drawing soft random notes from them. Then she sat down and played a simple melody. Her playing was very characteristic of her – hesitant at first, yet growing in confidence.

Mary leant her head against the high back of her chair and listened, relieved that she no longer had to try to make conversation with Lucinda. Too many confusing emotions were churning within her, and she knew she was as concerned about her own problems as she was about her friend's.

When this ugly business was over she would finally have to confront her feelings for Justin. None of her doubts or uncertainties had resolved themselves. Now that she had seen the house he lived in she believed more firmly than ever that their union would be a mismatch – unless she accepted the role of his mistress.

That thought reminded her of the unknown Bernadette and her hands tightened instinctively into fists. It was unreasonable to feel such violent antipathy towards the woman, but she did. Bernadette had had what Mary wanted yet was afraid to take.

And why did Justin wish to marry her? Was it simply because he'd been frustrated in his attempt to do so seven years ago? Did he love her? Or did he think he owed it to her? He must know how unsuitable and outrageous their marriage would be.

Because even if she discounted her life in St Giles there was still the unalterable fact that she was no more than the landlady of a coaching inn. And everyone who met her would know that – and whisper about her behind her back. Justin might think he loved her now, but would his love withstand years of knowing that his friends and family disapproved of her?

She suddenly realised that instead of becoming calmer she was growing more agitated, and she tried to force herself to listen more attentively to the piano. But there was a certain passionate energy in the way in which Lucinda was playing which echoed Mary's heightened emotions. Mary suspected that the girl was using the music to exorcise some of her own feelings about the day's events. She was pleased for Lucinda's sake, but the torrent of music did nothing to soothe her own restlessness.

She got up and went to admire a fine porcelain clock above the fireplace. It was all she could do not to pace up and down the room. But then the chords modulated, and Lucinda moved into a quieter, more melodic piece. It was familiar, but at first Mary couldn't place it.

Then she remembered. With unexpected, heart-wrenching force she was drawn back to her childhood. She stood frozen, one hand still reaching up to the mantelpiece, as she recalled the last time she had heard that tune.

She had been sitting in the garden with her father, listening to him working on his sermon. They had been surrounded by sweet-smelling honeysuckle and lavender. And through the open window of the house she could hear her mother playing the piano. It was a scene which, with slight variations, had been repeated hundreds of times in her childhood.

She had been happy then, with no awareness of how precarious her happiness really was. She had listened to her father preach about the importance of building one's spiritual house upon the rock – not the sand – and she had never questioned the security of her physical surroundings. After all, God dressed the lilies of the field, and watched over the smallest sparrow. Naturally He was watching over her.

But then her mother had died. And two years later her father had died – and her uncle had taken her to Church Lane.

She very rarely allowed herself to think about her first uncomprehending horror at being confronted with the rookeries of St Giles. It was still too unbelievably painful for her. But the combined stimuli of Lucinda's earlier terror in response to a similar shock and the sound of the achingly familiar melody stripped away her defences.

'*Mary*?'

Justin closed the door behind him and strode across the room, taking her into his arms without any hesitation.

Her face was bleached and her eyes were blank with distress. She was shaking with remembered fear and dread, but she made no sound. Justin wasn't even sure if she knew he was there, although he was holding her and speaking softly to her, and she was clinging to him in white-knuckled desperation.

The music stopped with a jarring chord and Lucinda started up. Justin met her eyes across Mary's head. 'It's all right,' he said quietly, and he was speaking to both women.

He held Mary close to him, his hand moving gently against her hair as he waited for the uncontrollable shaking of her body to ease. Lucinda watched, her lower lip caught between her teeth in painful concern. It was clear that she wanted to help yet she didn't know what to do. Justin smiled at her reassuringly, although his eyes were sombre, and glanced at a nearby chair. Lucinda perched on the edge of it, her hands gripped together in her lap, and waited.

Mary slowly became aware that she was in Justin's arms. She didn't yet know where she was, or how he came to be with her, but she didn't care. She could hear his voice, and the remembered voices of all her tormenters from the past began to recede. In the worst of her horror she had not wept, but now tears of relief sprang to her eyes and she gave a sobbing gasp.

'Mary, it's over,' said Justin softly. 'You're here now. You'll never have to go back. My love, I'm not letting you go again,' he added unevenly, a crooked half-smile on his lips.

Mary pushed herself away from him, her hand laid flat against his chest. She looked up at him, still confused and shaken – and then, in one flashing instant, she remembered where she was and realised what had just happened.

She glanced round wildly and saw Lucinda watching her anxiously.

'Mrs Drayton. . .' the girl said very tentatively.

At that moment Mary reached breaking point. She no longer had any resources left to deal with anyone or anythng. She just wanted to escape.

She wrenched herself out of Justin's arms and ran. She fumbled desperately with the door-handle for a few seconds, then she fled up the stairs to the bedchamber that the housekeeper had earlier assigned to her.

Lucinda jumped up.

'I must go. . .'

'No.' Justin caught her arm and drew her back.

'But. . .'

'She's too upset just now,' he said. He sighed. 'Come and sit down again, Miss Burleigh. I hope you've been well looked after in my absence.'

'Oh, yes,' she said, but her expression was distracted. 'It was like the time at my party,' she said slowly. 'Only this time was much worse. I'm so glad you were here. But what distressed her so much? I'm sorry,' she added, flushing, as she realised how inquisitive she was being. 'I didn't mean. . .'

'I think it was the music,' said Justin bleakly. 'I remember her telling me once that her mother was very fond of the piano.'

'Then it was my fault?' Lucinda exclaimed.

Justin had been gazing into space, trying to imagine what nightmares Mary had seen, but now he turned his head and focused on Lucinda.

'No,' he said firmly. 'It wasn't the music, Miss Burleigh. It was what happened when the music stopped. Please don't worry that you did anything wrong.'

'You know her very well,' said Lucinda shyly.

'But not, perhaps, well enough,' Justin replied. 'Did Henry take a message to your mother?'

It was after midnight. Mary was sitting up in her room. The fire had been lit earlier, but she had done nothing to maintain it and it had nearly burnt out. She was wearing a borrowed nightgown, and a borrowed dressing-gown, and she had been brushing her hair with a borrowed brush – but now her hair was falling in disarray across her shoulders and her hands rested motionless in her lap.

Her eyes were blank as her thoughts roamed without discipline or direction over everything that had ever happened to her. She had made no effort to go downstairs again after her precipitate departure. She knew she must have alarmed her companions, but she had no strength left to reassure them. She didn't even have the strength left to get out of the chair and go to bed.

The door opened quietly and Justin came in. She turned her head and looked at him without surprise, but she didn't say anything. His eyes rested on her consideringly for a moment, then he went over to the fire and busied himself for several minutes in relighting it. It was very cold in the bedroom.

After that he rubbed his hands clean on his handkerchief and went over to Mary. He took the brush from her and held her chilly hands in a warm, strong grasp.

'If you're not going to attend to the fire, perhaps you should take to wearing your muff indoors,' he said, gently chiding.

She stared at him blankly, her eyes wide and desolate. He gave a muttered exclamation and swept her up in his arms, sitting down in the chair himself and holding her comfortingly on his lap, her head against his shoulder.

'It's over,' he said hoarsely. 'Don't you understand, my love? Alf is dead. Penrose is dead. You're safe here with me, and there's nothing left to hurt you.'

Mary started to cry. The ice which seemed to have encased her cracked and disintegrated in the fierce warmth of Justin's embrace. All her pent-up anxiety over Lucinda, her horror at shooting Samuel, and her fears about Justin while he'd been away from her, flooded out from her.

He held her tight, kissing her hair, murmuring reassurances. He rubbed her cold hands between his to bring life and warmth back into them. And at last, when the worst of her tears had abated, he said, 'Shush. I've only got one handkerchief, and you're going to have a sooty face if you dry your eyes with that.'

'I've had worse,' Mary replied unsteadily, blinking to clear her hazy vision. 'Thank you.'

She took it and wiped her eyes and blew her nose. Even now she couldn't help noticing what fine linen it was. There was a monogram embroidered in one corner. Another reminder of Justin's status.

She was so comfortable on his lap. She could have stayed within the shelter of his arms forever, but it still wasn't a dream she could give any credence to. With a supreme effort of will she struggled to get to her feet. His hold on her tightened, and for a moment she thought he wasn't going to permit her to do so – but then he released her.

She took a few steps away from him, suddenly feeling the chill of the room now that she was no longer close to him. Would she always feel cold when she wasn't near Justin?

'Mary.' He stood up. 'I wish you wouldn't keep turning away from me,' he said quietly. 'Is it that difficult to trust me?' He put his hand on her shoulder, looking down at her with a penetrating gaze, and she closed her eyes. He released her and took a couple of hasty paces away from her. Mary was aware of the familiar coiled, impatient energy within him.

'You said Samuel was dead?' she said questioningly. It was better to talk of something solid and practical rather than her muddled, undisciplined emotions.

'Yes. Come and sit down again.' He drew her back to the chair. Then he took the stool from in front of the dressing-table and went to sit next to her.

'Did I kill him?' Mary asked fearfully, wondering if she had injured Samuel more grievously than she'd realised.

'No,' Justin replied quickly. 'It wasn't a very serious wound – barely more than a scratch. I hope you'd have aimed nearer the heart if you'd been alone,' he added almost humorously.

'Yes,' Mary admitted, pain and reluctance in her eyes. 'I knew you were there so I didn't have to, but. . .'

'It's over. Don't think about it,' said Justin firmly, taking her hands again.

'So how did he die?' Mary asked. She thought she ought to withdraw her hands from Justin's grasp, but she couldn't quite bring herself to do so.

'I killed him,' he said grimly, his eyes briefly losing focus as he remembered the ugly scene on the road. 'I didn't mean to. . .but when I saw him charging at you like that. . .I must have hit him too hard. I didn't even realise at first. But when I bent down to see how badly he was hurt. . .'

Justin didn't attempt to finish his sentence, but his grip on Mary's hands tightened almost painfully, and she knew how disturbed he was by what had happened.

She shivered, remembering the look in Samuel's eyes when he'd tried to attack her, and the threats Lucinda said he'd made against her. 'I certainly earned his hatred, didn't I?' she whispered.

Justin's troubled expression cleared immediately. His attention focused once more on her. 'In the unlikely event that something like this ever happens again, you are *not* going to deal with it alone – or even at all,' he said categorically. 'I knew I should have sent you home before he came to Bath.'

A spark of indignation flared in Mary's eyes.

'You have no business sending me anywhere,' she said sharply, drawing her hands away from him. 'I'm quite capable of looking after myself. I don't need you – or any other rich protector,' she added hotly, remembering the way he'd been so reluctant to believe that she'd sold the Blue Boar. 'I still can't believe you thought it was more likely I'd run off with another man than that——'

'I'm sorry!' he interrupted. 'For God's sake, Mary, I didn't believe the rumour easily! Only when I'd spent months searching for you and I couldn't find you.' He got up and took a hasty turn around the room. 'It was better to believe that than that you were dead,' he said fiercely, over his shoulder. 'They were the only two alternatives open to me, and I couldn't bear to think——' He broke off. 'You knew where I was,' he said tautly. 'I knew you could find me if you wanted to. And you clearly didn't want to.'

'But. . .'

'I know.' Justin flung up a hand. 'Donald said!' His hand clenched into a fist, then he let his arm drop to his side, some of the tension easing out of him. 'Every time I feel particularly murderous towards Donald I remember that you probably wouldn't have survived without him,' he said almost conversationally.

'Oh, yes, I would,' said Mary flatly. 'I can survive without anyone if I have to. What did you do about Samuel?'

Justin turned his head and looked at her. It was there in her eyes, the fundamental core of steel which had enabled her to endure the appalling hardships and betrayals of her life. Loving her and trying to protect her were not enough. The years of bitter struggle had given her the right to demand respect for her capacity to survive – and she would not lightly relinquish her claim.

Justin took a deep breath.

'Yes,' he said slowly. 'I believe you would have done. Do you know how hard it is for me to accept that? I don't mean that I wish you had less courage or strength,' he added almost impatiently. 'But it is very hard for me to accept that you are also ruthlessly capable of surviving without me.'

Mary's breath caught in her throat at the expression of raw pain in his eyes. She tried to speak, but she couldn't say anything. He came back and sat down in front of her again, once more taking her hands in his.

'Have I told you since we met again how much I love you?' he asked quietly. 'Please don't keep turning away from me and shutting me out.'

Mary reached out and gently touched his cheek with her fingertips. She was suffused with a wondering, overwhelming sense of love for him. He closed his eyes and leant his face against her hand, catching hold of her wrist as he turned his head to kiss her palm. Her lips curved in a trembling smile, and she stroked his crisp, dark hair with her other hand.

'Oh, my love,' he murmured hoarsely, and she felt a pang of almost unbearable yearning for him. She wanted him to sweep her up in his arms but, after a moment, he gathered her hands in his and bent his head to kiss her fingers. She felt glorious warmth radiating out from the touch of his lips.

He looked up and met her gaze, gold flecks warming his hazel eyes as he smiled at her.

'I'm sorry I ever doubted you,' he said, his voice low and deep. 'And if I ever do have to deal with such an ugly situation again, I hope you are beside me – with your pistol in your hand. I think I need your protection as much as I hope you need mine.' His expression became almost rueful. 'Even after everything I knew about him, you were still more ready for Samuel this afternoon than I was,' he added.

'Not really,' Mary replied quickly. 'It's different for me, Justin. I've never been able to rely on my strength or speed, the way you can. Only on my wits. I've always known I can't take chances, so I've become over-cautious.' She smiled self-mockingly. 'The first thing I did last night after Samuel left was run down and make sure the front door was bolted,' she confessed.

Justin laughed softly. 'I'm glad to hear it,' he said. 'I hope I would have had the sense to do the same.'

'So what did you do about Samuel?' Mary asked, getting impatient. She was quite confident that Justin would have sorted things out satisfactorily, but she wanted to know *how*. 'And why didn't you tell me Samuel was dead before we left you on the road?' she added. 'You must have known by then.'

'I did,' said Justin, 'but I didn't want to cause you or Lucinda any more distress. I knew you'd be worried, and I thought you might insist on coming with me to see Sir Edward. All right!' Although she'd made no attempt to speak, he lifted his hand in a quick gesture which seemed both defensive and apologetic. 'I know you'd have been more than equal to the task – but it was better for Lucinda to be spared any more distress.'

'Oh, Justin, I wasn't complaining!' Mary exclaimed quickly, her voice not quite steady. 'I'm glad you didn't tell me. I wouldn't have wanted to speak to the magistrate any more than I imagine Lucinda did.'

'You may have to give him a statement tomorrow,' Justin warned her. 'But he'll come here. There won't be any difficulty.' He paused, his eyes dark with recollection. 'I told Sir Edward what happened,' he continued after a moment, 'and we got a statement from the postilion which confirmed my account. *He* was very anxious to dissociate himself from Samuel and Phelps. And Phelps himself was remarkably talkative when he realised what a precarious situation he was in. He told us things about Samuel which——'

'What things?' Mary prompted him softly, when Justin broke off.

'Apparently he killed a maidservant last year,' said Justin harshly. 'She was pregnant, and she went to him for protection. But her demands infuriated Samuel and he struck her down. Phelps is quite eager to show us where they disposed of her body. I don't think he realised how deeply he is incriminating himself – he's so keen to lay all the blame on his late master.'

'There really isn't going to be any problem for you about Samuel's death, is there?' Mary asked anxiously. 'I couldn't bear. . .'

'No, no,' Justin assured her hastily. 'As I mentioned, Sir Edward may need a statement from you and Lucinda – and Henry, of course. But Samuel's death was an accident, and even if it hadn't been I doubt if any action would be taken against me. Don't forget Samuel was in the process of abducting an heiress at the time he died. No jury would convict me for what happened.'

'They'd probably give you a medal,' Mary

replied firmly, trying not to let him see how upset she was on his behalf.

She knew that what had happened would not be easy for Justin to come to terms with. He could hardly help being relieved by Samuel's death, but she knew he would never be able to take pleasure or pride in being responsible for it. She thought bitterly that if she had aimed truer she would have spared him a great deal of pain.

'I'm sorry,' she said, instinctively voicing her thoughts. 'If I'd killed him on the road you wouldn't have had to. . .'

Justin looked up swiftly, and laid his fingers gently across her lips.

'You can't deny me any opportunity to demonstrate my ability to deal with a brutal world,' he said lightly. 'Between us we have managed to preserve Lucinda, and Penrose, relatively unharmed from Samuel's malice. I think we should be satisfied with that.'

'I am satisfied with it,' said Mary firmly.

'Good.' He stood up again, his movements once more restless and impatient.

He went over to the fireplace, staring down at the dancing flames. Mary saw that his hand resting on the mantelpiece had closed into a fist. After a moment he looked at her.

'I said I'd take you back to the Lazy Cat before we discussed this any further,' he said tautly, 'but I can't wait that long. You are going to marry me, aren't you?'

Mary stared at him. She'd wondered earlier

whether he'd asked her to marry him because he felt he owed her a duty – or simply because he'd been frustrated seven years ago. But she knew now that that wasn't true. He was asking her because he loved her. He had said so, and she could feel his love for her as truly as she could feel her love for him.

But it had never been that easy, even seven years ago.

She thought of the austere, stately butler who had greeted her on her arrival, and the footmen in their magnificent livery. She thought of the lords and ladies with whom Justin would be on familiar terms. He must, she thought numbly, have met the King! Yes, she remembered him describing the corpulent George to her in the days when he'd still been Regent. And Justin was certainly a member of the House of Lords.

But she was only the landlady of a wayside inn. Even if no one ever found out about her life in St Giles, that fact alone would be enough to damn her. She imagined the endless, polite charade that her life would become, trying desperately to pretend that she was something she was not. Servants were quick to judge their masters. How would they feel about her if she became Justin's wife – Lady Hawkridge?

Lady Hawkridge!

Hardly aware of what she was doing, she pressed her hands against her cheeks.

'Are you thinking about my mistresses?' Justin asked tensely. 'I couldn't lie to you when you asked, Mary. I won't lie to you. But none of them meant anything to me.'

He came back to her and she stood up automatically.

'Why won't you answer?' he demanded impatiently, seizing her by the shoulders. 'For God's sake, Mary! Talk to me!'

She touched his cheek gently.

'I can't marry you,' she said sadly. 'I don't belong here.'

He took a hasty breath, and then chopped off what he'd been about to say. He bent his head and closed his eyes for a moment as if he was struggling to maintain his self-control, then he looked up and met her steady gaze.

'You belong with me,' he said harshly. 'Or I belong with you, if you prefer.'

'No.' Inside she felt as if her heart was breaking, but the familiar implacable expression had returned to her eyes. In her bitter anguish she was holding him more at bay than ever.

'Love isn't enough,' she said painfully. 'I don't know how to live in your world – and I don't think I want to. I would be a disgrace to you and to myself. No, wait!' She saw him start to speak. 'Justin, do you know what it is like to live with deception? To pretend to be something you're not – with the constant fear that one day you'll be found out? I do. I've done it for years. I cannot. . .' Her voice faltered.

'Are you telling me you're not fit to be my

wife?' Justin demanded gratingly. 'Don't you think I have a right to make that decision?'

'You have a right to ask me,' said Mary. 'I have the right. . .to refuse.'

She could see the hurt, thwarted, disbelieving look in his eyes, his fierce rejection of what she had said, and she was filled with bitter, agonising pain. But she was thinking of the day when her presence by Justin's side would bring shame to him. She could not endure that for his sake – or her own.

'You are the woman I love. You are the woman I want to marry. You are the woman I would be proud to claim as my wife,' said Justin categorically. 'You have spent the last week insisting you've lived a respectable life – why are you so determined to deny that now?'

'I don't deny it,' Mary said hardly. 'I have been a respectable landlady for seven years. An *innkeeper*, Justin. Can you imagine what your friends would say if they knew? And before that I was a thief's whore,' she continued harshly. 'You're not the first man who's laid hands on me, and not the first man who's made love to me – but I'm not a widow.'

She could see from the look in his eyes that she'd hurt him with her savage reminder of her past. She wanted to cry bitter tears of remorse for wounding him so badly. She wanted to put her arms around him and tell him that she didn't mean it. But she couldn't.

She stared at him with the same fierce, aloof,

implacable gaze she had used to keep the world at bay for over twelve years.

There were never any half-measures in her dealings with people. As Samuel had already discovered to his cost. When she had once made up her mind about a course of action, she never allowed herself the luxury of uncertainty – and she didn't indulge in it now.

'Do you seriously imagine I'm going to let you walk out on me again?' Justin demanded wildly. 'Do you think that after everything that's happened I'm just going to let you *go*? My God!' He shook her in his frustration. 'You know I love you. Do you think I care about your past? I'd still want you if you'd lived with a different man for every year we've been apart! Don't you understand that?'

'Don't.' Mary stretched her hands out to him imploringly and he released her so suddenly that she staggered and nearly overbalanced.

'I can only think of one good reason why you won't marry me,' he said, his voice cold and empty. 'And that's that you don't love me enough. And now I come to think about it you never have told me you love me. Ever. Not in St Giles. Not in Bath. And not tonight. Do you love me, Mary?'

She looked up briefly, but she couldn't meet his eyes. Nothing had ever hurt her as badly as this, because tonight she was hurting someone she loved. It was so much easier to endure suffering herself than to impose it upon the one person she cared about more than any other.

But she'd already set her course. Perhaps she'd done so all those years ago in Church Lane when she'd repeatedly told Justin that it would be a scandalous, unsuitable marriage – and Donald had quoted her own words back to her to destroy all her hopes of happiness.

And nothing had happened to change her mind. All she'd done was grow older and more conscious of the hazards of such a union. And now she'd even seen, and been daunted by, the splendour of Justin's world.

But he'd made it easier for her. He had handed her the one weapon with which she could end this bitter dispute forever. But she couldn't use it. She couldn't lie to him and say she didn't love him.

She lifted her chin to meet his eyes, not realising how chillingly cold and distant her gaze was because she was trying so hard not to let him see how much she was hurting.

'I'm here. Now,' she said. Without realising she was doing so, she glanced at the bed. 'Tomorrow I'll go home. But tonight. . .'

'Dear God!' Justin exclaimed, a stunned, horrified expression in his eyes. 'Are you so sick of me that you're prepared to sacrifice yourself to me to get rid of me?'

He took a step back, staring at her in shaken disbelief. Then he turned on his heel and strode out of the room.

For a moment after he'd gone, Mary continued to stand as cold and immobile as a pillar of ice. Then her face crumpled and she fell on her knees beside the bed, giving way to an outburst of tears as wild and despairing as the one with which she had responded to Donald's message all those years ago.

CHAPTER THIRTEEN

MARY didn't know how long she'd been huddled beside the bed, her face hot with tears, her hands clutching at the coverlet, when she felt a gentle touch on her shoulder.

'Don't,' Justin said. 'I can't bear it.'

He was on one knee beside her. She turned and flung herself into his arms.

'I'm sorry!' she wept. 'I'm sorry, I'm sorry!'

'Oh, my love,' he whispered unsteadily.

He gathered her against him, rocking slightly to ease the desperate flood of her tears. She'd thought that nothing could assuage the pain that had wounded her to the depth of her soul – but she'd also been afraid that she'd driven him away forever. She could feel the warmth of his body, and the rough texture of his waistcoat beneath her hand. She could hear the strong beat of his heart beneath her head.

He was still holding her when she'd done everything she could to force him away from her. He gave her back sweet for sour. No one else in her life had ever been so steadfast. Least of all those people from whom she'd had the most right to expect protection.

She lifted her head and he stroked her tear-stained cheek with gentle fingers, and then kissed her hot, swollen eyelids with the utmost tenderness.

'Why did you come back?' she whispered.

'Because I can't stay away,' he replied simply. 'Mary, you don't have to give me anything you don't want to. If you don't love me. . .' he paused, and she saw the pain in his eyes '. . .I can't force you to,' he finished with quiet agony. 'If you want to go back to the Lazy Cat I'll take you. But please don't shut me out of your life. I just. . .need to know you're safe. I'll always need to know you're safe.'

Fresh tears started in Mary's eyes, and she raised herself in his embrace, slipping her arms around his neck. Then she drew his head down to hers.

He kissed her, and she felt the yearning, hope and pain of his love for her in the way his lips caressed her mouth. She lifted herself a little more towards him, her lips parting in response to his gently questing tongue.

He drew back.

'Mary. . .?' he said questioningly.

'Take me to bed,' she told him softly.

'No.'

She saw the instant, uncompromising refusal in his eyes, and for a moment she was afraid that he no longer wanted her. But his arms tightened instinctively around her and she was reassured.

She looked down for a moment, trying to collect her emotions, then she lifted her head to meet his intent, searching gaze. She smiled unsteadily and touched his lips with slender, hesitant fingers.

'I can't talk to you,' she said helplessly. 'I can't *tell* you... Justin, I don't know what I think any more – or what I ought to do. You keep telling me not to turn away from you. Don't turn away from me.'

He stood up in one swift movement, carrying her with him. A brief, incoherent thought flickered through her mind that, even after all the exertions of the day, he still had energy to spare. Then he was laying her down on the bed.

He sat down beside her, his hand on her waist, and she felt a pulse of excitement begin to beat steadily through her.

'Are you sure?' he asked, looking deep into her eyes, doubt in his own. 'I haven't forgotten how distressed you were in the drawing-room in Queen Square yesterday. Mary, I never want to hurt you.'

She laid her hand on his arm. He'd discarded his coat long ago and she could feel the strong, firm warmth of his forearm beneath his fine linen sleeve.

'Is lust the same as love?' she asked, and saw a measure of illumination dawn in his eyes.

'No,' he said in a shaken, comprehending voice. 'No, my love, it isn't. But you already knew that. That's not really the question, is it?'

She hesitated, unsure of how to reply. Several of the candles had guttered out by now, and the light in the room was quite uncertain. He smiled and stroked her hair back from her face, touching her cheek with gentle fingers. She felt the breathless pulse of expectation within her begin to beat faster.

'Are you sure this is what you want?' he asked again.

She nodded, and then answered out loud, so that he could be in no doubt as to her response. 'Yes.'

He bent forward and kissed her. His lips were gentle and coaxing on hers, but she felt the barely contained force of desire within him, and her hands caught at his shoulders. Then she buried her fingers in his hair. She still wasn't sure whether the burning, desperate longing he aroused in her was shameful or joyous. But she knew it was what he wanted, and making Justin happy was more important to her than anything else. She had hurt him and spurned him and denied him – and she couldn't deny him any more. Nor could she deny herself. Whether she went back to the Lazy Cat or whether she stayed, they would still have had this night of love.

His lips became more demanding, his tongue probing deeper into her mouth, and fresh fires began to smoulder within her. She clung to him, raising her torso to press more closely against him. He slipped an arm beneath her shoulders and sat up, lifting her with him. Her head fell back as he kissed her throat. She shivered responsively, longing for the moment when she could feel his body more closely against hers.

He must have discarded his cravat with his coat. She'd hardly noticed before, but now she was grateful. She let her fingers slide tentatively beneath the open neck of his shirt, delighting in the firm play of the muscles in his chest and shoulders. She felt the shuddering response that jolted through him at her touch, and for an instant she was afraid that she had done something wrong. But then he found the fastenings of the dressing-gown and quickly slipped it back from her shoulders. Now all that separated her heated body from his questing hands was her borrowed nightdress.

He touched her breast very lightly through the material, and she gasped at the instant wave of pleasure that flooded over her. Her fingers dug into his shoulders, and she leant impatiently into his hand, her hair falling in wild abandon all around her. His other hand was warm on her back, urging her up. She curled her legs beneath her and he lifted her across on to his lap.

With his hand still on her breast and her arms around his neck she raised herself to kiss him. She felt his tongue sear across her burning lip, and his hand gently kneaded her swollen breast until she was conscious of nothing but the glorious, sensual delight claiming all her awareness.

She moaned softly, her eyes half closed and heavy with desire.

At last he drew back slightly and looked down at her, lying pliant and trembling in his arms. His breathing was quick and uneven, and she could feel the fierce thudding of his heart as he held her against him. She had a dim sense that he was fighting to maintain some semblance of control, and then he smiled wonderingly.

'When you decide to do something, you don't do it in half-measures, do you?' he asked. His voice was hoarse, but his tone was light, almost joking.

Shameful colour flooded Mary's body. She made a quick movement as if she intended to escape, and he tightened his hold on her.

'There is nothing you or I can do tonight, born of love, that would seem sinful in the eyes of heaven,' he said softly, his eyes holding hers in an infinitely tender gaze. 'Do you believe that, Mary?'

She stared at him in amazed wonder.

'How did you know?' she whispered disbelievingly.

'After all the lectures the rector's daughter must have had on the sins of the flesh?' he asked wryly. 'And I've never liked the sound of Lady Moorcock. Being thrown from the rectory straight into the hell of St Giles would confuse anyone's moral standards. I'm sorry, love,' he said regretfully. 'If I'd been paying more attention to what you were really feeling, instead of what I wanted you to feel, I might have served you better.'

'You've always served me well,' Mary replied unsteadily.

Her hand covered his where it still rested on her breast, and she smiled up into his eyes, shyly, but

without any doubt. He gave a wordless exclamation and caught her hand in his, lifting it to
press a fervent kiss on her palm. Warm ribbons of
delight coursed up her arm and she turned more
fully towards him, suddenly impatient of words.

He found the hem of her nightgown and slipped
his hand beneath, his fingers sliding lightly and
sensuously up her leg to her thigh. She caught her
breath, clinging to him. His touch was causing
waves of almost unbearable delight to flood
through her, yet he was simultaneously arousing
an unnamed and as yet unfulfilled longing to
experience even greater pleasure.

She suddenly realised that part of his delay was
caused by a wish not to hurt or frighten her.

'You can't hurt me,' she reminded him, half
shy, half impatient.

He laughed unsteadily and laid his head
between her breasts for a moment. She cradled
him against her. She was vividly aware of his
arousal, and the urgent, powerful desire he was
rigidly controlling. She felt a rush of love and
tenderness for him. His strength exhilarated her,
but without his compassion and care it would have
been worse than meaningless.

Then he caught the bottom of her nightgown
and began to ride it up her legs. She lifted her hips
and he eased it up to her waist and then over her
head. She felt embarrassed and closed her eyes,
turning her face into his shoulder, because she
knew he was looking at her in the flickering
candlelight. It didn't occur to her that she should

deny him the opportunity to do so. She knew – none better – how much he lived through his eyes and what he saw, but it was difficult to be naked beneath his scrutiny.

He sighed, and her eyes flew open in consternation.

'I don't suppose you'll ever let me sketch you like this, will you?' he said sadly, and she saw the loving, teasing light in his eyes. 'I told you,' he reminded her, softly chiding, 'it always gives me pleasure to look at you.'

'Justin!' She gasped with embarrassed indignation, and tried to huddle her arms across her breasts. 'Why do you always know what I'm thinking?'

'I don't. Only when you let me. And you're not trying very hard to shut me out right now, are you?'

He smiled at her. Then she saw his expression change. His hazel eyes began to burn with intense, urgent longing. Not just for her body. She knew he wanted more than that. But she caught his shoulders and lifted herself up against him, pressing a kiss against his mouth.

He responded hungrily. His hands moved urgently against her naked back. The desire which he had aroused in her earlier began to throb even more insistently through her body. She wanted to feel his touch on every part of her. She wanted to see and touch him as he was seeing and touching her. She tugged impatiently at his shirt.

He turned with her still in his arms, and then

she uttered a soft sound of protest as she found herself lying alone across the bed. He stood up and swiftly discarded his clothes, then he pulled back the covers and lifted her so that she was inside the bed rather than on top of it. A second later he had joined her between the crisp linen sheets.

She was lying on her back. He was lying beside her, on his side, and they were touching for the whole length of their bodies. The fire in the hearth had long since died down again, and Justin hadn't pulled the covers very high, but Mary wasn't cold.

Her hair was spread wildly across the pillow, and her skin glowed with eager excitement. Justin gently nudged her legs apart with his knee, and she felt a surge of satisfaction and expectation.

His hand cupped her breast and he rubbed her nipple gently with his thumb. She arched her back, thrusting herself against him, and he leant down to brush her aching flesh with his lips. She caught her breath as she was pushed to another level of pleasure and longing. His lips closed around her nipple, and she felt the soft rasp of his tongue against the hard, sensitive peaks of her breasts.

She gave a soft moan, half in yearning, half in protest at the experience of so much pleasure, and he lifted himself up until he was poised above her. She parted her legs willingly – eagerly – and raised her hips to meet his deep thrust.

A feeling of overwhelming satisfaction and contentment filled her as he entered her, but she had no time to reflect upon it before he began to urge her to new heights of ecstasy. Her hands clutched at his back, clenching and relaxing in an involuntary rhythm which echoed the rhythm of their bodies. She had surrendered all her control to Justin. She had been swept away from her familiar bearings, and everything she knew which gave her security, but she was not afraid, and she did not try to claw her way back to rational normality.

Her world had exploded. Her body was no longer a mundane, earthly vessel for her soul. It had become a glorious means by which she could give and receive love. A physical expression of every passionate, tender feeling she had ever had for Justin.

She seemed to hover on the edge of a blinding revelation. Then Justin raised her to the last, culminating moment of ecstasy, and an unbelievable warmth and contentment filled her.

There was no hasty separation. Justin withdrew slowly. But he slipped his arm beneath her and took her with him, so that she lay with her head resting on his shoulder, her leg resting casually across his.

Her hand drifted across his muscular chest. She was thinking, incongruously enough, of Bill Crawford. The cracksman had only been five years older than Justin when she'd known him, but his wiry body had been scarred and coarsened by the life he'd led. He'd seemed very alien and unattractive to Mary – but then she'd only been fifteen at the time.

'Bill Crawford?' said Justin softly.

She lifted her head in surprise and looked down at him.

'What?'

'Aren't you making a comparison?' he asked, a crooked, self-deprecating smile on his lips. He pushed her wildly tangled hair back as it fell over her face and on to his.

'But this wasn't the first time for us!' Mary exclaimed, disconcerted. 'Why. . .?'

'The last and only time we made love you weren't there,' said Justin quietly. 'You gave yourself to me so wearily. As if your body was nothing more than a means of silencing my importunities. I loved you so much. It was one of the most soul-destroying experiences of my life. I promised myself I'd never repeat it unless. . .'

'It was different this time, wasn't it?' said Mary, her heart aching for the hurt she had unknowingly inflicted upon him.

He smiled tenderly.

'You were here, weren't you?' he said softly.

She nodded, and her hair fell forward again, tickling his nose. He blew at it in mock-exasperation and she giggled, settling down to rest once more with her head on his shoulder.

Then she sat up again.

'If you knew I was thinking about Bill Crawford, you must have been thinking about Bernadette,' she said accusingly.

'No,' he denied immediately. 'Well. . .' He hesitated. 'Not Bernadette, exactly. The question you mentioned earlier, about the difference between love and lust.' He sighed. 'If I could undo. . .'

Mary laid her fingers across his lips.

'Whatever happens, we must never talk about the past to be undone,' she warned softly. 'There's too much that should have been different.'

'Whatever happens?' Justin repeated sharply. A question sprang into his eyes, but he didn't voice it.

Mary was grateful. Some things she still didn't know the answer to. Justin loved her, she loved him, but that didn't mean she was any more suitable to be his wife now than she had been two hours ago. She needed time to think. She needed time to get used to the idea that for the first time in her life she really did have someone who would never betray her.

'Who taught you to shoot?' Justin asked idly.

Mary blinked, the question was so unexpected. Then she raised her head and looked at him, and an almost mischievous smile spread across her face.

'I know,' he declared, just before she could speak.

'Bill Crawford,' they said in unison.

Mary laughed and nestled down beside Justin again. They were cooler now, and he reached down to pull the covers over them. Only two candles were still burning, and neither would last much longer.

'I've never heard you speak badly of him,' said Justin quietly. 'For all you described it to me as a practical bargain, I think you were fond of him – and it wasn't pain you were afraid of in my arms.'

'He was never unkind to me,' said Mary slowly, looking back across the years. 'You're right. He gave me no pleasure, but he gave me no pain either. I think he cared about me. And he was the only one who never made me promises he could not keep. He gave me the pistol and he taught me to use it because he said he might not always be there to protect me. He said I should know how to protect myself.'

'He showed a better understanding of you, and your situation, than I always have,' said Justin sadly. 'And his gift is still protecting you ten years later. You've never had anything of mine to comfort you in my absence.'

Mary's hand moved on his chest as she instinctively began to touch the ring on her third finger with her thumb. As soon as she realised what she was doing she stilled the gesture. She wondered if Justin had noticed. If he had, he didn't comment.

'You must go to sleep,' he said almost regretfully. 'There isn't much of the night left.'

'No.' Mary felt a moment of panic. The night was passing and tomorrow she would have so many decisions to make. She was suddenly very afraid, and full of desperate longing that this beautiful interlude need never come to an end.

Justin stroked her back reassuringly and she realised that her distress had communicated itself to him.

'Tomorrow's just another day,' he said softly.

'You don't have to make any decisions. You don't have to do anything but sit in a sunny spot in the garden and watch the blackbirds eat last year's apples. Mrs Marlowe's fond of blackbirds. She says they sing sweeter than any other kind. But for myself, I'm not so sure. They seem a fussy bird to me, always clucking anxiously in the hedgerows. I prefer the storm bird – the missel-thrush that sings in the teeth of even the worst winter gales. I've seen her many times in the park, singing as if her life depended on never giving way to the storm – perhaps it does.'

Tears glistened in Mary's eyes. She knew he was telling her far more than he was saying. But she kept her head down on his shoulder so that he wouldn't see how deeply his words had affected her.

'What about Lucinda?' she reminded him unsteadily.

'We'll wait for word from Bath before we do anything,' Justin replied. 'She told me that she wrote in her letter to her mother that she was quite well, unhurt and safe, but that she couldn't return to Bath until she knew what had been done about Samuel. She thought she might be needed as a witness, or to give a statement. She's a brave girl.'

'Did you tell her about Samuel?' Mary asked.

'Yes.'

She felt Justin's muscles tense beneath her and she moved her hand instinctively in a reassuring caress. His hand captured hers, holding it in a warm, strong grasp.

'I think she was relieved,' he said after a few seconds, 'although she inevitably found it distressing. I'm afraid she may have a few nightmares before she can put the whole thing behind her completely.'

'Will you have nightmares?' Mary asked, thinking how much more unpleasant his involvement in Samuel's death had been.

'I don't know yet,' he replied quietly, his hand gentle on her hair, and suddenly she knew he wasn't talking about Samuel. 'Go to sleep, love. You need a certain amount of energy, even to watch the blackbirds.'

Mary closed her eyes, still feeling his light touch on her hair. They had made a tacit agreement not to discuss the subject which was uppermost in both their minds. But the issue of whether Mary would marry Justin still lay unresolved between them.

She knew how much he wanted that, and she knew what it would do to him if she refused. But the decision was ultimately hers. He had acknowledged as much when he'd come back into the room what seemed a lifetime ago and found her weeping on the floor by the bed.

But he'd said that he needed to know that she was safe. And as she listened to his quiet breathing beneath her head she knew that she needed to know at least that much about him also. But she didn't have to marry him to ensure that. He could visit her sometimes at the Lazy Cat. Perhaps even stay at the inn. And she would have the comfort of seeing him, without the anguish and fear of bringing shame to him.

And he would have...what? An opportunity to see her but not to touch her? It would destroy him, just as surely as it would destroy her. She sighed, and felt Justin's hand pause for a moment in its soothing caress. An arrangement like that would be even more disastrous for their love than the strains that would be imposed on their marriage by malicious scandal. They had to be together, or apart. There could be no half-measures between them.

Which left one, final possibility. She had declared so vehemently that she would never be his mistress. Yet it was also true that seven years ago she had tried to persuade him that it was the only possible relationship between them.

As his mistress, her past could never be used as a weapon against him. He would be free to live his normal life and she would have the satisfaction of knowing that he was free to do so.

And their children would be nameless bastards.

There was no way out. No way that didn't involve hurting someone. She didn't know the answer to his question. She was tired and confused, and she could see only calamity whichever way she turned.

She was drifting through a succession of uneasy dreams, half awake, half asleep, when he gently lifted her away from him and slipped out of the bed. She was aware of him going, and a silent cry of loss filled her. But she was still only half awake and she made no move to stop him.

He dressed in silence and went out of the room before any of the servants were stirring.

CHAPTER FOURTEEN

MARY woke after a few hours of fitful sleep. No one had come to disturb her. She wondered if Justin had given orders to that effect. If he had, she could only be grateful. She was still naked between the fine linen sheets. She had never before in her life slept naked.

She rolled over, taking almost guilty pleasure in the caress of the linen against her skin. It took no effort of the imagination for her to remember what it had been like when Justin had shared the bed with her. Her body glowed with the remembered feel of him – and the desire to feel his ardent touch again.

She could not feel ashamed of that. She remembered Lady Moorcock's tight-lipped, elliptical comments – and then she remembered Sir Richard Moorcock. A reprehensible smile flitted across her lips. If she'd been married to Sir Richard she might have felt the same way as Lady Moorcock.

Then she thought about St Paul and the many exhortations in his epistles to practise the virtue of celibacy – his repeated warnings that it was better to be celibate than to marry, but better to marry than to burn in hell.

As a child she had never really understood the significance of those admonishments. Now she did, and she could not accept them. She was more than a suffering soul struggling to be free of the unclean, sensuous demands of her body. Her heart, her mind and her body could be as united in love as they had always been in her determination to survive.

She had never flinched from forcing her body to undertake the hard, back-breaking work of building up the Lazy Cat into a successful business. Why should she hesitate to use it now to give pleasure to herself and the man she loved?

She smiled up at the canopy of the bed. One uncertainty, at least, had finally been resolved for her. She had learnt a great deal about herself – and the meaning of love – these last few days. Was she ready to take the great gamble of marrying Justin?

Half an hour later she walked down the grand, sweeping staircase, trying not to look as nervous as she felt. It was ironic that in some ways she had been less worried at the thought of confronting Samuel than she was at the possibility of meeting Dibley again. But she'd always had the option of shooting Samuel. She could hardly do that to the butler if he upset her.

A footman sprang to open the door to the breakfast-room for her, and she sailed past with a courteous smile, trying to look as if expressionless young men in magnificent livery had been opening doors for her all her life.

Lucinda was sitting at the table alone. She smiled when she saw Mary, but there was a worried question in her eyes. Mary glanced around, but they were alone.

'I'm so sorry I rushed out like that last night,' she said seriously, and with a certain amount of embarrassment. 'After all you'd been through yesterday, it was hardly fair. . . But my mother used——'

'Please don't,' said Lucinda quickly as Mary stumbled over the words. 'Please don't feel you need to apologise – or explain. Not unless you really want to. And not after everything you've done for me. Would you like some coffee?' she added, picking up the coffee-pot.

'Yes, thank you.' Mary sat down, looking round in puzzlement. 'Where. . .?'

'Lord Hawkridge sent all the servants away,' Lucinda explained blithely. 'I told him last night how uncomfortable they'd made us feel at dinner.'

'You did?' said Mary faintly.

'I didn't think he'd mind,' Lucinda said, passing her a cup. 'He's never been at all grand.'

'What did he say?' Mary asked.

'He laughed and apologised and said he only kept such a large household to satisfy Dibley's notions of baronial splendour,' Lucinda replied. 'He said that, since Dibley had been butler here before *he'd* even been born, he felt he owed it to him – especially as he spent so much of the rest of his time setting things in an uproar by *not* behaving conventionally. Lord Hawkridge, I mean. I shouldn't think Dibley's ever done anything unconventional in his life. Mind you. . .' she paused thoughtfully '...when I met him this morning, when Lord Hawkridge was with me, I thought perhaps he wasn't as austere as he likes to appear.'

Mary was watching Lucinda, a curious half-smile in her eyes.

'You're very observant,' she said.

'I must develop my skills,' said Lucinda serenely. 'Lord Hawkridge says that it's very important to learn to see things truly if you want to produce an accurate likeness.'

'Lord Hawkridge has been practising those skills all his life,' said Mary quietly. 'I'm sorry,' she added a few moments later, the distracted expression clearing from her eyes. 'I haven't asked you how *you* are this morning. Did you sleep well?'

'I had some bad dreams,' Lucinda admitted, her eyes clouding. 'I'll be glad to go home – even to Cousin Emma. But I spoke to his lordship, and he said it would be best if we wait for Henry to come back. Just in case Mama has decided to come here. I begged her not to do so in my letter, but it would be dreadful if she did and we missed each other on the road.'

'I'm sure Henry will be back very soon,' said Mary reassuringly. 'He'll have ridden hard all the way to Bath. And I'm sure he knows you're just as anxious to hear from your mother as she will have been to know you're safe.'

Lucinda smiled. 'Do you really think he had an uncle with a woodwormy leg?' she asked.

'I think he may have embellished his story slightly,' Mary replied. 'I embellished mine – well, actually I made it up completely,' she confessed.

'I thought you did.' A twinkle danced in Lucinda's eyes. 'You were trying to distract me. Ma'am, you couldn't...you couldn't teach me how to shoot, could you?'

Mary choked on her coffee.

'I hope you'll never have any reason to need to know how!' she exclaimed.

'Oh, so do I,' Lucinda agreed fervently. 'But it does seem a useful accomplishment to possess.'

'I haven't got my pistol any more,' said Mary. 'Justin took it away from me yesterday. But I'll see what I can do.'

It suddenly occurred to her to wonder where he was. She glanced around almost as if she expected him to appear beside her, a puzzled, uncertain expression in her eyes.

'He said he was going to sketch the blackbirds in the kitchen garden,' Lucinda told her, buttering another slice of toast. 'Are you sure you wouldn't like something to eat, ma'am?'

'No – no, thank you,' said Mary vaguely. 'I'm not hungry. The coffee is fine. I really think you ought to stop calling me ma'am,' she added. 'I'm beginning to feel like an octogenarian dowager! My name's Mary.'

'Thank you!' Lucinda replied warmly. 'You know, I almost think it was worth being abducted if it meant I got to meet you and Lord Hawkridge,' she said reflectively. 'Oh, for heaven's sake go and look at his sketches,' she added with impatient affection. 'It was bad enough having breakfast with one distracted companion; two in less than half an hour is excessive!'

Justin was sitting in the sheltered lee of the kitchen garden wall. The wind was keen, but the sun was bright, and it was warm on the stone bench.

He was sketching the birds as they pecked at last year's rotting apples which Mrs Marlowe had thrown out to them. Mary paused for a moment, watching. There was a missel-thrush among the blackbirds. Its pale brown plumage was drab and unexciting beside the glossy blackbirds, but she too had heard it singing in the winter storms.

She had seen it, but she had never given it a second's thought. Justin had not only seen it, he had remembered it. Perhaps he would always see more than most of his fellow men.

Then the wind caught her skirts, alarming the birds, and Justin looked up. When he saw her he smiled, and her heart turned over at the love and affection in his gold-flecked eyes. She glanced down at his sketch, trying to find some inner balance before she spoke to him.

'"To see a World in a Grain of Sand",' she quoted, '"And a Heaven in a Wild Flower". I've always wondered what the world looks like to you.'

He laid aside his sketchbook and took her hand, drawing her to sit down beside him.

'The trick is learning to see the world through

your eyes,' he said almost humorously. 'I've been trying to understand why you're so determined to resist me.'

'I. . .'

'No, let me speak.' He smiled into her doubting eyes with loving certainty. 'I think, after all the years of fending for yourself, it must be difficult to surrender even a limited degree of control over your life to someone else. And marriage means so much more than that, doesn't it?'

She caught her breath, her eyes fixed in wonder on his face, because she hadn't expected him to understand that aspect of her reluctance.

'You can't go on running the Lazy Cat,' said Justin reasonably. 'But you can keep it if you like. And I'll never expect you to stop thinking for yourself – I'm not interested in a wife who's nothing more than an ornament in my drawing-room.'

He saw the renewed doubt in her eyes and reached out to cup her cheek gently in the palm of his hand.

'But that's the real problem, isn't it?' he said softly. 'You don't think you're fit to be an ornament in my drawing-room, or anywhere else.'

Mary caught his wrist in her hand.

'We can't change the past,' she whispered desperately.

'We don't have to. Do you really think I care what anyone else thinks?' he asked. He spoke quietly, but there was a fierce undercurrent of passion in his voice. 'I don't give a damn about the rest of the world, Mary. They can say what they like about us behind our backs – but if I ever hear anyone abuse you in my presence they'll rue the day they learnt to speak.'

Mary's heart was beating with wild, all-consuming happiness. She could hear the throbbing sincerity in his declaration; she knew he meant every word he said.

'You asked me if I knew what it was like to live a lie, all the time in fear that you might be found out,' he continued, his voice strong and uncompromising. 'And you're right, I don't know. But it doesn't matter. Because I'm not asking you to live a lie. You don't have to pretend to be anything you're not. All I'm asking is for you to be my wife, with all the love and courage at your disposal – as I will try to be your husband with all my heart and soul.'

Mary bent her head because the burning intensity of his love-filled gaze was almost too much to bear. She was too full of emotion to speak. She couldn't deny him now. He deserved nothing less from her than the same commitment with which he had pledged himself to her.

'I can only think of one reason for you not to marry me,' said Justin more quietly. 'And that is that you don't love me. Give me your hand. No, the left one.'

She smiled unsteadily and gave it to him, letting him slip the ring from her finger. Then she watched, her eyes locked on his face, as he held it up to look at it. He was still holding her hand in his, and when the pressure of his fingers on hers suddenly became almost painful in the fierce surge of his relief she knew that he had recognised the inscription.

Ruth 1 v 16. He quoted it from memory in a soft, confident voice.

'Intreat me not to leave thee, or to return from following after thee: for whither thou goest, I will go; and where thou lodgest, I will lodge: thy people shall be my people, and thy God my God: Where thou diest, will I die, and there will I be buried: the Lord do so to me, and more also, if ought but death part thee and me.'

He let his hand fall, and turned to meet Mary's glistening, tear-filled eyes, love and understanding blazing in his own eyes.

'Donald didn't want me to take it,' said Mary unsteadily, because now she really had no more secrets from Justin. 'But it was more respectable to be a widow than a spinster. And I said if I was going to be anyone's widow it would be yours.'

'You're not going to be my widow, you're going to be my wife!' Justin declared triumphantly.

He pulled her into his arms, or perhaps she threw herself there. Her arms were locked around him. His head bent protectively and possessively over hers. He rubbed his cheek against her hair, and she felt his hold on her tighten until she could scarcely breathe. At that moment she knew there was only one power on earth that would ever part them again.

Just for one agonising instant the dreadful possibility of losing Justin gripped her heart. She had lost too much already, and she knew better than anyone the uncertainties of life.

Then she put the fear aside. It was not worthy of her love. If God willed it, they would share decades of happiness together. But if, by some dreadful fate, it was not to be, then their love would protect and comfort them. Nothing, not even the shadowy presence of suffering or death, could change that.

Justin released his hold on her slightly, and lifted her head with one hand beneath her chin to look deep into her eyes.

'Tell me!' he said insistently.

'I love you,' she replied, without hesitancy or doubt. 'I have always loved you. I always will.'

His expression was transfigured, his burning eyes swam before her face, and then he kissed her.

Some time later, when Mary was leaning quietly against Justin's shoulder, his arm firmly around her waist, they heard the drumming of distant hoofbeats on the other side of the wall. She looked at Justin, startled, and he shook his head.

'I don't know,' he said. 'It might be Henry, but I doubt he'd be coming quite so urgently – unless something's wrong in Bath.'

He stood up and went to a gate in the wall. Mary went with him, her hand still resting in his.

'Well, well,' he murmured in amusement.

'What is it?' she demanded impatiently.

'Look.' He drew her to stand in front of him, his arm around her, and bent to kiss her hair as she gazed across the expanse of park beyond towards the road.

'But who. . .?' Mary watched the distant, hastening horseman with narrowed eyes. He looked familiar, but she was sure it wasn't Henry.

'Peter King,' said Justin helpfully.

Mary gasped and turned round to look up at him in amazement. But before she had time to speak he slipped one hand behind her head and kissed her parted lips, his other hand pressing warmly into the small of her back. Her arms instinctively slid around his neck, and for a long, timeless moment she was lost in his embrace.

At last he drew back, laughing softly.

'The sooner we get that ring back on your finger the better, I think,' he said humorously. 'What I was going to say, before you drove every other thought out of my head by looking at me so beguilingly, was that he'll have to follow the road round to get to the front of the house. So we have a bit of time in hand. Except that I don't think it's either of us he's riding so urgently to see.'

'Nor do I,' Mary agreed. 'I wonder if Lucinda will be pleased to see him?'

'Oh, I think so,' said Justin, grinning. 'We had an interesting though typically allusive conversation last night which seemed to touch on the subject of how a young man might feel if a lady he had a high regard for had just been abducted.'

'You did, did you?' said Mary with a certain amount of resigned amusement in her voice. 'Now I come to think about it, this isn't the first time Lucinda has confided in you. How on earth do you always manage to get people to talk to you?'

'I don't. Always.' There was a flicker of remembered torment in his eyes, and Mary knew what he was thinking.

'I'm sorry,' she whispered. 'Justin, if I'd had more faith in your love. . .if I hadn't been so sure I wasn't suitable. . . I wouldn't have been so ready to believe Donald all those years ago. I could have spared you so much pain.'

He smiled down at her tenderly. 'But we aren't going to talk of things to be undone,' he reminded her softly. 'And if I had once thought to go and claim the ring, I would have found out that you'd already done so – and then I'd never have given up my search. But I didn't even remember it when I came back to London and couldn't find you. And later, when I did, I couldn't bear the thought of having the ring without also having you.'

Mary slipped her arms around his neck and drew his head down to hers, kissing him with all the love and passion at her disposal.

Eventually he dragged his lips away from hers.

'I am *not* going to make love to you in the vegetable patch,' he said firmly. His breathing was ragged, but there was a hint of amusement in his eyes.

'Are you going to make us wait until we're married?' Mary asked, a laughing, almost brazen twinkle in her own eyes. 'I seem to remember you making some such decree last time.'

'Last time was different,' he pointed out, but there was no condemnation in his voice – only love. 'And no, I don't think I could – even if I wanted to. We'll have to get a special licence.' He kissed her quickly and stepped away from her. 'Come and sit down again,' he said. 'We'd better give Lucinda some time to greet her beau before we go in. If she needs us, she knows where to find us.'

When they returned to the bench, Mary picked up the discarded sketchbook, flipping idly through the pages.

'Do your servants know about me?' she asked, recalling her fears of the previous evening.

'No,' he said reassuringly. 'Only Henry.'

'Henry?' She looked at him swiftly.

'He doesn't know everything,' said Justin, answering her unspoken question. 'But it was when I was looking for you that I found him. He's been with me ever since.' He grinned. 'He's expressed his approval of you in the strongest possible terms,' he added. 'He'll never forgive either of us if we don't get married.'

'I wouldn't want to disappoint Henry,' said Mary teasingly. 'Does. . .is there anyone else who knows?' she asked hesitantly.

'None of the servants in this house – or any other,' Justin told her, drawing her back within the security of his arm. 'And nobody else. I've never had much inclination to talk about you. You've always been too important to me.'

'Oh, Justin.' She turned impulsively towards him. 'I do love you.'

He kissed her. And then reluctantly drew back.

'I was going to offer to be your mistress,' she confessed after a moment. 'But then. . .'

'You thought about the children,' he said for her, smiling crookedly.

'How on earth did you know?' she demanded, amazed. There was no possible way he could have guessed that. They'd never discussed the issue of children. 'Can you read my mind?'

'No, but I'm learning how it works,' he said affectionately. 'You can endure almost any shame or hardship for yourself, but you can't bear to inflict it on those you love. And you will love our children.'

'Yes.' Tears sparkled in Mary's eyes. 'You've second-guessed me at every turn,' she said, feeling overwhelming love and tenderness for him.

'Do you mind?'

'No.' She took a deep breath, remembering all the women who had gone before her. There was something she needed to know, but she wasn't sure how to ask it.

'What is it?' he asked, seeing the change in her expression. 'Mary?' he added as she hesitated.

'Do you have any children?' she asked in a rush,

her voice sounding rather harsh in her distress at asking such a question.

He held her gaze with his for a long moment. She saw the troubled look in his eyes and realised he was caught between the need to be honest with her and the fear of hurting her. She felt a wave of sickening anxiety sweep over her. If Justin had children, he would be a good father to them, whether or not they had been born in wedlock. Was there someone else in his life who had a claim on his heart?

'One. Perhaps,' he said at last.

'Perhaps?' Relief was hammering through her body, but she tried not to show how much the question had mattered to her.

'His mother claimed he was mine, but I don't think she was in a position to know for certain,' he explained. 'Certainly as the boy has grown older he has never looked like me.'

'Do you. . .see him often?' Mary asked.

'No, not often.' Justin held her hands in his, as if he was aware of how difficult she was finding this revelation. 'His mother didn't want him. I took him and put him in the care of a good couple who've brought him up as their own. He knows me only as a friend of the family. And no one but his parents know he is not their child. They'd already got two daughters, and their only son was stillborn. I've known them all my life.'

He frowned, his eyes losing focus as he looked back on what had happened. 'It was very. . .strange,' he said at last. 'Something which to me was a source of shame and distress brought them great happiness. I've never really been able to resolve my feelings on the matter. I only know that it made me more careful in future.'

He met Mary's gaze and smiled, and she knew that his thoughts had returned to the present.

'It was before I knew you,' he said. 'The lad's ten years old now. And after that... Well, if you must know, I think some of the women I've had in my keeping have often been disappointed in the demands I've made upon them,' he admitted, half laughingly, half reluctantly. 'I won't be at all surprised if I get back to London to discover that Bernadette has already found someone to replace me.'

'Justin!' Mary exclaimed.

She tried to sound shocked, and certainly she was relieved. But all the same her first, reprehensible thought was that she couldn't imagine how any woman could leave Justin for another man.

He smiled lopsidedly. 'The truth is,' he said, 'that all I ever really wanted was to lie with love. But the only time I lay with you...'

'I never meant to hurt you,' Mary said urgently, seizing his hand impulsively.

'I know.' He squeezed her hand warmly. 'And then I lost you, and I was angry as well as hurt, hence the succession of mistresses – but it never really worked. At first, perhaps. But in the end they became more ornamental than functional. Bernadette's probably had fewer demands made upon her than the average vicar's wife. Although she is extremely ornamental,' he added wickedly.

'What does she look like?' Mary asked jealously.

'Fast,' said Justin, grinning. 'But she has no heart——' he laid his hand gently on Mary's breast, and she felt an instant leaping response ' – so she isn't beautiful. Or perhaps she would be if she was with the right man.'

'I see,' Mary murmured, determined not to ask the question that was hovering on her lips.

'Yes, you're beautiful,' he said instantly, smiling teasingly at her. 'I wonder how many times I'll have to tell you before you believe me?'

'But you love me,' Mary pointed out, though she was warm with happiness at his words. 'And you said. . .'

'I can still, with difficulty, look at you objectively,' said Justin with mock-severity. 'Or do you suppose my powers of observation, as well as my heart, are completely overwhelmed by you? I'll prove it to you if you like,' he added, picking up the sketchbook again.

She smiled, making no objection when he started to draw her. She knew he would do so many times in the years to come, and she was no longer afraid of what he might see. She leant back comfortably against the sun-warmed wall and looked out thoughtfully across the kitchen garden. She had always been fond of gardening and, although she knew there would be an army of servants to take care of the grounds, she hoped that perhaps she would be allowed a small corner for herself.

Then she laughed inwardly at the absurdity of the thought – and finally, almost unexpectedly, surrendered to the glorious, swelling certainty that she had come home. She was suddenly filled with such joyous energy that she wanted to leap up and run before the wind like a hare, but she kept her feet tucked demurely beneath her and her hands folded modestly in her lap. If she moved now, she would spoil the picture, and she was aware that Justin was working with swift, intense concentration on his sketch.

At last he laid down his pen. She flexed her arms luxuriously at her release, and reached out for the sketchbook.

'May I see it?'

'Of course.'

He was about to put it into her hand, when he glanced past her and smiled. She turned and saw Lucinda and Peter coming slowly towards them. Lucinda's hand was resting demurely on Peter's arm, but there was an indefinable air of happiness about them which was very revealing.

'It seems to have been a satisfactory morning all round,' Justin murmured, letting Mary take the sketchbook.

She glanced down, and saw herself as Justin had seen her. Her head uplifted, poised for whatever lay ahead. Behind her the tempest still raged. But before her, already casting a glow upon her cheek, the summer sunshine was bringing warmth and happiness.

'You've survived the storms, the dark and the shadows,' Justin said to her softly. 'Now it's your turn to come out into the light. Or perhaps I should say it's *our* turn. Because wherever you go, and whatever you do, I will be with you. Forever.'

THE LOVE CHILD
by
Meg Alexander

After living in southern Spain for many years, **Meg Alexander** now makes her home in Kent, although having been born in Lancashire, she feels that her roots are in the north of England. Meg's career has encompassed a wide variety of roles, from professional cook to assistant director of a conference centre. She has always been a voracious reader, and loves to write. Other loves include history, cats, gardening, cooking and travel. She has a son and two grandchildren.

Also by Meg Alexander
in Mills & Boon® Historical Romance™

THE GENTLEMAN'S DEMAND
THE RELUCTANT BRIDE ★
MR RUSHFORD'S HONOUR ★
THE REBELLIOUS DEBUTANTE

★ **The Steepwood Scandal** mini-series

Look for

THE MATCHMAKER'S MARRIAGE

Coming June 2003

Chapter One

1789

They made a sorry pair as they trudged along the road. It had been the worst of summers, and even now, on this late September day, the rain had fallen unceasingly since dawn.

Prudence glanced at her companion. It was difficult to decide which of them looked worse…she in the ragged coat and breeches taken from a scarecrow on the previous day, or Dan, in his rapidly shrinking hand-me-downs, his red hair plastered to his skull.

She tugged off her old moleskin cap and offered it to him, but he shook his head.

"You'd best wear it," he said firmly. "When you take it off, your head looks like a hedgehog."

"I know it!" Prudence glared at him. "But how could I pretend to be a boy with long curls hanging down my back?"

"At least your other clothes didn't smell of horses." Dan wrinkled his nose. "That scarecrow must have been stuffed with straw from the stables."

"Then you'd best walk on the other side of the lane if the smell offends you." Her voice was sharper than she had intended and the boy's face fell at once.

"I'm sorry," she said quickly. "I'm tired and my feet hurt, but I don't mean to be mifty."

"We could rest for a bit," he suggested. "It's drier under that big tree and there's a stream. You could bathe your feet."

"I don't know…" Prudence looked doubtful as she hobbled along beside him. "If I take off my boots, I might not get them on again." She winced. To say that her feet hurt was an understatement. Every step was agony.

As they reached the shelter of the tree she sank down gratefully on to a soft bed of leaf litter. Beside her the little stream looked inviting and the temptation was too much to resist. She unlaced her boots and pulled them off. A quick inspection showed her that the blisters on her heels had broken, chafed by the sodden leather, and now the flesh was raw and bleeding.

The pain was so intense that tears came to her eyes, but she forced them back, plunging her feet into the icy water. It gave her some relief, but at that moment her spirits were at their lowest ebb. How could they go on?

Three days of tramping south had left them both exhausted. The few crusts which they'd managed to save from their meagre suppers at the mill had long since been eaten. Since then, the only food which had passed their lips was the loaf and the cold fat bacon given to them by a farmer on the previous day.

Prudence shuddered at the memory. The man had been quick to offer them shelter in his barn, and she had put it down to pity for two cold and hungry fellow-creatures.

Then he had begun to question them, his eyes intent upon the slender girl who stood before him, neat in her cotton pinafore and worn brown cloak. The cloud of tawny hair had escaped the confines of the plain white cap tied with strings beneath her chin, and tumbled in a mass of gleaming curls almost to her waist.

It was her eyes which had held him. Of a clear hazel, and fringed with long dark lashes, they'd shone with gratitude as she'd thanked him for his kindness.

Then he'd slipped an arm about her waist, and his strange hot look had frightened her.

"I'll take a kiss in payment." The coarse red face had come close to hers and he had been breathing hard.

"Let me go!" she'd cried in panic. She had still been holding the kitchen knife. "I'll use this if you touch me!"

"No, you won't, you little vixen!" As he had reached for the knife she'd twisted out of his grasp and taken to her heels.

"Run!" she'd cried, and Dan had followed her. They had been too swift for their pursuer, who had soon given up the chase, but Prudence had still been trembling when they stopped.

The experience had shaken her. Hunger, thirst, exhaustion and even recapture were to be expected on their journey. It hadn't occurred to her that her sex might put her at risk.

The answer had come when she saw the scarecrow in the field. She'd seized the clothes, including the greasy cap, and had changed behind a hedge, much to Dan's astonishment.

"Why are you doing that?" he'd asked.

"It's a disguise. They'll be looking for a boy and a girl, rather than two boys."

To her relief the explanation had satisfied him. It would have been difficult to explain the danger to a twelve-year-old.

"Now cut off my hair!" She had handed him the knife.

"Oh, Pru, I can't!"

"You must. It won't fit under the cap."

He'd obeyed her, struggling with the heavy locks until they had lain in a heap at her feet. Then he'd begun to laugh.

"Must you make game of me?" she had reproached him. "I know it must look strange."

"It's worse than that. The ends are sticking up in spikes."

"Then it's lucky I have no mirror." She had picked up the ancient cap, crammed it on her head, and scowled at him.

He had been contrite at once, and she had soon recovered her good humour. With a grin she had begun to quote the guardians of the Foundling Home on the dread evils of vanity. She was an excellent mimic, and he had laughed aloud.

That night they'd slept beneath the crumbling roof of a deserted cow byre, huddling together for warmth. Then, spurred on by gnawing hunger, they'd pushed on at first light.

The sight of an elderly woman spreading her washing beneath a makeshift lean-to had tempted her to beg for bread, but the woman had set her dogs on them.

The same thing had happened at the next two farms and now she felt a sense of desperation. She should have come alone. She had put Dan at risk. It wasn't fair to subject a child to the possibility of starvation, and even physical assault.

Dan sensed her mood and gave her a cheerful grin.

"Don't worry, Pru!" he cried. "Watch me!"

Before she could stop him, he ran into the middle of the road and began to turn cartwheels. "I think I'll become an acrobat," he shouted.

Neither of them heard the sound of the oncoming carriage. Then a team of horses rounded the bend ahead of them, travelling at speed.

Prudence tried to scream a warning, but no sound issued from her lips. She watched in horror as Dan froze. He was too terrified to move.

The carriage swerved, but the driver was too late. She heard a sickening thump. As if in slow motion, Dan's small figure rose in the air and landed by the roadside.

Forgetful of her blistered feet, Prudence flew towards him, falling to her knees in the wet grass. Dan was lying dreadfully still, and she could see no sign of life.

The silence which followed was broken only by the stamping of the frightened team of thoroughbreds. Then she heard the sound of footsteps.

She looked up through a haze of tears as the driver walked towards her.

"Murderer!" she cried. She rose to her feet, wild with rage, and threw herself upon him, striking at his face in an uncontrollable frenzy. "You've killed Dan!"

The man brushed her aside without a word. Then, careless of his immaculate buckskins, he knelt down in the muddy lane, and turned Dan over. With gentle fingers he began to probe for any possible injury.

"He isn't dead," he said at last. "And there is nothing broken. That's a deep cut upon his brow. He must have hit it when he fell."

"You did that!" she shouted. "I heard the sound as the carriage struck him—"

"He was lucky not to have been trampled beneath the horses' hooves. As it was, my mudguard caught him a glancing blow. We'd best get him out of this…"

"Don't touch him!" Prudence yelled. "Haven't you done enough? I'll take care of him."

The man looked up at her. "To date, your efforts in that direction don't seem to have been too successful. Be quiet! Hysteria won't help him."

Then he looked beyond her with a changed expression. Prudence followed his glance and was surprised to find a silent crowd of people close behind them.

They were a motley crew, and though they made no move she had a sudden feeling of unease.

These were not local farmers, nor were they respectable cottagers or labourers. Most were dressed in rags or coarse sacking, and their skins were ingrained with dirt.

Among them she noticed a number of cripples, and some of the women had babies slung upon their hips. This did nothing to reassure her. Without exception they wore fiercely predatory expressions, and she could guess what they were thinking.

Here was a prize indeed. A wealthy traveller off his guard, and obviously alone. A dozen pairs of eyes gleamed at the prospect of such rich pickings.

As her companion rose to his feet, one of the men stepped forward.

"Your honour has suffered an accident?" he enquired. "I trust your horses came to no harm?"

Receiving no reply, he moved closer. "Will you spare a coin or two for poor men injured in the service of their country, sir? It's shabby treatment we've had from them as used us…"

Involuntarily Prudence sidled closer to her companion. The leader of the beggars was a fearsome sight. Long greasy locks half-obscured his face. A black patch covered one eye, but from beneath the tangled mass of hair the other gleamed out as bright and wary as that of some wild animal. He had lost a leg, and was leaning heavily on a crutch, but as she looked at his deep chest and powerful shoulders she guessed him to be no mean adversary.

His story might be true, but she doubted it. His restless shifting gaze alarmed her and she sensed that he was waiting…

She half-turned to look at the wood behind them, only to see stealthy figures slipping between the trees.

"There are more of them," she whispered.

"I know it. They intend to rush us." Her companion slid his hands into the pockets of his greatcoat.

The leader of the beggars stiffened. He gave a shout and the group moved forward. Then they stopped.

Prudence looked down to find two small but deadly looking pistols in the hands of the elegant figure of the man beside her.

"Stand back!" he ordered. "I'll drop the first one who takes another step."

"Now, sir, there's no need for that." An ingratiating

smile appeared on the face of the one-legged man. "We mean you no harm." As he spoke his gaze shifted slightly to one side.

Then there was a rush of feet and one of the women came at them from behind. Tall and grossly fat, her bulk made no difference to the speed with which she covered the ground. In one huge hand she brandished a fearsome-looking cudgel, and in the other she held a knife.

Prudence screamed as her companion stepped aside to avoid the onslaught. Then, almost without thinking, she thrust out a foot. Neatly tripped, the woman fell to the ground and lay there, winded.

The distraction offered their only opportunity to the beggars. One of them leaped forward, striking at the pistols with his stick. The sharp crack of a pistol shot was followed by a yelp of agony. Then the man fell back, clutching at his arm.

"A foolish move, your honour." The smile of the one-eyed man was filled with menace. "Now you have only one shot left."

"But I have reinforcements." The gentleman kept him covered as he gave a careless wave towards the coach.

All eyes followed his gesture. Then panic seized the crowd. A liveried groom was standing by the horses' heads, and in his arms he held a massive blunderbuss.

"Now, my young friend, you will oblige me by walking slowly to my carriage and getting inside." The gentleman's voice was calm.

"No, I won't leave Dan."

"Commendable, but foolish. Kindly do as you are told." Her companion raised his voice. "Sam, you may fire!"

As the great gun roared the beggars scattered, and within seconds the lane was deserted.

Without more ado the gentleman returned his guns to his pockets and bent to take Dan in his arms.

"Stop! Where are you taking him?" Prudence demanded. She had no alternative but to hobble after him towards the carriage.

"Your friend needs attention," he told her briefly. "There must be an inn along this road."

"But...but we can't go with you," she cried.

The elderly groom was quick to echo her sentiments. "They've tricked you once, my lord," he muttered darkly. "Doubtless they was set to stop the coach for the others."

Worn out by terror and exhaustion, Prudence lost her temper.

"We were not!" she shouted. "If your employer had not been driving like a madman, Dan would not be injured."

"Why, you impudent young cub, his lordship drives to an inch." The groom raised a hand to box her ears, but his master stopped him with a look.

"This is no time for argument," he said coldly. "Sam, I don't care to be kept waiting. You will open the carriage door at once."

His servant obeyed him with extreme reluctance, but he couldn't resist a final gibe as he looked at Prudence.

"This one stinks," he announced. "He'd best ride on the box. You'll not get the smell out of the coach."

"Of course I won't," his lordship agreed pleasantly. "I shall leave that task to you, unless the smell of horses suddenly offends you. Now stop complaining and help me with this child."

He motioned Prudence into the carriage and laid Dan on the seat beside her with his head resting in her lap.

Undaunted, Sam continued with his dire predictions of treachery, all of which were ignored. Then, as the coach moved off, his lordship swung aboard and took the opposite seat.

Prudence did not look at him. Her thoughts were all for Dan. The bruise upon his head was swelling visibly and a thin trickle of blood ran from the cut into the roots of his hair. His eyes were closed, and against his pallor the childish freckles stood out sharply.

A lump came to her throat and she bent her head to hide the tears which threatened to overcome her. In her worst nightmares she had not envisaged such a predicament. Was this how their journey was to end? With Dan injured and her feet in their present parlous state they could not go on.

And she had left her boots by the roadside. Suddenly it was the last straw. With the back of her hand she tried to dry her eyes, but the tears flowed faster and began to fall upon Dan's head.

"You'll drown the lad!" A clean white handkerchief was thrust into her hand. "Cheer up! I hadn't thought you lacking in courage."

She tried to reply, but choked upon her words.

"You did well back there," the quiet voice continued. "As a murderer I thought you might have left me to the mercy of the beggars." There was a hint of humour in his lordship's tone.

Prudence found her voice at last. "You were driving too fast," she whispered. "I thought you'd killed him."

"Understandable…but then, I did not expect to find

a small boy turning somersaults in the middle of the road.''

"He was trying to cheer me up." Prudence choked again. "I was tired and out of temper."

"I see. You have come far?"

The question caught her unprepared and she was at a loss for an answer.

"Some distance," she murmured in confusion. Then she glanced down at her feet. "And now I have forgot my boots. I left them by the roadside." It was all too much, and her eyes filled again.

A small quiver of emotion disturbed the gravity of his lordship's expression.

"That, I should imagine, is the least of your present problems. You won't get far with your feet in that condition."

He spoke no more than the truth. Blood was already seeping through the rags which she had bound about her heels.

"The blisters broke," she said simply. "Sir, where are you taking us?"

"As I mentioned before, the boy needs attention. He is badly shocked, and that bruise will be the better for a cold compress. Have you friends or family in the neighbourhood?"

Prudence shook her head. "I don't know where we are. Is this Derbyshire?"

"It is, indeed. Where are you making for?"

"We are travelling south. To…er…to the coast."

"Then you have some way to go. How long have you been on the road?"

"Three days."

"So you have come from Cheshire?"

Prudence stiffened. Her reply had been incautious. This man had been quick to estimate how far they were likely to have travelled in so short a time. With every sense alert she looked at him fully for the first time.

He had taken off his many-caped driving coat to lay it over Dan, and now, from his starched cravat to the tips of his gleaming Hessian boots, she saw before her a man who was the epitome of fashion. He might have been poured into the perfectly fitting coat of corbeau-coloured cloth. She had never seen such fabric in her life, nor met anyone who wore his garments with such careless grace.

She guessed his age at not much more than thirty, but it was his face which held her attention. Whilst not precisely handsome, the clear-cut features lent it an air of character and distinction. Dark glossy locks fell forward on to a wide brow, but their tousled disarray did not deceive her for an instant. This was no idle fop. She could sense the energy in him, held in control, but flexed and ready.

The dark eyes which inspected her with such remarkable clarity might have been black, but closer inspection revealed them to be blue.

Even had she been foolish enough to imagine that this man might be easily deceived, the firm mouth above a strong jaw told her otherwise.

She shifted uneasily in her seat. She must be more wary. This man, with his air of authority, might so easily be a magistrate, and she'd hoped to avoid all contact with the forces of the law. His questioning had disturbed her. She knew that her replies had been less than satisfactory. Now he was waiting for an answer.

She nodded. Then Dan opened his eyes.

"My head hurts," he complained. "Pru…?"

"No, it is not prudent for you to move," she told him quickly. He must not mention her name. "You fell and bumped your head, but we are safe and you will soon feel better."

"Where are we going?"

"Don't try to talk," the gentleman advised. "I believe we've reached an inn. Now we can make you comfortable."

It was a startled landlady who inspected the little group of travellers. A glance had shown her the coat of arms upon the door panel of the carriage and she curtsied low as his lordship carried Dan indoors. Then the smell of the stables assailed her nostrils and she barred the way to Prudence.

"The lad had best go round the back," she said. "He can wash up in the yard."

"I beg your pardon, madam?" The glance which was levelled at her caused the woman to wilt.

"Of course, if your lordship should prefer…?" she faltered.

"I do. The young man will accompany me. We shall need a bedroom and a private parlour." He followed the woman up the stairs and into a small chamber. "Is this the best you have?"

"'Tis the largest, sir. We don't see much of the Quality, but you may use my own parlour."

"Thank you." The stern face relaxed into a smile of surprising sweetness, and Prudence was astonished. It was like sunlight breaking through the clouds. Perhaps, after all, this formidable creature had a gentler side.

"The boy has been injured, set upon by thieves along

the road,'' he continued. ''We shall need hot and cold water and some cloths.''

''Must I send for the surgeon, sir?''

''Not yet. We'll see how he goes on.''

''Poor lad. These are terrible times we live in, sir, when a body ain't safe in his own country.''

The landlady was becoming aware of her good fortune. The Quality, so she'd heard, sometimes took odd notions into their heads. If the gentleman cared to bestow his munificence upon a pair of urchins, she might yet reap the benefits of his generosity.

''Quite so! Now the water, if you please.''

As the woman bustled from the room he laid Dan upon the bed. ''Do you bathe his head,'' he told Prudence. ''I must speak to Sam.''

Prudence did as she was bidden. She washed away the blood from the ugly cut and was relieved to find that it was not as deep as she had feared. Dan's bruised face was swollen, but he appeared to have suffered no other ill effects.

Dan reached out for her hand. ''Who is that man?'' he murmured.

''I don't know yet, but he was driving the coach which hit you. Do be careful, Dan! He mustn't guess that I'm a girl.''

A knock at the door stopped her from saying more. Sam was still muttering as he came into the room with his master's portmanteau on his shoulder. He dumped it by the bed and then withdrew as his lordship entered the chamber.

A swift glance assured him that the boy was feeling better. Then he turned to Prudence.

''Now, my young friend,'' he said. ''You will oblige

me by getting out of those appalling rags and washing away the smell of the stables. Have you no other clothing?''

Prudence shook her head. ''I left my bundle by the roadside with my boots.''

She was quick to realise that the loss of her cap and pinafore was a blessing in disguise. This sharp-witted man might recognise them for what they were—the type of garments worn by inmates of an institution. She'd left her telltale cloak in the farmer's barn.

Her lip curled. It was unlikely that this elegant member of the nobility had ever seen an orphan. Even so, she must be careful.

She was unprepared for his next move. With a sweep of his hand he knocked the old cap from her head.

''I should point out that it is customary to remove one's headgear when indoors,…'' he began. Then his face changed. ''Good God!'' he said faintly. ''Pray give me the name of your barber, sir. I must avoid him at all costs!''

''It was me!'' A peal of laughter came from the bed. ''I said it wasn't a good idea to cut it with a knife.''

''How right you were!'' his lordship said with feeling. ''May I express the fervent hope that you do not intend to make barbering your profession, Dan?''

The boy shook his head. ''No, I'm going to join the navy.''

''Thank heavens for that! As a sailor you may give your savage instincts full rein.'' He turned his attention to Prudence, ignoring her look of indignation.

''Here!'' He threw open his portmanteau and drew out a frilled shirt. ''This will be too big for you, but it will serve for the moment. I can offer you only a pair of drawers in place of breeches, but you may tie them about your waist." He glanced at her feet and shook his head. "You must go barefoot for tonight."

"For tonight, my lord? I had thought you would go on." Prudence felt a stirring of alarm.

"I can't," he told her easily. "One of my team has an injured fetlock. Sam has gone for the farrier…"

"I'm sorry to hear it, sir, but Dan and I must leave. We can't stay here…"

"Why not? This is as convenient a place as any, and doubtless our hostess will be able to provide a meal."

Prudence gave him a hunted look.

"Come now!" he continued. "You must be reasonable. Dan is unfit to travel further and so are you. As for me, I should have no objection to a hearty dinner. Nor would you, I imagine."

A sound from the bed brought them round to look at Dan. He was sitting upright with his face alight. Then he made as if to throw the coverlet aside.

"I'm so hungry," he announced. "When shall we eat, my lord?"

"All in good time, but you shall have your meal upon a tray. I don't wish to find you out of bed today. To date your friend has kept his name a secret, but no matter. He will dine with me—that is, if he will bestir himself to wash and change his clothing." With these peremptory orders he strode out of the room.

Prudence bristled with indignation. Did this arrogant creature think that she had no will of her own? Without a by-your-leave he had taken all decisions from her. The fact that he was right was merely an extra source of irritation. What was more, he had insulted her.

"What's the matter, Pru?" Dan was quick to notice her frown.

Prudence could only look at him in dismay. She had no wish to spend the rest of the day in his lordship's company. He had much too keen an intellect, and she might betray herself. She was under no illusions. He would see through any subterfuge.

"He seems kind," Dan told her. "You don't think that he intends us any harm?"

"Not exactly...I mean...not intentionally, but he's been asking questions. I don't trust him."

"You don't trust anyone."

"I haven't had much cause to do so. He could send back word about us."

"He can't. He doesn't know who we are. Besides, he's right. We couldn't go on today, and this bed is so comfortable." Dan snuggled down among his pillows. "He said that we should have some food..."

Prudence gave up the struggle, although it was against her better judgement. As she well knew, there were worse things than cold, hunger, a pair of blistered heels, or even a bump upon the head, but the temptation to sleep beneath a roof and to allay her gnawing need for sustenance was much too strong.

She stepped behind a corner screen and peeled off her ragged garments, handling them with distaste. The water in the ewer was tepid by this time, but she washed herself from head to toe, scrubbing until her skin was pink. Then she doused her head. With any luck she could smooth down her wet hair until it lay flat.

It was a vain hope. As the short crop dried the spiky ends sprang up again, defying all her efforts. A glance in the mirror made her gasp. She scarcely recognised herself. The hazel eyes looked enormous in a face made gaunt by worry and exhaustion. Then she shrugged. This was no time to consider her appearance.

She threw the frilled shirt over her head. As his lordship had predicted it was far too large, and it fell below her knees. The shoulders extended far beyond her own and her hands were lost in the sleeves. She rolled them up and turned her attention to her feet. By tearing one of the clean cloths into strips, she managed to bandage her heels. Finally she stepped into the drawers.

The waist, she found to her surprise, was not excessively large, but the legs were so very long. As she pulled them up to hang in folds she heard his lordship at the door.

It took all her courage to step out from behind the screen. It was one thing to tell herself that her appearance did not matter, but quite another to present a figure of fun. If that wretched creature laughed, she would never forgive him.

Chapter Two

Prudence found that her fears were unwarranted. Although a small muscle quivered at the corner of his lordship's mouth, he made no comment.

And Dan had no eyes for her. His attention was fixed upon the laden tray which was, at that moment, being laid across his knees by a serving wench.

As the woman left the room, their companion turned to Prudence. "Sit down!" he ordered. "I refuse to face that head across a dinner table."

A strong hand forced her into a chair. Then his lordship extracted a pair of scissors from his bag. She glared at him in mutinous silence as he snipped at her hair for several minutes. Then he stepped back to inspect his handiwork.

"I think that's better, Dan, don't you?"

"Much better!" Dan spared only a brief glance for the offending head. He was fully occupied in devouring a leg of chicken.

"I think so, too. Shall we dine?" Without waiting for an answer he led the way into the adjoining room, motioning to Prudence to follow him.

Uncomfortably aware of her bizarre appearance, she

could not look at him. She had never thought herself a beauty, or even passable in looks, but she could scarcely have appeared to worse advantage than at that moment.

Her rescuer had changed his clothing, and the contrast between them made her doubly ill-at-ease.

His lordship had an excellent leg for the coming fashion of pantaloons, and that, combined with yet another well-cut coat and a profusion of snowy linen, succeeded in reducing her to silence.

The sight of a table laid for two did nothing to reassure her. Nor did the array of dishes on the sideboard. A juicy ham was flanked by pies and pasties and an open raspberry tart. Clearly the landlady intended that her noble visitor should dine on the best she could provide.

Hungry though she was, Prudence could not repress a feeling of alarm. That this member of the aristocracy should invite a common urchin to dine with him was not at all in the usual way of things.

"You look troubled. Is something wrong?" the deep voice enquired.

"My lord, why are you doing this? You cannot wish for my company—"

"You are mistaken. Did you not save my life? Had you not tripped that monstrous creature, I might be lying dead upon the road."

"Oh, no! You think they would have killed us?"

"Nothing is more certain. They could not let us live to identify them."

Prudence shuddered. "I was terrified," she admitted. "They were like a pack of wolves…"

Her companion smiled at that. "You are letting your imagination run away with you. I agree that they were a motley crew—mostly deserters, I should think, with a number of thieves among them."

He lifted the lid from a tureen and inspected the contents.

"We are in luck," he announced. "Our hostess would appear to be an excellent cook, to judge by this aroma. Will you take soup? I suggested that we served ourselves this evening in the interests of privacy."

Prudence threw him a suspicious look, but he did not seem to notice. To hide her confusion she took the ladle from him.

"I will do that," she said. "Will you be seated, sir?"

She laid a steaming bowl before him, wondering too late if he would find it strange that a boy should be so deft. Then she filled her own.

"You will take wine with me?" Without waiting for an answer, he filled her glass. "To you, with my thanks." He lifted his own in a salute.

Prudence flushed. "Sir, you exaggerate my part in our escape. You were in no danger. Your groom had the beggars covered."

She saw the gleam of teeth as her companion threw back his head and laughed.

"Sam rode guard on the mail coach before he came to me. He won't be parted from his blunderbuss."

"When he fired, it sounded like a cannon," Prudence said with feeling.

"A useful weapon! Now I suggest that you eat before the soup grows cold."

For once Prudence was happy to obey him. The soup was delicious and she ate with relish.

"More?" He lifted an eyebrow in enquiry.

She shook her head.

"Then let me carve you a slice or two of ham." He filled her plate from the dishes on the sideboard. "You do not care for the wine?" he asked.

"Sir, I am not used to it."

"Try it!" He watched as she sipped obediently at the contents of her glass.

She was very thirsty and the cold liquid was delicious. Unaware of the possible effects, she swallowed more than half of the wine.

"That's better!" He wore an absent expression as he re-filled her glass, but his eyes were intent upon her face.

Prudence did not notice. She was well, well fed, and decidedly drowsy. It was hard to fight off the desire to sleep.

She must think. Though her companion had been more than kind, her limited experience of human nature had warned her not to expect too much from others. This stranger was making too much of what had been an instinctive act upon her part. He knew as well as she did that he had not been at serious risk with Sam on guard, so his present interest in her was a mystery. She longed to question him again.

He seemed to read her mind. "What would you have had me do?" he asked. "Should I have left you by the roadside?"

"I suppose not." Her reply was less than gracious.

"You suppose correctly. Tell me, what are you afraid of?"

"I'm not afraid!" she cried hotly. "It's just that…well…things have not turned out as I expected."

"I find that they seldom do, don't you? Life is full of surprises. Take my own case, for example! At one moment I was driving peacefully along the road. At the next I am attacked by a wild creature who accuses me of murder."

"You deserved it! You have forgot to mention what happened in between."

"I haven't forgotten, and now I wish to make amends in some small way." He filled up her glass again.

Prudence was seized with an unaccountable desire to giggle. "The landlady isn't pleased to have us here," she said inconsequentially.

"On the contrary, she is filled with sympathy for your plight. She deplores the fact that my two young relatives were set upon by thieves when taking a walk to stretch their legs after long hours in the coach."

"She must have thought us very oddly dressed!"

"You were stripped and left for dead. When I found you, I covered you as best I could with the discarded rags which the beggars left behind."

"She believed you?" Prudence gave him a sleepy smile. "You don't look like a relative of ours."

"You are my brother's children," he told her smoothly. "I hope you don't mind being provided with a ready-made uncle."

Prudence found that she was nodding. Her eyelids felt so heavy that she could keep them open only with the greatest difficulty.

"It was a lie," she murmured.

"So it was! I'll do penance for it later. Sam will make sure of that…"

"He doesn't trust us." She was already half-asleep. "He's right, you know. We might be planning to murder you in your bed."

"I plan to take every precaution. I saw you at once for a pair of desperate characters." He glanced across the table and was not surprised to find her sound asleep, the cropped head resting on one arm.

With a curious little smile he lifted Prudence in his arms and carried her into the adjoining room. There he laid her beside Dan's sleeping form and pulled the coverlet over both of them.

With a last look at his unlikely charges he left them to their slumbers.

Prudence wakened to a tumult in the yard below. For a second she lay still, gazing blankly at her unfamiliar surroundings.

Then memory flooded back and she was seized with panic. The noisy cackling of geese told her at once that strangers were about. She wondered with a sense of dread if the beggars had attacked the inn. Worse, had she and Dan been traced?

A moment's reflection convinced her that it was unlikely. Knowing that they were penniless, no one would enquire for them at a hostelry, unless it was to ask if they'd been seen in the neighbourhood.

She peeped through the curtains to find that Sam was the cause of the indignant squawking.

As he walked across the yard, his master issued from the door beneath her window. Immaculate as always, he nodded to his groom.

"Your lordship has breakfasted?" Sam asked hopefully.

"Not yet. There are some matters to which I must attend. I won't need the carriage for another hour at least."

Sam's face fell. "I shan't be sorry to leave this place," he muttered. "Nor to be shot of those two young hellions. They ain't to be trusted, as I said before."

His master smiled. "Your concern for my safety does you the greatest credit, but, as you see, I have survived the night with my throat uncut, and with all my possessions intact."

"I made sure of that, my lord. I slept across their doorway."

"Dear me! You must have spent a most uncomfortable night. That would account for your ill humour. There was not the slightest need for you to do so. I took the precaution of locking their door."

"Hmm! I didn't think—"

"You didn't suppose I had so much sense?" His lordship laughed. "It wasn't for the reasons you imagined. Come, man, find yourself a chop or two and a flagon of ale. Then you'll feel much more yourself."

He turned and re-entered the inn, unaware that above his head Prudence was seething with anger.

She hurried to the door and tried to open it, but it was still firmly locked.

"What is it, Pru?" Dan gave her an anxious look.

"We are prisoners," she said slowly. "We must have been discovered. Where are your clothes?"

"That woman took them away to dry them."

"So that's it! She must have realised that they were pauper's garments. Oh, if only they had not locked us in. We might have slipped away…"

"I can't go without my breeches, and you have no shoes."

"I can go barefoot," she retorted. "My feet are better today. How is your head?"

"The bump has gone down." Dan fingered his brow. "What are we to do?"

"We must seize our chance. When the woman brings your clothes, you must be ready, Dan. When I give the word, you must run."

He nodded. "I'll follow you, but I hope we get our breakfast first."

As the key turned in the lock Prudence swung round,

expecting to see the maid. Instead, it was Sam who stood there with a bundle of clothing over his arm.

"You're to put these on," he told them sourly. "And be quick about it. His lordship wants his breakfast." He dumped the clothing on the bed and went into the parlour.

As the sound of voices reached her, Prudence raised a finger to her lips. Then she crept across the room to listen at the door. Sam's voice was raised in protest. Then she heard his master's deeper tones, but she could not tell what they were saying.

"Get dressed quickly!" she ordered. "He's forgotten to lock the door behind him."

She examined the clothing on the bed. Dan's coat and breeches had been dried, so she threw them over to him. Among the other garments she found a pair of corduroy trousers, a flannel shirt, and a rough homespun jacket. Then her eye fell upon a pair of worsted stockings. She slipped them over her bandaged feet. They would be better than nothing.

The trousers fitted snugly over her slender hips, but the shirt was long enough to hide the outlines of her figure, as did the bulky jacket.

She glanced in the mirror. To her surprise the short clustered curls now seemed to frame her face, giving her a boyish look. She would pass a casual inspection.

"Aren't you ready yet?" she cried impatiently. "We haven't got much time."

"I can't fasten anything. My clothes have shrunk. Oh, Pru, must we go without our breakfast? I can smell the food from here…"

"Of course we must. You know what will happen if they catch us."

She hurried to the outer door and opened it as quietly

as she could, only to find that her caution had been wasted.

"Good morning!" his lordship said cheerfully. "You slept well, I trust?"

"Why...er...yes, my lord." Prudence threw a warning look at Dan.

"Then let us break our fast without delay. I hope to reach Stevenage by nightfall." He led the way into the parlour, nodding a greeting to the landlady who was busy with the chafing dishes.

Prudence realised at once that her previous fears were groundless. The woman smiled at them.

"Sir, your nephews look much recovered after their ordeal..."

"Indeed, they do. You may leave us, ma'am. We shall manage to serve ourselves."

It was a clear dismissal, but the charm of his lordship's smile robbed his words of all offence. The woman curtsied low and left them.

"Dan, you haven't buttoned up your shirt." Under cover of helping him, Prudence hissed a warning. "Take care! Let me answer any questions."

Dan nodded, but his eyes were on the steaming dishes. He needed no second invitation to fill his plate, but Prudence made no move to join him.

"Not hungry?" Their tall companion was smiling down at her. "You surprise me!"

She could contain her anger no longer.

"Why did you lock us in?" she demanded.

"Merely a precaution. I do not know this inn and nor do you. You had no wish to be joined by drunken revellers, I imagine?"

"No, of course not, but I thought...well, I thought..."

"You thought that I expected you to attack me during

the hours of darkness. What a poor opinion you have of me!'' His smile infuriated her.

''I know that you expected nothing of the kind. Nor were you thinking of our safety. Did you suspect that we might run away?''

''A curious idea. Do you make a habit of running away?''

''Don't lie to me!'' she answered shortly.

''Well, to tell the truth I thought it unlikely. You were sound asleep when I left you, but the possibility had crossed my mind.''

''Was that why you made me drink the wine?''

''My friend, I did not force you. On the contrary, you seemed to be enjoying it.''

''Did you have wine?'' Dan demanded in disbelief.

Prudence coloured. ''Yes, I did, but I shall not take it again.''

''Not at breakfast, certainly,'' his lordship agreed. ''Chocolate is much to be preferred at the start of a long journey, unless you care for a flagon of ale?''

Prudence glared at him.

''Do not look black at me, I beg of you. It is much too early. Are you always such a crosspatch in a morning?'' He rose and began to fill a plate for her. ''Eat this! It will help to cure your headache.''

She longed to refuse, but it would have been the height of folly. She had no idea when they would eat again. The experience of the past three days had convinced her that it would be easy to starve to death without friends or money for their journey.

As she ate her mind was racing. It was clear that this peculiar stranger had kept up the pretence that she and Dan were his nephews, and she could not think why.

She finished her meal and pushed the plate away.

Then she looked up to find that he was watching her. With a feeling of dread she awaited the expected questioning, but he did not begin at once.

Prudence waited as the silence lengthened. Then she could bear it no longer. It was better to get it over with.

"My lord?" She gave him a limpid look of innocence, and was displeased to see a twinkle in his eyes.

"You fell asleep whilst we were talking," he replied. "You did not tell me much about yourselves."

"I did! I told you in the coach. We are making for the coast."

"Which one?"

"Er...the south coast."

"That is a large area. What is your destination?"

"Dover," she said promptly. It was the only coastal town she knew in Kent.

"I see. And what to you intend to do there?"

"Dan wants to join the navy."

"And you?"

"I shall do the same."

"Really?" he said mildly. "I had not realised that the navy was recruiting females."

Prudence froze. Her face paled and she turned her head away. Even Dan was silent.

"When did you guess?" she whispered.

"My dear, you hurled yourself into my arms at our first meeting. I am not in my dotage yet. I can still distinguish a man from a woman."

Prudence was too stunned to speak.

"I did not find it difficult," his lordship continued. "Even though you were accusing me of murder at the time."

"Was she?" Dan was unperturbed to find that the secret was out at last. "Why did she do that?"

"She thought I'd killed you."

Dan grinned. "Pru is a terror when she loses her temper."

"Pru?"

"It's short for Prudence," Dan explained helpfully.

"Prudence?" His lordship's voice was oddly hollow. His shoulders began to shake and a hand went up to cover his eyes.

"You have the headache, sir?" Prudence asked in tart tones.

"Just a momentary affliction. Forgive me, it was the shock!" With a supreme effort he recovered his composure.

"I can't imagine why you should find my name so amusing." Prudence was furious with him.

"No, you would not. Now that we have cleared up that small matter, perhaps you will tell me why you found it necessary to disguise yourself as a boy?"

She did not reply, and his lordship looked at Dan.

"Prudence thought it best. They won't be looking for two boys, you see…" He stopped, aware that he had been guilty of an indiscretion.

"You are being pursued? By whom?"

Prudence threw him a goaded look. "It need not concern you," she said stiffly.

"But it does," he insisted. "You must put it down to my insatiable curiosity. Dan, you will please to tell me the whole." His voice had the ring of authority and Dan hung his head.

"Pru said that I must not."

"And I say that you will. Now, let us have done with this nonsense. I don't intend you any harm."

"Then you won't send us back?" Dan looked up hopefully.

"I'd find that difficult, since I don't know where you've come from."

"Exactly! And you shan't find out!" Prudence sat with hunched shoulders as shame and misery possessed her. It was one thing to dress as a boy when no one knew her secret. It was quite another to appear before this elegant creature in trousers which were much too tight, and a shirt which had lost the top two buttons. She pulled it closed, railing inwardly at her own folly. This was no time to worry about her clothing.

"Don't be too sure of that! I'd prefer to hear the story from you, but failing that I can send Sam to make enquiries."

"That would please him," she cried bitterly. "He thinks us no better than the vagabonds."

"You could prove him wrong. Won't you trust me?"

Prudence was silent. Dan's eyes pleaded with her, but she would not be persuaded.

"Very well, then." His lordship walked over to the bell-pull. "Sam shall retrace your route. It won't take him long, since you have travelled on foot, and he will be on horseback."

"Pru, please tell him." Dan was trembling. "I don't want to be locked up again with a dead man."

"Did I hear you aright?" His lordship turned, his hand already upon the rope.

"Yes, my lord. It was when we ran away before. They caught us not far from the mill. It was a punishment—"

"That I can believe!" There was more than a hint of anger in his voice. "Who were these people?"

"The superintendent and his wife. They have charge of the apprentices."

"Where?"

"It was at the cotton mill."

"How came you to be there?"

Prudence glared at him, but she was seized with a feeling of despair. By now he knew enough to return them to a life of drudgery if he cared to do so. Most of the industry was situated further north. It would not be so difficult to trace a spinning mill in Cheshire.

"We are foundlings," she told him in a sullen tone. "The parish sent us to the mill."

He studied her with his calm, dark gaze and something in his expression persuaded her to plead with him.

"My lord, won't you let us go?" she begged. "Our fate cannot matter to you. We shall find work in the south of England. Anything would be better than the life we've led."

"I must believe you." He rose and began to pace the room. "But what am I to do with you? At the mill you were sure of food and shelter..."

"The food was horrible," Dan said. "The bread had weevils in it, and the milk was mixed with chalk and flour and water."

His lordship sat down again and Prudence noticed that his mouth had hardened. "Go on!" he said abruptly. "How many were you?"

"Nearly a hundred sometimes, but some were hurt and could not work. Once I crushed my fingers in the straps." Dan held up his right hand to show that he had lost a fingertip.

"The straps?"

"They were a part of the machinery," Prudence told him. "It was dangerous when the youngest children fell asleep. They got so tired in the heat and the dust. Sometimes they fainted."

"What happened then?"

"They were dragged away and others took their

places. My lord, we worked from six in the morning until seven at night. You will not send us back to that?''

He smiled then, and suddenly there was nothing but warmth in his expression. For the first time she felt something of his charm.

''I don't believe I will,'' he told her lightly. ''You had best travel on with me. I go as far as Canterbury.''

''Where is that?''

''It is in Kent.''

Prudence stared at him. ''You cannot mean to take us on with you?''

''Why not? Shall I leave you here to be discovered? Of course, the search for you may already have been abandoned.''

''Then we shall no longer be in danger.''

His lordship lifted an eyebrow. ''You think not? Has your experience taught you nothing?''

''I don't know what you mean.''

He sighed. ''I had thought it must be obvious. How long will it take you to travel the length of England, and how are you to live? Admit it, you were starving when I found you.''

It was impossible to argue. She knew that he was right.

''And another thing. Suppose you had met that group of beggars when you were alone? What then?''

''We had nothing worth their taking.''

''You are mistaken. They would soon have discovered your secret. You are young, and comely enough to appeal to—''

''To a thief?'' she snarled.

''I was about to say...to any unprincipled rogue for whom your youth would be no barrier. At best you and

Dan would have been set to beg for them. And at worst? Need I go on?''

Prudence flushed to the roots of her hair, but he ignored her.

''What do you say to riding in my carriage, Dan?''

''Yes, please!'' came the prompt reply. ''Don't be so mifty, Pru. You can't walk far without your boots, you know.''

''I agree. Prudence must not be…er…mifty. Pull the bell-rope, Dan. I'll tell Sam to set the horses to.''

Prudence was unconvinced. ''We don't even know your name,'' she said uncertainly.

''A shocking omission on my part. I crave your pardon. I am Sebastian Wentworth…''

''Lord… Lord Wentworth?''

He bowed. ''Very much at your service, Miss Prudence. I hate to press the matter, but I believe we should make haste. Sam is sure to prophesy disaster unless, or even if, we leave at once.''

Dan looked mystified. ''Why should he do that?''

Wentworth laughed. ''He will warn me of the certain wrath of the authorities for taking up a couple of runaways.''

''But he doesn't know that we are runaways.''

''That's true! We must think up a story for him. That task we shall leave to Prudence. I suspect that she has a certain talent for it. Now, where is Sam?'' He left them to go in search of his henchman.

''I can hear Sam,'' Dan announced. ''He's in the yard below.'' He ran over to the window. Then Prudence heard a low cry.

''What is it?'' she asked quickly.

''They've found us. Sam is talking to Superintendent Henshaw.''

Chapter Three

Prudence seized Dan's hand. Sick with dread, she hurried him towards the door, but he hung back.

"I don't want to go down there," he cried. "Can't we hide?"

"Where? There isn't room in here, and Sam is sure to give us away. Be quick! They'll be up here at any minute. Our only chance is to run…"

She dragged him behind her down the stairs, but her way was barred as a figure came towards her.

"Going somewhere?" Wentworth enquired pleasantly.

Prudence tried to slip behind him, but he stood four-square across the passage to the servants' quarters.

"Don't be a fool!" he said softly. "Stay here, and don't make a sound."

With that he strolled towards his groom, flicking away an imaginary speck of dust from his sleeve as he did so.

"Sam, I am grown tired of waiting. Where is my carriage?" His voice reached them clearly in the still morning air.

"Beg pardon, my lord. 'Twas this gentleman as stopped me…"

"Indeed!" His lordship's voice was cool. "May I ask why?"

He received an obsequious bow. "Your lordship, I am searching for two runaways…a young boy and a girl…"

"Really? You feel, perhaps, that my groom has them concealed about his person?"

The sarcasm brought a flush to the superintendent's face, but he persevered. "I thought he might have seen them," he said doggedly.

"Sam?" At a glance from his employer Sam shook his head.

"And your lordship has not passed them on the road? The lad is twelve years old or thereabouts and has red hair. The girl is seventeen and taller."

"Sam, would I have noticed them?" his lordship asked in languid tones. It was clear that the conversation bored him.

"I think not, my lord." Sam's expression was wooden.

"Quite! One cannot, after all, take note of every urchin. Would they have come this far?"

"They were seen by a farmer on the Cheshire border. The girl was up to her old tricks…"

"Spare me the details, my good man. We are now in Derbyshire. Have you considered? Your charges may have met with some accident. Why, only yesterday I myself was attacked by a pack of thieves…"

"They'd be safe enough," the superintendent's reply was sour. "They have nothing worth stealing."

"No money and no food? Your optimism is refreshing. Yet I suppose they might be set to begging for the others. Perhaps if you followed the band of thieves? No…on second thoughts…perhaps not! They are a rascally mob. You are armed, I hope?"

"I am not, my lord."

"Dear me! I must admire your courage, sir. Your horse and your clothing must be a temptation, to say nothing of your purse."

"I...I had not thought of that." The superintendent began to look uneasy. He cast a furtive look about the stable yard as if expecting the beggars to appear at any moment.

"Well, it will not deter you from your duty, I expect. Personally I should not care to travel alone. Had it not been for Sam here, I might have lost all my possessions and possibly my life... But I must not go on. I see that you are determined to continue with your search, and we must not delay you."

"You advise against it, your lordship?"

"Good heavens! Of course not! The decision must be yours, though I own I should not care to risk my own skin for these two missing children. Your dedication does you credit, and you have my warmest wishes for your safety."

The superintendent gave him a hunted look as he re-mounted. "I may have been over-hasty in setting off alone, sir. These are sad times we live in when apprentices are so far lost to their obligations as to run away from those who would care for them."

"Worthless creatures, and hardly worth your trouble, I imagine." Wentworth nodded pleasantly and turned away.

"Oh, it ain't that, sir." An ugly note crept into the man's voice. "We always catch them. Let one escape and we'd have no end of trouble. We make an example of those who try it. When I get my hands on that hell-cat of a girl...!" His expression was vicious as he spurred away.

Sam turned to his employer. "My lord, I almost gave them up," he said slowly. "But I didn't like the look of him."

Wentworth clapped him on the shoulder. "You are an excellent judge of character, Sam. Apart from that, you would have incurred my most severe displeasure. Now bring the carriage round. It's time we were on our way."

"Do you think he'll be back?" He gazed after the horseman, who was disappearing with almost indecent haste.

"I doubt it. If I'm not mistaken, he won't draw rein until he reaches safety. But even if he does it will avail him nothing. We shall be miles away."

Sam looked at him in horror. "Sir, you can't be meaning to take them on with us?"

Wentworth nodded.

"But, my lord, they are parish children and bound apprentices."

"So?"

"You'll be breaking the law," Sam said heavily.

"It's a poor law that binds children to a life of slavery. Now, Sam, will you fetch the carriage, or shall I ask the stable-lad?"

"He'll not touch your team, my lord." Shaking his head, Sam walked off across the yard.

"Oh, Pru, we're safe!" Dan crept out from his hiding place. "Lord Wentworth sent old Henshaw about his business. I like him very much, don't you?"

"I think him very strange," Prudence said slowly. "Why should he help us?"

"He looked sad when we told him about the mill."

"What can he know about it? Cheap sympathy means nothing. He won't think of those we've left behind."

"When I'm rich I'll buy the mill and set them free," Dan told her stoutly.

"Then I must help you make your fortune." Prudence grasped his arm and led him into the yard.

Wentworth took the reins and they made good time that day, reaching Stamford by noon.

For the first part of the journey Dan occupied himself by looking out for rabbits and foxes. When that palled, he began to count the number of crows and magpies in the trees.

Finally he became aware of Pru's unusual silence.

"What's wrong?" he asked. "This is better than walking, isn't it? And it's such a fine carriage." He settled himself more comfortably among the squab cushions and began to examine the brass fittings on the doors.

"Don't touch anything," Prudence warned. "You know how things have a way of coming to pieces in your hands."

"It's only because I like to find out how they work," he replied in an injured tone. Then his face brightened. "Do you suppose that his lordship will stop for food?" he asked.

Prudence laughed. "Don't you think of anything but your stomach, you greedy creature?"

"Well, I liked the chicken we had last night. I hadn't tasted it before, and I could have eaten the whole of that raspberry tart…"

"You almost did so. I thought you would get the stomach-ache."

"Did you? Is that why you are so quiet?"

"No, I was just wondering what we are to do."

"You'll think of something, Pru. You always do." He

smiled at her with total confidence and returned to his counting.

Prudence did not pursue the subject. His faith in her was touching, but often it worried her. He was so sure of her ability to surmount all obstacles.

Her mouth curved in a rueful smile. From the moment she'd first seen the frightened nine-year-old, something about him had touched her heart. His stocky little figure had looked so gallant as he'd tried to keep up with the others at the mill, taking full bobbins off the spindles and replacing them with empty ones.

Even when his hand had been caught in the straps, which turned the wheels of the machinery, he hadn't cried.

She'd nursed him then, stealing extra food and watching over him until the injury had healed. Since that time he'd been devoted to her, and their mutual affection had comforted her throughout their darkest days.

Later he'd been set to work on two machines, each of which spun fifty threads. His task was to guide the threads and to twist them when they snapped. He'd learned to take the machinery to pieces and to apply the oil. At an early age his talent for repairs had been apparent. It was small wonder that Superintendent Henshaw had tried to find them, apart from a wish to discourage runaways. In time Dan would have become a valuable asset to the workforce.

She herself would be no loss, she thought with fierce pleasure. From the day of her arrival she had fallen foul of the authorities. The memory made her smile.

"Have you thought of something funny? Tell me!"

"It's nothing! I wondered if Mr Henshaw was relieved because he couldn't find me."

Dan grinned at her. "I expect he was. He said that you were a dis—a dis—"

"A disruptive influence? I expect I am and always have been. I made up my mind that he would not beat the spirit out of me."

"He couldn't do that," Dan assured her. "I'm glad that we ran away, aren't you?"

"Of course I am." It was the truth. With every mile that passed they were putting that life of misery behind them. Her spirits lifted. "Look, we are coming to a town."

"And see, there is a fair!" Dan craned his head out of the window. "There's sure to be bear-baiting and cock-fighting…"

"You bloodthirsty little monster! Where did you hear about such things?"

"From the men at the mill."

"Well, you would not like them," she told him firmly. "And nor should I. In any case, Lord Wentworth will not wish to stop for long."

She was mistaken. They had reached Stamford, and his lordship guided his team through the entrance to the Ram Jam Inn. As he drew up a team of ostlers ran towards him. Wentworth threw them the reins and sprang down from his seat.

Before Sam could let down the steps he'd opened the door and reached up his arms to Prudence.

"I don't need help," she announced with dignity. Then she caught her foot upon the sill and tumbled headlong.

A pair of strong arms closed about her and she found herself held firmly against his lordship's chest.

"Pride goes before a fall," he mocked as he released her.

The physical contact had been brief, but none the less it was disturbing. For the last year or so the men at the mill had made advances to her and they filled her with disgust, smelling as they did of dirt and sweat.

Wentworth was different. As he held her in his arms she'd been aware of the scent of clean fresh skin and soap, mixed with faint traces of tobacco. It was not unpleasant, but she was quick to move away from him. She had no wish to find herself so close to any man. Past experience had warned her of the danger.

His eyes flickered to her face with a queer disarming smile which made them dance. She could not guess what he was thinking. Then he turned to Dan.

"Hungry?" he asked.

"Yes, sir." Dan's reply was prompt. "Will they have raspberry tart here?"

"I think it not unlikely. Shall we go in?" He led the way into the crowded inn.

"My lord, it is a pleasure to see you again!" The press of travellers parted as the landlord came towards them. "You'll find your team in peak condition, sir."

"I know it, otherwise I should not leave them in your care. I'd like a private parlour, Briggs, and a meal as quickly as you like. There are three of us."

The landlord bowed.

"One other thing," his lordship continued. "Do you have raspberry tart?"

"Of course, my lord."

"Then a large one, if you please, or possibly two…"

Dan's eyes sparkled. Then he tugged at Wentworth's sleeve.

"We may not be able to eat them both," he whispered.

"Then we shall carry one of them away with us. It may help to sustain you on the road to Stevenage."

"But I shan't be hungry if we eat our dinner here."

"Forgive me if I place no reliance at all upon that statement." Wentworth followed the landlord to an upper room and his companions followed.

All three of them did justice to the meal. Then Dan leaned back with a sigh of satisfaction.

"Sir, is it far to Stevenage?" he asked.

"Some long distance, but we'll reach the town by nightfall. Why do you ask?"

"Well, my lord, did you not see the fair and all the people?"

"Dan, the fair is of no interest to Lord Wentworth." Prudence frowned at him.

"Oh, I don't know…" Wentworth considered her out of the corners of his eyes. "I have been thinking. Are you handy with your needle?"

Prudence stared at him. "I can sew," she told him stiffly.

"There will be pedlars here. They sell such things as fabrics, ribbons, thread and needles. You might make yourself a skirt."

"But I have no money, sir."

"That does not signify." He forestalled a refusal with his next words. "Hear me out! I am offering you a loan. When you find employment you may repay me."

He looked at her from under lazy eyelids, aware of the tension in her figure. "I have no ulterior motives, if that is what is worrying you."

"We are already too much in your debt. I cannot—"

"But I must insist. You cannot be comfortable in your present garb, and it reflects upon my consequence, you know."

She saw the gleam of amusement in his eyes and it angered her. She longed to refuse his offer. Consequence, indeed! Nothing would shake his self-assurance.

Still, she must not cut off her nose to spite her face. The tight breeches were uncomfortable, and were likely to chafe her badly if she wore them for much longer.

"Then if it is to be a loan…?" She forced out a belated word of thanks with her acceptance of his offer.

"Very well. Shall we walk about the town? A half-hour should suffice, I think."

Dan was elated. Half an hour was better than nothing, and he might yet see the bear. He found it difficult to hide his impatience as Prudence made her purchases, but his wish was gratified at last. He found himself at the front of the crowd as the huge animal was paraded before them.

"Come away!" Prudence tried to extricate him from the milling throng. She'd heard tales of the snapping dogs being ripped to pieces by those fearsome claws, and the thought made her shudder.

"But, Pru, the bear is going to dance…" He looked so disappointed that she had not the heart to drag him away. At least there were no dogs, and the beast appeared to be well cared for. Her relief showed in her face.

"Satisfied?" Wentworth's expression was unfathomable as he looked down at her. "The bear is the keeper's livelihood. What did you expect?"

"I thought it might be used for baiting."

"Not this one. The sport, if such it may be called, is a sickening sight. I should not have let Dan watch it."

Prudence looked at the animal's long, curved claws.

"I suppose it must defend itself," she murmured. "I hate to see it chained in such a way."

Wentworth studied her with his calm dark gaze. Then he reached into the crowd and pulled Dan away.

"There is a juggler further on," he said. "You may watch him for a little while. Then we must go." His eyes roved over the roadside stalls. Then he drew Prudence to one side, pointing to a cobbler sitting at his last.

"Have you something to fit this lad?" he asked. "He's lost his boots."

"These young 'uns!" The cobbler shook his head in disapproval as he examined the unshod feet.

Prudence felt ashamed. The walk about the fair had worn her stockings through, and her toes poked through the holes.

"My boots will be too big for him," the cobbler said in disappointment. He was unwilling to lose a sale.

"What of these?" Wentworth picked up a pair of soft leather slippers.

"Those be ladies' slippers, your honour."

"No matter! The lad has blisters on his feet." He motioned to Prudence to try them on. Upon her assurance that they fit he paid the asking price, knowing full well that it was double the true value.

The man bowed them away. It was rare for such good fortune to befall him, and if the gentleman cared to waste his blunt on shoes which the lad would kick through in a couple of days it was none of his concern.

"My lord, they were very expensive," Prudence announced in shocked surprise. "I should not have taken them."

"Your feet are almost bare," Wentworth pointed out. "Will you run the risk of getting an infection in those blisters?"

She could not argue. Instead she seized Dan's hand

and followed his lordship as he strode back to the inn. His long legs made it difficult to keep up with him, but he now seemed to be in a hurry.

Sam was waiting in the courtyard, and he looked at his master in enquiry.

"Yes, put them to. I'll settle up and then we'll be away." He entered the main doorway of the inn, leaving Dan and Prudence standing by the arched entrance from the busy road.

Prudence clutched her purchases to her as she gazed at the noisy crowd of travellers. All seemed to be bustle and confusion at first sight, but the ostlers knew their work. As one coach after another swept in to the courtyard, steaming glasses of punch were handed up to the occupants whilst teams were changed with such speed that it amazed her. It was clear that the Ram Jam Inn had a high reputation to uphold.

Then she saw Sam. He was leading four of the most beautiful horses she had ever seen. The matched bays drew all eyes, and she heard gasps of admiration from the men about her.

"Oh, Dan, do look!" she cried.

To her consternation there was no reply.

"Dan?" she called in panic. She could see no sign of him.

"It's all right, I'm here…" He scrambled out from beneath his lordship's carriage. He had a smear of grease across his cheek and his clothes were covered in grit.

"Drat the lad!" Sam shouted. "Get out of it!"

"I wanted to see how the coach was made." Dan gave him a sunny smile. "It rides so well…I thought there must be some special way of springing it."

Sam was slightly mollified by such admiration. "'Tis

his lordship's own design. He'll have nothing but the best.''

''I can see that.'' Dan moved over to stand beside him. ''These horses? Are they what is called blood-stock?''

''Aye…they have Arab blood. Look about you, lad! You'll see the difference in the cattle round you.''

''On your favourite subject, Sam?'' Wentworth had reappeared. He looked surprised to find Dan deep in conversation with his groom, but he refrained from comment. He handed Prudence up into the coach, bestowing her purchases beside her. Then he raised an eyebrow in enquiry.

''Dan was admiring your horses,'' she explained. ''He scrambled beneath the carriage, too. I hope you do not mind.''

''Why did he do that?''

''He likes to know how things are made.''

''I see. Would he care to ride up top with Sam for an hour or so, do you suppose?''

''You need only ask him.'' Her expression softened and a smile peeped out. ''You must not spoil him, sir. He is in the way of becoming a perfect nuisance.''

''I have no fears for Dan, or for his future. Anyone who can make a friend of Sam in less than half a day is likely to go far.'' He perched Dan up beside his groom and climbed into the coach.

''You will not drive yourself, my lord?'' Prudence was alarmed by the prospect of spending time alone with this exquisite stranger. She guessed that he intended to question her.

''Not for the moment, unless you have some objection to my company?'' His eyes were twinkling and she looked away. He seemed to have an uncanny ability to read her mind. "You may spring 'em, Sam," he called.

"What does that mean?" asked Prudence. "I have not heard it said before." She was casting about her for some topic of conversation which would divert his attention from herself.

"It means that Sam will give the bays their heads. They are fresh and much in need of exercise."

"Then we shall be travelling fast?"

"We shall. I hope the prospect does not frighten you." He consulted his watch. "We must reach Stevenage by nightfall."

"Why so?"

"I intend to stay there overnight. Then we press on to London."

She looked dismayed. "I thought you meant to go to Kent?"

"This is the easiest way. The main roads are faster than the country lanes. Once we have crossed the Thames River there is a good route to the south."

She nodded, satisfied with his explanation and content for the moment to look through the window at the passing countryside. Her companion seemed disposed to continue their conversation.

"Won't you tell me something about yourself?" he asked.

"There is no more to tell," came the guarded reply. "As I mentioned, Dan and I are foundlings, sent from the parish to the mill."

"You know no more than that…nothing about your parentage?"

"I was told that I was found in a basket beside the parish church."

"And Dan?"

"His parents died of smallpox when he was five. No one would enter the house. He stayed by their bodies for three days before they found him."

"My dear!" He reached forward and took her hand. "I am surprised that he is sane."

"He had nightmares for a long time after that. They started again when Superindendent locked him up with the dead body of one of the men."

"There can be no excuse for that!" Wentworth's face had paled and Prudence saw the sparks of anger in his eyes.

"There was nowhere else to put him. It was the second time we'd run away. The first time it was just a beating. Since that did not serve we were locked up in darkness without food."

"You were with him?"

She stared at him in astonishment. "Oh, no! That would not have been allowed. They shut me in a cupboard. We spoke to each other through the door. He was crying, but I told him that if the old man hadn't hurt us when he was alive he couldn't do so when he was dead."

She dismissed the incident from her mind. It was evidently just one more event in a long history of abuse.

"It is an incredible story...and terrible to hear. I had no idea that such things occurred."

Prudence eyed him squarely. "I don't suppose you had. Have you ever visited a mill, my lord?" She knew the answer before he spoke.

"No! I had no occasion to do so." He was silent for some time.

"It must have taken all your courage to run away again," he said at last.

"I had no choice. As the girls at the mill grow older

the men…er…make free with them.'' She turned her head away, unwilling to meet his gaze.

''But the superintendent?'' he protested. ''You were his responsibility. He must have known what was happening.''

Her glance was one of pure disdain. ''Of course he did, but more bastards mean more workers in the end. He did not care, and it was becoming more difficult to refuse…''

''But you did so?''

''Oh, yes, I am not in the family way. The overseer was the worst, but I hit him with a brick and then we ran away.''

Anger fought with amusement in Wentworth's mind. ''You seem to be a redoubtable adversary, my dear. What a sensible solution!''

''I thought so then, but now I'm not so sure. I should have come alone. Had we not met you, Dan might have starved.''

''That won't happen now,'' he assured her. ''If I am not mistaken, that raspberry tart is at this moment disappearing fast.''

Prudence gave him a sleepy smile. It was warm inside the coach and she felt very drowsy.

''I didn't thank you properly,'' she murmured.

''For what?''

''For not betraying us, and for my lovely shoes.'' She stuck out her feet and examined them with satisfaction. ''I've never worn anything half so fine.''

She clutched her bundle to her. This evening she would make herself a skirt from the roll of pale blue cambric purchased at the fair. It was the best that the pedlar had to offer. She would have chosen something cheaper, but Wentworth had insisted on the blue.

Looking at the bent head, his lordship was surprised by an emotion new to him. He was no stranger to compassion, and her story had moved him deeply. Yet there was something else. This absurd little creature in her ridiculous clothing had a curious quality all her own.

She could be as stiff and awkward as any boy, the cropped head and the clean lines of her face adding to the illusion. The next instant she was all woman, feminine enough to take pleasure in her new shoes and the trifling gift of fabric for a gown.

He studied her through half-closed lids. Prudence was not a pretty girl. Her mouth was too generous for beauty and freckles sprinkled her nose. Yet beneath those dark brows the wonderful hazel eyes were widely spaced and huge, giving her the look of a young fawn. Yet there was determination in that strong little jaw. It was an arresting face, and one which would always demand a second look. An unusual creature, he decided.

Unaware of the keen scrutiny, Prudence fell asleep.

She wakened to find that the coach had stopped and Dan was tugging at her arm.

"Are we at Stevenage already?" she asked. "I thought it would take longer."

"Of course not, silly! But you've been asleep for hours. Lord Wentworth thought that you might like a drink." He held out a glass of lemonade.

Prudence sipped at the refreshing liquid as Dan continued to chatter.

"You should see Lord Wentworth drive! He's a member of the Four Horse Club, you know, and he drives to an inch! Sam says that he is a Nonesuch. This team of his are real goers."

Prudence smiled at his use of horsey cant. Sam's influence was obvious.

"And he's very rich. He keeps teams along the Great North Road at all the staging posts, Sam says."

"Sam says?" she teased. "Is he become your greatest friend?"

"No, you are my best friend, but Sam knows such a lot. He's promised to show me how the carriage is sprung when we have more time." He vanished as a shout recalled him to his seat upon the box.

As they picked up speed Prudence drifted into a dreamlike state. She tried to gather her wandering thoughts. She ought to be making plans. When his lordship set them down at Canterbury she and Dan would be left to their own devices and she must find work without delay. If the town was large enough, she would ask at some of the inns.

She had no experience of such work, but perhaps it would not matter. She could do scullery work and serve at table, and Dan might find employment as a pot-boy.

She thought of the noisy bustle at the Ram Jam Inn and her spirits sank. It was a daunting prospect, but it could be no worse than working at the mill. And it would not be for long, she promised herself fiercely.

Her hand went up to finger the small brooch which was pinned to her under-bodice. It was little enough to go on, but it was her only hope of finding those who had abandoned her.

For the hundredth time she wondered why it had been hidden in the tight folds of her swaddling clothes. Had it been a last despairing effort to tell her of her parentage? Perhaps her mother had hoped that one day she might set out on her present quest.

Her face hardened. There was no tenderness in her

heart for the woman who had abandoned a week-old child to the mercy of others. At best she'd been left to face an uncertain future. At worst she might have perished on that cold March day. The death of a foundling was not uncommon.

Yet she had survived, often by strength of will alone. Her own resolve had sustained her through the long years of repression, of beatings, of poor food and incessant drudgery.

She'd shivered through northern winters in the icy attic which she'd shared with twenty other girls, sleeping in all her clothing to avoid the freezing draughts. Her one thin blanket had been useless.

In summer the heat in the attic room was suffocating as the sun beat down upon the roof. In the mill itself it was unbearable. The children often fainted and accidents were frequent.

She closed her eyes as if to shut out some of the dreadful sights she'd seen. Small bodies were so easily crushed in the machinery.

Through it all her burning anger never left her. It was wrong to feed on hatred, so the parson said. It was not only a sin, but it was self-destructive. She'd shrugged. To have her spirit crushed was even more destructive. She was determined that it would not happen to her.

And she'd had one stroke of luck. When all attempts at discipline had failed, she'd been sent off to the vicarage to be frightened by the threat of hellfire if she persisted in rebellion.

Chapter Four

To her surprise the old parson had been gentle, though she'd stood before him with a sullen face, and her chin held high.

He'd talked to her with infinite patience, but there was nothing he could do to change her lot. At least he didn't repeat the pious homilies which hung on every wall of the attics and the mill. Once, in a fury, she'd torn them down, refusing to believe that the Lord was merciful. That day Dan's friend had been crushed beneath a roller beam.

Unmoved by Mr Henshaw's claim that she was an agent of the devil, the parson had questioned her at length. He'd tried to convince her that burdens were placed only on shoulders strong enough to bear them.

"That isn't true!" she'd said defiantly. "Did not Mag Wilkins kill herself rather than bear the overseer's child?"

He'd made haste to change the subject, feeling that it was unsuitable for a young girl.

"Won't you tell me what is troubling you?" he'd asked.

"Oh, sir, you found me by the church. Was there nothing…nothing at all to say where I had come from?"

He'd hesitated. "There was a brooch. I've kept it for you. We found it in your clothing." He opened a drawer in his desk and handed the trinket to her.

The small medallion glistened softly in the candlelight and Prudence turned it over in her fingers. It was attached to a bar fitting at the back and it felt heavy to the touch.

"What is it made of?" It was like nothing she had seen before.

"It is gold, my child. You must take great care of it. Would you prefer to leave it with me?"

Her hand closed about it. "I'd like to keep it, if you please. Was there nothing else?"

"Just a broadsheet beneath the blanket in the basket." He paused uncertainly, but he could not resist her pleading look. "It was printed in Kent."

As the hope grew in her eyes he shook his head in sorrow.

"Prudence, you should give up hope of finding out your ancestry. I should not have told you of these things, but you have the right to know."

Prudence was studying the medallion. "There is some carving on it," she murmured. "Sir, what is this beast?"

"It is some heraldic emblem. I have no knowledge of such things. I beg that you will put these questions out of your mind."

She gave him a steady look and he sighed.

"Headstrong as always, I fear! Pray consider, my dear, that when a child is given up as you have been there is always a reason. Let us suppose that you found your natural parents…you might not be welcomed at their hearth."

Undeterred by her bitter smile he felt obliged to continue.

"Men and women marry…or re-marry…a bas—I mean, a previous child can be an embarrassment."

When she made no reply he renewed his efforts.

"Happiness lies within ourselves," he told her quietly. "If you would but try to make the best of your present situation, you might find peace of mind. In time you will marry and have children of your own…"

She shook her head. "I shall not marry…not here, at least. No child of mine shall be forced into the mill."

The parson laid a hand upon her head. He had counselled her as best he could, but this slender child had a strength of will which he found astonishing in one so young.

"Remember the willow trees," he said at last. "They bend in the fury of the storm, but they don't break. Will you not learn to bend a little?"

"I'll try." Prudence was grateful for his understanding, but it did not alter her determination to discover the secrets of her ancestry. "I thank you, sir, for your kindness to me."

"It is little enough, my dear, but I hope that you will come and talk to me whenever you feel the need. In the meantime, you have my blessing."

He'd dismissed her then, but he hadn't forgotten her, and she'd formed the habit of calling at the vicarage on occasion, grateful for his interest in her education.

He'd talked to her for hours, lent her books, and taught her to write a fair hand. Under his influence her manners had been refined, and with her quick ear she had been swift to realise that the rough northern dialect in common use at the mill was unacceptable in polite society. In his company she'd learned to speak as he did himself, though she kept this knowledge to herself.

Her only regret was that she and Dan had left without the old man's blessing. It troubled her, but it could not be helped. He would have tried to stop her.

She prayed that he had not mentioned Kent to the superintendent, though she guessed that the search for the two runaways had already been abandoned.

She must put such fears behind her. There was no point in meeting trouble half-way. Their encounter with Lord Wentworth had been a miraculous stroke of luck. Now they might be sure of reaching Kent without further mishap. Left to their own efforts it would have taken weeks to reach the south coast, if they had ever succeeded.

Even today the journey had seemed endless in spite of the comfort of the carriage. She felt stiff, and, as she had feared, the tight breeches had begun to cut into her flesh. When they reached Stevenage she would make her skirt without delay.

At their destination she was delighted to find that she had a bedchamber to herself. She unpacked her bundle quickly and spread out the cotton fabric on the carpet. A single seam would serve, and if she turned down the top of the skirt she could run a ribbon through to gather it into her waist.

Then she frowned. She had no scissors. Dan must ask Lord Wentworth if she might borrow his. She opened the door, but Dan was nowhere to be found. Doubtless he was with Sam.

She glanced through the window and saw them standing by the carriage, but her efforts to attract Dan's attention were unavailing.

There was nothing for it. She must go herself.

In the corridor she stopped a chambermaid and was directed to his lordship's chamber. She tapped at the door and upon a muffled command to enter she walked into the room.

To her horror she discovered that Wentworth was half-naked. Stripped to the waist, he was dousing his head in a china basin filled with water.

She began to make a hasty retreat, startled by the sight of his splendid torso. His lordship had the body of an athlete. Broad shoulders tapered to a slim waist and beneath his tanned skin she was aware of the play of muscles on both his back and arms.

In confusion she turned back to the door, intending to slip away before her presence was detected. Then Wentworth spoke.

"I've finished, Sam. You may pour the water over my head." He gestured towards a steaming ewer.

In silence, Prudence picked up the jug and tipped the contents over the dark curls.

"Now the towel! Be quick about it, man!" He reached out blindly for the cloth.

Prudence thrust it into his fumbling hand. He stiffened as his fingers touched her own. Then her wrist was seized in an iron grip and Wentworth swept the hair out of his eyes.

"What are you doing in here?" he demanded roughly. "Was I mistaken in you? Would you rob me whilst my back was turned?"

Prudence could have struck him though she was badly frightened. There was a cold glitter in his eyes which filled her with dread.

She had paled to the lips, but she would not allow him to see her terror.

"I had no such intention," she replied in icy tones. "I came to ask if I might borrow your scissors."

For a long moment his eyes searched her face. Then he released her.

"Have you no sense at all?" he demanded harshly. "You should have sent Dan."

"I couldn't find him. He's with Sam." She was ready to weep with rage. "I beg your pardon for the intrusion, but I see now that you do not trust us. From here we shall make our way alone."

"Don't be a fool!" Wentworth thrust his arms into his shirt. "If you want an apology you shall have it. Here…" He reached into his bag and held out the scissors.

"Keep them!" she retorted. "You may also have the cloth you bought for me, and my slippers." She kicked them off and stood before him in her bare feet.

"Good God! What a hot-head! I wonder that you have survived so long. Has anyone ever boxed your ears?"

"Frequently, my lord, and I gave as good as I got."

"Threats, my dear? Don't try your strength with me! Let me warn you, I am unaccustomed to defiance."

"Then I had best leave you. I won't be called a thief." Her eyes were sparkling with wrath.

"Are you suffering from injured pride?" Wentworth drew on a splendid scarlet dressing-gown. "I said I was sorry for misjudging you. Is not that enough?"

When she did not reply he picked up the water-jug. "Would you like to throw this at my head? It might relieve your feelings…"

He was laughing down at her and suddenly she felt breathless and oddly disturbed by some emotion which she did not understand. Against the magnificence of the dark red robe his skin looked firm and smooth. She could see a small pulse beating in the hollow of his throat, and with his hair still damp and tousled he looked much younger.

"You caught me at a disadvantage," he admitted. "I am not used to have a young lady break in upon me when I am bathing…"

"The fault was mine, sir." Prudence felt the hot colour rising to her cheeks. She should have left the room without delay, but she felt rooted to the spot.

"Then you won't throw the jug? Warn me if you decide to do so. I plan to take evasive action." His eyes were full of amusement.

"You are being foolish, sir. It would break your head…" Her mouth began to curve at the corners.

"I don't think so. I never met a woman yet who could hit a barn door at ten paces, but I had forgot. You have had some practice with your trusty brick. Had I remembered it earlier I should not have offered you the jug."

"Now you are gammoning me, my lord."

"Do you mind?" He reached out a hand and ruffled her hair. "Sometimes the temptation to do so is irresistible. Now off you go and take the scissors with you."

"Yes, sir."

Wentworth looked thoughtful. "And Prudence, there is one more thing. You must learn to be more careful. Fortunately, I have no designs upon your person…"

"I…I never thought you had, my lord." She was scarlet with embarrassment.

"Well, there is no harm done, but another time, and with another man, you might find yourself in difficulties. A brick is not always readily available, you know." His chuckle brought an answering smile from her.

"That is unfair!" she reproached. "I should not have

told you of the way I stopped the overseer. Will you not forget it, sir?''

''On the contrary, it is often at the forefront of my mind. You may rest assured that your virtue is safe with me.'' His lips twitched. ''Are we friends again?''

She nodded.

''Off you go, then. If Sam comes in and finds you here he will be scandalised. To date he has been unable to accuse me of snatching a babe from the cradle.''

''I am not a babe!'' she cried indignantly. ''And Sam does not know that I'm a girl…''

''Of course he does. The superintendent told him… Don't let it worry you. Sam may be rough and ready, but he's a model of discretion.'' A hand reached out to rest upon her shoulder and he pushed her gently towards the door. ''We dine in an hour,'' he said. ''Hurry, or you will have no time to make use of those scissors.''

Prudence needed no further persuasion. Working quickly, she soon fashioned a skirt from the roll of cloth. She had no time to do more than to secure the seams with running stitches, praying that they would hold.

The bodice was more difficult. She solved the problem by cutting a length of fabric, folding it, and making a slit for her head. The result was a disaster. Throwing caution to the winds she slashed at the neck and folded back the edges to make a v-shape. A triangle made from the remaining fabric served as a fichu, and helped to hide the makeshift effort. She caught it at the bosom with her brooch.

The finished garment was barely passable, but certainly it was more comfortable to wear a skirt again. The colour suited her, and she had lost the haunted look which made her eyes look much too large in the delicate face.

She glanced in the mirror. Wentworth would be forced

to admit that she was not a child, though, of course, his opinion could not matter in the least.

Even so, she was gratified by his look of surprise.

"Well done!" he said. "I foresee that you might make your fortune as a mantua maker, Prudence. Was I not right to insist upon the blue? It becomes you well."

Unused to compliments, she blushed at his remarks, but the moment passed as Dan engaged him with questions about the design of the carriage.

It gave her time to recover her composure. It wavered again later when she found the deep-set eyes studying her intently.

"Sir, is something wrong?" she asked at last.

"Not at all! Was I staring? I beg your pardon, but I have not seen you in a gown before. You look very different."

"More feminine?" she asked hopefully. It was pleasant to bask in the glow of his admiration, but his next words brought her down to earth.

"By the heavens, you women are all alike! Give you a new gown and you are all charm and fragility." He grinned at her. "What happened to the termagant I knew?"

"What's a termagant?" asked Dan.

"A fearsome creature who makes men shudder in their boots." Wentworth's voice was solemn.

"Oh, Prudence can do that," Dan told him. "Superintendent Henshaw walked the other way when he saw her coming."

"Amazing!" Wentworth mused. "Why was that, I wonder?"

"Pru always does what she says she'll do. She told him she'd be sick if he made her finish up the gristle on her plate. He did, and she was...all over him!"

"Fascinating!" A quiver of emotion disturbed for a moment the gravity of his lordship's expression. "A warning to the entire male sex, I make no doubt."

"Dan, how could you?" Prudence threw him a goaded look. "Must you tell these stories?"

"Well, it's true, isn't it? I thought that it was splendid."

"Whatever you may think, it is not a suitable subject for the supper-table." Her look of reproof was intended to discourage Dan from making further revelations, but he did not notice. He was about to speak again when Wentworth intervened.

"I've been admiring your brooch," he told Prudence. "It's most unusual. May I take a closer look at it?"

In silence Prudence handed it to him.

As he felt the weight of the medallion his expression changed. "Gold?" he said in an altered tone. "How came you by this?" The question was apparently casual, but she was quick to notice the suspicion in his eyes.

"I did not steal it, if that is what you mean," she told him in haughty tones. "It was found among my clothing when I was abandoned."

"It's an heirloom," Dan confided. "Prudence says so. I wish I had one like it. Not a brooch, of course, but perhaps a watch and chain…"

"You haven't got the stomach for a watch and chain." Wentworth laughed. "It will come in time and to help it along you must eat more of this curd pudding." He pushed the dish towards Dan, but Prudence sensed that his thoughts were elsewhere.

A wild hope seized her. "Sir, have you seen this crest before?" she asked.

Wentworth shook his head. "One crest is much like

another. I may have seen something similar in the past, but I don't recall the occasion.''

''Oh, please, my lord, will you not try to remember?'' In her excitement she sprang to her feet and as she did so there was an ominous tearing sound.

Looking down she could see that the stitches in the hastily sewn seam had given way. The fabric of her skirt gaped wide, revealing a shapely leg from thigh to ankle.

Wentworth was equal to the occasion. He dispatched Dan at once to fetch his dressing-gown. Then he turned to Prudence.

''Sit down!'' he ordered. ''The chambermaid will attend to your skirt.''

Prudence was close to tears. Her humiliation was complete, but his lordship did not laugh, nor did he look at her again. Instead he strolled across the room to pull upon the bell-rope.

Minutes later she was seated once more at the dining-table, clad in the red silk dressing-gown. The luxurious feel of the soft material was seductive, but it was poor compensation for her shame.

''Cheer up! All is not lost! The chambermaid will stitch the seams for you,'' Wentworth said soothingly, but she would not look at him. He decided to change the subject.

''I've been wondering about the crest upon your brooch,'' he murmured. ''It would not be impossible to trace it…''

He had her full attention at once. The disaster to her gown was forgotten as she leaned towards him.

''How?'' she demanded.

''There are books on heraldry…and one might make enquiries, though there is no guarantee of success.''

''You know of such a book?''

"I own one," he admitted. "That may be where I saw the crest…"

Something in his tone made her suspect him of evasion. She was beginning to feel that he knew more than he was prepared to reveal.

It could not be true that one device was much like another, else why would the nobility set such store upon their own? Had Wentworth recognised the emblem? She could not be sure, though it seemed far beyond the bounds of possibility that she should meet by chance a man who could help her in her quest.

And she could not blame him if he still mistrusted her. A valuable brooch was the last thing he might expect to find in the possession of an orphan girl. It was no wonder that he'd thought that she had stolen it.

It did not matter what he thought, she told herself with a little spurt of anger. Then honesty compelled her to admit that it wasn't true. She wanted him to think well of her and…well…to admire her.

There was little hope of that. Not only had she accused him of being a murderer, but some inner turmoil made her fight with him incessantly. Instead of gratitude she'd offered only rebellion and sharp words.

And only that evening she'd burst in upon his privacy without a by-your-leave and snapped at him when she was in the wrong.

She blushed deeply at the memory of that distressing confrontation in his bedchamber. How fortunate that he was a gentleman. Most of the other men of her acquaintance would have taken full advantage of the opportunity to tumble her upon the bed.

He'd been quick to assure her that he had no designs upon her person. It was a relief, though at the same time it was somewhat mortifying.

"Prudence, you are miles away...won't you come back to us?" Wentworth addressed her with a question in his eyes.

"I beg your pardon," she said hurriedly. "I find that I am tired, sir. Will you excuse me if I leave you?"

"It's time we were all abed," he agreed. "Tomorrow we must leave betimes. I'd like to cross the river before noon."

"The river?" Dan's eyes shone with anticipation.

"The River Thames. There will be much for you to see upon the water...barges, ferrymen and, best of all, the tall ships. If you fall asleep, you'll miss the sight."

"I won't do that, my lord. I'll go to bed this instant." He hurried away.

Prudence rose from her chair. Then she hesitated.

"You have a problem?" Wentworth asked.

"No, sir, but Dan is not used to sleeping alone. He has never done so in his life. At the mill he shared an attic with the others. If he should have another nightmare...?"

"I thought of that. His chamber leads into yours. Why not leave the connecting door ajar?"

"You must think me foolish beyond permission."

"No, I think you sensible of your responsibilities."

"Please don't think me ungrateful, my lord. It was good of you to bespeak a room of my own for me."

"Young ladies do not share a bedchamber, even with a twelve-year-old boy," he told her lightly.

Her colour rushed up again, and it was in some confusion that she left him.

On the following day Wentworth took a seat in the coach beside her, leaving Dan to ride upon the box with Sam.

She could not feel at ease with him, and he was quick to sense it.

"It's only for the first part of the journey," he explained. "Dan's happy in his favourite perch and I wish to speak to you in private."

Prudence smoothed her skirt. It had been returned to her that morning neatly stitched, and the bodice had been fashioned into a more becoming style. Now she studied her fingers, waiting for the questions which she guessed must follow.

"Have you thought about your future?" Wentworth asked. "What will you do when we reach Kent?"

"I must find employment, sir. At the fair in Stamford I saw men and women waiting in the street. They seemed to be offering themselves for hire."

"They were. The farmers come to town to bind them to a contract for a year or more."

"I could do the same."

"Could you? Did you not notice that all of them wore something to indicate their skills?"

"You mean on their jackets? Yes, I did. I wondered at the time..."

"And what would you wear, Prudence?"

She stared at him in dismay. "I...I don't know."

"Well, it cannot be a battleaxe, though that would be most suitable. Can you milk a cow, or wring a chicken's neck?"

"No...but I could learn," she told him stiffly.

"Pray do not consider it. Life on the land is hard. You'd be exchanging one form of slavery for another."

She looked at him uncertainly. "I thought of trying the inns at Canterbury, my lord. I was used to wait on table at the vicarage."

Wentworth looked surprised. "Then you were not always in the spinning mill?"

"Not always. When there was a fever in the village some of the vicar's servants died. He asked if I would go to him."

"You weren't afraid of the fever?"

"Oh, no, I'm never ill."

"And the superintendent did not object to losing you?"

A mischievous smile lifted the corners of her mouth. "He was glad to be rid of me. He said…"

"Yes?"

"Well, he said that the vicar would be better advised to wear a hairshirt if he wished to suffer."

Wentworth's laugh rang out. "What a reputation!" he teased. "Were you happier at the vicarage?"

"Oh, yes, but it was not for long. They were short-handed at the mill as well, but at least I learned something about the running of a household. It was not so difficult to make sure that everything was kept in order, so, you see, some innkeeper might employ me…"

"And Dan? Is he to be a pot-boy or a turnspit?"

"A turnspit? What is that?"

"A boy who sits beside a blazing fire for hours on end, roasting himself as well as the meat which turns upon the spit."

"He shan't do that!" Prudence said decisively. "A pot-boy might be better."

"I must doubt it. Would you have him at the mercy of some ill-tempered creature who worked him until he dropped?"

"We are both used to that, my lord."

"But I thought you wished to escape a life of drudgery?"

"We do." She sighed with exasperation. "I wish you will not throw cold water upon all my plans. I know it will be hard at first, but nothing could be worse than the life we left behind."

"Don't be too sure of that!" Under their heavy lids his eyes were veiled, but they did not leave her face.

She could not guess what he was thinking, but under his scrutiny she felt uneasy. In some curious way he seemed to be assessing her and she did not like it.

It was fortunate that she could not read his mind. The female sex held few secrets as far as Wentworth was concerned, but this girl was unusual. She spoke with a frankness which he had not found in any other woman, and he could not doubt her courage.

She had some quality…something more than mere looks. Child though she was, it would draw men to her like flies to a honeypot. It was unthinkable that she should seek employment at an inn. She would not last a week before some man would force his attentions on her, and a refusal would probably mean dismissal.

"Not an inn!" he said sharply. "You must think of something else…"

Prudence glared at him. "You've already pointed out that I can't join the navy, sir. Must I try the army?"

"Don't be pert! We shall think of something. I'll give it my consideration."

A plan was already forming in his mind, but it was too soon to speak of it. Another person was concerned. He must consult with her before the decision could be made.

"There isn't much time," Prudence told him. "I must start to earn at once."

"Did you earn nothing at the mill?"

"They were supposed to pay us. I think it should have

been a shilling or two each week, but there were fines for everything. We never saw the money. Mrs Henshaw said that they were saving it, in case we frittered it away…''

''On what?''

''I'd have spent mine on food,'' she said quickly. ''Dan was always starving…''

''He is already making up for that.'' Wentworth gave her the queer disarming smile which was peculiarly his own, and suddenly she felt breathless.

She turned her head away. She was growing foolish. This was not the time to lower her guard, allowing herself to be lured into trusting this enigmatic creature.

''Whatever I do, it will not be for long,'' she murmured.

The remark was incautious and he picked it up at once. Realising that he would learn nothing by challenging her direct, he approached the subject from another angle.

''I found the story of your brooch intriguing,'' he said lightly. ''How strange that it should have been hidden in your clothing!''

Her head went up at once and she gave him a straight look. ''Have you remembered where you saw the crest before, my lord?''

''Sadly, I have not. You believe it to be significant?''

''It must be! It was not hidden there by chance.''

''There was nothing else to give some indication?''

''Only a broadsheet, printed in Kent…'' Her hand flew to her mouth. She had given herself away and she knew it. Wentworth's next words confirmed it.

''You have not been honest with me, Prudence.'' His voice was grave. ''Why did you not tell me your true reason for wishing to come to Kent?''

"Why should it concern you? You cannot help me, but if you had recognised the crest you might have warned others against me. I had to take that chance."

He ignored the accusation. "I see it now. You are determined to find your natural parents. Is that wise?"

"Spare me the arguments, my lord. I heard them from the vicar. It may not be wise, but it is what I intend to do."

"But how can it profit you? When a child is abandoned…"

"I don't expect you to understand. Doubtless you can trace your ancestry for generations. I don't know who I am. It is like living in limbo. I can think of nothing else."

"But what can you hope for if you succeed? Money, perhaps…?"

"I don't want money," she replied in icy tones. "I would not take it if it were offered, but I need to know my parentage."

"You might be disappointed," he warned.

Her smile was bitter. "There can be no doubt of that. Who would leave a week-old child in the doorway of a church, not knowing if it would be found before it died of cold and hunger?"

"Then you seek revenge?"

Faced with the question Prudence felt confused. "I don't know," she admitted. "I want to confront my mother and to know the story of my birth…. To find out why…?"

"You could be the cause of much unhappiness."

"And what is that compared with mine? I have told you something of my life, Lord Wentworth. You do not know the whole…"

He reached out to rest his hands upon her shoulders. "I know that you have suffered, but will you let hate destroy you? You are strong. You do not need it to sustain you."

"I have nothing else." She pulled away from him, resolved that his words should not soften her determination.

"But you have, if you would but see it. Have you considered how this search may end?"

Prudence was silent. She would not argue with him further. Nothing he had said had changed her mind. She and Dan must survive. That was her immediate objective. Later she would decide on a further course of action.

Chapter Five

At the first staging post he offered her refreshment. Then he took the reins again, leaving her to her own thoughts.

They were not pleasant. She felt troubled and confused and also a little frightened by the prospect of what might lie ahead.

During these last few days she had come to rely on Lord Wentworth to a degree that she had not realised until she was forced to face the fact that their parting could not be far distant.

It was agreeable to travel in such comfort, secure in the knowledge that for the moment she and Dan were safe. Wentworth's air of authority combined with his obvious wealth would always smooth his path in life, she thought with some resentment. She doubted if he would ever understand how others were forced to exist.

Yet that was unjust. She has seen his expression as he listened to her story. Anger had mingled with pity in his eyes, but would he help her further?

She had no idea how he could do so, though she was beginning to believe that for his lordship nothing was impossible. Her head went up proudly. If he tried to offer her money she would not take it. It would be an insult...a blow to her self-respect. Then common sense returned. She could not let Dan starve.

She pressed her fingers to her temples, trying in vain to think of some solution. Her thoughts were going round in circles.

If only Wentworth had not dismissed her suggestions out of hand. Until then her hopes of finding employment had been high, but his advice could not be ignored. He was right. Without experience she had little to offer in the workplace.

It was a lowering thought, and she thrust it from her mind at once. If she gave way to despair, both she and Dan would perish.

She tried to rouse herself. She had been lucky. With Wentworth's help they would be in Kent by nightfall. The thought of reaching their destination should have cheered her, but it didn't, and the reason was not far to seek.

Honesty compelled her to admit that she would miss his lordship's greeting in a morning, his laughter, and even his teasing manner. In his company the world took on a different aspect. Everything about her seemed new and vivid. Life without him would be bleak indeed.

She forced her wandering thoughts into safer channels. If she was now in charity with Wentworth, it was simply gratitude. He'd been kind to Dan, and it was the relief of knowing that the boy was in safe hands which had caused her to think better of their rescuer.

His lordship's charm was undeniable, but she found it difficult to understand him. Doubtless his decision to take them up had been a whim, but the novelty would not last. She'd heard stories of the gentry, and had marvelled at their eccentricities. Wentworth, she suspected, would drop them with casual unconcern when he tired of his unlikely charges.

Well, it would soon be over. Then he need trouble himself no longer.

She must have dozed for several hours. When she awoke it was to find that they'd left the countryside behind. Now they were passing through mean streets and she looked about her in surprise. Surely this could not be London?

In her imagination she has always thought of it as a city of gleaming gold, with fine palaces and churches to delight the eye. The huddle of filthy hovels by the roadside was divided only by narrow alleyways piled high with dirt and excrement. The stench was appalling, and she was forced to hold a handkerchief to her nose.

Sullen faces stared at the carriage as it passed along the road, reminding her of the beggars who'd attacked them. These people were as ragged and as watchful as the thieves, apart from those who lay prone in the gutters.

At first she though that they were sick. Dying perhaps from some outbreak of fever? Then she heard wild laughter as a group of men and women tumbled out in to the road, and she realised that they were almost insensible with drink.

Wentworth swerved to avoid them, but their curses followed him long after they had been left behind. She looked back to find that the revellers had joined the others in the gutters.

She recovered her spirits as the carriage moved on towards the heart of the city. London must be enormous, she decided. Here the buildings were all that she had dreamed of. In the distance she could see St Paul's Cathedral and also the Tower of London.

Then they were crossing the river—as Wentworth had foretold, it was a fascinating sight. She marvelled at the traffic on the water as ferrymen shot from one bank to the other, avoiding lighters, barges and the great ships which had the right of way.

Her eyes followed in their wake with wonder, trying to guess where they were bound as they sailed down river towards the open sea.

Perhaps when her quest was ended she and Dan might take passage on one such ship. Life might be very different in another land. If she could save enough…? The idea gave her thoughts a new direction.

When they reached Southwark, Wentworth stopped to bait the horses.

"There is still some way to go," he said. "And, as always, Dan is hungry. We'll eat here."

The stop did not delay them long, and when they resumed their journey Wentworth rejoined Prudence.

"My home is to the south of Canterbury," he told her. "I plan to avoid the city by taking the country roads."

"I see. Then, sir, if you will set us down at some convenient point we shall find our way from there."

He shook his head. "I won't leave you by the roadside. It will be nightfall soon. You had best come with me, for tonight, at least."

An enormous feeling of relief swept over her. She need not shoulder her burden just yet, but it was not right to impose upon him further.

Her indecision showed upon her face. "My lord, you need not—" she began.

"I know that I need not," he intervened. "But I wish to do so. Come, Prudence, you must be reasonable. You cannot wander about in darkness in a place you do not know."

"But, sir, your wife? We may not be welcome…"

"I have no wife, and my mother will most certainly make you welcome. Now let us have no more argument. Are we agreed?"

Her eyes filled. "Thank you!" she choked out.

"Great heavens, Prudence, don't destroy my faith in you! I came prepared for anger in return for my untoward suggestion, but not for tears…"

She managed a watery smile. "Now you are making game of me," she reproached.

"Perish the thought! Would I dare to do so? A black eye would be my just reward…that is, after you had flown into your high ropes and had me quaking in my boots…" His eyes were twinkling.

At that she laughed aloud.

"That's better! Do you know, that is the first time I've seen you laugh…really laugh, I mean. You should do it more often. It's a great improvement."

"I go into whoops quite often, sir…when there is anything to laugh at."

"You will find a good deal to amuse you at Hallwood…if the place is still standing."

Prudence grew serious at once. "Oh, sir, do you fear an accident?"

He grinned at her. "Not exactly, but my dear mama has a passion for building. I am never too sure that I shall find one stone standing upon another."

He was teasing again, trying to divert her, and she found herself laughing with him.

"Is yours a large family?" she asked shyly.

"I have an older brother, but Frederick dislikes country life. He cannot tear himself away from Whitehall. Peregrine is the youngest. Then there is my sister, Sophie, but she is married and lives in France."

His face changed, and she was at a loss to understand his altered tone. Possibly his sister was ill. She had no wish to pry.

He was silent for some time. Then he looked up and saw her worried expression.

"Forgive me!" he murmured. "I am a poor companion, but Sophie is much upon our minds at present."

"She is not well, my lord?"

"It is not that. You must have heard of the present troubles in France?"

"No, sir. News was slow to reach us in the north of England. In any case, we were not told of what was happening in the outside world."

"There's been a revolution," he explained. "Some weeks ago the mob stormed the Bastille."

"The Bastille? What is that?"

"It's a fortress, used for holding prisoners. They promised quarter to the Governor if he surrendered..." Wentworth's face grew dark. "Instead they murdered him and those of his men who would not join them."

"How horrible! But, my lord, your sister would not be near that place..."

"No, she was not in the city at the time, but heaven alone knows where it will end. There is rioting throughout the country, with peasants shouting for liberty, brotherhood and equality. They are burning and killing as they go."

"Is nothing to be done? The King—?"

"King Louis is helpless. He can place no reliance on

his troops. Most of the army is disaffected. The law is flouted everywhere…''

''And you think your sister may be in danger?''

''No person of means is safe, least of all an aristocrat. That is why I came down from the north. I must fetch Sophie back to England.''

''That would be best,'' she agreed. ''She must be terrified, but you will bring her back to safety, I'm sure of it.''

He looked so grave that she longed to comfort him…to banish his sombre thoughts. Then he gave her a crooked little smile, sensing what she found it hard to put into words.

''Have you such faith in me?'' he asked lightly.

Her colour rushed up at that. ''I believe you will do what you set out to do,'' she murmured in confusion.

''Then we are two of a kind. Let us leave this distressing subject. I must not burden you with my problems. You have enough of your own…''

''But I like to hear about families,'' she said warmly. ''It must be wonderful to have brothers and sisters, and…and a mother.''

''You will like her. She has a gentle heart, and Hallwood is well known as a refuge…''

''Sir?''

''My mother keeps open house,'' he explained. ''She seems to have taken over the work of the old monasteries before King Henry destroyed them. No one is turned away, deserving or not. There is always food for the needy. I believe they put a mark upon the gates to show others that help is always to be had.''

Prudence saw the twinkle in his eyes, and she begged him to go on.

''You'll find the oddest characters about the place,''

he continued. "Some are permanent residents. Naturally, my mother assures me that they earn their keep. Doubtless those I find dozing in the gardens are recruiting their strength before a next assault upon the weeds!"

She laughed at that, pleased to see that his mood had lightened.

"Perhaps your sister is not in the danger you imagine?" she offered shyly.

"Possibly not. Gilles, her husband, is the best of men. His workers are well treated, against the usual way of things in France."

"Then may they not protect him and his family?"

"I cannot say. Pressures may be brought to bear on them from a handful of fanatics. I won't be satisfied until I see the situation for myself." He looked out into the dusk. "We are almost there. Soon you will be able to rest."

Prudence followed his glance to find that the coach was turning off the road through a pair of massive ornamental gates, supported by stone pillars.

Each pillar was crowned by the oval sculpture of some fruit which she did not recognise.

"What are those?" she asked.

"Pineapples!" he told her drily. "They are a well-known symbol of hospitality, and most appropriate, I feel, although my mother was indignant when I teased her."

Prudence caught his eye, and went off into peals of laughter as the comic implications struck her. Then he was laughing too, his eyes warm with affection for the person who was the cause of all this merriment.

They were moving swiftly down a long straight avenue lined with beeches, and sensing that they were close to home the horses picked up their pace.

Then Prudence caught her first sight of the house. For a moment she was dazzled. The last rays of the setting sun had caught the windows, turning them to flame. She caught her breath. The place seemed to be afire with reddish light.

As the carriage rounded the curved forecourt in front of the building, she was able to appreciate its situation. Nestling closely in the shelter of the hillside, it was long and low, and well protected from the east winds.

She guessed that the main part of the house was very old, but there were a number of additions. Wings had been built on, but they were in keeping with the original structure, though one of them was clearly recent.

Wentworth chuckled. ''My mother at the peak of her enthusiasm,'' he explained. ''I tell her that she is a second Bess of Hardwick. I don't think it detracts, do you? She has followed the intentions of the earliest builders.''

''It's beautiful!'' Prudence sighed with pleasure. ''How happy you must be to live here! It looks so peaceful.''

''I hope that you may find it so,'' he joked. ''I've noticed that tranquillity flees at your approach.''

A sharp retort died on her lips as the great door opened and a woman came down the steps towards them. She was almost as tall as Wentworth and she had the same dark eyes. Now they were alight with pleasure.

''Sebastian! At last! My dear, you can't imagine how I've longed to see you.''

Wentworth sprang down from the coach and enveloped her in a bear hug, dropping a kiss upon her cheek.

''Are you well, my dearest? I confess that I'm relieved to see that our four walls are still standing…''

She smiled at the raillery, but then her face grew

grave. "I haven't the heart to think of anything but Sophie. Oh, love, I have so much to tell you…"

"And I you." Wentworth turned to hand Prudence down from the carriage. "This is Prudence Consett. If you have no objection, she will stay with us for this one night at least. Prudence, this is my mother, the Dowager Countess Brandon…"

Prudence felt uneasy as the dark eyes inspected her. There was no warmth in that look. Was this the gentle creature who welcomed those in need?

She tugged at Wentworth's sleeve. "If it is not convenient, we can go on to Canterbury," she murmured in a low voice.

"Nonsense! Dan, come here…!" Wentworth walked round to the box and lifted up his arms. "Jump!" he ordered. "This, my dear Mama, is another friend of mine. He, too, will stay with us tonight. He and Prudence have had a long and tiring journey, so I suggest that we go indoors."

Dan was dropping with exhaustion and her ladyship's expression softened. She moved ahead of them to lead the way through a long low hall and into a pleasant sitting-room.

"Ring the bell, Sebastian!" she said quietly. "Your friends will wish for some refreshment." Her words were civil enough, but her voice was cold and Wentworth looked surprised, though he made no comment.

Prudence was under no illusions. They were not welcome here. Her cheeks were burning. It wasn't difficult to read her ladyship's mind. She suspected her son of bringing some lightskirt into her home. Prudence could not blame her. Gentlemen did not normally travel in the company of an unknown girl without some ulterior motive.

She did not look at the hastily summoned servant. Then Wentworth addressed his mother.

"I believe that Dan and Prudence will prefer to see where they are to sleep before all else. Where is Ellen to bestow them?"

Lady Brandon flushed, but a glance at her son's face persuaded her to think it wiser not to refuse his request. She gave her instructions at once, but as Dan and Prudence left the room they heard her clear tones.

"Sebastian, what are you about? Who is this girl?"

They did not hear his reply, and it was perhaps as well. When he spoke it was only filial devotion which prevented him from giving full vent to his anger.

"You disappoint me, ma'am. Prudence is not what you imagine. Would I insult you by asking you to receive a woman with whom I had an illicit connection?"

His mother looked at his set face. "You have never done so, but this is all so strange. Where did you meet these people? The girl is not in the common way... There is something about her...something which I cannot place..."

"I don't think her beautiful in the least."

"No, she is not, but she has something beyond mere beauty. Do you not see it?"

"Her looks are well enough, but, my dear, she is a mere child..."

"She must be eighteen. Many girls are married at that age."

"She is seventeen, I believe, but she knows nothing of the world. One might as well point the finger of scorn at a babe-in-arms."

"Sebastian, you have not answered my question. Why did you bring them here?"

"I had little choice. They do not know this part of the country. I could not abandon them."

"My dear boy, you will drive me to distraction. I demand an explanation. How can you be responsible for them?"

Wentworth began to pace the room. "It's a long story," he admitted. "I brought them down with me from Derbyshire."

"For what reason?" His statement did nothing to reassure her ladyship. They must have spent several nights upon the road.

"They are foundlings," he told her shortly. "I took a bend at speed and almost killed the boy. He was playing in the road."

The Dowager Countess paled. "You were not hurt?"

"No, and nor was he, thank God! He suffered only a cut upon the head, though he was unconscious for some time."

"Would it not have been wiser to have left him with his friends?"

"He has none...only Prudence."

"But are not foundlings cared for by the parish? Surely...?"

"The parish sent them at nine years old to a life of slavery in the local cotton mill."

"Slavery? Sebastian, that is coming it too strong. This is seventeen eighty-nine. Such things do not happen in this country."

"Don't they? You must ask them to tell you about their lives. Like you, I had no idea..."

"But they would be apprenticed, would they not, and given food and shelter? Someone would care for them."

"To such an extent that they were forced to run away?"

"Oh, my love, you have not taken up two runaways? Is that not abduction? It must be against the law!"

Wentworth's expression hardened. "A law which condemns young children to a life of misery? I had no scruples about breaking it."

"But what are you to do with them?"

"I don't know yet, but they can't fend for themselves."

Her ladyship grew thoughtful. "No, I see that now, but to bring them so far? Was that wise?"

He grinned at her suddenly. "No, it was not, but they would have come south in any case. That is, if they were not attacked or murdered along the road."

"But why should they wish to come to this part of the world?"

He sat down then and took her hands in his. "Put it down to my curiosity if you will, but there is some mystery about the girl. She wears a brooch which bears a coat-of-arms. With it she hopes to trace her family."

Lady Brandon was startled. "Did you recognise it?"

"I can't be sure, but I think so. I lied, saying that one such device was much like another. I don't know if she believed me."

"Then, who…?"

"No, I shall not tell you. It is merely a suspicion. I should need to know much more before I can be certain."

With that she was forced to leave the subject, though she shook her head at him. "More lame dogs, my dear?"

"Say rather a kitten and a puppy!" His eyes were teasing. "Is not this a case of the pot calling the kettle black? I am most truly your son, you know. Would you not have done the same?"

She bridled. Then, disarmed by his amusement, she patted his hand.

"Have you no respect for your aged mother?" she asked.

"I have, though aged is not a word I would use to describe her."

"Flatterer!"

"I mean it. You are still a great beauty, my dear."

"I don't feel it at the moment. Oh, Sebastian, the news from France is getting worse. I am so afraid for Sophie and her children." She signed heavily. "Perhaps that is why I was not as kind to your foundlings as I might have been."

Wentworth threw an arm about her shoulders. "I knew there was something on your mind. Tell me, has Perry been over to see Sophie?"

"He is but just returned. I should have dissuaded him. Foreigners, and especially the English, are unwelcome there, but I was desperate for word of her."

"And what did he find?"

"Both Sophie and Gilles believe that they are in no present danger, but it is all so uncertain. The situation changes from day to day. Gilles has great faith in the loyalty of his people, but the tide of feeling in the country is so strong."

"It's hardly to be wondered at. For centuries the peasants have been heavily taxed whilst their masters and the clergy pay no tax at all. And what is worse, the nobility think themselves above the law."

"Gilles does not."

"He is an exception, my dearest."

"That may not save him, or my darling Sophie and her children. There have been abuses which should be stopped, but that is no excuse for murder."

"Does Perry share your fears?"

Her worried frown deepened. "He came back in a dreadful rage. Sophie only just restrained him when some fellow addressed her as citizeness. He was about to give the man a thrashing."

"If that is all she has to bear, you need not be afraid for her," Wentworth told her lightly.

"I suspect that it will not be all. Fanatics travel from town to town inflaming the passions of the mob. Perry attended one such meeting in disguise. He did it for a lark. You know what he is like, but even he was shocked by what he heard. Oh, my dear, if only Sophie might come to England…at least until conditions in France improve."

Her son looked grave. "That may take some time. Would Gilles allow her to bring the children for a visit?"

"He might…if you could persuade him."

"Then I'll pay them a visit without delay. I may be able to bring her back with me."

"Oh, Sebastian, if you could! I should not ask it of you, but Perry must not go again. He is such a hot-head. He'd be certain to fall foul of one of these new committees."

"Dearest, you may ask anything you wish of me. I had intended to pay my sister a visit in any case—"

He broke off as Dan and Prudence entered the room.

Prudence advanced towards her hostess with her head held high, but he was quick to notice her uncertainty.

Her ladyship held out her hand. "Come and sit down," she said in a kindly tone. "Sebastian has been telling me about your journey. You must be very tired. Are you comfortably bestowed? Our rooms are always kept in readiness for visitors."

Prudence murmured her thanks. She was embarrassed,

and acutely aware that she and Dan looked out of place in the splendid setting of the drawing-room.

Her ladyship seemed unaware of it. "You will be glad to seek your beds tonight," she continued. "We dined earlier, but Ellen has brought a tray. You will take some refreshment?"

Dan's eyes lit up and Wentworth laughed.

"I should warn you, my dear Mama. This boy has hollow legs. His stomach is a bottomless pit…"

This brought a look of reproach from her ladyship.

"Boys are always hungry. Who should know it better than I? Sebastian, it is unkind of you to tease. You have a hearty appetite yourself."

"That's milled me down! I stand corrected." He glanced at Prudence with a twinkle, and was pleased to see that she was becoming more at ease.

He pressed his mother's hand in wordless gratitude. Then, pretending to be famished, he began to eat, urging Dan and Prudence to follow his example.

Dan needed no persuasion, but Prudence appeared to have lost her appetite. He was about to make some comment but his mother caught his eye and he was silent.

Lady Brandon turned to Dan. Undaunted by his surroundings, he did full justice to the delicacies upon the tray, but his interest in her conversation quickened when she mentioned the new foal, born that very morning.

"Shall I see him?" he questioned her eagerly. "Is he on his feet? What colour is he?"

"So many questions!" Her ladyship chuckled. "Let me take them one at a time. He was on his feet within minutes of his arrival, and you may see him in the morning. He is a beautiful chestnut."

Dan reached out for another macaroon. Then, at a look from Prudence, he withdrew his hand.

Lady Brandon was aware of the exchange.

"Pray don't discourage him," she begged. "The macaroons are very light. They can do no harm."

Realising that he had found an ally, Dan beamed at her, but Prudence shook her head in mock reproach.

"Dan will explode!" she said with a faint smile.

Lady Brandon glanced at her. She smiled in reply, but this girl would not be easily won over. She had known it from the moment of their meeting.

Wentworth was well aware of the tension between the two women. He had a sudden inspiration. Stretching out his long legs he leaned back in the wing chair and closed his eyes.

"I'm glad that we are come to the end of our adventures," he murmured in a weary voice. "Three days ago we were in greater danger than we might have been in France. These days one cannot travel the roads with any degree of safety—"

"My dear boy! Were you harmed? What happened?"

"We were attacked by a group of beggars. That was when Prudence saved my life, at some risk to her own."

Lady Brandon whitened to the lips. Then she turned to Prudence. "You saved my son? Oh, my dear, how can I ever thank you?"

Prudence blushed. "His lordship exaggerates," she murmured. "Sir, you were in no danger. Your groom was armed—"

"You are mistaken as to the danger. Sam could not have fired into the crowd without the risk of hitting us. Had you not been so quick, we might have been overwhelmed…"

Her ladyship stretched out a shaking hand to Prudence.

"How brave you were!"

"Ma'am, it was nothing. I merely put out a foot to trip the woman."

"Now, Prudence, you shall not dismiss all claim to valour." One lean hand reached out to ruffle her hair. "I appreciated it, if you did not."

"And so do I!" Lady Brandon rose to her feet. "Come, let me show you to your rooms. We shall speak again in the morning."

Wentworth smiled to himself. He had hit upon the one circumstance which would persuade his mother to think more kindly of her unexpected visitors. He was soon proved right.

"You might have explained that Prudence saved your life," she reproached him on her return.

"I had no wish to worry you unduly. In any case, it might have seemed like blackmail. I wanted you to form your own opinion. This is your home. I have no right to foist them on you if you find them unacceptable."

"Unacceptable? My dear, I am ashamed. I was less than gracious when they first arrived. I shall not easily forgive myself."

"You are not to blame. It must have been a shock to see a young girl travelling in my carriage."

"It was. That is what surprised me."

"And now? Will you give me your opinion?"

"The boy is a merry little soul, but Prudence seems so distant. Do you not find her so?"

He laughed then. "Distant? That is an understatement. She is prickly, difficult and proud, and possessed of an iron will."

His mother's eyes went to his face. "Yet you like her?"

"Yes, I do! I admire her spirit. It is amazing, especially when one considers how she has been treated. A lesser character would have been crushed.''

''I understand. But what is to happen to her now?''

Wentworth hesitated. ''I don't know. I've been trying to think of something. I hoped you might advise me...''

Her ladyship studied her fingers. ''It will be difficult. But I think you have no wish to turn them out.''

''I can't. How would they survive? As I said before, I won't abandon them.''

''Of course not. You owe her so much...''

''Then you will allow them to stay?''

''That would be one solution, but what are they to do? Prudence does not strike me as a girl who will accept charity, however well meant.''

He frowned. ''You are right, but—''

''I am sure of it. She is not in the common way at all. You may be right about her ancestry. Have you noticed her features and her beautiful hands? They are not those of a peasant girl. She speaks well and, in spite of her past life, I cannot fault her excellent manners. You do not find it hard to believe her story?''

''Prudence is not a liar,'' Wentworth said harshly. ''Apparently the local parson took an interest in her. She has learned from him. He saw her quality and did his best for her.''

''Then what now?''

He was silent for some time. ''I don't know. She spoke of finding field work, or seeking employment at some inn, but it would not serve.''

''I agree.''

Her son gave her a straight look. ''Would you consider making her your paid companion?''

''My dear boy!'' His mother's expression changed. ''Do I need a companion? I am not yet in my dotage!''

"I know it well." Wentworth began to smile. "But, dearest, you always do too much. Prudence might fetch and carry for you, and she tells me that she knows something about the running of a household."

"Is she able to read and write?"

"I don't know. I didn't ask her…"

"Very well. I'll see her in the morning, though I doubt if she will wish to stay here."

"You might mention that you will be much in need of help if Sophie brings her babes to stay with you," he said slyly. "Prudence has a gift with children."

His mother gave him a quizzical look.

"Pray don't allow her brusqueness to deceive you," he said quickly. "Prudence has learned to hide her feelings behind a mask of indifference. She does not dare to let it slip."

"It is scarcely to be wondered at. The vulnerable must be always on their guard." For a few moments she was lost in thought. "I'll mention Sophie to her," she said at last. "Though we can't be sure that Gilles will let her come to us. I wrote to him as soon as Perry returned. Perhaps we should wait for his reply before you go. I don't wish him to think that I am an interfering mother-in-law."

"He'd never think that!" Wentworth threw an affectionate arm about her shoulders. "He'll understand your concern. When do you expect to hear?"

"Within a day or two. I sent Tollard with the letter."

"The lawyer's son?"

"Yes, he has some French, and he's a steady fellow. He understood that I could not send Perry back again."

"Quite right! Now go to bed, my love. You have done all you can. You must leave the rest to me."

Chapter Six

It was in no easy frame of mind that she climbed the stairs. The situation troubled her. Sebastian was a kindly man, but he was also a respecter of the law. It must have taken some powerful emotion to persuade him to break it by taking up these two young runaways.

Their story had shocked him, as it had herself, but was pity enough? She found herself wondering if he had examined his true motives. His warm defence of Prudence had startled her. He had left her in no doubt that the girl's character had impressed him.

After all, she had saved his life. That must put him forever in her debt. She herself would not forget it, but the incident had blinded him to the dangers of keeping the girl beneath his roof.

True, he appeared to think of her as no more than a child. His manner towards Prudence was friendly, but nothing more. Sadly, children grew up and Prudence might conceive a *tendre* for him, if only out of gratitude for her deliverance.

It was all most unfortunate, but it would have been impossible not to agree to his request. Sebastian would have found some other way to help his charges, and it was wiser to keep the girl at Hallwood, where she would be under her own watchful eye.

It was such a pity that Sebastian had not married. So many suitable girls had set their caps at him, dazzled by his charm, his looks and also by his wealth, and urged on by their ambitious mammas. Invariably courteous, his heart had remained untouched.

In fact, she reflected, it was not until today that she had heard him express his feelings about any female quite so openly.

She sighed. Perhaps it was not so strange that Sebastian had avoided marriage. That dreadful business with Amelia must have soured him. Yet to form an attachment for this unknown girl would be nothing short of disaster.

As she submitted to the ministrations of her maid, her heart lay heavy within her breast. Worries about one's children did not lessen even when they were fully grown. She must take some action.

Maria Selincourt might be persuaded to bring her daughters for a visit. Sebastian had not seen the girls since they were children, and if they had but a half of their mother's delightful disposition, he could not fail to be impressed.

On that comforting thought she fell asleep.

When she entered the drawing-room next day, she found Prudence poring over a broadsheet. Evidently the girl could read. That, at least, removed the need to ask humiliating questions.

"Have you breakfasted?" she asked.

"Yes, thank you, ma'am. I will call Dan. We waited only to thank you again and bid you farewell."

"My dear, won't you sit down? Must you rush away

so soon? There is not the least necessity for you to do so.''

''On the contrary, ma'am. Lord Wentworth may have mentioned…I must find employment without delay. We are quite without means, Dan and I, and I must find some way to earn a living for both of us.''

''You could stay here,'' her ladyship suggested.

''No, ma'am. We cannot live on charity.''

''That was not what I had in mind. Prudence, I am in need of help. Sebastian gets so cross with me. He thinks I do too much.''

''But, your ladyship, I have no skills. I can't dress hair, or repair fine lace…''

''Nor can I, but my dresser deals with all such things.''

''You think I might become a chambermaid? I cannot cook, you know.''

''I have another plan. What do you say to becoming my companion? The work would not be difficult.''

Prudence flushed painfully. ''I have no experience. I've never met a companion. What should I be required to do?''

''You might help me with my correspondence. I see that you can read. Do you write a fair hand?''

''Yes, ma'am. The vicar taught me. He said…'' She stopped in confusion.

''Yes?''

''He believed that…he said that…it was a pity to let intelligence go to waste. I'm sorry if it sounds boastful.''

''Not at all. You must have made a good impression on him.''

''He was good to me,'' Prudence told her simply. ''Now I am teaching Dan.''

''You could go on with that.'' A thought occurred to

her. "Then there is the library. Since the death of my late husband it has been much neglected."

"Ma'am?"

"Some of the books are in need of attention. You might check through them. I have no time myself. Then they should be catalogued—"

"Your ladyship, such work would be beyond me. Does it not require expert knowledge?"

"Not to make a simple list. You would soon learn."

Prudence held her breath. To be offered such a position was beyond her wildest dreams, but she hesitated.

"There is Dan," she murmured.

"Dan will make himself useful. Sam will see to that. They are friends, so I hear. That in itself is an achievement." She began to smile.

"Lady Brandon, may I ask you something?"

"Anything, my dear."

"This offer? Is it because Lord Wentworth told you that I saved his life? I wish you will not let that weigh with you. It is not true. He carried pistols, and Sam was on guard. His lordship was in no danger."

"I see that you are determined to be honest with me. Let me be equally so with you. I'd like to keep you here with me. If Sophie comes to us I shall be much in need of help, and Sebastian tells me that you have a gift with children."

Prudence blinked away her tears. She could not mistake her ladyship's sincerity, and to be offered refuge at Hallwood brought an overwhelming sensation of relief. She curtsied.

"If that is what you wish, ma'am, I shall be happy to accept. I cannot tell you—" She broke off then, unable to say more for fear of breaking down completely.

"So we are agreed?" Her ladyship stretched out a

hand to draw Prudence to her feet. "Off you go! You will wish to tell Dan. I believe he's in the stables."

Prudence stumbled blindly out of the room. At that moment she needed time to come to terms with her good fortune. Once out of sight of the main house, she sat down upon a stone bench and gave way to her tears. That Wentworth was behind this splendid offer she could not doubt. Her previous distrust vanished. Now she must admit that he was the best of men.

At last she dried her eyes and made her way towards the stables. There she found Dan upon his knees beside the new foal, with Wentworth watching in amusement.

Dan did not notice her at first. Then, as Wentworth greeted her, he rose to his feet.

"Must we go so soon?" he asked wistfully.

"I have a surprise for you. We are not to go at all." Prudence looked up at his tall companion. "My lord, this is your doing, I believe?"

Dan interrupted before he could reply. "You mean we are to stay here?" At first he didn't understand. "Oh, Pru, you can't mean it…?"

"Yes, I do. Lady Brandon wishes me to help her."

"You agreed?" Wentworth looked down at her with laughing eyes.

"I did, my lord. I am to help with correspondence and also to…to begin to catalogue the library."

"What a relief! I have been overcome with worry about the library."

"You kept those worries to yourself, sir." Prudence gave him an answering smile, but was determined to leave him in no doubt that she knew the true state of affairs.

"I have had other things on my mind." His hands rested lightly on her shoulders. "I'm glad that you've agreed to stay. It's much the wisest course for the present. Shall you be happy here?''

''Of course, my lord. How could it be otherwise? Things might have been so different for us, and we are grateful, Dan and I.'' She turned to the boy beside her. ''What do you say to Lord Wentworth?''

Dan reached up to take his lordship's hand. ''Sir, I like it here. I'm glad you are our friend. May I tell Sam?''

''He'll be glad to hear that he won't lose his assistant.'' Sebastian grinned at him. Then he looked at Prudence, and saw that her lips were trembling.

''Cheer up, my little Amazon! It isn't like you to turn into a watering-pot. Where is my lion-hearted friend?'' Gently, he took her in his arms. ''I promise not to beat you more than once a day whilst you are at Hallwood.''

''Do you often beat your servants, sir?'' Prudence struggled to match his attempt at humour.

''Frequently! What is it they say? 'A woman, a dog, and a walnut tree, the more you beat them, the better they be.' You won't agree with that, of course.''

His arms were still about her, and suddenly she was conscious of the impropriety of their situation. This would not do at all. She tried to move away, blushing as she did so. It was comforting to be held so close within that strong embrace, but past experience had taught her that a light caress could turn to something more…something dark and ugly.

She had found it frightening, but now nothing seemed more natural than to cling to her protector, to be aware of the thudding of the heart so close to hers. She longed to throw her arms about his neck…

She was trembling in the grip of some emotion new

to her and he sensed it instantly, though he mistook the reason.

"You are cold," he said. "You should not be out of doors in that thin gown. Let us find my mother. She will have something to suggest."

Lady Brandon had anticipated his concern. After sending him away to find some occupation, she took Prudence to an airy bedchamber on the first floor of the west wing.

"This was my daughter's room," she explained. "Sophie is grown a little stouter since she had her children. Some of her clothing is sure to fit you."

"But, ma'am, she will not like to think…"

"Nonsense! She will not wear her girlhood gowns again. I kept them just for sentimental reasons. Now, what do you say to this?" She lifted out a high-necked garment in a charming shade of green. The small ruffle at the throat was repeated in the trimming of the cuffs.

"It is much too fine," Prudence answered doubtfully. She had guessed correctly that the fabric was expensive.

"It is warm, my dear. We cannot have you falling ill, and that cotton is unsuitable for cold weather. If we should have a winter like the last?" She shuddered at the memory.

Prudence remembered it well. Those winter months had been the coldest for many a year. In the attic rooms ice had formed thickly on the inside of the windows, and the snow had been too deep for any of them to reach the outside privy. Even so, they had been forced to try.

The bitter weather had taken its toll upon undernourished bodies made weaker by exhaustion and exposure to extremes of heat and cold. Long before the arrival of spring, many of the younger ones had succumbed. Now they lay beneath the earth in the silent graveyard.

That fate should not be hers, she thought grimly. What would Dan do without her? She swallowed her pride and did not argue further as the pile of clothing grew.

By the end of that morning she was the bewildered owner of a heavy woollen hooded cloak and several more morning dresses.

"Ma'am, that is more than enough," she protested at last. "I have no need...I mean...I shall make myself ridiculous if I pretend to be a lady."

"Why so?" Lady Brandon was adding undergarments, bedgowns, and even a charming ribboned nightcap. "Your figure is excellent, and if you are to be my companion...well, you must think of my consequence, you know."

Prudence smiled in spite of her misgivings.

"Something amuses you?"

"I beg your pardon. Lord Wentworth said much the same when he too showed me kindness. When we met I was wearing garments taken from a scarecrow. He bought me the blue cambric, saying that it did not suit his dignity to be seen with me in...er...breeches."

"I should think not, indeed. But tell me, why were you dressed as a boy?"

"It was safer, your ladyship. A farmer made advances to me—"

"I understand. There is no need to say more." Indeed there was not, Lady Brandon thought privately. There was something about this girl which would make such advances inevitable. She was surprised that Sebastian had not noticed it.

Thank heavens he thought her still a child, at risk because of her innocence and her youth.

With an effort she turned her mind to the matter in

hand. "There, that will serve you for the present," she said finally. "Shall you wish to change at once?"

"If you please, ma'am. I have worn this gown for days and it is sadly crumpled."

"I think we might dispose of it, don't you?"

"Oh, no!" The protest was immediate. "I should like to keep it, if you please. It will remind me of our journey."

"You do not prefer to forget it? It must have been a dreadful experience."

"It was at first, but then his lordship found us…" Her voice tailed off and she turned away.

Lady Brandon felt disturbed. Prudence might not know it yet, but she was not indifferent to Sebastian's charm. There was danger here. The blue gown was his gift, and as such it would be treasured.

She went downstairs to find Sebastian in the best of spirits.

"When I leave for France I thought I might take Sam and your new man, John," he announced. "Where did you find him, dearest? I've seldom seen such a villainous-looking creature. Apart from that, I can't understand a word he says. Dan had to translate for me."

"John is from the north of England. Pray do not hold his appearance against him. He is a gentle soul."

"I should not have guessed it. He looks well able to give a good account of himself in case of trouble." Wentworth looked up as Prudence came to join them. He was too well-mannered to do more than greet her in his usual calm way, but his surprise was evident.

Prudence felt ill at ease in her borrowed plumage. Her mirror had shown her that the gown was a perfect fit, and the subtle shade of green became her delicate col-

ouring, but his lordship might consider it unsuitable for
an orphan girl.

A glance at his expression convinced her otherwise.
She could not mistake the admiration in his eyes, and
she felt oddly breathless.

"Come in, my dear!" His mother was aware of the
exchange and made haste to change the subject. "Sebastian has been telling me of his plan to leave for
France," she said lightly.

"No, Mother, I was asking you about your latest
henchman…" Sebastian's eyes were twinkling. "Tell
me more!"

"I can't think that it is of any consequence…but if
you must know, John escaped from a press-gang. There
was a fight and one of the men was injured."

"Badly?"

"John does not know."

"So you are harbouring a fugitive?" Wentworth's
shoulders began to shake. "Did I not mention something
about the pot calling the kettle black? And here you
are…with a possible murderer in your service."

"What have I said that is so amusing?" his mother
demanded. "I wish you will be serious."

"I am all concern."

"Well, there is no need to be so. John is as gentle as
a lamb. You cannot expect him to like the idea of being
pressed against his will. Do you wish me to dismiss
him?"

"Not at all. He will suit my purpose very well. He
looks able to give a good account of himself, and he has
one other great advantage…"

"What is that?"

"He must be forty years younger than any of your
other servants." He gave her a wicked look.

"Go away, you odious creature! You are utterly without conduct or propriety of taste."

Wentworth was unrepentant. He kissed his mother's hand. Then, as he passed Prudence he reached out a hand to ruffle her hair.

"How grown-up you look," he said. "That gown becomes you well."

He was gone before she could reply, but her blush did not go unnoticed by Lady Brandon.

Prudence was the first to break the silence.

"Ma'am, when Lord Wentworth goes to France...will he be in danger?"

"We must hope not. He tells me that I must not worry...perhaps he is right." She tried to smile but it was clear that she was unconvinced. "Sebastian is so dear to me. He is sensible, of course, but I am glad that Sam and John are to go with him. You have seen John?"

"No, ma'am."

"He is a great hulk of a man. Sam tells me that he can fell an ox with one blow of his fist." This unusual accomplishment seemed to offer her some comfort. She rose to her feet.

"Let us take nuncheon," she said more cheerfully. "Doubtless we shall hear from Gilles within the week. This afternoon you may see the library and make a start upon your task."

She knew that Prudence needed some diversion. The girl must not be allowed to dwell upon the possible dangers of Sebastian's coming trip to France.

She had misjudged her companion. Beneath the close attention which she was forced to pay to her ladyship's instructions later that afternoon, Prudence felt a sense of dread.

Suppose some accident should befall Lord Wentworth? It did not bear thinking about. The sweetness of his smile, the way his eyes lit up when he was amused? She had learned to take his banter in good part, and even to return it in some measure. Her thoughts were wandering, and Lady Brandon sensed it.

"I must not weary you with too much detail for the present," she said kindly. "Do your best, my dear. You might make a start by looking out the volumes most in need of repair."

Prudence nodded, but when her ladyship had left the library she sat down suddenly and buried her face in her hands. What was happening to her? Until today she had thought only of finding her natural parents. Now it was Wentworth who filled her mind to the exclusion of all else.

She made an effort to recover her composure. If this was gratitude, it was like nothing she had known before. She should not have agreed to stay at Hallwood, she thought sadly. Yet it was such an opportunity, and the alternative was too horrible to contemplate.

She dared not attempt to look into the future, but her present good fortune could not last. Wentworth would marry in time. It was unlikely that his wife would look with any favour upon a pair of foundlings.

A feeling of desolation threatened to overwhelm her, but she thrust it aside and made a start upon the books. She would take one shelf at a time, and examine the dustiest volumes first.

Lady Brandon had explained that she must look for signs of damp or insect damage. She soon discovered a bloom of mould upon some of the fine morocco leather covers, and she laid these to one side. Later she would ask for a cloth to wipe them down.

Some were weighty tomes, and she found it difficult to lift them. Clouds of dust flew out as she opened and then closed them, and without thinking she wiped a grimy hand across her cheek.

After a couple of hours she felt exhausted and she leaned against the table to survey the results of her efforts. The library was large and it was lined with books from floor to ceiling. As she looked at the few shelves she'd cleared, she knew that to catalogue the entire collection would be the work of many months.

At first she had listed the volumes in the loose-leaved book which Lady Brandon had provided for that purpose, but now her hands were too dirty to touch the paper. She found the library steps and pushed them over to the corner. The last three shelves of that section were beyond her reach, but it seemed a pity not to fetch them down that day.

She found that climbing up and down the steps was tiring. Another pair of hands would be a help and she resolved to press Dan into service for the future. With Sam away he would be glad to help her.

She looked up at the top shelf. A single book remained and she was loath to leave it. She mounted the steps again and picked it up. It was heavier than she had expected and she swayed. With both hands occupied it was impossible to hold on either to the ladder or the shelf.

Then the door opened and the sound startled her.

''Prudence!''

At Wentworth's shout she turned and missed her footing. She gave a cry as she tumbled down. Then she was in his arms.

For what seemed a lifetime she lay there trembling. Then he carried her over to a low oak settle.

"Are you trying to kill yourself?" he demanded furiously. "Of all the *stupid* things to do!"

"You startled me!" she snapped. It was easier to fly at him than to admit that she found his touch disturbing. As he held against his massive chest, she seemed to have lost all power of rational thought. It was strange, but her world was bounded by his nearness. She thrust him away and began to struggle to her feet.

Without ceremony he pushed her back against the settle. "Idiot!" he uttered savagely. "If you dare to climb those steps again, you will answer to me."

"My lord, I must examine the books. That is why her ladyship employed me—"

"She did not employ you to break your neck. I did not think you capable of such folly." His face was dark with anger.

"Why should you care?" she cried hotly. "How dare you order me about? You don't own me!"

"That is my only satisfaction. Ever since we met you have been in one scrape or another. It will serve you right if I let you dash your brains out. That is, if you have any at all, which I take leave to doubt."

Prudence glared at him. Her eyes were snapping with rage. Wentworth was being unreasonable. He was making a ridiculous fuss about a tumble. She said as much, and was taken aback when he took a step towards her.

"If you were not a female, I'd give you the thrashing of your life!" His hands were clenched.

"That would help, of course," she told him sweetly. "I'm unhurt, but you seem to be determined that I shall have some bruises."

"You were fortunate not to break a leg," he growled. "What then?"

"I expect you'd have broken the other one, just to teach me a lesson..."

A suspicious quiver touched the corner of his mouth, but he would not be mollified so easily.

"Come here!" he ordered roughly. "You look as if you have been working in a coal mine. Your hands are black with dust, and you have a grimy mark on your cheek. Where is your handkerchief?"

"I haven't got one." Her eyes were defiant.

"Great heavens, are we back in the nursery again? Here, spit on this!" He gave her his own handkerchief.

"Where is the mark?" she demanded.

"Sit still!" He scrubbed none too gently at the offending mark. "That's better. You had best make haste to wash your hands. We dine early in the country."

"Then if you will excuse me, sir?" Prudence stalked away with all the dignity at her command. His lordship had treated her as if she were some recalcitrant child and she felt mortified.

It didn't help to know that she'd been in the wrong. It had been foolish of her to attempt to balance at that height, especially when she was alone, but there was no necessity for Wentworth to be so unpleasant about it. The danger hadn't occurred to her.

Later, it was a relief to find that he hadn't mentioned her mishap. His talk was all of his coming journey to France, making light of possible difficulties, and vowing to bring his sister back to England without delay.

Lady Brandon changed the subject.

"Where is Dan?" she asked.

Wentworth laughed. "In the kitchens, I expect. He's already a favourite with Cook."

"He mustn't be allowed to make a nuisance of himself," Prudence murmured.

"Then keep him with you." His lordship's tone was sharp. "He may climb the steps and hand the books to you."

His mother was startled by his tone. Sebastian's customary good humour appeared to have deserted him. She glanced from one face to the other. Something had happened between these two.

As neither of them seemed disposed to mention the cause of their disagreement, she turned to Prudence.

"My dear, you must not feel obliged to stay indoors all day. Tomorrow you might ask the gardener for some flowers for the house, though there is little for cutting at this time of year."

"If you ask, he may allow you to use the knife yourself, Prudence." Sebastian's tone was sardonic. "There is another opportunity for you to harm yourself."

A look from his mother silenced him.

"Why not take Dan with you?" her ladyship suggested. "You will wish to assure yourself that all is well with him."

"Thank you, ma'am. If you'll excuse me I'll tell him now." Prudence made her escape.

She could not wait to get away from Sebastian. He was being hateful, and all because she had climbed that wretched ladder. His icy sarcasm was too much to bear.

Perhaps he was regretting his offer to let them stay at Hallwood. Well, that was easily remedied. She would speak to Lady Brandon at the earliest opportunity. To leave now would appear ungrateful, but it could not be helped.

"You have upset that child, Sebastian." Her ladyship

frowned at her son. "I am surprised at you. You think she has not suffered misery enough?"

He had the grace to look discomfited. "My apologies, my dear. I am not myself today. I should have left for France at once. My ill humour is nothing to do with Prudence."

"Then why vent it upon her?"

"She is too sensitive," he said roughly. "I can't understand it. In the usual way she is only too ready to fly out at me…"

"You had best make your peace with her," his mother observed. "I won't have quarrelling in my household."

He dropped a kiss upon her brow. "It won't happen again, but why she should take my words so much to heart I can't imagine."

Lady Brandon had no such difficulty. She was beginning to realise that Prudence valued her tall son's good opinion above all else.

Meantime, his lordship went in search of Prudence but he could not find her. He toyed with the idea of sending to her room. Perhaps she had retired to enjoy her misery in private.

He felt aggrieved. By this time she should know him well enough to realise that his manner could be…well…perhaps a little forthright. He had not meant to hurt her feelings, but women were the very devil. They read meanings into the slightest word.

And it did not take long, he thought bitterly. Here was this child, not yet grown to womanhood, and already capable of irritating him like some burr upon his skin.

Yet that was not entirely true. He was forced to admit it in all honesty. There was a freshness about her which was disarming. She had no airs and graces, she was not obsessed with her appearance, nor did she simper and agree with his every word like most of the girls of his acquaintance. With Prudence it would always be straight dealing, however maddening she was at times.

Doubtless with the years she would lose that childlike innocence. Meantime he must watch his tongue. He had hurt her, and he could not understand himself.

That very morning he had awakened in the best of humours—that is, until he had found her in imminent danger of breaking her neck. His anger was well justified, but he should not have allowed it to betray him into a lack of courtesy.

His alarm grew as he realised that she was no longer in the house. He stepped out through the French windows and gazed into the gathering dusk. The wind was chill and he shivered, though not entirely from the cold. Surely she had not taken it into her head to run away again?

Chapter Seven

It was with an overwhelming sense of relief that he heard Dan's laughter from the stables. Prudence would never leave without the boy. He hurried across the stable yard, but Dan was alone.

"I was stroking Foxglove, sir. Sam said that I might do so..." Dan looked anxious as he noticed Wentworth's frown.

"Yes, of course. Have you seen Prudence?"

"I thought she was indoors, my lord."

"Most probably. It is no matter..." He would not alarm the boy, but Prudence must be found.

She could not have wandered far. There had not been time enough for that, but she did not know the grounds. She might trip, or stumble into the stream. Then there was the lake.

He cursed himself for his sharp words as he took the path through the shrubbery. Then he saw her.

She was standing by the wooden bridge, gazing into the water. As he approached she did not move, but he turned her round to face him.

"What a goose you are!" he teased. "I thought you knew me better than to take offence at my ill humour."

"I don't know you at all." Prudence wore a closed expression, but her chin went up and he saw the anger in her eyes. Memory took him back to the moment of their first meeting. Now she wore her courage like a cloak. He guessed at once that she had come to some decision.

"Was I truly hateful?" he said softly. "I am sorry for it. Won't you say that I'm forgiven?"

"There is nothing to forgive," she told him briefly. "You may do and say whatever you wish. I know that I annoyed you."

"You frightened me, my dear. I don't wish any harm to come to you."

"It need not concern you, sir. I see now that I was mistaken in agreeing to stay here. This life is not for me. I shall speak to Lady Brandon in the morning."

"So hasty?" Wentworth glanced at the tense little figure. She had moved away from him and her eyes were intent upon the flowing water of the stream. "To be courageous is one thing, Prudence, but to be a hot-head is another. Don't decide now, when you are angry. Won't you sleep on it?"

"You don't understand." She faced him squarely. "I have been thinking... If I stay, I shall grow accustomed to a life of ease, but Dan and I have our way to make alone... We must do so without delay."

It was but half the truth. Her own reaction to his coldness had dismayed her. In those few moments the bottom had dropped out of her world, leaving her bereft.

Harsh words were nothing new to her. She had endured them all her life, shrugging them aside. This was something different and she was wise enough to see the danger. If she left Hallwood now, she might regain her peace of mind. If she stayed, she would grow more attached to this man who now confronted her, and that would lead to misery.

The present ache in her heart would grow into intolerable anguish. She had no wish to suffer it, and now she had the choice.

"All this for just a few harsh words?" he whispered. "Have you considered Dan? He is so happy here."

She threw him a reproachful look. That was hitting below the belt. He was well aware that Dan must always be her first concern.

"I shall look after him," she said stoutly.

"As you did before? Forgive me, but I must be plain. Would it not be wiser to have something in mind before you leave Hallwood? You cannot allow him to starve."

For the first time she wavered, and he saw the indecision in her face.

"May we not strike a bargain, Prudence? Stay here for a month. I promise that you may bound about on ladders without let or hindrance. I shall place the fieriest steed in my stables at your disposal, and you may drive the gig to your heart's content. No one shall accuse me of cosseting you."

His old disarming smile stole her heart from her breast, and her mouth curved.

"You are gammoning me, my lord."

"I mean every word of it. I shall lay in a good supply of liniment and bandages. Then all will be well..." He slipped her arm through his. "Are we friends again?"

Prudence made no demur, and for the moment he was satisfied, though he suspected that he had lost her trust. It would take some time to win it back again.

All her old defences were back in place, and there was now some intangible barrier between them. He was at a loss to account for it.

"Shall we say a month then? It will soon pass, and your time will not be wasted. As she told you, my mother will be glad of your help when Sophie comes to us. Meantime, I shall make enquiries for you. As I mentioned, we may be able to trace your ancestry."

Her face lit up at once. "Do you mean it, sir? You will do that for me?"

"Only if you cease giving me those dagger-looks," he teased. "Seriously, Prudence, I promise to do my best, but I'd like your word that you will do nothing hasty."

"Sir?"

"I have no wish to search the countryside if you should decide to run away again. My nerves will not stand it."

She laughed at that, and he sensed that some of their old easy relationship had been restored. Absentmindedly he began to stroke the back of her hand with his thumb. "Are we agreed?"

Prudence looked down at the hand which held her own. It was firm and strong and very capable. If anyone could help her solve the mystery of her parentage, it would be Sebastian. She nodded.

"Good! Then let us go indoors. The night air is growing cold."

It was in a much happier frame of mind that she accompanied him back to the house.

On the following day she began to work once more upon her lists. The piles of books around her were sufficient for the moment, and she was soon absorbed in the work.

Unaware that the door had opened, she was startled when a strange voice greeted her.

"Am I interrupting? My mother said that I might introduce myself. I am Sebastian's brother."

Prudence found herself smiling at the impish face.

"Then you must be Mr Peregrine. I'm sorry, sir. I don't know your title."

"Everyone calls me Perry. I say, you do look busy. Is there anything I can do?" He was clearly determined to be friendly, and Prudence liked him at once.

"I am forbidden to climb the ladder," she told him drily. "Yet I don't see how I am to reach the books without it."

"That's no problem!" he told her gaily. "Which ones do you want?" He sprang up the ladder and stood there, laughing down at her.

Prudence looked at him with interest. She guessed that he was not much older than herself, but the family resemblance to both Lord Wentworth and his mother was unmistakable. He had the same dark eyes and clean-cut features, and he was very tall. Yet there was a difference. For a moment she could not place it...something about the mouth, perhaps?

For a time he chatted easily, and with his help the work went quickly, but after a while he grimaced.

"This is dull work, Prudence. I may call you Prudence, may I not? Don't you prefer to be out of doors? I do myself."

"I hear that you are fond of sailing."

"There's nothing like it. To catch the breeze and skim along with the deck of a fine yacht beneath your feet...is like...it's like the flight of a bird. Don't you agree?"

"I don't know. I've never seen the sea."

He was startled by her words, but he made a quick recovery.

"You lived far inland, I suppose? Never mind, it will

be my pleasure to take you to the coast. You do ride, don't you?''

''I'm afraid not.'' It was becoming clear that Perry knew nothing of her past life. Lady Brandon must have intended to be tactful, but it would not do to let this young man think her other than she was.

''Sir, I am not here on holiday,'' she explained. ''Her ladyship has been kind enough to take us in—''

''Us?''

''I have a boy with me. His name is Dan.''

''Is he yours?'' Perry spoke without thinking and then flushed to the roots of his hair. ''I beg your pardon! I have no right to pry.''

''It was a natural question. Dan is not a relative. He is my friend.''

She saw the speculation in his eyes, but it was impossible to be offended. ''He is twelve years old,'' she said.

''Then that's all right. He can't object if I teach you to ride.'' Perry was grinning at her.

''Sir, I think you cannot have understood me perfectly. Dan and I are beholden to Lord Wentworth and her ladyship for saving us from penury...''

''My mother often does the same for me,'' he told her carelessly. ''Now, for example, my pockets are to let until quarter-day. I haven't a feather to fly with.''

Prudence tried to control a sudden spurt of anger. ''I think you will not starve,'' she said sharply. ''Nor will you find yourself without a roof above your head...''

She saw his look of bewilderment, and was sorry for her caustic tone. This charming young man had no more idea of true hardship than any others of his breeding. She could not blame him for that.

''I spoke in haste,'' she apologised. ''You see, Dan

and I were in sad case when Lord Wentworth found us—''

''Seb found you? I don't understand.''

''We were running away…we were apprentices.''

Peregrine eyed her with fresh interest. ''And old Seb helped you? It ain't like him to go against the law. I'm the one for that. Won't I roast him! He shan't take me to task again.''

''I beg that you will say nothing of the matter unless Lord Wentworth speaks of it himself. He knew that it was wrong to take us up. It was an act of kindness on his part.''

''Oh, Seb's all right until he gets upon his high ropes. Then he looks down his nose just so.'' He mimicked his brother's sternest look so accurately that Prudence began to laugh.

''You've seen it too?'' Perry's frown deepened and he began to pace the room in a fair imitation of Wentworth's easy stride. ''Miss Prudence, you will obey me to the letter, else it will be the worse for you,'' he announced. ''And now it's time for the downing stare… Is this severe enough?'' He drew his brows together and gave her an icy glance.

Prudence made an unsuccessful attempt to hide her amusement. ''One of these days you will go too far,'' she warned. ''Suppose your brother should catch you at this mimicry?''

''It will be the stocks for me. He'd enjoy nothing more than to pelt me with rotten fruit.''

''And won't you deserve it?'' she teased.

''I expect so. Sam will be happy to join in. He ain't forgiven me for taking out Seb's black stallion. You should have seen his face when I came off. He was hopping up and down with rage.''

His mock dismay put an end to her attempts to recover her composure. Helpless with laughter, she gave up the unequal struggle.

"Sir, you are the most complete hand!" She was drying her eyes when Wentworth entered the room.

"You've met, I see!" There was a certain stiffness in his manner which Prudence found hard to understand. Perhaps he did not care to find her upon such easy terms with his young brother.

Unrepentant, Perry turned to him. "Prudence was working too hard. I thought I'd take her mind off this dull task."

"You appear to have succeeded. Prudence may leave the work at any time, as she well knows."

"But I have no wish to do so." Prudence looked at Peregrine. "You are mistaken, I do not find it dull. Lord Wentworth, please, I beg you will not heed…"

Peregrine looked from one face to the other. "Have I put my foot in it again? I beg your pardon, Prudence. From now on you shall climb the ladders, struggle with the heavy books, and cover yourself in dust to your heart's content."

"She will not," his lordship said repressively. "Perry, am I to understand that you have been helping?"

"You might say so. Look at what we've done today!" He gestured towards the many volumes now restored to the shelves. "I tell you…I am quite worn out."

"It must be almost as exhausting as sailing from Dover to Calais," came the ironic reply.

"Yes, that's another thing. I hear you to are to go to France for Sophie. Will you take me with you?"

"I will not. I prefer that you stay here. Our mother has enough upon her mind."

Peregrine's good humour vanished. "Seb, it ain't fair!

Just because I threatened to mill some fellow down? He deserved it. You don't know what it's like in France at present. I tell you—''

''Pray allow me to find out for myself. Your quarrel with some peasant has nothing to do with my decision. I need you here to keep an eye on things.''

''They go on much as usual,'' Perry said sulkily. ''You ain't expecting revolution here, I hope?''

''It can't be ruled out. Frederick sends word from Whitehall that the Government is concerned. I think it unlikely that there will be disaffection here, but others are not so sanguine in their hopes.''

''Those old women in the Cabinet?'' Perry's voice was scornful. ''If they had anything about them, they'd have sent help to the French king.''

''And plunged this country into war? Remind me to persuade you never to enter politics, Perry.''

His brother grinned. ''There's no chance of that. What a life those fellows must lead…cooped up all day…with nothing to do but jaw!'' Sebastian's irony was lost on him.

''I'm glad to hear that my fears are groundless,'' came the smooth reply. ''In one thing you are right. Prudence has done quite enough for today.''

She looked up at him, but he forestalled her protest.

''Dan is looking for you, my dear. He has much to tell you. It seems that you must exchange one chatterbox for another.'' He was smiling as she left the room.

''She's great fun, isn't she?'' Perry gave his brother a quizzical look.

''Do you find her so?''

''Don't you? I suppose you've treated her to some of your homilies, but she seems to think the world of you.'' He chuckled. ''I can't think why!''

"Merely gratitude. She has had a hard time of it."
Wentworth began to turn the pages of one of the books
upon the table.

"Well, if you had to bring a woman here, I'm glad it
ain't some bran-faced, swivel-eyed creature."

"Dear me! You have even less elegance of mind than
I had supposed."

"Well, it's true, ain't it? She has the kind of face that
you look at twice. There's something about her...I
wanted to—"

"Yes?" The question was apparently casual, but
Wentworth's jaw had tightened.

"Oh, I don't know...make a friend of her, I suppose."

"Prudence is much in need of friends, especially if
they wish no harm to come to her."

It was a clear warning, and Perry flushed. "You don't
imagine I'd do anything to upset her?"

"I hope not, Peregrine."

"Damn it, Seb! When you give me my full name I
know I'm on dangerous ground. I ain't a rake, you
know."

His brother smiled at that. "I know it well, but Prudence is just a child, and she is vulnerable."

"She need not be afraid of me. It's you she worries
about."

"I beg your pardon?" Wentworth's eyebrows went
up.

"Don't look black at me! I meant only that when I
offered to teach her to ride, or to take her to the coast,
she refused. She thought you might not like it."

"I have no objection. She must not stay indoors all
day."

"Well, I hope you'll tell her so. She's got some nonsense into her head about not being here to enjoy herself.''

"She is a stubborn creature, and as proud as Lucifer." There was an odd note in his lordship's voice and Perry picked it up at once. He could not understand it, and it made him hesitate before he spoke again.

"Sure you don't mind?" he asked at last.

"Of course not."

"Then you'll speak to her?"

"Leave it to me! Must we go on with this?" Wentworth sounded impatient as he turned away. Apparently he was anxious to bring the discussion to an end.

Perry hid a smile. He had got his way. There would be no further argument from Prudence. He was sure of it. Privately, he suspected that she would walk through fire for this tall brother of his. Certainly she would fall in with his wishes.

Then Wentworth stopped with his hand upon the door.

"There is just one other thing. If Prudence is to learn to ride, you must be firm. Sometimes she is inclined to let her courage get the better of her judgment."

"Don't worry! I'll put her up on the oldest nag in the stables. She won't come to any harm."

As his brother walked away, Peregrine gave a low whistle. He was not given to examining the private motives of those about him, but there was something strange about all this. Sebastian was preoccupied, and seemed to have acquired a curious habit of gazing into space.

He shrugged. Sebastian would not tell him, even if he asked. Perhaps he was thinking of his coming journey to France. His sense of injury at being forbidden to make one of the party sent him in search of Prudence.

He found her throwing a ball to a boy with carroty

hair, who tossed it back to her so quickly that she missed the catch.

Perry ran across the lawn, lifted an arm, rolled over and regained his feet, brandishing the ball with a shout of triumph.

"I say! Well done!" Dan looked at him with admiration. "Do you play cricket?"

"My dear sir, you see before you the star of the local team! You must be Dan."

Prudence nudged the boy. "Make your bow," she urged.

"This gentleman is Lord Wentworth's brother. Sir, I still don't know your title."

"If I tell you, you will forever call me by it," he grinned. "Won't Perry do? After all, I call you by your given name. Perhaps I should mind my manners and address you as Miss...?"

"My name is Prudence Consett, sir, but I beg that you will continue to call me Prudence."

"Is it apt?" He could not resist a sly dig at her. "My brother does not seem to think so."

"His lordship likes to joke." Prudence refused to be drawn, though she was not pleased. The two brothers must have been discussing her.

"Then that is settled? I am Perry, you are Prudence, and this is Dan."

"Am I to call you Perry, too?" Dan looked a little doubtful.

"You will do so, if you please. If not, I shall put you in to bat, and bowl some fearful corkers at your head."

Dan was soon at ease with his new friend. "Have you seen the foal?" he asked.

"Not yet, but you shall show him to me." As he led

the way across the stable-yard Sam ignored his cheerful greeting.

"Am I still in your black books, Sam? Here I am come to make amends with two pupils for your riding-school."

Sam sniffed. "It's to be hoped that you don't intend to teach 'em, Master Perry. They'll break their necks."

"No, no! We shall rely on you. What we need is a quiet mare suitable for Miss Prudence here, and a pony for Dan. I thought of Firedance and the cob."

"The cob ain't suitable for the lad," Sam announced at once. "I'll find him something else. Firedance is quiet enough."

"She doesn't sound it." Prudence felt a twinge of apprehension. "And I've never ridden a horse before."

"Don't worry! Firedance is as gentle as a lamb. Her name belies her nature. She isn't fiery, and nor does she dance. In fact, she is a slug."

Sam snorted in disgust. "I don't know why we keep her, but her ladyship will have it."

Dan glanced up at him with shining eyes. "Will you really find me a pony, Sam? That's famous! I never thought I'd be so lucky!"

His hero unbent a little. "The lad is good with horses," he announced to no one in particular. "We'll have no trouble with him."

Prudence was amused. No such assurance had been given on her behalf.

"I shall have no trouble with either of my pupils, though I expect they'll eat their suppers standing by the mantelshelf for the next few days."

"Not if you use your head, sir. We shan't keep them at it for too long."

"Of course not. We'll start tomorrow. You have a good supply of horse liniment?"

"What's that for?" Dan asked.

"To rub away your aches and pains, that is, if you can stand the smell. It's very strong."

"Give over with your nonsense, Master Perry." Sam permitted himself the faintest of smiles. "There'll be no need for that."

"Not if you help us, Sam. Can we rely on you?"

"Please, Sam! I shan't be afraid if you are there." Dan fixed his eyes upon his idol, and Sam could not resist their pleading.

"I expect I'll be around," he said gruffly. "Now, lad, how about grooming Firedance?"

As they went off happily together, Perry threw his eyes to heaven.

"That boy is a magician," he announced. "Evidently he doesn't qualify for Sam's usual description of a dratted nuisance."

"Did you?" she chuckled.

"I still do, I fear. But I intend to mend my ways. Do you still need help in the library?"

"Only if you feel that you won't be bored."

"With you? I doubt it. Confess it, you are a catalyst!"

"I beg your pardon?" Her eyes had begun to twinkle.

"Oh, I don't know. It's just that I get the impression that when you are around things begin to happen…to change."

"You have a vivid imagination, sir," she said demurely.

"I don't think so. Here is old Seb…acting quite out of character. It must be your doing."

She was spared the need to reply when Dan came running back to them.

"I forgot to show you the foal," he said. With evident pride he led them into the stall, pointing out the finer points of the little colt, and laughing as the creature galloped about, kicking up its heels.

"He's splendid, isn't he?" Dan said with satisfaction. "He stands well, and he's deep in the chest... Sam thinks him a true thoroughbred."

"I bow to expert opinion." Perry led them back to the house. "We're late for nuncheon. Cook will be calling down curses upon our heads."

"No, she won't. I'll tell her that we're back." Dan disappeared in the direction of the kitchen.

"More conquests?" Perry shook his head in mock amazement. "That boy will go far. First Sam, and now our highly temperamental cook? I must ask him for some lessons."

"Dan has the most amazing appetite." Prudence smiled at him.

"So have I, but I shouldn't care to tackle Cook."

"You speak from experience?" she asked wryly.

"Of course. You must have heard. I am the black sheep of the family."

"I don't believe that for a moment." Prudence was still laughing as they joined the others.

Wentworth's eyes rested upon her face. He made no comment, but as they left the dining-room he drew her to one side.

"I must speak to you alone," he said. "Perhaps this evening...in the library after dinner?"

She nodded her assent, but the request surprised her. Was he about to point out some impropriety? Perhaps he intended to forbid her growing friendship with his brother. Prudence flushed. She had no wish to be thought encroaching.

* * *

For the rest of the afternoon she was kept busy with Lady Brandon's correspondence, but when the family gathered for their evening meal she found herself uneasy about the coming interview.

Wentworth did not linger over his wine, and when she slipped away to join him in the library she found him waiting for her.

"Can you draw?" he asked without preamble.

The question was so unexpected that she stared at him. "My lord?"

"I asked if you could draw?"

Prudence began to smile. "I can draw a cat, with one circle for the head, another for the body, and two triangles for the ears, but that is all. Why do you ask?"

"I need a drawing of the crest upon your brooch if I'm to make enquiries. I intend to keep my word, you see."

Prudence unpinned her brooch and laid it on the table. "Did you not tell me that you had a book on heraldry, sir?"

Wentworth grimaced. "Look about you, Prudence." He gestured towards the crowded shelves. "I see no sign of it. Since my father died, this room has remained untouched. Even the cupboards are filled with ancient volumes. I can't be sure that the book is still here."

"I see." Prudence drew a sheet of paper towards her. "I'll do my best..." After a few moments she handed him the crude drawing. "It isn't very good," she told him ruefully.

"It will serve." His lordship folded the paper and tucked it into his breast pocket. For some moments he was lost in thought. Then he gave her a searching look.

"You are sure about this?" he asked. "If we are successful, the result may be distressing for you."

"I am prepared for that," she told him proudly. "It can't be worse than never to know the truth."

"Don't be too certain of that, my dear. I wouldn't have you hurt again."

She shook her head. "I must find out."

Her face was set, and he knew that it would be useless to argue further. "Shall we join the others?" he said quietly.

In their absence Perry had been questioning his mother.

"Old Seb has surprised me," he observed with interest. "He clucks over Prudence like a hen with a single chick. I've never known him to go on like this before."

"Sebastian takes his responsibilities seriously, and so he must. The boy and the girl are in his charge, since he has chosen to make them so."

"I wonder why he did it? You don't think that he and Prudence...?"

"No, I do not," his mother said sharply. "Under those circumstances he would not have brought her here to me. There was some accident and Prudence saved his life."

Perry whistled in surprise. "Does it not seem strange to you?"

"I think we need not speculate upon his motives. I'm sure he acted with the best of intentions. Whether or not it was a wise decision it is impossible to say."

Perry looked at her troubled face. "Don't worry about it, Mother. Sebastian always knows what he is doing."

"Does he, my love? I wonder. At present, he thinks of Prudence as a charming child."

"Then he must be blind," Perry told her bluntly. "I

know he ain't much in the petticoat line as far as marriage is concerned, but even he must see…''

''Not as yet. Prudence was dressed as a boy when they first met.''

''She ain't wearing breeches now,'' Perry murmured significantly.

''Must you be so indelicate? Pray keep a still tongue in your head. Sebastian is not my sole concern, you know. I have no wish for Prudence to be hurt.''

''He's careful of her feelings. He warned me off, you know.''

His mother smiled at that.

''I can't see why you are amused,'' he said in an injured tone. ''Prudence enjoys my company…''

''I'm sure she does, my darling boy, but I know that you would not make unwelcome advances to her.''

''Sebastian would flatten me if I tried it.'' He gave her a cheerful grin. ''You see, you have nothing to worry about.''

''Possibly not, but I cannot like this situation. If only Sebastian had married! Heaven knows that I have tried to bring him to it!''

''You try too hard,'' her son said wisely. ''Old Seb is a stubborn brute. He'll make his choice in his own good time.''

''I know it!'' she admitted sadly. Then she summoned up a smile as Prudence and Sebastian came to join them. She would hide her misgivings for the present.

Chapter Eight

Prudence slept late next day. When she came down it was to find Perry pacing about the hall.

"Had you forgot your riding lesson? Or were you hoping that we'd start without you?" His face was full of mischief.

"I hadn't forgotten," she said primly. "Just give me time to eat my breakfast." She hoped that her face did not betray her anxiety. On the previous day even the gentle Firedance had looked enormous to her inexperienced eyes.

"Nervous?" Perry teased.

"Not in the least," she lied.

It was a different matter when Perry tossed her up into the saddle. She looked with envy at Dan, who was already seated astride his pony.

"Can't I ride like that?" she protested. "I'm sure it must be easier."

"Certainly not! Sebastian would have my skin. Ladies ride side-saddle, as I'm sure you know."

"Well, I think them very foolish," she snapped. Seated high above the ground, with one leg crooked over the pommel, she felt that her position was precarious.

"Oh, come on, Pru! Sam will take you on the leading rein. I thought Sebastian might be here, but he's gone off on some business of his own. You'll soon feel easy with your mount. Then we can go out every day."

This promise did not cheer her, and she clung to the reins as if her very life depended on it.

"Just relax, miss," Sam advised. "These beasts can sense if you feel nervous. They ain't so very different from the rest of us."

Prudence gritted her teeth.

"Just get to know her, miss. She wouldn't mind a kind word, and a pat or two. She's got feelings too."

Prudence took him at his word, and when her lesson was over she felt more confident.

"Shall I show you something?" Dan ran over as she dismounted. "Sam showed me this trick."

Beneath her astonished gaze he blew gently into the horse's nostrils.

"Why are you doing that?" she asked.

"In the American colonies the savages do this to tame wild horses. '"The finest light cavalry in the world', aren't they, Sam?"

"So I've heard said." Sam's reply was gruff. He seemed none too pleased by this revelation of his past, but Prudence was intrigued.

"You have visited the Americas?"

"Only during the late rebellion, miss. I was in the army."

"You met the savages?"

"They ain't all savages, miss…not compared with some of ours." He turned away.

"You are on dangerous ground," Perry whispered. "Sam admires the red men. He couldn't believe that they'd never seen a horse until the Spaniards came."

"Shall we go there, Pru?" Dan's face was alight with interest. "I should like to see them."

Perry laughed. "Aren't you afraid of losing your top-notch, Dan? Some Indian chief would be proud to have that fine red hair hanging from his belt."

Dan looked puzzled. "Is that why Sam has no hair at the front?"

"Nay, lad!" Even Sam was amused. "I managed to hold on to my scalp, but the hair was gone long since."

Prudence pulled Dan aside. "Sam is bald," she whispered. "You must not comment on it. That would be rude. He can't help it."

At the sight of Dan's stricken face, the old groom felt moved to comfort him. He winked. "It's a sure sign of brains. They say that no grass grows on a busy street. Come on! I'll tell you about the savages whilst we feed the horses."

"Will you? Oh, Sam, I wish you didn't need to go to France. I shan't know what to do without you…"

It was an unfortunate remark. Perry's face clouded at once. "Sam has no need to go," he snapped. "I can take his place. At least, I could if my loving brother would agree."

Prudence was quick to intervene. "Lord Wentworth has no plans to leave at present," she soothed. "Besides, you are needed here. Did you not promise me your help? I suspect that you have changed your mind. I see it all now…standing on a ladder makes you dizzy…"

She gave him her most enchanting smile and he was not proof against her charm. His face cleared.

"Pru, if you believe that you'll believe anything. Shall we go now? I see that I must make amends."

As Prudence turned she caught Sam's eye. He was looking at her with new respect. Mr Perry was not the easiest of men to handle, but this slight girl seemed to have the secret. Who would have thought it of the ragged urchin he'd been so keen to leave behind in Derbyshire? Not for the first time he was amazed at Lord Wentworth's perspicacity. His master must have seen something in her, and he'd been right, as always.

He favoured Prudence with a brief nod as he walked away, stroking his bald head. He'd been tempted to announce that his loss of hair was due as much to Mr Perry's antics in the past as to anything else, but wisdom prevailed and he held his tongue.

Perry watched the ill-assorted couple out of sight.

"He's not a bad old stick," he said grudgingly. "Even if he is inclined to think that my brother can walk on water."

"Can't he?" Prudence teased. Laughing, she fled into the house to avoid the playful blow he aimed at her.

Together they worked on, with a brief pause for nuncheon. It was late in the afternoon when Wentworth returned and came to find them.

As Prudence looked up at him with a question in her eyes he gave an almost imperceptible shake of his head. She made no comment, sensing that he wished to keep her search from Perry.

It surprised her a little, but as yet she knew neither brother well. Perhaps Perry was too volatile to be trusted with the secret. She guessed that it would intrigue him, promising unknown adventure. For all she knew, he might scour the countryside, asking questions which could not fail to give offence to some of the old Kentish families.

Sebastian was more cautious. His search would be steady, but thorough, and undertaken with tact. She gave him a shy smile. It was good of him to trouble, and she must not be impatient. It was too much to hope that he would glean the information which she needed at a first attempt.

"You look tired," he said briefly. "Have you been in here all day?"

"Not at all!" Perry answered for her. "You see before you an intrepid horsewoman. In no time at all she'll be taken fences like a good 'un."

"You had your first riding lesson, then?" Wentworth threw himself into a chair and stretched out his long legs. "Did you enjoy it?"

"Only in parts, my lord." Prudence dimpled at him. "I doubt if I shall take fences with Sam holding the leading rein. And…and the horse seemed so big."

Wentworth smiled at that. "Firedance will appear to shrink as you get used to her. Skill will come with practice…"

"And then we shall be off," Perry assured him. "Did you know that Prudence has never seen the sea? I'm dangling that treat before her like a carrot if she will but persevere."

"Oh, I don't think we need wait until Prudence learns to ride," his brother murmured in casual tones. "We can take the gig. Dan will enjoy it, too."

Perry raised his eyebrows. He was about to express his astonishment at this suggestion, but a glance at his brother's face decided him against it. He contented himself with a single question.

"Will you have time?" he asked wickedly.

"I think so." Sebastian refused to rise to the provocation. "If there is any urgent business to be done, we can always send you into Canterbury."

Perry knew when he was routed. He laughed and

raised his hands in protest. "No, I'll go with you. It will be like old times. Shall we take them to the cove?"

Sebastian nodded.

"You'll love it, Pru," Perry announced eagerly. "Seb and I used to swim from there."

Prudence looked from one face to the other. In spite of the difference in their ages, these two were clearly good friends. She sensed that Perry idolised his elder brother. Any differences between them arose from the fact that Perry was so young and had not yet learned discretion. It would come with time.

"It would be a wonderful treat for us," she agreed. "May I tell Dan?"

"I'll tell him." Perry rose to his feet. "If I sit here much longer the dust will settle on me, too."

As the door closed behind him Sebastian looked at Prudence. "How did you persuade him into this?" He gestured about the room.

"Your brother offered his help, my lord. He needed no persuasion…"

"Then I suggest that you make the most of it. I don't know when he was last absorbed in such pursuits." Wentworth regarded her from under lazy eyelids. "I think you must be a witch. Have you some secret magic which enables you to tame the wild?"

Prudence laughed. "I learned of such a thing today. Sam has been showing Dan the Indian way of taming horses."

"And who tried it on my brother?"

"Not me!" Her eyes were dancing. "You must give him credit for a kindly impulse, sir."

"I am suitably impressed. Even so, I think it best not to mention the crest upon your brooch to him. He knows little of your story…" He was silent for some time.

"I will do as you suggest," she agreed. "But, why?"

"Perry might appoint himself your knight in shining armour," he said drily. "I shudder to think what skeletons he might uncover among the local gentry."

"You found nothing yourself, my lord?"

"Not yet, my dear, but these are early days." He reached out and took her hand. "Don't give up hope, but don't build too much upon it. There is no guarantee that we shall be successful."

"I know that you are right." Her face was wistful. "But deep inside I feel that you won't fail."

"Such faith!" he teased. "I'm not infallible, you know. One of these days someone will tie a little string four inches above the ground and I shall trip over it."

Prudence laughed and shook her head. "I suspect that you are as great a tease as your brother, sir." Her eye fell upon the clock. "Good heavens! Is it so late? I must change or I shall keep her ladyship waiting this evening."

She hurried away, leaving Sebastian to wonder why their proposed trip to the coast should fill him with such pleasure.

His mother was equally surprised.

"In October, my dears? At this time of year the winds from the Channel can be bitter. Prudence, I hope you have not allowed my sons to persuade you into this trip against your better judgment?"

"I am looking forward to it," Prudence told her shyly.

"Then you shall wear your warmest clothing, and you must not stay out too long."

"Mother, won't you join us?" Sebastien suggested.

"Certainly not! I have too much regard for my old

bones.'' Her smile robbed her words of all severity, but she would not be persuaded.

Prudence was enchanted by the prospect of the drive. She hadn't left the house since the day of her arrival, and her spirits rose at the thought of a change of scene.

The idea of travelling in the gig had been discarded in favour of a spanking new curricle, and as they climbed aboard Dan's glowing face served to cheer her even more.

Mindful of his mother's instructions, Perry took them along at a steady pace, and even Sebastian found himself unable to criticise his driving.

Dan had no eyes for the rolling countryside through which they passed. His thoughts were upon the treat ahead.

''Are we really to see the sea?'' he asked. ''Prudence has promised that one day we shall take a tall ship to a far country, like the ones we saw on the London river. You remember them, sir?'' He appealed to Wentworth.

''Yes, Dan, I do. But shall you like to leave England?''

''Prudence thinks it may be best for us, don't you, Pru? She's going to help me make my fortune.''

''And how will you do that?''

''I haven't decided yet. Perhaps I'll think of a special way to build a ship, or to design a new carriage...''

''I hope you'll allow me to be the first to know.'' Wentworth smiled down at him. ''In one of your carriages I might be the envy of all my friends.''

''And I'll give you an order for a ship.'' Perry joined in the delightful fantasy. ''Unless, of course, you go so far away that you forget your friends.''

"Oh, we shan't do that, shall we, Pru?" Dan was firm in his resolve. "Sam wouldn't like it at all."

This brought a smile from his companions, but Dan was gazing through the window.

"Where is the sea?" he asked anxiously.

"It's still out there, unless someone has moved it." Perry was in a jovial mood, and he kept up his nonsense until they reached the coast. Then, as they gained the crest of a hill, he stopped the curricle.

"There!" he announced with an expansive gesture. "What do you say to that?"

Far below them lay the waters of the English Channel, sparkling in the autumn sunlight. A number of different craft plied up and down the shipping lanes, from cargo vessels to pleasure yachts, but they were too distant for Prudence to distinguish the ports of origin listed on their hulls.

"I didn't think the sea would be so big." Dan was awestruck. "It seems to go on for ever, but the water is grey. I thought the sea was blue…"

"It is in some parts of the world." Wentworth smiled down at him. "One day you may go there. Then you'll see the size of the great oceans. This is a narrow stretch of water. On a clear day you can see the coast of France."

Prudence peered into the distance. "Then it isn't so very far away. Is the water rough today?"

"Calm as a mill-pond!" Perry wetted a finger and held it up. "There's just a slight breeze. It's perfect for sailing…"

"And it's settled. I doubt if it will change." Sebastian looked thoughtful and Prudence guessed that he was thinking of his sister. If he was to bring her back to England, it must be before the onset of the winter gales.

"See, there is France!" He pointed out a faint line on the horizon, darker than the shimmering sea below them.

"Have you been there many times?" she asked.

"Frequently!" Sebastian clapped his brother on the shoulder. "Perry is a dedicated sailor. There's nothing he likes better than to feel a deck beneath his feet and a following wind."

He received no answering smile.

"Then why not take me when you go?" the younger man demanded. "If you don't want me ashore, I could wait in harbour for you."

"We'll see! It will all depend on Gilles...we can't be sure that he will let Sophie come to us."

"Come off it, Seb! You won't be satisfied with that. You'll go yourself...I know it."

Sensing that an argument was about to develop, Prudence changed the subject.

"Is it possible to get closer to the sea?" she asked eagerly. "I confess that I should like to walk along the shore."

"Oh, please!" Dan begged. "I could throw stones into the water."

Perry's face cleared. "We can go down to the beach. There's a small cove close by. We used to swim from there when we were boys."

Dan gazed at him in admiration. "Can you really swim?" he asked.

"Like a fish!" Perry grinned at him. "I'll throw you in if you like...that's the way to learn."

"You'll do no such thing," Sebastian told him firmly. "I've no intention of wading out to rescue Dan, and probably you as well."

Perry pretended to be crushed. "You see how it is," he told Dan. "I'm always receiving set-downs, and not only from my brother. I can't impress Prudence, no matter what I say. She's as bad as Sebastian.''

"She doesn't mean it," Dan assured him. "The vicar used to say that her bark was worse than her bite.''

"Well, her bark is bad enough. I shouldn't like to suffer her bite." He pretended to shudder in terror until Dan was convulsed with laughter.

Prudence looked at her companions. Then she joined in the merriment, though she gave a mock scowl at Dan and Perry.

"Ignore them, Prudence!" Sebastian took the reins from his brother to guide his team up the narrow track towards the cliff-top. There he stopped beside a single stunted tree to which he secured the pair.

"Shall you like to leave them here?" Perry asked.

"They'll come to no harm for a short time. Of course, if you prefer to walk them up and down…?

"No, no, I'll take your word for it. I'm just as keen as Dan to get down to the beach." He set off towards the edge of the cliff at a fast pace.

"Check first if there's been a rock fall," Sebastian called after him. "The path may be blocked—"

"I ain't a complete fool, brother." Perry sounded impatient. Then he shouted back to reassure the others. "It's clear right down to the shore."

As Dan started after him, Prudence caught his sleeve.

"Is it safe, my lord?"

"If Perry says so, you may be sure of it. He knows the danger well enough, and he won't take chances with your safety."

"He did say that the path was clear," she murmured.

"That wasn't quite what I meant. In some parts of the coastline the cliff face is unstable."

"You mean that the rock could fall away to the shore below?" Prudence clutched Dan's sleeve more tightly.

"Perry will have checked that the cove is still unchanged, but if it worries you we need not venture down there."

Dan's face fell. "Oh, Pru, you promised! And you, too, sir. I thought that was why we came."

Sebastian smiled at Prudence. "We did promise, didn't we? Believe me, the path will be safe. The problems have arisen in the past when storms have lashed the coast and undermined the cliffs. I will go first, to help you down."

Dan tugged at her hand. "Come on!" he urged. "Perry said we might find things like crabs or small fish in the rock-pools."

Prudence could not resist his pleas and some of his excitement communicated itself to her. Even so, she drew back a little as they started down the winding path.

Perry had already gained the beach and was waving to them. He looked no bigger than a child's toy from that height.

"Don't look down!" Sebastian said quickly. "Just concentrate on Dan. We'll keep him between us."

In single file they made their way down to the shore, with Prudence grasping firmly at the strong tufts of grass on the banks beside them to steady her descent.

Her confidence grew with every step, hampered though she was by her long skirts. This was one occasion when she would have preferred to wear a pair of breeches.

Then Sebastian jumped down to the sand and turned to help her. "Well done!" he said. "I hope you didn't feel too dizzy."

She gave him a trusting smile. "I didn't expect to feel

like that," she admitted. "I can't remember looking down from such a height before. My head began to spin and the drop seemed to be drawing me…"

"Heights can have that effect. But look about you, Prudence—was it worth it?"

Her look of delight gave him his answer. "I wish I could follow Dan's example," she said wistfully.

Dan had already taken off his boots and stockings and was leaping over the rocks in Perry's direction. Within minutes they had squatted down, the red head and the dark one close together, as they peered into a small pool.

"You'd regret it," her companion assured her. "The sea water is freezing off the English coast. Won't you walk with me instead?"

Prudence took his proffered arm and they began to stroll along the shore. His lordship was surprisingly knowledgeable about both plant and animal life within the cove, and Prudence was so absorbed in learning all she could that she did not notice how the time had passed.

"We should be going soon," he said at last. "Though I doubt if that suggestion will meet with much approval." He nodded towards Dan and Perry, who had wandered further away.

"Oh dear, Dan's feet are blue with cold. I'll call to him."

Dan came running back at once but, as his lordship had predicted, he had no wish to leave. Prudence frowned at his protests. Then Perry intervened.

"We can't go yet," he announced. "We ain't had our game of beach cricket."

"True," said Sebastian. "But for that we need a ball."

"I thought of that." His brother grinned. "The magician will oblige…'' He produced a cricket ball from his pocket. ''Now just three pieces of driftwood for the stumps, and a wider one for the bat, and then I'll take you on, Dan. You bat, and I shall bowl.''

''So Prudence and I are to make up the other team? Which do you prefer, my dear? Will you keep wicket, or stay in the outfield?''

Prudence stared at him, but he had already taken off his coat and was rolling up his sleeves. Her lips curved in amusement. It appeared that the game was on. What a pair they were, these Wentworths! They never lost the ability to surprise her.

''I'll stay back here,'' she laughed. ''I can catch, but I know nothing about keeping wicket.''

''And, Perry, you can't bowl to me if you're on my team.'' Dan had picked up his makeshift bat and was waiting by the stumps.

''In beach cricket we have other rules,'' Perry told him solemnly. ''We're a few men short of a full team. Now, are you ready?'' Without more ado he sent a few gentle balls towards the batsman.

Dan hit them without difficulty, and Prudence was moved to protest.

''Perry, you aren't trying! That's cheating! Here, let me…!'' She threw off her cloak and tossed aside her bonnet. Then she took the ball from Perry.

She beat Dan with her first throw, delivered at a run. The stumps flew wide and Perry gazed at her in mock awe. Then he looked at his brother.

''This girl has hidden talents,'' he announced. ''I'm not surprised you chose her for your team.''

Prudence flushed as he and Sebastian began to clap.

''I expect it was a fluke,'' she said shyly. ''Now it's Perry's turn. Will you bowl to him, my lord?''

"No, Prudence! The bowler must finish the over."
Sebastian's eyes were twinkling.

Prudence tried again, but Perry was on his mettle. He
hit the next five balls almost into the surf.

"I can't beat him, sir, but if you tempt him into a rash
stroke I might catch him." Prudence threw the ball to
her partner.

"No chance of that!" Perry announced, but success
had made him overconfident. He struck the next ball
high into the air and Prudence raced across the beach.
She was running backwards as she caught it. Then the
heel of her boot became entangled in her skirt. She
tripped and fell headlong.

With a sharp exclamation Perry threw aside his bat,
but Sebastian was the first to reach her. He fell to his
knees in the sand, and raised her tenderly in his arms.

"Are you hurt, my dear?"

Something in his tone caused Perry to glance at his
brother's face. Then he looked away. That glimpse of
raw emotion had told him more than any words could
say. Sebastian was in love with Prudence, even though
he might not be aware of it.

"Just winded, sir, but I caught Perry out." Prudence
brandished the ball. "I should have worn my breeches,
but I did not know that we were to play cricket…"

"I thought we had already decided that you were
never to wear them again!" Sebastian said shortly.

"But I tripped over my skirt. In breeches…"

"Prudence! I'll hear no more of this." He lifted Prudence to her feet and began to dust the sand from her
gown. "Why, your hair is full of the stuff…" He ruffled
the short curls to clear it away and handed her her bonnet. "Now, put on your cloak. We've kept the horses
waiting for too long…"

Dan looked from one face to the other. Then Perry winked at him and shrugged his shoulders. "Come on," he said. "Next thing we shall be in trouble with Sam…"

He glanced ahead and was amused. Sebastian had Prudence by the hand and was already halfway up the path to the cliff-top.

"You go too fast," she protested. "I can't keep up with you…"

She heard a noncommittal grunt, but her companion slowed his pace. For some reason he seemed out of temper, and she could not understand it. A sigh escaped her lips.

"What's wrong now?"

"I was wondering why you were so cross, my lord. I'm sorry I'm so clumsy. I didn't mean to fall."

"You might have hurt yourself badly."

"On the sand?"

"Didn't you see the rocks? One was so close to your head that I thought you must have struck it when you fell."

"Lord Wentworth, I'm not made of porcelain—"

"No, you are made of flesh and blood, and I wish that you would remember it!" He almost threw her up into the carriage.

"Don't look black at me!" she coaxed. "This has been such a happy day. I'll remember it all my life."

"You are easily pleased." He gave her a reluctant smile. "I suspect you have more lives than a cat. How many have you used up now?"

"Not more than three or four, I think. I'll try to save the others."

"Well, warn me in good time if you decide to use them. You are adding to my grey hairs, you know."

"I haven't noticed any yet." Her eyes were dancing. "I think you are teasing me."

"Minx!" He shook his head in mild reproof. "What am I to do with you?"

She was spared the need to answer as the others reached them, and under cover of Dan's chatter she felt at leisure to reflect upon the day.

Her pleasure in the outing had been genuine. It was difficult to believe that she, Prudence Consett, had taken to her present delightful way of life so easily. A month ago she could not have imagined it. She'd had no idea of the way in which some other human beings lived. In surroundings of great elegance, and owning land as far as the eye could see, they were able to pursue their interests without interference, and, she guessed, without financial worries.

Well, one day she would have a lovely home. She began to daydream. It would be very much like Hallwood. From the moment she had stepped inside, the house had seemed to reach out to her, enveloping her in a welcome of its own. Perhaps it was because she'd loved it from the start, from the Great Hall with its wonderful plastered ceiling, to the polished wood and intricate carving of the massive staircase. It would be a wrench to leave it all, yet leave she must.

She glanced down at Dan, his face alight with enthusiasm as he questioned Perry endlessly about the wonders he had seen. He, too, was happy in his new life. To take him away would tear at his very heartstrings. Should she leave him behind with those who would care for him? She gave a little shake of her head. How could she break the ties of affection which had held them together for so long? Dan would feel betrayed, and to her, betrayal was the worst of sins. Her own experience had taught her that.

When they reached Hallwood it was already dusk and the lamps were lit, throwing long fingers of light from every window. Prudence felt a renewed surge of affection for the place as it nestled against the sheltering hillside. In a few short days she had come to think of it as a haven of peace and safety.

She must think carefully about Dan's interests. He would be welcome to stay here. Lord Wentworth had made that clear, and it might mean a better future for him. In time he would forget her.

She was still lost in thought when they entered the Great Hall. Then Lady Brandon came towards them with a letter in her hand.

Chapter Nine

"You've heard from Gilles?" Sebastian asked quickly.

"No, my dear. This letter is from Frederick. He plans to visit us before the week is out…"

"Oh, Lord, the belted Earl himself!" Perry winked at Prudence. "I hope he don't intend to bring his lady."

"He does, and the children, too."

"My God! Are we to have the Gorgon and her monsters?"

His mother gave him a stern look of reproof. "Peregrine, do try for a little conduct! You really must not speak of Amelia in that way. As for my grandchildren…they may have improved…"

"Unlikely!" Perry was unrepentant. "I think I'll make myself scarce."

"You will do no such thing. Prudence must think you entirely lacking in good manners, as I do myself."

Prudence made no reply. She was looking at Sebastian. His mouth had tightened into a thin line, and the crease between his brows was marked.

"Does Frederick give a reason for this sudden visit?" he asked.

"Should he need one to visit his mother?" Lady Brandon was on the defensive. Neither of her younger sons had welcomed her news.

"Of course not, dearest!" Sebastian threw an affectionate arm about her shoulders. "Perry and I were surprised, that's all. Frederick doesn't often visit us at this time of year, but it will be good to see him again."

"It would be if he'd decided to come alone…" Perry grimaced. "Prudence will soon see that I'm right." He turned, but she was already out of earshot.

She'd been quick to sense the tension in the air. There was some mystery here, and she wanted no part of it. A family quarrel would distress her.

Perry was given to exaggeration, but he was good-natured, and inclined to believe the best of his fellow human beings. She had not heard him speak so ill of anyone before, but his dislike of his sister-in-law seemed to be acute.

And Sebastian had looked so strange. He'd tried to retrieve the situation, but to her ears his words were unconvincing.

Prudence resolved to make herself invisible, as far as possible, for the duration of the Earl's visit. She would keep Dan with her, out of sight, and she would eat alone.

She broached the subject later to her hostess.

"Lady Brandon, I'm sure that you will wish to have your family to yourself when the Earl arrives. With your permission I will eat with Dan in the servants' quarters—"

"You will do no such thing, my dear. You must pay no heed to Perry. It's true that my daughter-in-law can be most trying, but you are my guest, and you must not hide yourself away. Don't allow Perry to frighten you with his nonsense. He and Amelia are not the best of friends, but I'm sure he will behave himself.''

Prudence did not argue, although she suspected that her presence and that of Dan would be frowned upon by the fearsome Amelia.

Later, when Perry spoke to her alone, she was convinced of it.

"I hope you didn't think me unkind," he said frankly. "But Amelia is a hateful creature. You'll discover that for yourself.''

"Perry, please!" Prudence held up a hand to stop any further confidences. "I can't listen to gossip about your family—''

"Just thought you should be prepared. And now old Seb must suffer, too. She can't have any tact at all, to come when he is here.''

"Lord Wentworth would never be less than courteous," Prudence said stiffly. "If you tell me otherwise, I shan't believe you.''

Perry grinned at her. "Oh, he'll be courteous all right...in fact, so damned polite that it's frightening. It don't stop him thinking just as I do.''

"The Countess must have some good qualities...after all, your brother married her." It was a useless attempt to stop Perry in full flow.

"Second-best!" he said darkly. "She wanted Seb, you know, but he would have none of it. What do they say? 'Hell hath no fury like a woman scorned?' '' She turned on him, accusing him of trifling with her. There were some ugly scenes, I can tell you.''

Prudence knew that she should change the subject, but the temptation to hear the full story was too much for her.

"Well, at least she has found happiness with the Earl," she murmured.

"Don't you believe it! Frederick found her out too late. He blamed Sebastian and felt sorry for her. Then he discovered she'd been lying, but that was after they were married."

Prudence was silent. There was little she could say.

"And to come here now!" Perry threw his eyes to heaven. "That is all we need."

There was something in his tone which caused Prudence to give him a suspicious look.

"Why now, in particular? Do you mean because of me and Dan? You think she will not like it?"

"Amelia don't like anything," he told her hastily. He had said too much, and he cursed his idle tongue. In future he would keep his own counsel, but if he could see the growing affection between Prudence and Sebastian he was certain that Amelia would not miss it. Then there would be fireworks.

"Don't mind me," he continued. "My mother won't stand any nonsense, and nor will Seb. Shall I help you again in the library tomorrow?"

Prudence welcomed the change of subject, and she nodded her agreement. At dinner that evening the Earl's proposed visit was not mentioned again, and the atmosphere appeared to have returned to normal.

She was up betimes on the following morning, anxious to make up for lost time. Dan was nowhere to be found, nor was Perry. Then Lady Brandon came to join her.

"Let me see how you go on, my dear." Her ladyship bent over the carefully copied lists. "You write a fair hand, Prudence. Sadly, my own looks as though a spider had fallen in the ink and crawled across the page.''

Her eye fell upon the piles of heavy books, and she looked startled. ''I must hope that you did not lift these down yourself…?''

''No, Peregrine helped me,'' Prudence told her shyly. ''Ma'am, he will not allow me to use his title. Indeed, I do not know it.''

''Perry dislikes formality. It is no matter. You have done him good, you know. He has grown up in the shadow of his elder brother and, being so much younger, sometimes he feels ill used.''

''His help was most welcome,'' Prudence murmured.

''And most surprising, but today the novelty has worn off, I fear. He and Dan were making for the lake when last I saw them.'' She drew a small key from her pocket and unlocked the cupboards beneath the shelves. ''You might look through these if the others are beyond your reach. No one has glanced at them in years.''

They were interrupted as the door burst open. Perry hurried into the room with Dan at his heels.

''Sorry, Pru!'' he cried cheerfully. ''I didn't think you'd start so early. We've been swimming…''

''In the lake? My dear Perry, it must have been freezing!'' Lady Brandon looked at Dan's shivering figure.

''It was a bit,'' the boy admitted. ''But I learned to float.'' His teeth were chattering.

''Ask Cook to give you a hot drink.'' Her ladyship waited until the door had closed upon him. Then she rounded upon her son. ''Have you run mad?'' she demanded. ''The child is none too strong and to take him swimming in October…? Sometimes I wonder at your lack of common sense.''

''I expect that Dan was to blame for that.'' Prudence

was quick to intervene. "You must not let him tease you, sir. You spoil him—"

"I don't think so!" Perry's anger flared and he flung out of the room.

Prudence was dismayed. "I had no wish to upset him…" she said falteringly.

"It is easily done at this present time. He is nursing a sense of injury since Sebastian would not allow him to go to France. Dan has diverted his attention, but he must not tire the boy beyond his strength."

"I'll keep Dan with me for the next few days. It will be a struggle, ma'am. He grows indignant if he suspects that I am trying to cosset him."

"Did you not tell me that you were teaching him to read? Perhaps the lessons should begin again?"

"Of course…that is the answer…and Peregrine will understand."

"You are too mindful of his feelings," her ladyship said quietly. "Meantime, I will send him into Canterbury. That should occupy him for the rest of the day."

She was as good as her word; with Perry dispatched upon his errand, Dan was persuaded to give his attention to a primer which Lady Brandon sent down from the nursery.

He was eager to learn, but after an hour Prudence judged that the lesson had lasted long enough. She settled him in the window-seat with some illustrated volumes of ancient maps, believing that the monsters illustrated beside the oceans would keep him occupied for some time. Half an hour later he was asleep.

Prudence returned to her lists. She had begun to realise that there was more to cataloguing than she had at first imagined. Cross-referencing was beyond her and so was the task of researching dates. It wasn't always easy to guess when a volume had been printed, and she decided to make notes on a separate sheet of paper. Later she would question Lady Brandon as to how she might find out.

Absorbed in her work, she did not at first pay much attention when Dan called to her.

"Are you listening, Pru? I thought you wanted to know about your brooch…"

She was on her feet at once. "What do you mean?"

"Come and look at this! The drawing looks the same to me…"

Leaning over his shoulder, she found herself gazing at the brightly coloured plates in a book on heraldry. With shaking fingers she unpinned her brooch and laid it beside the page.

"No…it is not the same…" Her disappointment was intense. "It is quite like…but not exactly so, and the inscription is different."

"Let's look at the other pictures. There are hundreds of them…"

"We must take great care." A glance at the leather binding and the quality of the paper had shown her that the book was valuable. "Let us bring it over to the desk and lay it flat. I hope that her ladyship will not mind us handling it."

"She unlocked the cupboards for you, didn't she?"

Prudence nodded. The temptation to examine the book in detail was overwhelming.

"Is this it?" Dan asked on more than one occasion.

Each time she shook her head. She was beginning to despair. Their search had taken more than an hour and they were almost at the end of the book. Perhaps she was not destined ever to find the secret of her birth.

She turned another page or two, then she gasped.

There it was! There could be no possibility of mistake. She knew every detail of the drawing upon the page. It was identical with the pattern on her brooch.

As she stared at it, she found that she was trembling. Her face was ashen, and as the colours blurred before her eyes she thought that she must faint.

"Pru, are you ill? You look so strangely…" Dan gave her an anxious look.

"No… It is just that I have waited for so long…I can't believe that we have found it."

"There is some writing underneath. Can you read it?"

"No, I think it must be Latin. Let me look again. See, here is a capital letter! Perhaps it is a name, but they put such strange endings on to words. This one is Manvel-lus."

"I've never heard of a name like that. Have you?"

"I suppose it could be Manvell in the English way. Let's see if there is something else…"

She was too preoccupied to be aware that the library door has opened. Then Dan nudged her.

"Oh, Lady Brandon! I am so sorry. I did not hear you come in."

"You were too absorbed." Her ladyship was amused. "What have you found that is so interesting?"

"It is a book on heraldry, ma'am. I was showing it to Dan. I hope you do not mind."

"Not in the least. You are at liberty to examine anything, my dear, though I fear that you are spending too much time indoors. You look excessively pale…"

As Dan was about to speak Prudence flashed him a look of warning. For the moment no one must learn of her discovery. Every instinct warned her against questioning Lady Brandon. She had no way of knowing how such questions might be received. If the name Manvell was known in the district and the family should learn of her arrival in Kent, some action might be taken against her.

She was under no illusions. At the instigation of some noble family the law might be invoked against her. She could be charged with being an impostor. Certainly she was a runaway, and so was Dan. At an order from a magistrate they would be returned to Cheshire.

She looked up to find that Lady Brandon's eyes were fixed upon the open book. Prudence closed it swiftly.

"It is nothing," she murmured. "Just a slight headache."

"Then you shall spend no more time in here today. Leave the books as they are. You may return to them tomorrow. Why not walk in the gardens this afternoon and take a rest before we dine this evening?"

Prudence was glad to be excused. Her mind was racing. On the following day she would examine the book again. Possibly she might find some clue as to the whereabouts of the family of Manvell, if that was indeed their name.

Next morning her hopes were dashed. The volume on heraldry had disappeared. Greatly troubled, she went to find Lady Brandon.

"Ma'am, I fear I have been careless. I left the books on the desk as you bid me, but one of them is missing. I have searched, but I cannot find it. At first I thought that one of the maids had restored it to the shelves, but it is not there…"

Her ladyship was full of apologies. "What will you think of me, my dear? I should have told you. I took the book away myself. Sebastian asked me to look it out. I put it in his room."

Her manner was not altogether easy, and Prudence wondered at it. Lady Brandon would not meet her eyes and her sense of indignation grew.

Sebastian must have given orders that she was not to be allowed to see the book. It was only with an effort that she hid a feeling of outrage.

"I'm glad to hear that it isn't lost," she said quietly. "I have made a note of the title and will fill in the details at some later date."

She saw the relief on Lady Brandon's face, and it confirmed her suspicions. Her anger grew as she considered the implications. It was clear that Sebastian did not trust her, although she had given him her word. Did he believe that she would run away if she discovered the secret for herself? Worse, was he trying to protect some family in the locality, possibly friends of his?

She would find out. She had intended to speak to him on the previous day, to tell him of her find, but he was gone from home, and did not return until the early hours of the morning.

Today she had not seen him at the breakfast table, and a casual enquiry elicited the information that he had left the house at first light.

Was he trying to avoid her? He would not succeed. She didn't need him now, and she would tell him so. Her discovery was a triumph or sorts, but she could take no pleasure in it. It was a shock to realise that the obsession which had sustained her for so long had lost much of its importance.

Was this what the old vicar meant about being very sure of what she wanted? When wishes were granted, the result could turn to dust and ashes. But did she know what she wanted? An insistent voice within her clamoured to be heard, but she refused to listen.

Back in the library, she found herself unable to concentrate on the work in front of her.

A dark face swam before her gaze, laughing, teasing, and very dear. In her mind's eye she traced the curve of Sebastian's mobile lips, his glowing eyes, and the errant way his black curls refused to stay in place. His presence was so real that he might have been in the room.

She must be mad to dream of him when she should be working at her task. Sternly, she gathered her wandering thoughts. Her first consideration now must be to find some way of finding out about the family of Manvell.

Perhaps she could question Perry. That might be the answer. He knew so little of her past that neither Sebastian nor his mother could have discussed it with him.

She must warn Dan not to mention her discovery to anyone, though that resolve made her feel uneasy. It seemed almost as if she were encouraging him to be deceitful.

She soon found that her fears were groundless. Dan had dismissed the discovery from his mind. He'd been promised a visit to the flour mill, and he could think of nothing else.

"Haven't you seen enough of mills?" she teased.

"This one is different, Pru. It's worked by a waterwheel and the stones come down to grind the flour. I want to find out how it works... Sam says that it's very interesting, and I'm to ride there on the pony."

Smiling, she sent him on his way. For once, she was glad to be alone. She'd slept little on the previous night in spite of her weariness, because when her head touched the pillow, her thoughts had begun to race in an endless circle.

The discovery of the Manvell coat-of-arms had dis-

turbed her deeply. The shock had turned her world upon
its head. Now that her long-cherished dream was made
reality, the thought of what might lay ahead was frightening.

Her chin went up and she straightened her shoulders.
Where was her courage? Was it not better to know the
truth, however distasteful that might be, than to wonder
for the rest of her life? She would not give up now.

The sound of moaning broke into her thoughts. It
came from beneath her window and it puzzled her. Was
it some animal in pain? She hurried across the room and
flung the window wide.

Perry was sitting on the balustrade outside, but he did
not raise his head.

"What is the matter?" Prudence called. "Are you
hurt?"

"Stricken to the heart!" he whispered. "You see before you a penitent. I couldn't find a hair shirt and I
haven't got a scourge, so I'm beating my breast in the
hope of forgiveness…" His shoulders were shaking;
when he looked up, she saw that he was laughing.

"Why, you…you deceiver! How can you be so foolish? I thought you in great pain!"

"I am, but the pain is in my heart! May I come in
and talk to you? I'm sorry about yesterday. I meant no
harm to come to Dan."

Prudence relented. "Come in if you must. Are you
longing to set to work again?" She gestured towards the
shelves.

"Back to the treadmill?" Perry assumed a virtuous
expression. "Do you think it a suitable punishment for
my ill-temper?" He threw a long leg over the window-
sill and climbed into the room. "Must I go on with it
until I am forgiven?"

"You need not ask for my forgiveness, sir."

"Oh, Lord! Now I know I'm in the mire. Must you call me sir?"

"A mere slip of the tongue...I beg your pardon..."

"It is I who should beg yours."

"But you have already done so." Prudence gave him her most enchanting smile. "I did not blame you for the swimming lesson. I know how persistent Dan can be. Unfortunately, he isn't strong, but he won't admit it."

It was pointless to explain that the years of hardship had taken their toll of Dan's thin body, but Perry saw her sad expression.

"I was thoughtless," he told her quietly. "I'll be more careful in future. Pru, you haven't told me much about your life before you came here. Was it very hard?"

"No more than that of many other foundling children, I imagine. We were always tired and cold and hungry. I doubt if I could make you understand."

"But it is all behind you now. In time Dan will grow strong. He is a favourite with Cook, you know. She'll soon put flesh upon his bones. Just look at me!" His grin was irresistible and her eyes began to twinkle.

"Are we friends again?" he asked eagerly.

She laughed and he was satisfied.

She was glad to have Perry to herself. It was the perfect opportunity to question him without arousing his suspicions.

"Ain't you tired of all this?" he asked. "There seems to be no end to it..."

"I enjoy the work," she protested. "I'm only sorry that I know nothing of research into names or dates. Where would I find such things?"

"I don't know." His brows creased in thought. "You

might try *Burke's Peerage*, though you won't find authors or publishers listed there.''

''*Burke's Peerage*? What is that?''

''I've never looked at it myself, but I doubt if it would help you. It tells of titles, dates of birth, number of children, where people live, and other dull stuff like that. There should be a copy somewhere...'' He looked about him vaguely.

''Pray do not trouble to find it,'' Prudence said in haste. It would not do to let him think her interested in the publication. Some chance remark of his might alert his mother.

She was being devious and it disturbed her, though she could not suppress a feeling of irritation. Her quest would not matter to these people who, with centuries of tradition behind them, would never understand it.

In their different ways, both Lord Wentworth and his mother had attempted to discourage her, but their opposition only made her more determined.

Later, when Perry had left her, she began to search for the missing book. Then she heard the sound of horses.

Had Sebastian returned? With a thumping heart she hurried to the window to find the driveway crowded with carriages and outriders.

In the gathering dusk it was difficult to see, but she thought she could distinguish Sebastian's tall figure descending from the first coach.

Then she realised her mistake. The man was heavier than Sebastian, although there was a strong resemblance. With a sinking heart, she realised that the Earl of Brandon and his Countess had arrived.

As the light from the flambeaux streamed across the

entrance to the house Prudence caught her first glimpse of Perry's *bête noire*.

Dressed in the height of fashion, the Countess was immensely tall and thin to the point of emaciation. She looked both proud and disagreeable. Her cold expression did not change even as her mother-in-law came to greet her. She inclined her head, permitting just one kiss upon her cheek. Then she swept indoors.

The Earl did not follow her. With an arm about his mother's waist, he hugged her to him, smiling as three children tumbled from the second coach.

Ignoring the expostulations of their nurse, they rushed towards their grandmother, each anxious to be the first to greet her, and clamouring for attention.

As Lady Brandon bent to kiss them, Prudence looked at the Earl with interest. He was an older, heavier version of Sebastian, but the family resemblance was strong.

As the three boys began to fight he gave them a look of exasperation. Then she heard his sharp tones. He cuffed each child in turn, but the blows were not hard enough to warrant the screams which followed.

Prudence was startled. The eldest boy must be ten years old and his brother just a year or so behind him. For that age they were surprisingly ill-behaved, and now the Earl's youngest son was yelling in sympathy. She could not help comparing them with Dan, much to the latter's advantage.

She sighed. Perry was right, after all. The peace of Hallwood was sure to be disrupted for the next few days, but it was none of her concern. She would stay out of sight as far as possible.

Every instinct told her that the woman who had just arrived would view her with disfavour if she deigned to notice her at all. She would ask again if she might be allowed to eat with Dan in the kitchens.

Later that day she went to find Lady Brandon.

"Ma'am, if you please, I should prefer to eat in the kitchen," she pleaded.

"My dear, you are not a servant. For Dan, it does not matter. He is just a child, but for you it is unsuitable. Sebastian would not like it."

"I'm sure he would understand," Prudence urged in desperation. "You don't treat me as a servant...but...but I am an employee."

"Well, what do you say to a tray in your room?"

"Oh, yes, please. I will fetch it myself."

"There is no need for that." The older woman smiled. She was about to continue when the door opened to admit the Countess.

Prudence looked up to find that she was under inspection. The Countess looked at her mother-in-law and raised her eyebrows in enquiry.

"Amelia, may I present Miss Consett? Prudence, this is the Countess of Brandon, the wife of my eldest son."

Prudence made her curtsy, uncomfortable under the keen scrutiny of a pair of slate-grey eyes. She received an almost imperceptible nod of acknowledgement.

"Prudence is my new companion," her ladyship continued hurriedly. "She helps with my correspondence and is at present working in the library."

The Countess turned to her mother-in-law and spoke as if they were alone.

"A librarian? That is a curious occupation for a woman, and she is over-young. Had you spoken to Frederick, he would have sent down a male person...much more suitable in every way."

"As a companion for me?" Lady Brandon could not resist the temptation to take the Countess up for her sharp comments. Her attempt at humour was ignored.

"Was this girl recommended to you? If so, by whom? I hope you may not regret it. I am not at all in favour of employing young women where there are unmarried sons…"

"Then it is fortunate that Prudence is in my employ, not yours." Lady Brandon's voice was gentle, but the Countess flushed an ugly shade of red. "Prudence, my dear, you may leave us for the moment."

Prudence was happy to be dismissed. If she was not mistaken, the next half-hour would prove to be uncomfortable for her kindly hostess.

She planned to stay in her room that evening, but she had forgotten that she had finished her book.

It was well beyond the usual hour for dinner and she guessed that the family must still be in the dining-room. There was time to slip down to the library before anyone was about.

Chapter Ten

Prudence had miscalculated. The Countess had no patience with country hours, and dinner had been put back to the more fashionable time of eight o'clock.

Prudence met her in the corridor. She bobbed a curtsy, hoping to avoid the need for speech, but the woman stopped her with an imperious gesture.

"Come here, girl!" she ordered. "I wish it to be understood that you will stay away from my children."

"Ma'am?" Prudence looked at her in surprise.

"Don't play the innocent with me! Heaven knows what your life was before Lord Wentworth found you. I have heard something of your history, and I may say that it shocked me."

Prudence bent her head to hide the fury in her eyes. She wanted to strike out…to announce that it would be a pleasure to be spared the company of such odious little brats, but she held her tongue.

"You may go, but take care that you remember my words." The Countess dismissed her with a contemptuous look.

Neither had noticed that the door of the Earl's bedroom was ajar. As Prudence walked away, he came out to join his wife.

"Was that kind, Amelia?" he demanded. "The girl can do no harm. My mother is pleased with her—"

"Utter folly!" his wife snapped. "This is the result of yet another of Sebastian's distempered fits."

"I beg your pardon, madam?"

"You may well do so if you intend to defend your brother's actions. Have you no thought for your own position? As a member of the Government you cannot afford a scandal."

"Pray allow me to remind you that scandal feeds upon rumour carried by vicious tongues. You will oblige me, ma'am, by refraining from criticism of my family."

The Countess tossed her head. "I am well aware that no one is allowed to censure Sebastian, but I am sorry to find that your mother is so easily taken in. My own family would not indulge in such freakish behaviour."

"I believe you. They are not noted for their charity, are they?" His words were sufficient to silence her as they made their way down the staircase.

Prudence clenched her fists. Unable to pass them to reach her own bedchamber, she had been forced to wait in an alcove further along the corridor. Every word had reached her clearly.

Her face burned with humiliation. The Countess had made her feel unclean. She must find Dan and warn him not to speak to the children. This woman would be glad of any excuse to have them turned away. Thank heavens she was to be excused from dining in such unpleasant company.

Her relief was short-lived.

Later that evening Sebastian came to find her.

"Must you do this?" he asked without preamble.

She did not pretend to misunderstand him.

"Yours is a family gathering, sir. I should feel uncomfortable."

"You disappoint me. I hoped that we had made you welcome here." His voice was cold.

"You have, and I am grateful—"

"I don't want your gratitude," he said roughly. "I think you do not realise... By behaving in this way you give my sister-in-law cause to believe that you cannot conduct yourself in company."

Prudence flushed. "She may think whatever she wishes."

"No, she may not. Where is your courage? Are you afraid of her?"

Her eyes flashed then. "No, sir, but I have no wish to cause unpleasantness. The Countess will not care to dine with one she considers beneath her notice."

"That decision does not rest with her."

"My lord, this is a trivial matter. It is not worth a fuss."

"You are mistaken. The Countess of Brandon does not rule this household. In future you will dine as usual with the family."

Her temper rose. "You cannot force me!"

Their eyes locked, and then he smiled. "No, I should have learned my lesson, Prudence." He took her hand in his. "Won't you do this just to please me?"

She saw the old disarming smile and she was lost.

"Very well," she murmured.

He raised her hand to his lips and kissed it gently.

"I won't allow the dragon to eat you," he promised. "Sleep well! I'll see you in the morning."

He left her then, and for the next hour she was a prey

to conflicting thoughts. Why had he been so insistent that she joined the others? It could not be to settle an old score with the Countess. That would be unworthy of him.

Perhaps he was thinking only of her own comfort? She sighed. She'd been unable to make him understand that she'd be far more comfortable dining on her own.

And she'd forgotten to mention that she'd found the Manvell crest in the book on heraldry. Nor had she questioned him again about his own researches. She would do so on the following day.

Next morning she slipped down to the library by the back stairs. Dan came to her for his morning lesson, and then he disappeared in search of Perry.

That young man was giving the house the widest possible berth to avoid all contact with his sister-in-law. She missed his merry chatter, but in his absence she was free to search for the book she wanted.

It was an hour before she found it. Kneeling among the pile of books which lay about her, she reached to the back of the last cupboard and touched a thick volume bound in red morocco leather. She looked at the title with a sense of rising excitement. This was the book she sought.

It didn't take her long to find the entry. Avidly she scanned the details on Manvell of Longridge. Then she read them aloud.

Manvell of Longridge

Jonathan Manvell, born 3 November 1728. Married June 16 1750, Anne, daughter of Crispin Langhorne Esq., of Orford Chase in the County of Norfolk: by which lady (died 1754) he had issue, Frances, born

1751, and Henrietta, born 1754. Principal seat, Longridge Hall, in the County of Kent. Heir presump-
tive, William, Lord Woodforde, grandson of the
above.

Her own voice seemed to echo around the room,
mocking her with each syllable. Could she be related to
this family? The coat-of-arms upon her brooch was
clearly illustrated below the entry.

She read the words again. Either of the Manvell
daughters might have been her mother. They were the
right age…but why…why had she been abandoned?

There must have been some scandal…some unsuitable liaison which had resulted in the birth of a bastard.
She bit her lip. It was an ugly word, but she had faced
it long ago. The old vicar had suggested an alternative…he preferred to call her a love child, but Prudence
scorned the suggestion. Those who had abandoned her
knew nothing of love.

She pored over the entry again. Now she knew where
to find the Manvell family. Some time…somehow…she
would confront them, and she would savour every moment of their shame.

She was about to copy out the entry when the door
opened. Swiftly, she pushed the book beneath a pile of
papers, and turned to find Lady Brandon at her side.

"My dear, I shall need some help this afternoon. Frederick and Amelia are gone into Canterbury, Perry is out,
and Sebastien is away on some business of his own. I
thought it the perfect opportunity to get on with my correspondence. Shall you mind leaving your present
task?"

Prudence smiled and shook her head. It was a relief

to find that she and her ladyship were to lunch alone. She would copy out the entry later.

It was only in the dusk of the autumn evening that she found herself free to return to the library. It was the work of moments to write down the information that she needed. Then a thought struck her. She did not know the location of Longridge Hall, and the County of Kent was large.

She reached down the book of maps which had so enchanted Dan, but they were historic works, and owed more to the imagination of the ancient cartographers than to an orderly survey of the county. She could find no mention of Longridge. Perhaps it was just the name of the house. She had no way of finding out.

"Miss Consett, you will ruin your eyes by working in this light. Allow me to ring for candles." The Earl of Brandon was beside her.

"My lord, I have finished for the day." Prudence rose to her feet and dropped a curtsy.

"But I have not." He tugged at the bell-rope.

"I beg your pardon, sir. I had not realised that you wished to use the library. If you will excuse me…"

She was about to leave the room. This was her first encounter with Sebastian's elder brother, and she felt ill at ease.

"Don't run away. Won't you show me what you have been doing?" Prudence was grateful for his interest. She sensed that he wished to make up in some way for the insults offered by his wife.

She kept her explanations short, showing him her lists, and stroking the books with loving fingers. When she looked up, it was to find him smiling.

"An enthusiast, I see!" At that moment he looked so like Sebastian that her breath caught in her throat.

"It's difficult not to become so," she said shyly. "Some of these books are like old friends."

"And much less trying than new ones?"

"Oh, no!" she disclaimed quickly. "That is not true. Everyone at Hallwood has been kind to me."

"Everyone?" His tone was ironic, but he did not pursue the subject. Instead he laid his papers upon the desk, and as he did so she noticed his hands. They might have been Sebastian's. The Earl had the same long fingers and similar grace in all his movements.

She turned away, but he was already absorbed in his work and he did not see her expression.

Then, as she climbed the stairs to her room she heard wailing from the floor above. She guessed that it came from the nursery.

Since the children's arrival she'd learned to ignore the noise above her head as the three boys screamed and shouted, but there was something different about this cry. It was filled with pain.

She felt a sudden surge of pity, but there was nothing she could do. Her presence would not be welcomed in the nursery. The Countess had made her wishes clear.

She washed her face and hands, scrubbing away all traces of dust and printer's ink before she changed her gown for dinner.

"Is something wrong with one of the children?" she asked the maid who had come to help her dress. The wailing had increased.

"I don't know, miss. They'm allus crying about one thing or another."

"Perhaps so, but I can't help feeling that something is wrong."

"Well, that there nurse ain't with them. She be lying on her bed."

Prudence stared at the girl. "You had best come with me."

"But, miss, I'll be wanted in the dining-room."

"This won't take a moment," Prudence told her firmly. "Where is the nurse's room?"

The girl shrugged, but she led the way to the floor above and tapped at one of the doors.

Prudence heard a muffled sound. It was impossible to decide if it was an invitation to enter, or a plea for them to go away.

She opened the door and found herself in a darkened room. Over in the corner a huddled figure was lying upon a trestle bed. Then she heard a moan.

"Don't draw the curtains," the figure begged. "I can't bear the light."

Prudence lit a candle, shading the flame with her hand. Then she walked over to the bed.

"Nurse, what is the matter?" she asked.

For answer the woman turned towards her, revealing a flushed face covered in scarlet spots. She was feverish and clearly very ill.

Prudence was horrified. "How long have you been like this?" she asked.

"I've felt poorly for the past two days. The Countess said I was malingering. Now she can see for herself. I'm covered in these spots and they itch something awful…"

"Try not to scratch them. If you do they'll leave a scar. Have you told the Countess?"

"She don't like to be disturbed of an evening, miss." Tears of weakness trickled down the woman's face.

"Don't worry, I'll send word to her. Meantime you shall have some lemonade and a cooling lotion for the spots." Prudence dispatched the maid with the necessary orders.

It was too much to hope that the children had escaped the infection and her fears were confirmed when she opened the nursery door.

All three children were lying upon their beds, crying feebly. Their nightshirts were soaking to the touch and they were flushed and restless.

She looked about her swiftly. Then she poured some water from the ewer into a china bowl and began to sponge them down, stripping off their sodden clothing and throwing it aside.

Even the beds were damp with sweat. She would need help to change them, but first she must make the children comfortable. She tugged at the bell-rope before starting to search for their clean nightwear and was fastening the last of the buttons when someone entered the room.

Then she heard a gasp. When she turned, she thought that the Countess was about to strike her. The slate-grey eyes were venomous.

"So I was right!" Amelia hissed. "You and that other urchin have brought infection to this house." She carried a lighted candelabra to the bed and looked down at her sons.

"The light should be shaded," Prudence said quickly. "It may harm their eyes."

"Insolence! Would you give *me* orders? Leave this room at once and pack your bags. You won't spend another night beneath this roof."

"My dear Amelia, you sound quite distraught. What can have happened to disturb you?"

Wentworth was standing in the doorway, and as Prudence heard his deep voice she felt a surge of relief. She moved deeper into the shadows to hide the happiness in her eyes. Her expression would have betrayed the emotion which she wasn't anxious to reveal.

Her confusion went unnoticed as Sebastian faced Amelia. The Countess did not trouble to conceal her fury.

''This is all of your doing, Wentworth. Your precious paupers have brought their ailments with them. Now my children are at death's door!''

''I doubt it,'' he replied serenely. ''They are in remarkably good voice.''

He spoke no more than the truth. The wailing reached a crescendo as the boys heard their mother's dire prediction.

''Must you frighten them?'' he asked. ''I imagine that rest is what is needed...''

''As if you care!'' The Countess gave him a bitter look. ''I could not believe my ears when your mother told me that you had taken up two guttersnipes, and runaways at that. This is the result. Now others must suffer for your folly.''

Wentworth ignored her. Instead he turned to Prudence.

''Where is the nurse?'' he asked.

''She is suffering from the same complaint, my lord. I think it is the measles.''

''And have you had the measles, Prudence?''

''Yes, sir. Some years ago there was an epidemic at the mill.''

''Then you are safe from further infection. What of Dan?''

''He had measles at the same time.''

Sebastian turned to the Countess. ''Satisfied, Amelia? Neither Prudence nor Dan could have brought the infection with them.''

"Slum children!" Her voice was hot with anger. "Doubtless they are harbouring something worse. And who is to say that this is measles? It could be the small-pox—"

"Be quiet, woman! Will you cause a panic? Let us see what the doctor has to say before you give way to hysteria."

"That girl must go!" The Countess rounded on Prudence. "I won't have her near my children…"

"You intend to care for them yourself?" His voice was carefully neutral.

"Of course not! I employ others for that purpose. Besides, Frederick would not hear of it."

"Shall we ask him?" There was a note of deceptive sweetness in Sebastian's tone. "If you insist, I'm sure he won't object."

The Countess glared at him. "The nurse already has the measles, if that is what it is. It cannot signify to her…"

"Ma'am, she is not well enough to leave her bed." Prudence had not imagined that this statement would bring down upon her head the full fury of the Countess.

"Silence, you impudent wench! You will not interfere again. Did I not tell you to pack your bags?"

Sebastian stared at her, and she was the first to look away.

"Do you know, I was under the impression that my mother was the mistress of this household," he murmured. "Has she given such orders?"

Blue eyes and grey locked in total enmity. Then, her face contorted with rage, the Countess swept out of the room.

"Is Mamma cross?" a small voice quavered.

"She's sad to find you feeling ill, but you'll soon be

well again.'' Prudence gave the boys a reassuring smile. Then she felt a firm hand upon her shoulder.

"Will you stay with them for a while? I'll try to make some other arrangements."

"Pray don't trouble, sir. I'm used to boys. If her ladyship will excuse me from my duties in the library, I shall manage here."

"I know you will." Sebastian's eyes were warm as he looked down at her. "My dear, I can't begin to tell you…perhaps I should not try…" There was something in his voice which stirred her heart. She blushed and looked away.

"It is nothing, my lord." To hide her confusion she moved over to the boys. "We shall have a famous time. I know some exciting stories. Do you believe that a giant lives at Hallwood? His name is John. He can pick up a rogue in either hand and bang their heads together."

"Shall we see him?"

"I expect so," Sebastian replied. "But first you must get well again. John is a splendid fighter, but he won't like to catch your spots. You must rest up here for a day or two."

"But, Uncle, I can't stay in this bed. It's horrible…all wet and soggy."

"So it is. Out you get. Prudence and I will make things right." Without more ado he slipped off his coat. Then he picked up the two younger boys and carried them to an ancient sofa, tucking a coverlet around them. "You, too, Crispin. Under here. You'll keep each other warm. This won't take a moment."

He looked across at Prudence. "The bedlinen is kept in that large chest by the window. If you will help me…" Without waiting for a reply, he began to strip the beds.

"I will do that," she protested. "My lord, there is no need for you…"

"It is easier with two," he told her briefly.

She looked at him in surprise. How could he know? He could not have done such menial work before. Her astonishment was clear and he shook his head in mock exasperation.

"Still no faith in me? My dear, I haven't lived in an ivory tower, whatever you may think."

His actions proved it. His fingers were quicker than her own as he tucked in the corners of the sheets. Then he eyed his nephews.

"Jump in!" he ordered. "Since Prudence has been kind enough to stay with you I want you on your best behaviour. No more squalling! Soldiers on the battlefield feel worse than you do now. Later I'll come and tell you about our fight against the Frenchmen at Quebec in Canada."

With this promise he drew Prudence aside. "I'll send Sam for the doctor," he said quietly. "We must be sure that this is measles and nothing worse."

His face was grave and she longed to comfort him. "I'm sure of it, my lord. The symptoms are the same as those I saw before, and though the boys are uncomfortable and feverish, I cannot think that this is smallpox."

"I hope you may be right." His dark eyes held her own. "I have no right to ask this of you before we have the doctor's diagnosis…"

"Would I agree to stay here if I thought this was some dread disease?" she asked with a touch of humour.

"I know you would." He was gripping her hand so tightly that his fingers whitened. "What a staunch friend you are!"

"Pray do not worry, sir." Prudence coloured at the compliment. "I told you that I am never ill."

"And never daunted?" He was gazing down at her with an expression which she could not fathom. Then he released her hand and left her.

She turned back to the children to find them regarding her with solemn eyes.

"I don't know your names," she said cheerfully. "Won't you tell me?"

"I'm Crispin, this is Damian, and Gerard is the baby."

"No, I'm not!" This insult brought an immediate denial from the youngest child. "I'm a boy!"

"So you are…and a brave one, I expect. My name is Prudence."

"Will you read to us?" Crispin asked hopefully.

"It's too dark in here, but I'll tell you a story. Then we might sing some songs."

"I don't like the dark," Gerard told her. "The shadows look like monsters."

She heard a scornful exclamation from the eldest boy, and intervened before a quarrel could develop.

"There are four of us here," she chuckled. "No monsters would come near us. They'd be too afraid."

"Robbers might…" A watery eye peered out at her from beneath the coverlet.

"Then let's pretend that we are Bow Street Runners hiding in the robbers' cave, so that we can catch them."

As Prudence had expected, this led to an immediate demand to know all about the Bow Street Runners. She had not heard of them herself until the name had captured her attention in a book on famous crimes.

Now she allowed herself full licence, making up

imaginary stories of the exploits of that valiant band of men who were sworn to enforce the law.

"When I'm grown up I shall be a Bow Street Runner," Damian told her. "Papa will lend me one of his pistols."

"No, you won't. You are to go into the army. Papa said so."

"I might not want to…"

"Cowardy custard!" Crispin jeered.

"Be quiet, Crispin! The Runners are as brave as soldiers." Prudence quelled him with a look. "What will you do?"

"Oh, I'm to be the Earl of Brandon—"

"Not until Papa dies," his brother interrupted. "And I hope he won't just yet."

"He won't, will he, Prudence?" Gerard's lip was trembling.

"Of course not. Your papa is big and strong. He'll live for years and years and years."

"You are referring to me, I hope?" Sebastian had returned and was smiling down at the little group upon the bed.

Prudence had given up all notions of decorum. She was lying against the pillows with one arm around Gerard's small body. The older boys were sprawled beside her.

"Prudence, I hear that you have not eaten yet," Sebastian reproved her.

"I had forgot, my lord." She struggled to her feet.

"Well, off you go! Even a lady of iron constitution needs sustenance, you know."

Prudence warmed to the affection in his voice.

"You'll come back, won't you?" Gerard pleaded. "You said that we should sing some songs…"

"I promise! See, I'll cross my heart. I'll come back when the big finger of the clock is straight upwards, and the small one points to nine."

"That will be nine o'clock," Damian said proudly. "I've learned to tell the time."

Sebastian followed her to the door. "You need not hurry back so soon," he told her. "Will you not rest? I will see the doctor."

"I mustn't break my promise, sir."

He shook his head in mock reproof, but he did not argue further. The look in his blue eyes as they met her own was sufficient to turn her knees to water. She left him quickly. Her veil of serenity was fragile. He could rend it to shreds with a single touch. Now she was fighting a desperate longing to throw herself into his arms. She fled towards the sanctuary of her bedchamber.

Once there she found that her appetite had vanished. She could deceive herself no longer. The more she saw of Sebastian the more she loved him. It was nothing to do with his appearance, or the way his eyes smiled down at her, luring her heart from her breast. She would think him perfect if he were the ugliest man alive.

He was everything she had ever dreamed of in a man, but fate had not been kind to her. Nothing could come of this relationship, but she would remember him for the rest of her life.

Now she sensed a subtle change in him. In these past few days there had been something different in the way he looked at her.

Perhaps it was her imagination, but there was a special warmth in his expression. She thought back to their outing to the beach. He'd lifted her when she tripped and fell, and for a second she'd seen a strangeness upon his face. It was almost as if he'd dropped his guard, betraying something more than mere concern.

She shook her head. She must be dreaming. It would be folly to believe that he had grown to share her feelings.

Yet he had said that they were friends. She hugged the memory to her, treasuring his words. If only she might stay here for a little longer to see him, to hear his voice and to know that he slept beneath the same roof.

Hot colour rose to her cheeks as she recalled the day she had walked in upon him at the inn. It seemed a lifetime ago, but she could not banish the memory of that strong, athletic body.

She pressed her hands to her temples. She was allowing her imagination to run riot. It would be sweet to know the joy of lying in his arms whilst he whispered words of love. His eyes would look down at her, warming her with their inner glow...

She must stop this daydreaming. Such thoughts had never crossed Sebastian's mind. Had he not assured her on more than one occasion that her virtue was safe with him? He would always see her as the urchin he had found by chance, and never as a woman.

For her own peace of mind she must leave Hallwood as soon as possible. She was no longer bound by her promise not to run away in his absence. Yet her loving heart held her captive. She could not leave just yet. She had not discovered the whereabouts of Longridge... and...and there were the Earl's children to consider.

Those were excuses, she told herself fiercely. Honesty compelled her to admit it. She was becoming weak and self-indulgent. Where was her strength of will? Sadly, it seemed to have been swept away on a tide of love.

* * *

When she returned to the sick-room she found Sebastian reading by the light of a shaded candle. The children were asleep.

"My lord, was there no one else to sit with them?" she asked.

"The maids are nervous, Prudence. My mother will not force them. She would have come herself, but the doctor has forbidden it."

Prudence looked at him in dread, a question in her eyes.

"No, it isn't the plague. Just a severe attack of measles. He has given them a draught to help them sleep. Their nurse has suffered most."

"Then there is no need for you to stay here now. I will look after them."

She glanced up to find his eyes intent upon her face.

"Are you hiding something from me, Prudence?"

She blushed. "I...I don't know what you mean," she faltered.

"Say rather that you have no wish to tell me." His hand reached out to ruffle her hair in the old familiar gesture. Then he withdrew it quickly. "Your face is the mirror of your thoughts, you know."

"I hope that it is not." She managed a faint smile.

"Well, perhaps only to me. We have grown close in the time since we met."

A tingle of excitement ran from her shoulder blades down to the base of her spine. She had longed to hear those words, but she did not dare to hope that he meant more than friendship.

"Sir, you must have a taste for combat." She spoke with a lightness she was far from feeling. "Rather compare it to being hit on the head with a hammer. It feels so good when it has stopped.''

He laughed at that and the dangerous moment passed. In another moment she might have betrayed herself.

''Prudence, I should not ask it of you, but will you sleep next door? The children are unlikely to wake, but if you left the door ajar…?''

She was quick to murmur her assent. Then he rose to his feet, his hands resting upon her shoulders.

''I was mistaken,'' he said quietly. ''I thought you but a child, but now I find—'' He stopped as he saw the expression in her eyes. Raising her fingers to his lips, he left her to her thoughts.

Chapter Eleven

Prudence pressed her hands to her burning cheeks. Sebastian no longer thought of her as just a child. She felt herself unfolding like a flower in the sunlight. She had prayed for this, but she knew the risks.

She must hide her secret love for him. She knew now that he was not indifferent to her, and he was a man like any other. There was sensuality in that strong face, and he wanted her. She had well understood the look of passion in his eyes, though he had been quick to hide it.

A feeling of exultation seized her. She threw her arms out wide. How wonderful to be desired by this man whom she loved above all others. She was tempted to dance about the room.

Then common sense returned. Where would their mutual passion lead them? Marriage was out of the question, and much as she loved him she would never consent to become his mistress. Sebastian knew his duty. In time he would make some eligible connection. If she agreed to a liaison it would mean some hole-in-corner affair. That would sully both of them. To put temptation in his way could lead only to disaster.

She must spend the rest of her life without him, and

that would demand a wrenching effort of will. At least he could have no idea of her own feelings for him, otherwise he would not have spoken out so openly.

And he must never know. On that sombre thought she fell asleep.

It was after midnight when a cry aroused her from her slumbers. She hurried into the nursery to find Gerard tossing in his bed, coughing and feverish and scratching at his spots.

She gathered him into her arms and gave him a cooling drink. Then she slipped his fingers back into the cotton gloves.

"I can't sleep in gloves," he wailed.

"You shall be the conductor of the orchestra. He wears white gloves, you know. Here is your baton..." She handed him a spoon. "I will sing, but you must signal when to start."

The game diverted him for a time. Then he fell asleep again, heavy against her arm, but when she tried to move away his eyes re-opened time and again. She hugged him to her. She would stay with him till morning.

At last she fell asleep herself.

When she awoke it was to find Sebastian standing by the bed.

"Did we disturb you?" she asked in drowsy tones.

"No more than usual..." His voice was unaccountably harsh.

"I'm sorry, my lord. I thought I was singing softly." Then she realised that he was fully dressed.

"What time is it?" she asked.

"It's morning. Have you been here all night?"

"Oh, no, the children slept for hours. Then Gerard wakened."

"I see." His jaw was set in an expression which she did not understand.

Aware of the tension in him she followed his glance and was horrified to find that her nightgown had fallen open to the waist. She clutched it to her in confusion.

"Sir, I must get dressed. If you will look the other way, I'll go back to my room."

Obediently he turned his back as she slipped out of the bed.

"One moment, please!" he said. "I won't have you wearing yourself to the bone. You will please to rest this morning."

"It is not necessary—"

"Must you always argue?" He swung round upon her then and his tone was brutal. "You'd drive a man mad!!"

"I'm sorry!" she choked out. For some reason she had angered him, and shivering in her thin nightgown she felt vulnerable. A sob escaped her lips as she ran towards the adjoining room.

He caught her before she reached the doorway.

"You are sorry?" he cried wildly. "How do you think I feel? I wish I'd never met you."

"That's easily remedied," she said, weeping. "I'll go away…"

"I think not!" He threw his arms about her and held her close, showering kisses upon her eyelids and her lips until she was half-fainting. Against her conscious will she melted into his embrace, yielding to a passion which matched her own.

Lost to the world about them, they were unaware that the door to the corridor had opened, but a sharp exclamation of horror brought them back to reality.

The Countess was regarding them with a stony glare.

Then she smiled and there was malice in her eyes. Without a word she turned and walked away.

Sebastian was the first to recover his composure.

"Get dressed!" he said quickly. "I'll see if I can stop her."

"How will you do that?" Prudence was shaking with shame and humiliation. "Nothing will give her greater pleasure than to spread her tale throughout this house. She detests me, and has always done so."

"Leave it to me! The fault is entirely mine." With a formal bow he left her.

Prudence felt very cold. The fire in her room was not yet lit, and her teeth chattered as she struggled into her clothes.

Deliberately she made her mind a blank. She would wipe out all memory of the past hour. Sebastian had been quick to shoulder the blame for what had happened between them, but she too had been at fault.

She had welcomed his caresses, returning his kiss as if her very life depended on it. Her treacherous body had been aflame, and he must have sensed it. Now he would think her little better than a harlot, luring him on with little thought for the future.

She could not deceive herself. By now her ladyship would have the story. She might depend on it. Nothing would sway the Countess from her purpose, and she would revel in her triumph.

It was a bitter pill to swallow, but she could put an end to this impossible situation. She spread out the old blue skirt and began to make a bundle of her few possessions.

Thank heavens she had kept the old homespun jacket, her breeches and the flannel shirt. Slow tears fell upon the garments as she laid them on the bed. Memories of that day at the fair in Stamford were all too much to bear.

"Prudence, what are you doing?" Lady Brandon's voice recalled her to the present.

"Ma'am, the Countess will have told you. I can't stay here—"

"Am I to pay attention to the gossip of an ill-natured woman? I am disappointed in you..."

"What she said was true. She did find me undressed...and...and..."

"Sebastian stole a kiss from you? Is that so very dreadful? Young men are apt to do such things, and you are a most attractive girl. I'm sorry if you feel insulted."

"You don't understand." Prudence spoke in little more than a whisper.

"Believe me, I think I do."

"I wish it hadn't happened. What must you think of me?"

"I think you a sensible young woman who will not make too much of what was the impulse of a moment. Great heavens, Prudence, you will not tell me that no man has tried to snatch a kiss from you before?" Lady Brandon spoke in a rallying tone, with some amusement in her voice, but Prudence did not respond in similar vein. At last she forced herself to reply.

"They've tried...but..."

"Then if you are wise you will banish the matter from your mind. Sebastian was at fault, but he assures me that his behaviour will not be repeated. There now, are you satisfied?"

Prudence found no comfort in the assurance, though she was grateful to Lady Brandon for making light of the matter. She had no way of knowing that the older woman was troubled. Her ladyship was too wise to reveal that her worst fears were now confirmed.

It was only too clear that Sebastian's feelings had changed. He was no womaniser. He had never made advances even to the prettiest of her maids. And as for more eligible girls? She sighed. Of late she had begun to wonder if any woman would arouse his interest to the point of offering marriage.

Something must be done, but it would be madness to turn Prudence away as the Countess had insisted. Sebastian would spring at once to the girl's defence, and the whole situation would be given an importance which it did not merit.

The interview with her daughter-in-law had been most unpleasant, but Frederick had intervened, silencing his wife with a few sharp words.

''Will you make such a piece of work about nothing, Amelia?'' he'd asked. ''These matters are none of your concern. I wish you will not be so busy.''

''I am thinking about my children…''

''Are you? I had not noticed it. You have forgot, I think, that the girl is not afraid to nurse them.''

Later the Countess had returned to the attack. Both Prudence and Lady Brandon could hear the quarrel which was taking place even at that moment.

''Brandon, you are a fool!'' the shrill voice cried. ''The girl is a strumpet. She was almost naked in your brother's arms…''

His reply was indistinguishable.

''That's right! Make excuses! We all know that dear Sebastian is beyond criticism, but I had not thought that he would foist his light o' love upon your mother—''

The Earl's voice rose in anger. ''What a mind you

have! It is nothing of the sort. How dare you insult my family so?''

They heard a bitter laugh. ''Have it your own way, but I warn you…that girl will trap him yet.''

Prudence stood motionless beside her bed. Her eyes were dry, but she had never been so angry in her life. She longed to fly at the Countess, forcing her to retract the ugly accusation.

Lady Brandon made haste to close the door.

''What can I say, my dear? You must not allow the ravings of a vindictive woman to upset you. I am so sorry that you should have heard her.''

''Ma'am, I have no wish to be the cause of family quarrels. Dan and I must leave. We have been here too long.''

Lady Brandon played her last card. ''Won't you think of me?'' she said gently. ''I need your help with the children, and I ask it as a favour.''

Prudence looked at her in despair. How could she refuse? It would be base ingratitude. She owed this kindly woman so much. She made a last attempt to get her way.

''The Countess thinks me unfit to take care of her sons, your ladyship.''

''What she thinks is unimportant. Besides, she won't be here. Frederick is recalled to London and Amelia will go with him. They are to leave today.''

''I thought they were to stay for weeks…''

Lady Brandon frowned. ''Events are moving fast in France, and our Government is worried. Oh, my dear, I feel distraught. I can only pray that my darling Sophie and her babes are safe. If only we had heard from Gilles…''

Prudence was moved to pity. Lady Brandon seemed to have aged before her eyes. The lines upon her face were more pronounced and she was beginning to look gaunt.

On an impulse she reached out and laid a hand upon the older woman's sleeve.

"I'll stay," she said quietly. "At least until the boys are well again."

"Thank you, my dear. I'll take care that the burden does not fall entirely on your shoulders. Sebastian has gone to fetch our old nurse. She is somewhat frail, but she will help you."

Prudence nodded. The decision to stay was much against her better judgement, but it would have been churlish to refuse. She would avoid Sebastian's company, and with the Countess gone her life would not be made a misery.

"Will you not rest this morning? I think you did not sleep last night. Perry is with the boys, and Nurse will soon be here."

"Your ladyship, I am well able—"

"Yes, yes, I know you are, but we cannot have you falling sick yourself. Would that I could help, but I have not had the measles and the doctor has forbidden it."

"You should not consider exposing yourself to infection, ma'am. I will do as you ask when Nurse arrives."

When she went up to the nursery, she found Perry in possession of the floor. He'd found a box of paints and was dabbing scarlet spots upon his face, to the delight of all three boys.

As Prudence entered the room, he began to groan. "I'm ill!" he cried. "I must have lemonade and sherbet and jellies and fruit creams…"

"You shall have none of them," she said with mock severity. "A dose of the doctor's medicine is what you need."

This reduced the boys to helpless laughter.

"Make him take it!" Damian shouted. "It tastes horrible, Uncle Perry."

"Monster! Have you no pity for me?" Perry mourned. "Look at my face!" He closed his eyes and groaned again.

Prudence peered at him. "I think it a great improvement," she announced. "That colour suits you well."

"It's paint! It's paint! Did you think he had the measles?" Gerard was jumping up and down upon the bed.

"Not for a moment," Prudence said severely. "He is pretending to be a Red Indian on the warpath."

This was the signal for Perry to leap about the room, whooping and chanting as he danced.

"Master Perry, whatever are you up to? The noise is enough to frighten a body to death."

"I've never frightened you." Perry seized his old nurse about the waist and swung her off her feet.

"Adone, do! You silly boy! What will miss think of you?" The old woman straightened her cap and bobbed a curtsy to Prudence. "I take no notice of his nonsense, miss, and nor should you."

"I don't," Prudence smiled. "The boys must be so glad to see you, and so am I."

Nurse waddled over to the bed. "Well, Master Crispin, have you been painting up your face as well?"

"No, Ellie. These are real spots. I wish they did not itch so much."

"We'll soon put that to rights. Now, do you fancy anything to eat?"

They were quick to recite Perry's list of favourite foods.

Nurse shook her head, but she went away with a promise to see what she could do.

"Prudence tells exciting stories, Uncle Perry..." Damian gave her a hopeful look.

"Does she? Then I shall listen, too." He took a seat beside her.

"You are not otherwise engaged today?" she teased.

"No, I'm back in residence since I heard our heartening news." His eyes were twinkling.

Prudence frowned a warning at this reference to the departure of the Countess, but in reply he grinned at her.

"What about this story?" he asked cheerfully.

"Not yet. The boys must be washed and changed. Then they must take their medicine before they have their nuncheon."

This statement brought long faces, but the smiles returned when Perry insisted upon trying the obnoxious liquid. He held his nose and grimaced. Then he rolled upon the floor, clutching at his stomach. The three boys were convulsed.

"My dear sir, you are wasted here at Hallwood. You should be upon the stage." Prudence could not hide her own amusement.

"I know it." He jumped to his feet as Nurse returned with a laden tray. "What have we here? Is there some for me, or is this all for these greedy creatures?"

"Give over, Master Perry. The poor little mites ain't eaten a bite for days."

"I'm not a poor little mite...I'm a boy," Gerard announced with dignity.

"So you keep on telling us. Are you a boy who wants to hear a story about a dragon?" Prudence settled herself in a chair beside the bed and picked up a spoon.

"Yes, please!" Gerard opened his mouth obediently and took some of the jelly.

"Miss, I can do that," Nurse protested.

"Ellie, go and eat. You may come back later." Perry took the old woman by the arm and led her to the door. "Prudence, I hope this story isn't going to be too frightening. If it is, I shall put a pillow over my head!"

"It's *very* frightening," Prudence assured him. "Perhaps you should go away."

"No...I'll try to be brave."

"Very well. This is the story of the terrible dragon of...of Longridge." She hesitated, wondering if she should have used the name. "He lived in a cave high above the sea."

"With his friends?" Gerard interrupted.

"No, he had no friends. He was a wicked dragon. If he saw anyone on the shore, he would slither down and chase them."

"Did he catch them?"

"Never!" she said stoutly. "He couldn't run fast because he was so fat. That made him angry, so he decided to hide behind the rocks and breathe fire at the fisherman when they came in to land."

"Great heavens!" said Perry faintly. "A fat, fire-breathing dragon? I hope I never meet him."

"You might." Damian regarded his uncle with interest. "That is, if you sail your yacht too close to where he lives. If you should catch him, will you bring him back to Hallwood?"

"Certainly not! He'd frighten the horses. Besides, I've met one dragon. I don't care to meet up with another..."

Prudence gave him a goaded look. His wicked references to his sister-in-law were not in the best of taste, even though the children didn't understand them.

"Do you wish to hear this story?" she demanded. "If not, you may leave us!"

"Sorry, ma'am." He pretended to tug his forelock. "You won't hear another word from me."

"What happened then?" Damian was all attention.

"The dragon went for a swim in the sea. When he came out, he was so cold and wet that he decided to warm himself by making the biggest fire in the neighbourhood. He needed wood, of course, so he crawled into the forest, but all the woodcutters ran away."

"I wouldn't run away," said Damian. "I'd ask my father and Uncle Sebastian to come with me."

Perry laughed aloud. "An excellent choice! Both of them are expert at dealing with dragons."

"Will you be quiet? Perhaps you'd like to finish this tale yourself?" Prudence frowned at him.

"No, no! I am agog! Pray go on!"

Prudence had been thinking fast. She had mentioned Longridge. Perhaps there was a way to find out where it was.

"Then the dragon had another idea," she continued. "Why should he huff and puff and go to the trouble of making his own fire when there were huge fires at Longridge Hall? He could steal some fire from there."

"Was that a castle?"

"He didn't know, but he tried to find it. Then he lost his way, and there was no one he could ask."

"My father would have known," Crispin told her proudly. "He knows everything!"

"So does the Red Indian Chief." Perry grinned. "I could have taken him straight there. My tracking skills are legendary—"

Prudence seized her chance. "More exaggeration?" she teased. "I don't believe you, my good sir."

"No? Then let me inform you that Longridge Hall is not so very far from here. It's close to Dover." Perry began to laugh. "The old curmudgeon won't be too pleased to hear that he has a dragon in his woods."

"What's a curmudgeon, Uncle Perry?"

"He's a sourpuss, Damian, known in the neighbourhood for the miser that he is, or was. I wonder if he's still alive?"

"How strange!" Prudence could scarcely hide her excitement. "This man...he is not seen about the countryside?"

"Old Manvell is a recluse. He ain't been seen for years. He's probably been eaten by the dragon."

Gerard gulped. "Prudence, does the dragon really eat people?" His eyes were wide with fright.

"Of course not!" It was an effort to control her wandering thoughts. "He isn't very brave, you know. If anyone shouts at him, he runs away."

"But did he find the house with the fires?"

"No. He came to a clearing in the forest and there he met a boy..."

"A big boy?" Gerard breathed.

"He was about as big as Damian, and he was tending his pigs. When they squealed, he looked up and saw the dragon..."

Gerard pulled the covers over his head. "I don't want to hear any more," he shouted.

"But it is a splendid story." Prudence laid a comforting hand upon his shoulder. "He chased the dragon away so fast that it could not stop when it come to the edge of the cliff. It fell into the sea..."

"Was it drownded?" A fearful eye appeared from beneath the covers.

"Drowned dead! Now there are no more dragons at Longridge."

Sighs of satisfaction greeted the end of the story, although Crispin announced with scorn that it was just a fairy tale.

"I believed every word of it," Perry said solemnly. "I am quite worn out with the excitement. When are we to have another story?"

"Not until this afternoon," Prudence told him firmly. "The doctor is to pay another visit—"

"Then I'll be off. I've only had one dose of medicine and he'll be cross with me. He's put me through it in the past, I can tell you..."

"Master Perry, it was no more than you deserved." Nurse had come to join them. "Miss Prudence, you wouldn't believe what a lad he was...always falling out of trees, or into the lake. I never saw such a boy for breaking his limbs."

"But, Ellie, I've reformed. I haven't broken a bone for years...at least, not for months..."

"Get off with you!" The old woman eyed him with affection. Clearly Perry was her darling. "Her ladyship is waiting, and you mustn't keep her from her luncheon—"

She was interrupted as the door burst open and Sebastian came towards them. As she saw his expression Prudence half-rose to her feet.

"What is it?" she cried. "What has happened?"

"Sophie has arrived," he said briefly. "Gilles has sent her to us with young Tollard as her escort."

Perry looked startled. "That was a bit sudden, wasn't it? What changed his mind?"

"The mob took King Louis at Versailles. They brought him back to Paris. Now he's a prisoner in the Palace of the Tuileries."

Perry whistled in astonishment. "I can't believe it. How is Sophie?"

''She's unharmed. Come and see for yourself. She'll tell you all about it.'' He turned to Prudence. ''I'm sure you would like to meet my sister.'' Without waiting for a reply, he led the way downstairs.

Prudence hung back. As far as possible she wanted to avoid Sebastian's company, but Perry tucked her arm in his.

''You'll like Sophie,'' he announced. ''She's a great gun.'' This brotherly compliment appeared to be the highest which he could bestow, and Prudence hid a smile.

It faded as she entered the salon. The family gathering was larger than she had expected. Then Lady Brandon came towards her, leading a tall girl by the hand.

''Sophie, this is Prudence Consett. And this, my dear, is my daughter, the Comtesse de Verneuil.''

''I hope you will call me Sophie.'' The young woman's voice was low and musical. ''How are my brother's children today?''

''They are feeling better, ma'am.'' Prudence ventured a closer look at Sebastian's sister. How much alike they were. She would have recognised the young Comtesse anywhere.

Those dark eyes and the clean-cut features proclaimed her ancestry, and the firmly moulded lips were so like Sebastian's own. Yet Sophie did not look old enough to be the mother of two sons.

Although Sophie was smiling, Prudence gazed at her in some concern. Against the pallor of her cheeks the dark circles beneath her eyes stood out sharply. To Prudence, the young woman seemed to be on the point of fainting from a combination of worry and exhaustion.

Her own eyes sought Sebastian's, bringing him to her

side at once, but Sophie was quick to assure him that she felt quite well. She turned to Prudence.

"You must meet my husband's sister." Sophie led her towards the window, where Perry was already deep in conversation with another woman.

All that Prudence could see of her was a mass of fine blonde hair, and the impression of a striking toilette seen even from the back.

Then the woman turned and Prudence caught her breath. This was the loveliest creature she had ever seen. She might have been a Dresden shepherdess, with her porcelain complexion and a pair of glowing eyes which could only be described as aquamarine in colour. She was very tiny, and as Sebastian stood beside her her head barely reached his shoulder.

"What giants you are!" she complained prettily as she looked up at the two brothers. "Now here is a lady to whom I can speak without getting a crick in my neck. You will forgive my English, *mademoiselle*? It is not so very good."

"On the contrary, it is excellent." Sebastian smiled down at her. "May I present Miss Consett? Prudence, this is Mademoiselle de Verneuil…"

"Gabrielle, if you please. I think we do not stand on ceremony here. Is that so?" Her smile was disarming and Prudence warmed to her at once.

"Sebastian, won't you present me to this charming lady?" A young man came to join the little group. As he bowed over her hand, Prudence saw the look of admiration in his eyes.

She learned that he was Gabrielle's brother, Armand. He was as dark as she was fair, and he was a handsome creature, though little more than a boy. She guessed him to be not much older than herself, though his manner was more sophisticated than that of an English youth of similar age.

When she found him beside her at the dining-table, she was grateful for his easy conversation. Her own silence went unnoticed in the flow of talk.

With all the ease of a practised hostess Lady Brandon spoke only of uncontroversial matters, such as the latest gossip, Perry's recent exploits, the children's health, and reports of the most recent quarrels between the Prince of Wales and the old King.

Yet beneath the light-hearted banter Prudence was aware of a deep sense of unease in her companions. She glanced at Sophie, and was shocked to find her trembling.

She felt a surge of pity. She herself had only the sketchiest idea of what had happened in France, and what it might mean to the young Comtesse, but she recognised desperation when she saw it.

Her own worries paled into insignificance. She felt ashamed. Sophie had been forced to flee her home with her two babies, leaving her husband to an unknown future. What could be worse?

There was a brittle brilliance about Sophie which presaged disaster. Her nerves were as taut as bowstrings. Prudence cast about in her mind for some topic which would divert her.

"Ma'am, are your children well?" she asked shyly.

Sophie did not hear her. Then Armand leaned across the table.

"Miss Consett is addressing you," he murmured.

"I'm sorry…what did you say?"

"I asked about your children, ma'am. They have not suffered from the journey?"

"They slept for most of the way," Sophie whispered

vaguely. "They are so young. Denis is two, and Louis, my younger son, is three months old." Her lips were trembling, but she succeeded in forcing back her tears. "I hear you have been caring for Frederick's boys. We must all be grateful to you..."

"She deserves a medal," Perry intervened. "They are a handful, I may tell you."

"I do not find them so."

"And, Perry, you were *such* an angel. I remember your childhood well."

Sebastian's words brought a ripple of amusement from his family. It helped to lighten the atmosphere, but the dread was still there behind the laughter. It was intangible, but always present.

"You are quiet, Miss Consett." Armand turned to her. "I think you must be very tired—"

"Oh, no!" she protested instantly. "I prefer to listen. Won't you tell me something of your journey?"

She knew at once that she had hit upon an unfortunate topic. Armand's face darkened.

"I should not have come," he said shortly. "To leave was the action of a coward—"

"Nonsense!" Sebastian's voice cut across their conversation. "The ladies needed your protection, Armand. Had your party been attacked, young Tollard might have found it difficult to defend them on his own."

"I suppose so...but Gilles refused to leave."

"Your brother must have weighed the situation carefully. Sophie, is that not so?"

"He said...he said that if he left now his estates might be confiscated. As if that matters! I tried so hard to persuade him that his life was more important." Sophie's expression was pitiful.

"We should have gone out to him when the trouble

started," Perry announced in angry tones. "Gilles could have summoned his friends. Together we'd have been a match for any mob."

"But not for an entire country in the throes of revolution, I imagine." The biting sarcasm in Sebastian's voice brought a flush to Perry's cheeks.

He sprang to his feet. "I know you think me just a hot-head, but one day I'll show you—"

"*Stop it!*" The last traces of Sophie's self-control had vanished. "I can't bear to hear you quarrelling when Gilles...when Gilles..." She burst into tears, much to Perry's dismay.

"I'm sorry," he muttered.

"Then think before you speak!" Sebastian told him savagely.

"That's quite enough! Affairs in France may not be nearly so bad as we imagine..." Lady Brandon laid a comforting hand upon her daughter's arm.

"Of course they are!" Sophie was sobbing bitterly. "What is to happen now that the King is taken?"

"My darling, he and his family have not been harmed. They were simply moved from Versailles to the Palace of the Tuileries..."

"He is a prisoner, Mama. You can't deny it. And if the mob will use their sovereign so, what hope is there for those attached to his court?"

"Sophie, there is still support in France for King Louis. You are making too much of this. The people merely wanted him in Paris..."

"For what purpose? You have not seen the hatred on the faces of those peasants, but I have."

"But, darling, the hatred is more for the Queen, is it not? The Austrian woman, as they call her, has much to answer for."

"So has the King. He took no interest in affairs of state. His subjects might die of hunger for all he cared." Sophie's voice was rising in hysteria. "A day was wasted if he did not go hunting, or played at being a locksmith. They will have their revenge, and not only on the King…"

Prudence heard a little sigh. Then, before her horrified gaze, Gabrielle de Verneuil slumped sideways in her chair.

Sebastian caught her before she reached the ground, and on his face there was an expression of such tenderness that Prudence caught her breath. For one frozen moment she felt incapable of movement. Then she hurried to his side.

Chapter Twelve

"It has been too much for her," Sebastian said quietly. His eyes were fixed upon her lovely flower-face. Then he lifted Gabrielle in his arms and carried her from the room, followed by Sophie and his mother.

Prudence longed to offer her help, but clearly it wasn't needed. She looked at Perry.

"Don't say it!" he begged. "It was all my fault."

"You were not entirely to blame. Your family is worried, and nerves are on edge..."

He threw her a grateful glance. "That's true, but I should have been more tactful..."

"So should I!" Armand turned to him. "I wish I'd held my tongue."

"Will your sister be all right?"

"Of course, Miss Consett, but she shares the same fears as Sophie. The man to whom she is betrothed is attached to the French court. He, too, is imprisoned in the Tuileries with the royal family..."

"Gabrielle is betrothed?" Perry looked surprised.

"It isn't official. My parents haven't given their consent, but Lucien is devoted to her. We've known him all our lives—"

He broke off as Sebastian returned. His expression was thunderous.

"I'd like to speak to you, my lord," Prudence said quickly.

"Well?"

"In private, if you please…"

"Won't it wait?"

"I'm afraid it won't," she told him firmly.

He hesitated for only a moment, but good manners forced him to agree.

"As you wish! Shall we go into the library?"

Prudence led the way, then she closed the door and turned to face him. Her previous embarrassment was forgotten in her determination to prevent another family quarrel.

"What is it?" he demanded. His face was dark with anger.

"Pray don't be too hard on Perry," she began without preamble. "He meant no harm…"

"Must you concern yourself with what I intend to say to my brother?" His eyes were so cold that he might have been speaking to a stranger.

Prudence faced him squarely. "Yes, my lord. I was thinking of your mother and your sister. Will it help to have another dispute?"

"Madam, you take too much upon yourself! I'll teach my brother a lesson he won't forget!"

"You might begin by treating him as a man and not as a thoughtless boy. You hurt his pride." Prudence spoke with strong feeling, infuriated by Sebastian's icy manner.

"So he has a champion in you? I might have expected it…"

"Do you care to explain that remark?"

"Certainly! You and Perry have so much in common. You are both hot-headed, thoughtless, irresponsible creatures without any notion of the havoc you create."

"Anything else?" Prudence was breathing hard. She could have struck him.

"Much more, but I think you would not care to hear it."

"Pray don't consider my feelings, sir. It would be out of character."

"You have said quite enough." He gave her a look of quelling hauteur.

"I haven't begun to tell you what I think of you." Reckless with hurt pride and the bitter suspicion that he was in love with Gabrielle, she did not trouble to guard her tongue. "Why must you imagine that you are always in the right? People have failings, but you expect them to be perfect. I can't think why, when you behave so ill yourself."

He stiffened. "I understand. You are referring to that unfortunate incident this morning? I can't excuse myself. My behaviour was unforgivable, and I cannot blame you for your low opinion of my character."

Prudence was silent. He had mistaken the reason for her angry outburst. It had been caused by her fear of what he might say to Perry and an ugly little spurt of jealousy, but she could not explain. How could she tell him that she had longed for his embrace? Even now the memory stirred her blood.

When Sebastian spoke again, his voice was calm. "My mother tells me that you wish to leave when the boys are well again?"

Prudence could only nod. She did not trust herself to answer him.

"Then it shall be as you wish. After such an insult

you cannot wish to stay at Hallwood. Some arrangements will be made for you and Dan—''

Prudence lost the last shreds of her self-control. ''How dare you?'' she cried wildly. ''We want nothing more from you.''

''But, Prudence…'' He looked down at her bent head and reached out a hand to touch her curls. Then he withdrew it swiftly. With a formal bow he walked out of the room.

Prudence did not follow him. She felt numb with misery. That bitter quarrel had been devastating. Now she wished she could recall her angry words, but it was much too late.

And she had been unfair. In an unworthy desire to retaliate and to hurt him as she had been wounded herself, she had lashed out with deadly insults.

None of them were true. Sebastian did not expect perfection in others. Had he not made allowances time and again for her prickly nature and her hasty temper? She owed him everything.

Overcome by her feelings, she laid her head upon the desk and gave way to despair.

''Pru, what has happened to old Seb?'' Perry burst in upon her. ''I thought I was really in for it. What did you say to him?''

''I expect he'll tell you.'' She turned her face away so that he should not see her tears.

''No, he's rushed away without a word. I saw him making for the stables.''

Prudence did not reply and he gave her a nervous look. ''I thought I might take Armand into Canterbury this afternoon. My mother may have some commissions for us… It's a sort of olive branch, you know.''

"That is an excellent idea." Prudence gave him a feeble smile.

"Well, I won't say I care to meet Seb in his present mood. I think we had best wait until he's gone…"

His face cleared as they heard the sound of a horseman riding fast. "There he goes! Can't think why he's always on at me for risking my neck. If he goes at that pace he'll be brought back on a rail!"

"Will you excuse me?" Prudence stifled a sob. "I must go to the boys…"

"More stories?"

She rushed away without giving him an answer.

Perhaps it was her imagination, but the boys were more than usually fractious that afternoon. They were feeling better, and beginning to chafe at their confinement. After an hour of trying to entertain them, Nurse sent her away.

"You need some air, Miss Prudence. You look that peaked today! Leave these young rascals with me. We'll play at spillikins."

Prudence was glad to be relieved of her duties. With a pang of conscience she realised that she had been neglecting Dan. She wandered down to the kitchens, only to be told that Dan had returned to the flour mill with his friend the gardener.

The day was cold but it wasn't far to walk. She returned to her room for her warm cloak and left the house by the side door.

Dark clouds were looming overhead, but they matched her mood. An unpleasant task lay ahead of her. How was she to explain to Dan that within a week or so they must leave Hallwood? The boy had been so happy here. Now she was planning to take him away to face an uncertain future.

She could offer him the choice. Lady Brandon would keep him here if he wished to stay, but in her heart she knew that he would not.

She quickened her pace as a few drops of rain began to fall. Then the heavens opened and the downpour became torrential. The sheeting rain formed a veil, obscuring both the distant mill and the house behind her.

She dashed for the shelter of a massive oak, but her cloak was soaked before she reached it. Shivering with cold, she pulled the heavy folds about her. The shower was too violent to last for long, but her boots were already sodden.

"In distress again?" an ironic voice enquired. "Come over here!"

She looked up to find Sebastian standing not three yards away. Beside him his horse was cropping at the grass.

"What are you doing here?" she demanded stiffly.

"Following you. It did not occur to you that a storm was brewing?"

"Of course not!" she snapped. "This is just another example of my thoughtless, irresponsible behaviour—"

"Temper!" he reproved her. "We can't have sarcasm added to your other failings."

To her surprise she saw that he was laughing. Prudence turned her back on him, but he came towards her and laid his hands upon her shoulders.

"Take off your cloak!"

"I will do no such thing. It's much too cold."

"You prefer the damp to soak through all your clothing? Don't be an idiot!" He slipped off his many-caped riding coat. "Put this on!"

"No, I won't!"

"Then we'll use it as a tent." He spun her round, undid the fastening at her throat, and tossed the sodden cloak across his saddle. Then he flung his coat about his shoulders and held out an inviting arm.

Prudence looked at him uncertainly. "I thought you said that we should use it as a tent…"

"So we shall, but I don't plan to lay it on the ground. This is an emergency. We must forget our differences. If you will do me the honour to stand beside me, we shall share the coat." Sebastian did not wait for a refusal. He seized her arm without delay and drew her close.

Prudence tried to pull away, but he would not release her.

"Don't worry!" he said lightly. "This storm will soon be over."

There was an odd note in his voice, which made her wonder if he was referring to the weather, but his expression was bland.

"Still cross with me?" he asked.

"My lord, I said too much…" Prudence stood stiff and straight in the circle of his arms. "As I told you, I wished only to avert another quarrel."

"You didn't succeed very well. I was glad we weren't in the dining-room. If you'd had a knife, you would have stabbed me."

"I meant a family quarrel," she protested.

"That would have made a difference? I think not…" His voice changed and he spoke in an altered tone. "I'm glad you stopped me…I was angry…I should have said too much to Perry."

Prudence did not reply.

"Did you think me wrong in not allowing him to go

to France?" he asked. "My mother was much against it."

"Both you and she were right, I believe." Her face softened. "I expect you would not have travelled many miles before he felt obliged to break some fellow's head…"

"You are right. On his last visit he was lucky to get away with a whole skin, so you see…?"

"I understand. But, my lord, was it not possible to save his pride? If you had explained?"

"Yes, I was tactless. I forget that my young brother is a man full grown. I am too used to ordering him about…"

"Just your brother, sir?" Prudence twinkled.

"Yes, you baggage! Now you are chiding me again, and it is undeserved."

Prudence said nothing. Insensibly she had relaxed against him, more comfortable now that he had returned to his teasing ways. She was no longer shivering. The warmth of his body against her own was soothing, but all her senses were alert. His heart was so close to hers, and beneath the fine broadcloth she could feel it pounding.

Suddenly she pulled away.

"What is it?" he asked.

"The rain is not so heavy, sir. I think I might go on…"

"To the flour mill? You must be mad! You will come home with me at once and get into some dry clothing." He lifted her into the saddle and swung up behind her.

She did not argue, content to feel the strength of his arms about her. The moment was sweet. She would remember it for the rest of her life. Then he bent down until his lips were resting against her hair.

"You won't leave, will you?" he coaxed. "Prudence…what happened this morning was my fault and mine alone. I am not made of stone, you know. When I came to the nursery you were asleep. I watched you for a time and felt… Well, that is no matter. Suffice it to say that I forgot what is owed to you as a person I respect."

"You owe me nothing, sir. We shall always be grateful, Dan and I."

"I don't want gratitude."

"It is all I can give, my lord. You knew my purpose in coming to Kent. Now we must go on."

"Because of me?"

"No!" she lied. "Pray do not make it harder for me. We have been happy here…"

"Then why go?"

"We must," she insisted. "Now I must look to the future."

"But where will you go? What will you do? At least give me time to make some arrangements for your comfort."

"You have given us enough," she cried in desperation. "To do more would be wrong. I could not accept…"

"But I had planned to make enquiries on your behalf."

"Had you? Forgive me, but I can't believe you. You took good care that I should not make my own."

"I don't understand. You were free to ask anyone."

"But not to study the book on heraldry?"

He stiffened. "So that's it!" he said softly. "I knew that something had happened. You found the coat-of-arms?"

"I did, and I believe you knew the answer all along,"

she accused. Her lips were trembling. Sebastian was making it so hard for her to stick to her purpose. In another moment she would be in tears, but she would not allow him to suspect her weakness. A show of anger was preferable to that.

"I suspected it, but I could not be sure. That was why I asked my mother to find the book."

"But she was not to let me see it? That was not well done, sir. You had no right to keep the truth from me. Did you think I would not keep my word?"

"I regard your word as highly as I do my own." Sebastian's voice was grave. "But I suspected that you might read too much into the discovery. Prudence, you can't be sure that you are connected in any way with the Manvell family. I don't want you to be hurt. The brooch might have come from anywhere."

"It didn't. It was hidden in my clothing for a purpose. As to being hurt, my lord...it was more wounding to find that you didn't trust me."

"That was not my reason—"

"Then what? I am not afraid of the truth, and I will have it even if it means discovering that I am a bastard."

"Must you use that ugly word?"

"I've had to face it. A bastard...a love child...? The name cannot matter, but I must know the full story."

"So you are determined to go on?"

"Yes!" she muttered. "And you cannot keep me here against my will."

"I have not the least desire to do so. But I wish you will consider the difficulties. You would not get within a mile of Longridge Hall. Manvell keeps savage dogs, and trespassers are shot on sight."

"Then he is still alive?"

"I have heard nothing to the contrary, but it is hard to say. He is a recluse."

Sebastian's arms tightened about her waist. "I beg you will do nothing foolish. Stay here, and let me go—"

"No!" she cried sharply. "This is something I must do myself."

They had almost reached the house and he reined in at the entrance to the stable-yard.

"What of Dan? Do you intend to take him with you?"

Prudence did not reply.

"At least you should offer him the choice. He is happy here and we'd be glad to keep him with us."

"I'll speak to him," she murmured as Sebastian lifted her from the saddle. She did not trust herself to say more. With a heart full to overflowing she fled indoors. It was only later that she remembered that she had not thanked him for that generous offer.

She met no one as she hurried to her room. As she closed the door behind her she sighed with relief. The argument with Sebastian had drained her, but she could not allow her love for him to trap her into staying at Hallwood. In his company she would always be at risk.

She changed her clothing quickly and made her way to the nursery. Nurse was dozing in a chair and the boys were looking sullen.

"Here's Prudence!" Damian cried. "Now we'll have some fun."

At his words Nurse wakened with a start.

"Miss Prudence, I'm that glad to see you. I don't know what we are to do. Nothing pleases them today."

"Why should it?" Crispin snapped. "It's so boring lying here."

"Then don't! I see no reason why you can't get

dressed.'' Prudence turned to Ellie. ''Has the doctor been?''

''He found them better, miss, and the curtains may be drawn back tomorrow.''

''That's splendid!'' Prudence smiled at her three charges. ''Boys, weren't you happy with the news?''

''I suppose so.'' Crispin was not to be so easily won round. ''I'm tired of living in this dark room. We might as well be under the sea.''

''I suppose it is a bit like that with the light behind these green curtains. It looks quite mysterious. Of course, I've never been on a ship myself, so I can't imagine what it's like to look down through the water.''

''When the sea is calm you can see the pebbles on the bottom,'' Damian told her.

''And fish...I saw some little ones.'' Gerard bounced excitedly on his bed.

''Did you catch any?''

''Only in the rock pools, but Crispin caught a big one when Uncle Sebastian took us on his yacht.''

''It was a mackerel,'' Crispin volunteered.

Prudence looked at Ellie. ''Wouldn't you like to rest?'' she asked. ''I want to hear about these fish.''

As the woman left them, Prudence turned back to Crispin. ''It must be strange to catch a fish,'' she said. ''What was it like?''

Crispin forgot his boredom. ''They tug hard like a dog on the end of a rope. Sometimes they get away from the line, but the mackerel didn't.'' He sighed with pleasure. ''It was so beautiful...blue and silver...and it had a pattern on its back. Uncle caught dozens of them.''

''And we had them for our supper,'' Damian announced. ''I wish I'd caught one, but I only caught an eel.''

"Good heavens, Damian! I hope it wasn't very big."

"No, it was small, but it was strong. I couldn't pull it in myself, so Uncle did it for me. I touched it, though, and it was horrible…all squirming like a big, fat worm."

"I didn't touch it," Gerard told her. "Eels have teeth, you know. I thought that it might bite me."

"You're just a baby," Crispin jeered.

Prudence forestalled the coming argument. "Gerard is not a baby…he's a boy," she said firmly. "I expect that the eel was just as dangerous as some of the other creatures in the sea. They don't live round here, but far across the oceans there are sharks and whales."

Three pairs of eyes regarded her with fascination.

"Will you tell us about them?" Damian said.

For the next hour Prudence tried to recall everything she had read about the creatures of the sea until she ran out of inspiration.

"What shall we do next?" Crispin asked.

"Shall we play I-Spy?"

"We can't see in the dark," he objected.

"It isn't completely dark in here and it will make it more interesting. That is, unless you will find it too difficult for you?"

As she had expected, the challenge was too much for him and he entered into the game with enthusiasm. Gerard's efforts convulsed the older boys. His spelling was original, to say the least, but Prudence kept the peace, quelling Crispin and Damian with a look.

When Nurse returned with their supper, she glanced at the clock to find that it was growing late. Since the departure of the Countess, the family had returned to country hours for dining. She must hurry if she was not to keep them waiting.

She had almost completed her toilette when Lady Brandon came to find her.

Prudence greeted her with a smile. "How is Mademoiselle de Verneuil?" she asked at once.

"She is much better, my dear, and will dine with us this evening. The poor girl is full of apologies for her fainting fit, but I told her that we understood. Her parents are still in France, and so is our dear Gilles. She is so afraid for them."

"She must be distraught…" Prudence murmured in sympathy. "And your daughter, ma'am?"

"Sophie will not give way again. She feels that she owes it to the others to keep up her spirits."

"She is brave, but it is a worrying time for all of you."

"Indeed, but you have made it easier by giving me your help." Her ladyship hesitated. "Prudence, I have something to tell you. I hope you will not be offended by what I have to say."

"Lady Brandon, you could not possibly offend me."

"I wonder? I know how proud you are. The thing is that Frederick wished to make you a small gift, to show you his appreciation for your kindness to the boys."

"Ma'am, he must not think of it. There is no need…"

"He insisted, my dear." She produced a small purse from her pocket. "It was to have been a pretty trifle, but there was no time. He hopes that you will use the money to buy whatever pleases you."

Prudence coloured to the roots of her hair. "Ma'am, I can't take it."

"I think you must. You find it so easy to give to others. Won't you allow them the pleasure of giving to you? What would you say if your own generosity was refused?" She laid the purse beside the dressing-glass.

Prudence shook her head.

"You won't accept even to please me?"

"Lady Brandon, please don't ask it of me."

"I shall not press you as you feel so strongly, but Frederick will be hurt. Will you not use the money for Dan, if you won't take it for yourself?"

Prudence stared at her in desperation. Her ladyship was making it impossible to refuse.

"Now let us have enough of this nonsense!" the older woman said briskly. "Cook is on her mettle this evening. She hopes to convince our young visitors that English food is better than anything to be found in France. She will not thank us if we keep her waiting."

In obedience to her wishes, Prudence followed her from the room. She hoped that none of the others knew of the gift. If only she might have been allowed to refuse it. It made her feel like a servant, though she knew that it was not intended as a vail. And what else was she, after all?

Here at Hallwood she had been treated as a member of the family, but it was an illusion. She was out of place in this gathering of aristocrats. Even their kindness was given in charity.

Then she felt ashamed. Stubbornness and pride were her greatest failings, and she was well aware of it. It was high time that she learned to be more gracious in her dealings with other people. She forced a smile as she went to join the gathering in the salon.

Her good intentions were evidently shared by the other members of the party. Sophie had recovered her composure and greeted her arrival with a pleasant word of welcome, as did Armand. Gabrielle was chatting happily to Sebastian, who bent over her with an air of tender solicitude. Only Perry was subdued.

She looked at him and raised her eyebrows in enquiry.

"It's sackcloth and ashes for me this evening," he murmured. "How are the monsters?"

"Much better, I believe. I've been hearing about the joys of catching mackerel."

"Really?" His face lit up at once. "It's splendid sport. I'll take you fishing, if you like."

"Only if you promise that I shan't catch an eel!" She laughed up at him and was suddenly aware that Sebastian was watching her. There was something disturbing in his look.

He did not glance her way again. Instead he devoted himself to entertaining Gabrielle. Prudence forced herself to concentrate upon the banter between Armand and Perry who were seated either side of her.

The meal was all that Cook had promised. A Flemish soup was followed by oysters in batter. Dressed lobster followed, removed with a dish of broiled chickens in a mushroom sauce. There was a choice of mutton, or a goose and turkey pie.

Perry and Armand did full justice to each course, and she watched in wonder as they helped themselves to cheeses, fruit and nuts as the meal drew to a close. She herself took only a little of the syllabub for dessert, refusing the crisp apple pies which were such favourites with both young men.

"Well, Armand! What do you say now to English food?" Perry issued his challenge.

"You have the best raw ingredients in the world," his friend admitted.

"And the cooking?"

"What can I say?" Armand kissed his fingertips. "Nothing could be better."

Cook blushed as they raised their glasses to her, and made a hasty retreat when they had thanked her.

"You've made your point!" Sebastian grinned at his brother. "Is honour satisfied?"

Prudence felt relieved to find that the two brothers were in charity with each other once again. She accompanied the ladies from the dining-room with the feeling that something had been achieved that day, but her composure was soon shattered.

When the gentleman came to join them, Sebastian moved over to her side.

"You are still of the same mind?" he asked in a low voice.

"Yes, sir. I must go."

"But, Prudence, I have explained. My behaviour was inexcusable, but it won't happen again. Can't you forget it?"

"It is long forgotten," she lied. "You are not the first man who has tried to steal a kiss from me. I have learned to disregard it…"

She was stunned by his reaction. He paled as if she had struck him.

"It meant nothing to you?"

"Why should it, sir? You said yourself that it was a momentary impulse, and I accept your explanation."

"You are too generous." He bowed and moved away.

Chapter Thirteen

The exchange between Prudence and Sebastian had not gone unnoticed by Lady Brandon. Where her family was concerned she was quick to sense dissension and the expression on Sebastian's face alarmed her.

She moved across the room to sit by Prudence.

"Is something wrong?" she asked quietly.

"Lord Wentworth thinks I should not leave. He has been attempting to convince me of my folly."

"Pray don't allow him to upset you," her ladyship advised. "He means well. He is thinking only of your safety. If he seems brusque you must excuse his manner, and set it down to his concern for you and Dan."

Prudence sat perfectly still. If she moved her whole being would shatter into a thousand fragments. She felt as if something had died inside her, leaving her too numb to laugh and walk and talk like other people.

She prayed that the numbness would last. She longed to be spared the agony of starting to think again. Her cruel words had been deliberate and designed to hurt. If she could have found some other way to stop Sebastian's pleading she would have done so, but she was weakening.

It was better to be brutal. To sever all connection with a swift, clean stroke as one might cut off a limb too damaged ever to be restored to health. She had done it, but she would never recover.

Lady Brandon beckoned to her daughter. Something must be done to rescue Prudence from what appeared to be a state of shock.

"Here is Sophie, come to speak to you," she said gently. "I have told her something of your story, but she wishes to hear more…" She gave her daughter a speaking look.

Sophie was too wise to chat about anything other than inconsequential matters for a time. The fact that Prudence answered her in monosyllables did not appear to worry her. Then Sophie decided to dispense with the formalities.

"Prudence? I may call you Prudence, may I not? I want to understand… It must be so strange to be alone in the world and not to have a single relative to call your own. You must feel so isolated…as if you have no identity. Is that so?"

The words roused Prudence from her apathy. She stared at the sweet face of the older girl. "How could you know?" she asked slowly.

"I tried to think how I should feel if it had happened to me. Do you feel bitter about your natural parents?"

"I did, but now I'm not so sure. There must have been some reason for them to give me up. It was a dreadful thing to do, but…"

"But you want to know? I cannot blame you. I should feel the same myself."

"Ma'am, you are the first member of your family to agree with me…"

"Must it be 'Ma'am'? My name is Sophie. I had hoped we could be friends."

Prudence stared at her uncertainly. Before the undeniable charm of this tall girl she felt defenceless, but she pulled herself together.

"I must go on," she whispered. "I am so close, and I can't go on wondering for the rest of my life."

"I agree. I know so little of you, but I believe that you will always do as you think best. Don't allow anyone to stop you."

Her words had a heartening effect, surprising though they were. It was clear that Sophie had a mind of her own, and Prudence felt a rush of gratitude.

She took no further part in the conversation, but her despondency had vanished. It was simply the knowledge that someone understood what she was feeling… It made her believe that she was not alone.

With that knowledge came a softening in her attitude. The longing for revenge was gone, and so was the overwhelming sense of hatred. Now she would be satisfied just to know…to understand…

Her heart was in her eyes as she looked up at Sophie.

"Come and talk to me tomorrow," Sophie said. "I'll help you if I can."

It was then that Prudence felt the first stirring of suspicion. Had she been the subject of a family discussion? This was all too pat. First there had been the gift of money from the Earl. She hadn't examined the contents of the purse, but she guessed that it held gold. That was obvious from the weight. It should have warned her. She didn't need gold to buy herself the pretty trifle mentioned by Lady Brandon…a few shillings would have sufficed.

And now Sebastian's sister was offering her help.

That was even more extraordinary. Sophie did not know her.

It was unbelievable that in the midst of her own worries she should trouble to offer her assistance. Perhaps she had been asked to do so.

"Why should you wish to help me?" she asked. "I don't want pity."

"I don't offer out of pity," Sophie assured her. "I admire your spirit. My mother and Sebastian see it, too."

Her eyes flickered to the tall figure of her brother and Prudence followed her glance.

His annoyance apparently forgotten, Sebastian was deep in conversation with the beautiful Gabrielle. Prudence could not blame him. The girl was a vision of loveliness in a ravishing toilette of pale blue silk. The colour exactly matched her eyes, which were now lifted to Sebastian's as she hung upon his every word.

"They make a handsome couple, don't they?" Sophie murmured. "It is my mother's dearest wish that Sebastian will marry soon."

Prudence understood. A match between these two great families would please her ladyship. Perhaps she did not know of Gabrielle's previous attachment.

"Then Mademoiselle de Verneuil...? I mean...I thought...? Well, her brother said—"

"He spoke of Lucien? Nothing has been decided yet. Gabrielle is so young. I think she's still unsure of her own feelings." Sophie smiled. "She is my dearest friend, you know."

Prudence lifted her chin. Was this a warning? There was no need for it. Her plans were made, and Sebastian would not dissuade her.

He felt responsible for them, but Prudence was determined that the break should be complete. He might follow them as far as Longridge, knowing that it would be her initial destination, but she had no plans to stay there.

If she and Dan could leave in secret, they might be long gone before he could find them.

First she must speak to Dan. It would be best for him to stay at Hallwood, but in her heart she knew that he would refuse. Prudence was all he had, and she could not betray his trust in her. It would be too cruel to leave without telling him.

She was too preoccupied with her own thoughts to realise that the conversation had reverted to discussion of affairs in France. This time it was Armand, rather than Perry, who was the centre of attention. She was recalled to the present when he addressed her.

"Miss Prudence, don't you agree that it is the Austrian Queen who is the cause of all the troubles in my country?" His face was flushed as he appealed for her support.

Prudence shook her head. "I cannot say. I know so little of Queen Marie Antoinette, apart from what I have read—"

Gabrielle intervened at once. "Armand, you judge too harshly. She was married at fifteen, and surrounded by enemies from the start…think of the Du Barry, for example."

The impropriety of discussing the old King's powerful mistress was forgotten in the heated arguments which followed.

"She is a traitor," Armand cried fiercely. "All those letters from the Austrian ambassador to her mother? Why, Maria Theresa knew more about French affairs than the King himself."

"Whose fault was that?" Sophie demanded. "As I told you, he takes not the slightest interest—"

"She might have persuaded him. She herself is ready enough to interfere in politics—"

"Don't you think she deserves our sympathy at present?" Gabrielle's face was sad. "It isn't six months since she lost her eldest son…and now all this…?"

"I'm sorry for the death of the Dauphin, of course, but her behaviour has ruined all our lives."

"Forgive me, but you are mistaken, Armand." Sebastian spoke for the first time upon the thorny topic. "Whatever happens, you and Gabrielle are young enough to start again."

A silence followed his words. Then Sophie turned to Prudence.

"You must be so tired of our arguments," she said in a low voice. "This must be boring for you. We should try not to speak of it, but it is hard to banish it from our minds."

"Perhaps it's better to talk about it. I wish I understood more about affairs in France. Won't you tell me about the Queen?"

Prudence hoped that in speaking of Marie Antoinette, Sophie might forget the deadly danger which threatened her husband.

Sophie frowned. "Armand is right to a certain extent," she admitted with some reluctance. "Apart from meddling in affairs of state, the Queen's extravagance is legendary. Her friends are dissolute, and there have been scandals…"

"Yet you defend her?"

"I can't find it in my heart to judge her. As I said, she was very young when she first came to France. The old King and the Dauphin both adored her, and she was a target for those intriguers who hoped that she would use her influence."

"Did no one warn her?"

"No, alas! She made enemies from the first. She disliked court etiquette, you see, and scandalised the older, wiser members of the nobility. I believe her family tried to warn her to be more careful, but her mother died ten years ago…"

"And she had no one else?"

"Her brother, Joseph, came to visit her immediately afterwards. As Emperor of Austria he used all his influence and things were better for a time, but the damage was already done. Then he, too, died in the spring of this year. She is quite alone, except for Louis and her favourites."

"It is a sad story," Prudence murmured.

"You would think so if you knew of the hatred towards her. It frightens me. The revolutionaries make no distinction, you see. Any aristocrat must be their enemy."

"Enough, my dear!" Lady Brandon said in a low voice. "All this is most distressing to Gabrielle…"

"I did not think that she could hear me." Sophie was penitent at once. "How thoughtless I have been! Gilles, at least, is living upon his own estate, but Gabrielle's parents are in Paris." She rose and made her way across the room to sit beside her friend.

Gabrielle's pallor was alarming, and Prudence could well believe that she was on the verge of fainting once again. Then Sebastian leaned towards her and whispered something in her ear which brought a look of gratitude.

Prudence could bear no more. She made her excuses and fled for the sanctuary of her bedchamber. Once there, she recalled that she had quite forgotten her patients, but her concern was needless. All was quiet in the nursery and Nurse was asleep in the small trestle bed.

From the tread of feet outside her door, she guessed that the family gathering was breaking up. She would wait for a while before she ventured downstairs to the library to find a book. It was better to read than to lie awake for hours, a prey to memories of the past and fears for the future.

She hadn't even examined the contents of the purse which Lady Brandon had left with her. Now she opened it and tipped it out upon the bed. The Earl had been more than generous. She had never seen so much money in her life. Twenty golden guineas gleamed softly in the candlelight, but she was a loath to touch them.

To her they meant rejection. They hadn't been given out of kindness, but merely as an inducement to persuade her to go away.

Was she being unfair? The Earl was not a cruel man and he had no need to give her anything. If his wife had had her way, she would have been sent away without a penny to her name.

She looked at the gold again. Its soft gleam was tempting. For the first time she could understand why men would risk their lives to own it. It meant freedom and security. With these coins she could buy passage for herself and Dan on one of those splendid ships she had only dreamed about. How could she refuse to purchase a new life for him?

Her decision was made. She swept the guineas together and replaced them in the purse. Then she opened her door. In the hall below all was silent. Even the servants had retired. No one would see her if she crept downstairs. She need not carry a candle. The last flickering flames in the wall sconces would light her way.

It was only as she reached the foot of the staircase that she sensed that she was not alone. From the shadows she heard the murmur of voices, and she peered into the darkness.

Sebastian had his back to her and his broad shoulders obscured her view of his companion. Then she heard the rustle of silk and she was no longer in any doubt. He was holding Gabrielle in his arms.

Her own reaction shocked her. She swayed, and was forced to cling to the smooth mahogany of the staircase for support. She clenched her hands so tightly that the nails dug deep into her flesh. She must not faint. If she were discovered now, the lovers would believe that she was spying on them.

With a supreme effort of will she kept her footing and moved deeper into the shadows. She wanted to run…to flee into the night…to vanish into oblivion. Only then would she be able to blot out the memory of being held against Sebastian's heart whilst his warm lips found her own. Now his caresses were for Gabrielle de Verneuil alone.

Prudence thought that her heart must break with anguish, but human hearts did not break. They continued to beat, though their owners might feel that such exquisite torture would rob their minds of reason.

Somehow she regained her room and threw herself upon the bed, gazing at the ceiling with unseeing eyes. Later she could not recall how she had passed that night. She knew only that she must get away from Hallwood as soon as possible.

As soon as it was light she went in search of Dan. It would be difficult to explain her reasons for such a sudden departure, but it must be done.

Sam nodded to her pleasantly as she crossed the stable-yard, jerking his head in the direction of one of the stalls.

"I'm surprised he don't sleep with that there foal," he muttered with a grim smile. "Seems to think it'll vanish if he don't keep an eye on it."

She found Dan with his arms about the little creature's neck.

"He's growing, Pru. Can you see the difference?"

"He's very beautiful." Prudence stroked the gleaming chestnut coat. "Could you bear to leave him?"

A vigorous denial died on his lips as he looked up at her face. "Is it time for us to go?" he asked wistfully.

"It's time for me to go. You may stay here, if you wish…I know that you are happy at Hallwood."

"But I shouldn't be if you weren't here…" His lips began to quiver. "You wouldn't leave me, would you?"

Prudence hugged him to her. "I've hardly seen you for the past few days," she teased him gently. "Was that so very terrible?"

"But I knew that you were here. I don't want to stay without you." He turned his face away.

Prudence took his hand and stroked it. "I want to do what is best for you. We don't know what may lie ahead, and we came so close to starvation, Dan. That must not happen again."

"I don't care!" His passionate cry tore at her heartstrings. "I don't mind being hungry if I can be with you." He flung himself down upon the straw and began to sob.

Prudence gathered him up and held him close. "Don't fret!" she murmured tenderly. "I'll take you with me if that is what you really want, but I had to be sure."

"Well, I'm sure," he sniffled.

''Very well then, but we must be careful. You must tell no one of our plans. This time our journey will be easier. We shall have some money—''

''Where did you get it?''

''It was a gift. What do you say to travelling on some great ship to another country? Our lives might be better there…''

''Shall we have enough…enough money, I mean? Won't it cost a lot to go?''

''I think we might manage it,'' she told him cautiously.

''Do you really mean it?''

Prudence looked at his eager face. ''Of course I do, but it must be our secret for the present.''

''But why?''

''I can't tell you that just yet, but you must trust me.''

He nodded. ''When shall we go?''

''Very soon. Certainly within a day or two.''

She could not tell him that she was racking her brains to think of a way to leave the house without arousing suspicion. Even asking him to keep this secret was distasteful to her. It was encouraging him to be sly, but she dared not risk her plan becoming known.

Sebastian would be certain to object, though he would not keep her at Hallwood against her wishes. Doubtless he was already considering a post for her with some family in the neighbourhood. Then she would be forced to see him with his new bride and his children growing up around him.

She loved him enough to want him to be happy, but if time was to heal her aching heart she must go far away.

Still lost in thought, she walked back to the house.

Then she remembered. Sophie had offered to help her. That might be her only hope.

It was still too early for the ladies to appear, but Armand and Peregrine clattered past her in the hall in leggings and rough shooting coats. They waved a cheerful greeting and urged her to join Sebastian in the dining-room.

"He won't come out with us," Perry told her with a grimace. "I think he's feeling liverish this morning."

Prudence was glad that he had warned her. She felt too despondent to make a false attempt at conversation over the breakfast table, and she was in no mood for further argument.

With lagging steps she went up to the nursery. There, much to her surprise, she found Gabrielle already chatting to the boys. The curtains had been opened and a pile of picture books lay upon the beds.

Gabrielle saw her look of astonishment.

"You must not worry, mademoiselle," she cried gaily. "I have had this *rougeole*...this spotted thing...I do not know how you call it in English."

"It's measles!" the boys shouted in unison.

"Measles? I shall remember it. Miss Prudence, this morning you must have a holiday. Sophie would like to see you...she is in her boudoir."

Prudence made her way towards the west wing. She did not know this part of the house, but one of the doors was ajar and she peeped inside.

"Come in! I've been expecting you." Sophie was seated at her dressing-table, wearing a ravishing peignoir of yellow silk. "Have you breakfasted?"

Prudence shook her head.

"Then won't you join me?" Sophie filled a second cup with chocolate and gestured towards the freshly baked rolls. "Cook believes that I should eat for two. I am *enceinte* again, you see." She patted her flat stomach with a sigh of satisfaction.

"*Madame*, I am happy for you." Prudence took the cup and sipped at her chocolate. "To have a new baby will be wonderful."

"I hope to have many more…" Sophie's face clouded briefly. Then she shook her head as if to rid it of unwelcome thoughts, and smiled at her companion.

"We are not hear to speak of my affairs," she said frankly. "I meant what I told you yesterday. Is there any way that I can help you?"

Prudence hesitated. Would it be wise to trust Sebastian's sister? She could not be sure.

"I won't betray your confidence," Sophie told her quietly. "Anything you say will go no further."

Prudence looked into her eyes and was convinced.

"I mean to go to Longridge, *madame*. The family of Manvell may know the secret of my birth, but I don't know how to get away from here without…I mean…I don't want Lord Wentworth to fetch me back again, or try to stop me."

Sophie understood. Her eyes were filled with compassion as she looked at the younger girl.

"I expect he feels responsible for you and your friend," she murmured gently.

"Yes, *madame*, but he must not. You must not think me ungrateful, but he has done enough."

More than enough, if I am not mistaken, Sophie thought to herself. This girl was clearly in love with her brother. It must have taken all her courage to decide to go away, but it might be for the best.

"And what then?"

"*Madame?*"

"What will you do when you have seen Lord Manvell? Will you stay at Longridge? If you are right about your connection with the family, they must do something for you…"

"I want nothing from them," Prudence told her proudly. "Dan and I will go away. There are other countries. We shall take passage on some ship bound for the Americas or Australia."

"Alone, my dear?" Sophie was horrified.

"How else? I did not mean to speak of it, but you may know that the Earl of Brandon made me a gift of money."

"Oh, Prudence, won't you reconsider?" Sophie was beginning to doubt the wisdom of her offer of help. "I can understand your wish to find your natural parents, but to go halfway across the world…? Have you considered the dangers?"

"I have, and I will do it!"

A look at the set face told Sophie that further remonstrance would be useless. Prudence was determined, and all that she could do was to make the burden as light as possible.

"Let me think!" she said swiftly. "Longridge is close to Dover, I believe. Suppose we planned a trip to Canterbury, just you and myself and Dan? You have not seen the place, and it would cause no comment. From there the road leads straight to Dover."

"But how…?"

"Once we reached Canterbury you could disappear into the narrow streets. I should be distressed, of course, but then I should return to Hallwood to seek help."

"But, *madame*, in your condition you must not drive alone."

Sophie frowned. "You are right. I should not be allowed to take the reins myself. I'll ask for Sam to drive the carriage. Don't worry! I'll keep him occupied on one pretext or other whilst you get away."

"Are you quite sure?" Prudence asked slowly. "It would be the answer, but if Lord Wentworth should discover your part in this..."

"He won't! Now we must plan. What will you take with you?"

"As little as possible. We may need to walk some distance and we cannot carry much."

"In Canterbury you might hire a gig to take you out to Longridge. Do you drive?"

"No, *madame*."

"Then that won't do, but you are sure to find someone who plies for hire." Sophie walked over to a massive chest and began to throw clothing on the bed. "You will need warm things. Take anything you like."

Prudence protested, but she was overruled.

"I am salving my conscience," Sophie told her. "I should not encourage you in this project." She turned to Prudence. "I want you to know that I believed none of Amelia's accusations. She is a most unpleasant creature, and she has caused my mother much distress."

Prudence was silent. There was nothing she could say.

"Will you promise me one thing?" Sophie asked. "If anything should go wrong, will you send a message to me? No one else need know of it." She sighed. "Under other circumstances we might have become the best of friends..."

Prudence did not trust herself to speak. She had believed the worst of this generous-minded girl, thinking that her help had been offered just to protect her brother.

She had been mistaken. Sophie understood her feelings, and her heart was full as she gave her promise with a little nod.

Sophie did not press her further. Instead she busied herself by looking out warm petticoats and stockings and one or two woollen gowns.

"There!" she said at last. "There is no more than will fit into a single bag. Take this!" She produced a roomy leather satchel, and tucked the clothing inside.

The hardest question came last.

"When do you wish to go?" she said.

"As soon as possible, if you please." Prudence turned her head away to hide the anguish in her eyes.

"Not today, I think. A sudden decision to visit Canterbury might arouse suspicion. We shall speak of it this evening after dinner and we'll invite Gabrielle. A shopping expedition will be just the thing."

Her eyes were sparkling, and in spite of her suffering Prudence managed a faint smile.

"What is it?" Sophie asked.

"Pray don't think me impertinent, but you seem to have a gift for intrigue, *madame*."

"With three brothers one learns quickly," Sophie told her briskly. "I think you won't be seen with the bag if you go now. Perry and Armand are out with the guns, Mamma is in her garden, and Gabrielle is sitting with the boys. Sebastian has gone away on some errand of his own."

Prudence wanted to thank her, but the words would not come. She held out her hand, but Sophie gave her a quick hug.

"I wish you everything you wish yourself," she murmured. "Go now! We'll speak again tonight."

* * *

She was as good as her word. When the family assembled in the salon after dinner, the subject of a shopping expedition to Canterbury was introduced as if by chance.

Gabrielle clapped her hands. "I should like that above anything," she cried. "I brought so little to England with me."

"No more than a couple of wagons filled with trunks," her brother teased her. "I hadn't room enough for a pair of boots…"

"Then perhaps we should accompany the ladies?" Sebastian was lounging idly by the window, apparently at his ease, but his penetrating gaze roved from one face to another.

Prudence felt a twinge of alarm. Did he suspect the true purpose of this outing?

"You would hate it!" his sister told him firmly. "I won't have you pacing up and down if we keep you waiting. This is to be for women only, except that I thought we might take Dan. Prudence has seen so little of him lately, and the boy would enjoy an outing."

Prudence held her breath. This was the danger point. Would Sebastian think it strange if Dan were to accompany them? Her fears were quickly set at rest.

"Why make the boy suffer?" Sebastian chuckled. "He'll be bored."

"No, he won't. Prudence says that he likes to sit with Sam upon the box."

"That's true! Well, I wish you joy of your expedition. Let us hope that it doesn't rain. Mother, will you go, too?"

"I think not, Sebastian. The boys are to be allowed to come downstairs. I must find some occupation for them."

"Don't let them tire you out." Sebastian turned away to question Perry as to the prospect of a day's sport.

Sophie gave Prudence a brief, conspiratorial glance and the subject was dropped.

Alone in her bedchamber later that night Prudence had time to reflect. The first part of the plan had been accomplished, and it had passed off better than she expected.

She hadn't been able to warn Dan that they were to leave next day, but that was no bad thing. Unwittingly he might betray them by some chance remark. Now all they needed was a dry day. It would seem eccentric to set out for Canterbury in heavy rain, and the expedition would certainly be postponed.

She must still be careful. She waited until the house was silent before she removed the leather satchel from its hiding place behind a mahogany chest. It was not quite full, so she tucked the purse of guineas deep inside the folded clothing.

Then she looked about her at the familiar room. She would not see it again, but she would remember every detail for the rest of her life. And it would be a new life. She would not allow sadness to overwhelm her. She must look forward now.

She awoke to find faint rays of winter sunlight peeping through the curtains. The sky was clear.

They would go today. Then a thought struck her. How was she to smuggle her bag down to the carriage?

Sophie solved the problem for her. When she appeared she was carrying a warm rug. Prudence hid the bag beneath it.

"Where is Dan?" Sophie asked.

"I'll find him."

"Then make haste. I've ordered the carriage for ten o'clock."

Prudence hurried to the stables to find that Sam had already received his orders. Dan stood beside him with a radiant face.

"Pru, ain't this splendid?" he whispered. "I've forgot what it's like to ride upon the box."

She hadn't the heart to tell him of her plans. Later, there would be time enough for explanations. She went indoors to find Armand and Perry at the breakfast table.

"I can't think what's wrong with old Sebastian," Perry began in an injured tone. "I thought he'd come out with us today for a bit of sport, but he's got some maggot into his head. He's disappeared again…"

Prudence made no reply. She had screwed her courage to the sticking point and the fates were with her. She was to be spared the ordeal of a last meeting with her love. She pushed her plate away and excused herself with a muttered apology.

"Is it me, or is everyone peculiar today?" Perry demanded of Armand. "Now old Pru is behaving odd."

Prudence did not hear him. She had hurried away to hide her bag beneath the rug. Then she threw her cloak about her shoulders, and hurried out to the waiting carriage.

Chapter Fourteen

They set off at a spanking pace and Prudence did not look back. She was dangerously close to tears.

To her it seemed no time at all before the coach was rattling over the cobbled streets of Canterbury, and Sophie was too wise to attempt to engage her in conversation. When they reached the centre of town she signalled to Sam to stop.

"You may set us down here," she said. "We should not be above an hour or so."

"Must I take Dan with me, Miss Sophie...I mean, *madame*—"

"No! Dan is in need of clothing, too. You may come back for us at noon."

Sophie turned to Gabrielle. "The shops are all along this street," she said. "If you walk along I'll find you. You will not care to examine clothing for a boy."

As Gabrielle walked away Sophie turned to Prudence. "I'll give you all the time I can," she said quickly. "God be with you!" She held out her arms and for a moment the two girls clung together. Then Sophie turned away.

"What does she mean?" Dan asked.

"This is the start of our adventure," Prudence told him. "It won't be long before we are on the high seas."

"You mean, we are not to go back to Hallwood?"

Her face gave him the answer.

"Pru, you might have told me," he reproached. "I didn't say goodbye to Sam, or to Foxglove."

"Sam will take good care of Foxglove."

"I know it, but he'll miss me…" He looked so disconsolate that Prudence stopped.

"It isn't too late to change your mind," she said. "Sam will be back with the carriage at noon. You can wait here for the others…"

He gulped. "No! I want to go with you, but Sam will wonder…"

Sam would not be the only one, Prudence thought grimly. There would be consternation at Hallwood when their disappearance was reported. She would have given much not to have added to Lady Brandon's present worries, but there was no alternative. In the end it would be best for everyone.

"You could not have told him, Dan," she said gently. "It would have meant the end of all our plans. Now let us go quickly. We must be away from Canterbury before the search begins."

She took his hand and ducked into a little entry off the main street, hurrying him along at a pace which left him breathless.

Sophie had suggested that she hire a gig, or some such vehicle to take them along the Dover road, but where was she to find one? The inns in the town looked much too grand to rent such a modest form of transport, and she couldn't afford a chaise.

"A livery stable?" Dan suggested. "We could ask for directions…"

Prudence was doubtful. The fewer people they spoke to the less risk they ran of being found, but in the end she agreed.

It took some time to find the place as she didn't know the names of any of the streets, but they came upon it suddenly.

Prudence stopped outside. "Wait!" she said. "Stand in front of me for a moment whilst I find some money." She felt inside the satchel until her fingers touched the purse. Then she extracted a single coin and hid it in her glove. It would be unwise to produce the whole of her little hoard in full view of a stranger.

She explained her requirements to the burly individual who came towards them, but he was not encouraging.

"Can't be done!" he told her. "I've got a gig, but I can't spare a man to drive it."

"Prudence, I could drive... Sam taught me..." Dan's whispered words brought a swift reaction from the owner of the stables.

"Ho, yes? I'd be likely to trust my property to you, I don't think. You'd best take the mail coach, miss."

"It would take too long, and I'm in a hurry. Besides, Longridge is in the country outside Dover. I don't know the area. How am I to get there?"

"Don't know, miss. You might hire something in Dover..."

"But I can pay!" she cried in desperation. Slipping off her glove, she held up the piece of gold.

The man gave her a sharp look. "Well, I don't know..." A crafty expression flickered across his face. "It would cost you that...and more..." He seemed unable to take his eyes from the gleaming coin.

Prudence stared at him in dismay, sensing that he would increase the price to an extortionate level.

"Thank you!" she said coldly. "I shall ask elsewhere. Come, Dan!" She turned away, ignoring the protestations which followed her.

"Where are we going, Pru? Shall we take the mail coach?"

"I think we must." Prudence glanced up at the town clock. They had wasted too much time already, but with any luck they might not have too long to wait for the next coach out of Canterbury.

It would be slower than a gig, but the fare would be much less. She wished now that she had thought to ask Sophie to change some of the gold for smaller coins. The sight of a guinea could only arouse cupidity, and as a woman she would be considered easy prey.

And it was not yet noon. Sophie, she knew, would keep Sam waiting for as long as she dared. Then she would think up some pretext or other to account for their late arrival at the meeting place.

Even so, she could not afford a long delay. A lengthy wait for the mail coach was out of the question. If they had missed it she would be forced to hire a driver and a gig at any cost. Sam would not return to Hallwood until he had made an extensive search for them.

Luck was with her. As they passed the arched entrance of one of the inns she saw the coach about to leave. With a quick word to the driver she hurried Dan aboard and bought her tickets.

"Do you know Longridge?" she asked the guard.

"It's on the way, miss. We can set you down at the crossroads. It isn't much of a walk from there. Shall I take your bag?"

"Thank you, no. I'll keep it with me. Will you let me know when we reach the crossroads?"

He gave her a brief salute and helped her into a corner

seat. Then he blew his yard of tin and the coach rattled out into the main street.

Prudence attempted to conceal herself behind the leather curtain, but her eyes were anxious as she scanned the thoroughfare. It was only when they left the outskirts of the town that she felt able to relax. Sam had not seen them. She was sure of it.

Then Dan tugged her sleeve. "Why are we going to Longridge?" he whispered. "I thought we were to find a ship…"

"First there is something I must do. It won't take long. You must be patient."

He was satisfied with that, and smiled happily at a red-faced woman who was sitting opposite.

"You're a real carrot-top, aren't you? You remind me of my nephews." The woman returned his smile and offered him an apple.

Munching away, he was soon in conversation with her, her daughter and her daughter's husband.

Prudence closed her eyes, hoping that they would ignore her. She needed to think. So far her plans had gone smoothly, but greater obstacles lay ahead.

At best she might have half a day before the hue and cry began. When Sophie returned to Hallwood someone would come in search of her. It would not be Sebastian. Sophie had told her that he was out on some business of his own, but Perry and Armand could be reached.

Perry would not come to Longridge. He had no inkling of her destination. Then she remembered. Lady Brandon knew of her discovery.

She longed for the coach to travel faster, but the Dover road was good, and she guessed that the team of horses was already at the limit of its speed. It would take time, perhaps many hours, before the pursuit began, so she would not despair.

Her fear of discovery might be all in her imagination. It was possible that her disappearance might be greeted with relief by all concerned. It would solve so many problems.

But not her own. She was clutching at straws. Sebastian might be deeply in love with Gabrielle, but he would not shirk what he saw as his responsibilities. Nothing was more certain than that he would try to find her. She knew that he would come to Longridge.

And he always returned to Hallwood in time for dinner. Would he set out that night? It didn't matter. By then she would have left the place and be on the way to Dover.

The journey seemed to go on endlessly, but at last they were set down at the crossroads.

"It's half a mile up there, miss. You can't mistake the place. There's an eight-foot wall goes all round the estate…" As he jumped aboard, the coach picked up speed.

As Dan picked up the satchel, Prudence took it from him.

"I can manage," she said firmly. "Come on! We haven't far to go."

Dan was the first to see the wall. "It looks like a fortress or part of a castle," he said. "Do you think they have a drawbridge and a moat?"

"I hope they have a gate. We'd best walk round the wall and see if we can find it."

They came upon the gates almost immediately, and Dan stared up at them.

"Look!" he cried. "Look at that shield! The pattern is the same as yours…the one upon your brooch."

Prudence gazed up at the enormous iron structure. Set in the centre of each gate was the familiar coat-of-arms. The place looked impregnable and the gates were firmly closed, held together with a massive padlock.

There was no one visible in the lodge-house, so she tugged at the bell fixed to one of the stone pillars.

The clanging resulted in pandemonium. Prudence heard the rattle of chains and then she jumped back in alarm as two huge mastiffs raced towards her, snapping and barking as they thrust their heads through the bars.

The barking turned to yelps as the lodge-keeper kicked at them.

"What do you want?" he snarled.

"I wish to see Lord Manvell," Prudence said with dignity.

"So does many another!" His lips curled, baring a mouth full of discoloured teeth. "Be off, or I'll set the dogs on you."

Prudence would not be deterred. She had not come so far to be put off by this ill-natured wretch.

"You might at least ask," she retorted.

"I've had my orders. I've disobeyed 'em once today. I won't do it again."

"Then I shall stay here."

"I don't think so, miss. If you won't be told…" He produced a large key and inserted it into the padlock.

"Prudence, come away!" Dan's voice was sharp with fright. "Don't let him loose the dogs on us…"

"I'll be back," she promised.

"Suit yourself. You'll get the same answer." The man called off the dogs and disappeared behind the corner of the lodge.

"Can't we go now?" Dan whispered fearfully. "I don't like this place."

"I'm sorry, love." Prudence moved a little way up the lane and sat down on a grassy bank. "Don't you understand? I must see his lordship. I've waited all my life for this. He may be able to tell me who my parents are…"

"But the man won't let you in."

"There may be another way." Prudence looked up at the wall. "Let's walk along a little. I can see trees beyond the wall. If we could find an overhanging branch…?"

"It won't hang down to the ground on this side, and the wall is too high to climb. Pru, I wish you wouldn't think of it. There may be other dogs."

"It can do no harm to look," she insisted. "If there is any danger, we won't go on with it."

He trailed behind her with lagging feet, and was relieved to discover no overhanging branches.

"If you stood on my shoulders, you might be able to see the house," Prudence suggested.

"I won't go over the wall. For one thing, I couldn't pull you up—"

"I know that well enough," she cried impatiently. "Where is the harm in looking? You might see another pathway."

"If there is I expect it will be guarded just the same. Pru, can't we go now?"

"I suppose we must. Oh, Dan, I had such hopes…" She sat down suddenly and buried her face in her hands.

"If you stood just here, I think that I could see if I climbed on your shoulders." Dan was disturbed by her distress.

"No! You are right! It was a foolish notion in the first place. We'll walk back to the Dover road."

It was the end of all her hopes, but she had no right to put Dan in danger.

''I don't mind walking round the wall before we go,'' he offered generously.

''It may go on for miles and we can't afford the time. It grows dark so early, and we must find a place to stay.''

''Never mind!'' he comforted. ''Tomorrow we'll find a ship…''

Prudence straightened her shoulders. Perhaps it was for the best that they leave Longridge without delay. And what did it matter if she never discovered the secret of her birth?

Once it had been her dearest wish. She could not decide when that overwhelming obsession had begun to fade, but now it was not at the forefront of her mind.

''I say, Pru, look at this! If you stood on here you might be able to see over the wall.'' Dan pointed to a tree stump a few yards away. ''Do you want to try?''

Prudence gathered up her skirts and began to climb. It was not yet dusk and in the distance she could make out a building set high on rising ground. Then she heard a shot as something like an angry bee flew past her head.

''We've been seen!'' She jumped down from the stump and grabbed Dan's hand. ''Let's run!''

They had covered several yards before they heard the sound of approaching hooves.

''They're coming after us,'' Dan cried. ''Look, they are opening the gates!''

''Quick!'' she said. ''Into the ditch!'' She flung herself to the ground and pulled him down beside her. Then she heard a gasp.

''Pru, that was Lord Wentworth!''

''No! It can't be! What would he be doing here?''

''I don't know, but it's him. Look for yourself!''

Prudence lifted her head. The horseman was already vanishing into the distance, but there was no mistaking those broad shoulders or the careless ease with which Sebastian rode.

"He must have come to find us."

"That isn't possible. It's too soon…" Prudence found that she was trembling. She wanted to call out…to bring Sebastian back to her…but she did not.

Her thoughts were racing. He must have come to Longridge to find out all he could. The knowledge that he was still trying to help her was bittersweet. If only she had dared to call him back. Now it was too late.

It didn't matter anyhow. He could only confirm that she was illegitimate. Nothing could change that ugly fact.

She began to shiver. The recent rains had half-filled the ditch and her cloak and gown were soaked.

Dan regarded her with a critical eye. "You look very wet. I'm not so bad. I fell on top of you."

"Thank heavens for that! When we reach Dover I'll buy you some new clothes. Meantime, I'll change my own." She reached into the satchel. "Turn your back!"

A quick glance down the lane confirmed that no one was about, so she stripped off her clammy garments and rolled them into a bundle.

"I must have gained some weight." It was a struggle to fasten the breeches, but the shirt and jacket were long, and hid the outlines of her figure.

"You'd best carry this!" She handed Dan the bundle. "They'll soak everything if I put them in the satchel. Come on! It's late. We must reach Dover before dark."

Without the protection of the heavy woollen cloak she began to shiver again. The wind had dropped and she set off at a brisk pace.

"I can't keep up with you," Dan complained. "And I've got a stitch..."

"I'm sorry, love, but I don't know this place, and we'd get lost in the dark."

She hurried him along until they reached the crossroads where the coach had set them down. From there the main road led to Dover. It was growing dusk, but there was still traffic upon the highway.

They waved to one or two of the farmers, but no one stopped for them. Then Prudence saw the swaying lantern of a larger vehicle in the distance. Of course! The mail coaches ran at regular intervals from Canterbury to Dover. She stepped out into the roadway and flagged the driver down.

At first she thought he would not stop. She was about to jump aside when he reined in the team and gave her a sour look.

"What's up?" he asked. "Is something wrong ahead?"

"I want to go to Dover," Prudence told him firmly. "Have you room for two?"

"Be off with you, my lad! I don't give free rides, and you can be had up for stopping the mails..."

"I can pay." Prudence held out her hand towards the light and opened her palm to show the coins.

"You ain't stolen them?" The man eyed her suspiciously.

"No, I have not! Will you take us?"

"I suppose so!" He scooped up the money and put it in his pocket. No need to mention that he should have given a couple of tickets. The pay was low enough, and the extra would be welcome. He'd square it with the guard.

Prudence pushed Dan ahead of her and climbed

aboard herself, ignoring the sour looks of the other pas-
sengers. She could not account for their annoyance.
There was plenty of room. Then, as the woman beside
her drew her skirts away, she understood. In her worn
corduroys and the shabby shirt and jacket she was hardly
the type of fellow-traveller to be welcomed.

"They'll take up anyone these days," the woman
complained in angry tones. "Someone should protest to
the company. We've paid our fares—"

"So have we!" Prudence stared her down.

"Impudence! Thank heavens we haven't far to go."
With an indignant sniff the woman subsided.

Prudence did not spare her a second glance. She was
trying to plan ahead. When they reached Dover it would
be too late in the evening to seek passage on any of the
ships. They must seek shelter for the night, but who
would take in two such bedraggled creatures?

It was a pity that she had been forced to change her
clothing. Landlords were quick to assess the status of
their customers from their clothing. In Sebastian's company she had seen it often enough.

The expensive woollen cloak would have been an asset, but it was still damp. No matter. She would wear it.
It was plain enough to pass for male apparel.

Whatever happened, she must not give up her disguise. A woman of her tender age and a young boy need
expect no consideration at any of the hostelries.

In the end it was neither her youth nor her appearance
which was the stumbling-block. At Dover she found that
most of the inns were full. No offer of gold could sway
the landlord where the mail coach stopped. There were
many wealthier travellers than Prudence lying beneath
his roof that night.

The same thing happened at the second inn. It was

very grand, and she was informed abruptly that all the rooms were bespoken in advance.

"What are we to do?" Dan asked anxiously.

"We'll find somewhere," she assured him. "I can't believe that everywhere is full. Perhaps if we tried a smaller place..." She turned off the main street and began to walk downhill.

"Oh, look!" Dan breathed. "We must be near the harbour. Isn't that the rigging of a ship?"

"Yes! We must be close to the docks..." Prudence felt a twinge of alarm. She had read enough to know that the dock area in any port was not considered the safest of places. "I think we should turn back..."

At least it was full moonlight, and the streets were as bright as day, though the narrow alleyways lay in shadow. Then she stiffened as she heard a cry.

A small band of men poured out of a dark entry, struggling with someone in their midst.

Prudence stopped in terror. At first she thought it was a fight between a group of drunken revellers, and her instinct was to hurry away. Then the light fell on the ashen face of a young boy, held in the grip of two burly ruffians.

"Have mercy!" he was crying. "Don't take me! My mother has no one else..."

His pleas were answered with a shout of laughter.

"You'll see her in a year or two. A sea voyage will do you the world of good..." The leader of the group stepped up to him and struck him sharply across the face. "Stop your noise, or it will be the worse for you."

Prudence clutched at the arm of a passer-by. "Can't you help him?" she pleaded. "He is being taken away against his will..."

"I can't interfere with the law," the man muttered.

"The law?" She didn't believe her ears.

"Yes, lad. That's the press-gang. Make yourself scarce, or they'll have you next…"

"But are they allowed to behave like this?" Her voice had risen in anger, and it attracted the attention of the boatswain. He began to walk towards her.

"We're in luck tonight," he shouted to his crew. "Here's another one!"

Prudence turned to find herself alone except for Dan.

"We'll take the young 'un, too. Cap'n's short of a cabin boy," the man continued.

Prudence threw her satchel at Dan's head. "Run!" she screamed. Then she was caught in an iron grip, and the man's arm went around her throat.

Wild with terror, she bent her head and bit into his arm. She heard a curse and then the world went black as he struck out with a belaying-pin.

When she opened her eyes she thought that she was dreaming. She seemed to be caught in the middle of some horrific nightmare.

Bodies lay all about her in the darkness, and the cries and groaning were those of souls in torment. Some of the men were weeping, whilst others prayed.

The stench was frightful. Beside her one of the prisoners was vomiting into the darkness, and the smell of bodily functions was all-pervasive.

Then, unbelievably, she heard the sound of laughter, and she raised her head. A group of women were crouched in the corner of this barn-like space, swilling something from a bottle. As the smell of rum reached her she was overcome by nausea. She bent her head and forced it down between her knees.

The sickness passed, but she had a blinding headache.

She reached up gingerly to feel among her curls. Her fingers touched an enormous lump, and something warm and wet. She rubbed at the moisture trickling down her cheek and found that it was blood.

It didn't seem possible, but she had been taken by the press-gang. This must be the hold of one of His Majesty's ships. It was at anchor and rocking slightly on the swell. It was an effort to lift her head, but she glanced up to find a grating just above her. Beyond it she could see the stars.

Panic seized her. If she called out she might attract attention, but what was she to say? That the boatswain had made a mistake in capturing a woman? She shuddered. It was best to hide her sex within this crowded hold.

She was under no illusions. The women in the corner were here for just one purpose. She would be classed with them.

She looked about her anxiously. She could see no sign of Dan. He must have got away. That must be her only consolation. She guessed that they were still in Dover, but she had no hope of rescue, nor could she expect to keep up her pretence for long. Once her secret was discovered the fate which lay ahead was too terrible to contemplate.

She wouldn't be put ashore. Women were allowed on board, she knew. In time of war they took their chances with the others, caring for the wounded and helping where they could. That she could bear, but not the thought of being used for pleasure. She bent her head and wept.

The night seemed endless, but at last the first pale fingers of the dawn crept across the grating. Would they sail on the morning tide? She had no way of knowing.

Then a grinning face appeared above her. It was one of the midshipmen. He called his fellows over to enjoy the spectacle.

"Crying for your mother?" he jeered. "We'll knock that out of you."

Prudence stuck out her tongue at him.

"Why, you…" He spat a stream of tobacco juice towards her.

Prudence turned her head aside. The pungent brown liquid missed her face, but it spattered across her breeches and the front of her jacket.

"Just wait until you come on deck," he threatened. "I'll remember you…"

"Don't be a fool," the man beside her hissed. "He'll make your life a living hell."

Prudence ignored him. She strained her ears. Surely she had heard another voice…?

"My lord, it can't be done!" A man in splendid uniform was standing by the grating. "I have the authority to impress these men—"

"And women, too?" Sebastian's voice was cool.

"Sir, we have no women aboard, other than those…"

"I am not speaking of your drabs. I believe my sister is down there."

"Your lordship is certainly mistaken. My bosun is a man of much experience. There is no possibility that he would molest a lady."

"He might not have realised," Sebastian answered calmly. "My sister is eccentric. It amuses her to dress up as a boy. On this occasion she was running away…some foolish love affair…you understand…?"

"I can't believe it!"

"Then you can have no objection if we make quite sure."

The grating was drawn back, and a ladder lowered into the hold.

"Prudence!" Sebastian's voice held the ring of authority. In a trance-like state she climbed up to the deck.

Sebastian took her by the arm. "Here she is! My mother will have much to say to her!"

The Captain was clearly shaken. "What can I say, my lord? When I think that we might have sailed, not knowing—"

"Quite! But I beg that you will not blame yourself. This is an end of the matter. It will go no further."

The Captain murmured his thanks as he mopped his brow. It was not for him to point out that the young lady had spent the night locked up with men who were the dregs of Dover. Sebastian was quick to allay his fears.

"You are unharmed, Prudence?" he asked in icy tones.

She nodded.

"Then let this be a lesson to you." He walked towards the rail to hail his boat, leaving Prudence shivering on the deck.

The midshipman sidled up to her. He slipped an arm about her, squeezed her breast, and murmured an obscene suggestion.

"You should have spoken," he whispered. "There was no need for you to spend the night down there."

Prudence gave him a limpid glance. He was close to the ship's ladder. She appeared to stumble, fell against him, and knocked him over the side.

Her hand flew to her mouth. "What have I done?" she cried in pretty confusion. "Oh, dear, I am so clumsy...I do hope that the man can swim."

She hurried to the ship's rail to see her victim floundering in the water. Unseen by the others, she stuck out her tongue at him.

Sebastian helped her down the ladder. He did not speak again until they were seated in the bum-boat, being rowed ashore.

"Am I to be allowed to know how that particular young man annoyed you?" he enquired in neutral tones.

"Who? Oh, you mean the one who fell overboard?"

"I mean the one you pushed..." His smile did not reach his eyes and Prudence quailed.

She had expected anger and a violent quarrel, but nothing could be more frightening that this contained fury. Sebastian's face might have been carved from stone.

"He spat tobacco juice at me," she said defensively.

"Hardly enough to warrant an attempt to drown him! Suppose you tell me the truth?"

"He made remarks which I did not care to hear."

"He did not touch you?"

"No, of course not!" Prudence dismissed the suggestion as of no importance. "Sir, have you found Dan?"

"Dan found me. We met him along the road. He'd stolen a horse and was on his way to Hallwood."

"Poor Dan! He is unharmed?"

"Quite unharmed...no thanks to you. You might reserve some of your sympathy for me. A journey with a weeping horse-thief was something of a trial."

Prudence felt an overwhelming sensation of relief. Dan was safe. She turned to her companion.

"Sir, I am so grateful for your help. You can't imagine the horrors of that ship's hold..."

"I can imagine them all too well. Pray don't attempt to thank me, Prudence. At present it is only with the greatest difficulty that I have refrained from breaking your neck.''

"Then I'm surprised you didn't leave me where I was,'' she snapped.

"I wonder why I didn't. What a delightful prospect lay ahead of you! It was no more than you deserved.''

"I should have told them…I mean… I'd have explained…''

"Of course! Who could have doubted that you were a lady?'' Sebastian's tone was ironic. "After all, just look at you! That clothing must be the height of fashion!''

"My other things were wet,'' she told him sullenly. "There is no need to be sarcastic. After all, you said that you had no wish to keep me at Hallwood against my will.''

"I didn't mean that you and Dan should wander off alone! You see where it has led? I think you might have trusted me—''

"Well, I don't! You went to Longridge without telling me.''

Sebastian looked startled. "How did you know that?''

"We saw you. Dan and I were hiding in the ditch.''

"Why didn't you call to me?''

"You'd gone before we realised. Besides, I thought you were deceiving me…''

Sebastian's eyes were cold. "Thank you! That is all I needed… It did not occur to you that I might be trying to help you?''

"Yes, it did.'' Prudence forgot her anger. "Oh, sir, did you see Lord Manvell?''

"I did.''

"And what did he tell you?''

"He told me nothing.''

Prudence bent her head. "I know that you wish to punish me," she whispered. "But I think I have the right to know."

For the first time his voice softened. "I am not lying to you. I could learn nothing from him. You were not able to get inside the place?"

"No! The lodge-keeper threatened to set the dogs on us. Then someone fired a shot—"

"I heard it. That was fired at you? My God! You might have been killed…"

"Why should you care? You've just told me that you'd like to break my neck…"

"It is a severe temptation, Prudence. Could you not have called to me?"

"You'd have stopped us from coming to Dover."

"Most certainly! I can understand your wish for a sea voyage, but you might have chosen some other form of transport rather than a navy vessel."

"You need not mock me, sir. I think I've suffered enough."

"Not nearly enough, my dear! You will suffer more before I've done with you."

They had reached the dock and he handed her ashore. "Where are you taking me?" she demanded. "I won't go back to Hallwood."

"That is not our immediate destination," he agreed. "I imagine you will wish to change your clothing, and Sam is waiting for us."

Prudence looked up as a small figure erupted from the carriage. Then Dan was in her arms, sobbing wildly as he buried his face against her.

"I thought I'd never see you again," he wept. "Oh, Pru, I thought you'd gone without me!"

"Prudence is going nowhere, and nor are you, my

lad.'' Sebastian's voice was oddly gentle. ''Will you ride on the box with Sam?''

With Dan restored to his perch, Sebastian handed Prudence into the carriage.

She rounded on him at once. ''Why did you say that?'' she demanded. ''I told you that I won't go back to Hallwood.''

''Not even as my wife?'' He tried to take her hands but she snatched them away.

''That joke is in the poorest of taste,'' she cried. ''I had not thought you capable of such cruelty.''

''It isn't a joke, my darling. It is a serious proposal.''

Prudence covered her ears. ''I won't listen to any more of this. You said you'd make me suffer and you've done so.''

''Dear love, would it be so very dreadful? I daren't risk losing you again...and you aren't indifferent to me, I believe.''

''I hate you! If you say another word I'll jump out of the coach.''

Chapter Fifteen

Sebastian did not speak to her again until they reached the inn. Then he handed her a cloak.

"You'd best wear this," he said briefly.

Prudence was tempted to refuse, but it would be folly to enter the elegant hostelry in her stained garments.

"Afraid that I'll disgrace you?" she snapped as she flung it about her shoulders.

With her head held high she stalked indoors, ignoring the bowing landlord. The courtesy was not intended for her, but for the detestable creature who followed. How surprising that a suite of rooms was now at his disposal when only yesterday there was nothing to be had.

She was shaking with anger as she was shown into a splendid chamber and she banged the door behind her.

Her leather satchel was lying upon the bed, but when she felt inside it she found that the purse of guineas was gone. That was typical, she thought bitterly. Lord Wentworth would make sure that she had not the means to run away again, but the money was her own. She would force him to return it.

She never wanted to see him again. He was heartless. She had suffered much ill-treatment in her time, but nothing had wounded her so deeply. He must have guessed how much she cared for him. She had given herself away when he had held her in his arms and kissed her. And now to use her tenderest emotions against her? His false offer was a brutal mockery. She would never forgive him. Never!

Angrily, she tipped the contents of the satchel out upon the bed. Her gowns were crumpled, but it was no matter. The green wool had survived better than the others, and her under-garments were clean and fresh.

She stripped to the skin and washed away all traces of that stinking hold in the bowl of scented water on the dressing-stand. Her hair was still short enough to dry quickly, but she would take her time. For once his lordship could wait upon her pleasure.

It was Dan who tapped upon her door.

"Do hurry, Pru!" he said impatiently. "Breakfast is ready, and I'm starving."

Prudence felt that a single mouthful of the food would choke her. She had had more than enough of Lord Wentworth's charity, but she could not disappoint the boy. In silence she accompanied him to the private parlour. Neither she nor Dan had eaten since the previous day, and her stomach was protesting loudly.

That, together with an aching head, did nothing to improve her mood. The cut behind her ear was no longer bleeding, but the lump was huge. Suddenly she felt faint.

Sebastian caught her as she swayed. "Sit down and put your head between your knees," he ordered. Then he caught sight of the ugly swelling. "Why didn't you tell me you'd been hurt?"

"You didn't give me much of a chance," she murmured.

"Dan, go and ask for a vinaigrette, or burnt feathers."

"No, I shall be perfectly all right."

"Still arguing, Prudence? I believe you'll be doing so on your deathbed. You'd try the patience of a saint... Dan, you will please to do as I ask."

He waited until the door had closed. Then he took Prudence in his arms.

"Won't you listen to me?" he said softly. "I wasn't joking, Prudence. I want you to become my wife. See, I have the licence in my pocket..."

Prudence lifted her head and looked at him. As his eyes held her own she could no longer doubt him. Her sickness vanished and suddenly she felt very calm.

"Why are you doing this?" she asked. "I thought you were betrothed to Mademoiselle de Verneuil."

"To Gabrielle? Where did you get that idea?"

"I saw you...you were holding her."

"Gabrielle was in great distress," he explained quietly. "The man she loves was imprisoned in the Tuileries with the King and Marie Antoinette. I offered to see what I could do..."

Prudence only half-believed him. "Will you go back to France?" she asked.

"A friend went on my behalf. A message reached us yesterday. Lucien has been released."

"But how?"

"Money, my dear!" he told her simply. "Sadly, no amount of gold will save the King."

"It was a noble thing for you to do, my lord. I am happy for *mademoiselle* and for the man she loves."

"And what of the man who is in love with you?" His lips were against her hair. "Tell me I'm not mistaken, dear one. I've loved you for so long, but I wouldn't admit it, even to myself. Then, on that morning when I held you in my arms I could no longer doubt it, and when you returned my kiss…''

It was only with the most wrenching effort that Prudence forced herself to deny her love.

"You were mistaken," she whispered.

"Was I?" He took her in a long, hungry embrace, and his mouth came down on hers. That kiss lasted while the world reeled about them. Prudence felt that her very soul was being lured from her breast by the inexorable power of love.

Then Sebastian held her away from him. He looked deep into her eyes. "Deceiver!" he said fondly. "Will you deny me now?"

Prudence was too shaken to do more than gaze at him. He saw the anguish in her look.

"What is it?" he whispered. "You cannot still believe that I care for Gabrielle?"

She shook her head.

"Then what? My love, I promise to make you happy."

"No, it is impossible!" Prudence found her voice at last.

"But why? I love you dearly, and I know that you love me—"

"My lord, I think you have forgot…" Her voice was raw with pain. "I am a bastard! How can you marry me?"

"My darling, I don't care. Nothing must stand in the way of our happiness—"

"Don't!" she cried brokenly. "You have not considered. Now, at this moment, you may think it does not matter, but it does. How could you face your family, your friends…?"

"Ah, yes, my family! Always so considerate of my

welfare! They have been informed of my opinion as to their interference. It will not happen again.''

"You are wrong in blaming them for helping me. Your brother gave me the money out of kindness. He did not know that I would run away."

"And Sophie?"

"Sophie was concerned for me. It was only when she knew that I was quite determined to go that she agreed to fall in with my plan."

"And much good it has done you. If Sam had not remembered some of Dan's chatter, you might still be aboard that ship. It was only by chance that we took the Dover road."

Prudence rose to her feet and moved away from him.

"I meant it for the best," she said quietly. "I can't go on like this. We shall take passage in the morning if you will return my purse of gold."

"Will you give me one more day?" he pleaded. "It's important! If you are still of the same mind by this evening, I will book your passages myself. I give you my word on it."

She gave him an uncertain look, but the expression in his eyes robbed her of all power to resist. She turned away as Dan came back to join them.

"Don't you want your breakfast, Pru?" Dan asked cheerfully. "I thought you would be hungry."

Prudence allowed him to heap some food upon her plate. Later, she could not have described the meal, although she forced down a mouthful or two.

"Sam said that we were to leave at ten o'clock," Dan continued. "Are we going back to Hallwood, sir?"

"Not for the moment. Our route will take us across country, but you won't mind the drive, I think?"

"Oh, no, my lord." Dan was unaware of the tension in the room. "I like to ride on the box with Sam."

It was only as they were leaving Dover that Prudence permitted herself a question.

"Where are we going?" she asked. "Did you not promise to book passage for us?"

"Only upon condition that you are of the same mind this evening..." Sebastian relapsed into silence and she did not question him further.

There was nothing he could say or do which would alter her determination in the least, but for this one day she would humour him. And it was not just because he'd asked it of her. She was too weak to resist the longing to spend a few more hours in his company.

He said nothing to her as the carriage rolled through the autumn countryside. The first leaves were beginning to fall beneath a sky that was dark and threatening. It matched her mood, she thought in despair. This was the end of summer...an end of all that was bright and filled with life. From this day her path would be hard and lonely.

Her eyes were stinging with unshed tears and her throat ached. They might have been so happy. It had been bittersweet to discover that Sebastian's love for her was deep enough to persuade him to disregard all that was due to his family and himself.

She could not allow him to make that sacrifice. In time he would grow to hate her. He might be received in the world he knew, but she most certainly would not, and their children would be shunned.

She gazed through the window with unseeing eyes until they had been travelling for some time. Then something about the lie of the land attracted her attention. It should not have looked familiar but it did. When they reached the crossroads, she was sure of it.

"Isn't this the way to Longridge?" she exclaimed.

Sebastian nodded.

"Why have you brought me here? There is no point. If Lord Manvell would not speak to you, it isn't likely that he'll tell me anything. I doubt if we'll get through the gates…"

She was mistaken. The gates in the wall were already open. The dogs were silent, and there was no sign of the lodge-keeper.

Sam guided the team along the curving drive past an avenue of ancient oaks until they reached the building in the distance. As he drew up at the portico, Sebastian jumped down.

"Dan, will you stay with Sam? We shan't be long…" He turned to Prudence. "Come! We are to go straight in."

It was with the utmost trepidation that Prudence followed him. The sinking feeling in her stomach did not lessen as they walked through the empty hall. The place was as silent as a tomb. No servant came to greet them. Then she heard the creaking of a door.

"Lord Wentworth?" a low and musical voice enquired.

Sebastian turned and bowed. "It's a pleasure to meet you, Lady Woodforde. May I present Miss Consett?"

As Prudence sank into a curtsy, he swept back the hood from her face and hair with one swift gesture. Then she heard a low cry.

"Frances…?"

Prudence looked at the speaker in surprise.

"No, Lady Woodforde. My given name is Prudence."

Then she stepped forward to offer her assistance. Her ladyship was unwell, and seemed about to faint.

"Ma'am, won't you sit down?" she said. "May we ring for your maid?" She felt alarmed. Every vestige of colour had drained from the woman's face.

"No! Give me a moment!" The whisper from those pallid lips was almost inaudible. "Sir, will you help me? I must sit down…" She gestured towards an open door.

Sebastian took her arm. "My apologies, ma'am. I had hoped to prepare you. At your home they told me that you'd come to Longridge, but yesterday I was told that you were gone out."

"It was true! I had some matters to attend at Dover…" Lady Woodforde did not look at him. Her eyes were fixed on Prudence. "Let me look at you," she whispered. "Will you come into the light?"

She sank into a sofa by the window and drew Prudence down beside her. Then her eyes devoured the fine-boned face, as clear cut as that of a young lad's.

"You are so like her…there can be no mistake… Oh, my dear, you might be your own mother, returned to us after all these years…" Slow tears were trickling down her cheeks.

"Lady Woodforde, you are quite sure? I won't have Prudence hurt again." Sebastian stood before them, tall and straight, but there was a warning in his voice.

"Let me show you…I have a miniature which I keep always with me." Her ladyship reached into her reticule and handed him the trinket.

Sebastian's face was sad as he passed it on to Prudence, but she did not notice. The face which looked back at her was the image of her own.

"This is my mother?" she demanded eagerly. "Where is she, ma'am? I long to see her…"

Dread seized her as a silence followed her words.

"Oh, you will not tell me that she is dead?" Her expression was pitiful and Lady Woodforde took her hand.

"She died when you were born, my dear."

"Was that why I was given up? Could you not have kept me? What of my father?"

"Your father was killed some months before your birth. Prudence, you cannot wish to hear the details."

"But I do. I have waited all my life to learn the truth!"

"Will you ask me to relive my sister's suffering, child?" Lady Woodforde's face was a mask of agony.

"Ma'am, I think you must. Prudence has suffered, too. You cannot send her away without an explanation." Sebastian's voice was gentle, but he was insistent.

"Send her away? No! Never! To find her like this? You cannot know how much it means to me."

"Then, my dear ma'am, let us have the truth… You owe her that, at least."

"We owe her more, but it is a dreadful story…and another person is involved."

"Your ladyship, you must not fear to hurt me." Suddenly Prudence felt a rush of affection for this troubled woman. "Don't you understand? Anything is better than not knowing about my natural parents." She took Lady Woodforde's cold hand in her own.

"You may not think so…but if you will have it I must not deny you. Won't you sit down, sir? This may take some time… Let me ring for wine."

Prudence was about to refuse the offer of refreshment but a look from Sebastian silenced her. Lady Woodforde was badly in need of a restorative, and when the tray appeared he poured her a small glass of brandy. She took a sip or two and the colour returned to her cheeks.

"Prudence, when you were born your mother was just nineteen. Two years beforehand she had met the man she loved, but our father would not hear of the match."

"Why was that?"

"He'd promised her in wedlock to our neighbour, a man even older than himself. Your father was young, and had his way to make, though he came of an ancient family."

Her eyes were reflective as she looked at Prudence. "I think you must be like your mother in temperament. She was strong-willed and most determined. When John Herries suggested an elopement she didn't hesitate. I was fifteen at the time, and I thought it so romantic. If I had only known..." she stopped, unable to continue.

"Pray don't distress yourself," Prudence urged. "Do you wish to rest? We are in no hurry..."

"No! Let me go on." Lady Woodforde took another sip of brandy. "My...my father followed then. He found them three days later. They were married by then, of course, but it made no difference..."

"Married?" Prudence was shaken out of her fragile composure. "But I thought I was a bas—I mean, a love child?"

"You were indeed a child born of love, my dear. I never saw two people more devoted to each other. And they had so little time together..." Her eyes were glistening with tears.

"But surely Lord Manvell was too late? He could not come between husband and wife. My father must have told him so."

Lady Woodforde buried her face in her hands. She

was sobbing openly. "John was never given the chance. My father struck him down. He died that day."

Without thinking, Prudence reached out to Sebastian for support, and he took her hand in his.

"Are you telling me that Lord Manvell murdered him?" she whispered.

"It was hushed up and claimed to be an accident. There was some mention of a duel, but Frances told me later that your father was unarmed. She was brought back to Longridge, and shut away upstairs."

The memory was too much for her and she began to shudder, but she forced herself to continue.

"We didn't know at first that she was pregnant. The fashion then was concealing, and she was terrified for her child. My father found out in the end, of course, and he must have made his plans. He took you away on the day that you were born, and Frances was told that you were dead."

Prudence was shaking uncontrollably and Sebastian sat beside her to take her in his arms. As she was about to speak he shook his head.

"Let her go on," he said quietly. "This must be the first time she has told the story. It will help her."

Lady Woodforde seemed to have forgotten them. She was speaking aloud, but it was to herself.

"Darling Frances! It was the end for her. She'd heard her baby cry, and she didn't believe him. She thought he'd taken you away to kill you, as he did your father. She died a few days later. There was no reason for it. She did not have the fever. She just lost the will to live."

Prudence was too distressed to speak, though she knew what she must do.

"I want to see him," she said at last.

"My father? Oh, Prudence, please…you must not…"

"But I know he's still alive. Sebastian told me so, and I've promised myself this meeting. Are you afraid that he will injure you…that you should not have told me? Pray don't worry, ma'am. He shall not harm you."

"It isn't that! He cannot harm me now, but I beg of you to heed my words."

"My darling, it can do no good." Sebastian rested his hand upon her shoulder.

"I thought you said you loved me?" Her voice was high and clear. "Can you know so little of me? This is something I must do." The burning anger in her eyes convinced her listeners that she would not be deterred. "I will have justice! He shall learn what he has done to me and those who were entitled to my affections."

"Then come with me!" Lady Woodforde rose to her feet. She led the way through the gloomy hall and up a winding staircase. They walked for some distance along a corridor on the second floor until they reached a heavy oaken door at the end of the passageway. There she produced a massive key and inserted it into the lock.

"Go in!" she said quietly.

As Sebastian made to follow her, Lady Woodforde held him back.

"I think she must do this alone!" she said. "There is no danger. He is quiet this morning."

Prudence did not hear the low exchange. She walked quickly over the threshold and into the semi-darkness of an enormous bedchamber. A glance showed her that the bed was unoccupied, and at first she thought it was a trick. There was no one here.

She walked over to the windows and drew aside the heavy curtains. Then she heard a cry.

"No! Not the light! I don't want the light!"

She spun round. Then she stopped, transfixed by the

sight of the figure seated in one corner. He was huddled in an invalid chair, half-hidden by a mass of rugs.

Then, as she walked towards him, he threw up both his arms as if to ward off some dreadful vision.

"You've come at last?" he croaked. "I've been expecting you. For all these years I've been expecting you. You wouldn't rest easy in your grave, would you, Frances? Why have you waited so long? Was it to torture me?"

Prudence hadn't noticed the other occupant of the room until the man came towards her.

"He's rambling, miss. Don't let him upset you... He gets these strange notions, thinking he sees ghosts..."

He turned as two claw-like hands reached out for his throat.

"No, you don't, my lord. I've got eyes in the back of my head. You won't catch me again..."

Prudence shrank away. The speed of the sudden attack had shocked her. She had thought the old man incapable of such swift movement. Now he was babbling as he was thrust back into his chair.

The rugs had fallen away and she could see the strength in the short squat body, but it was his eyes which held her. They were wild with terror.

"He's best without visitors, Miss. They only frighten him, as her ladyship will tell you." The man began to replace the rugs, until only the old man's hands were visible.

Prudence could not take her eyes from them. Blood pulsed through the raised blue veins, and the skin was spotted with brown marks of age. Those hands had snuffed the life out of her father, and in doing so they had killed her mother, whilst she herself had been abandoned to a life of hardship.

But she had survived. Suddenly all her anger left her. This evil old man had paid and would go on paying for his wickedness. She could not have wished a worse fate upon him, living as he did in this half-world of horror and dread. She turned away.

"I'd like to go now, if you please," she said to Sebastian.

Lady Woodforde slipped an arm about her waist as they walked down the staircase. "That sight was not fit for your eyes, my love. I tried to warn you…"

"No, I understand, but I'm glad I came." Prudence was badly shaken, but now her thoughts were for her aunt. Her aunt? Impulsively she kissed the older woman.

"I have made you suffer, too," she said sadly. "I am sorry for it."

"My dear, you have brought great joy, in spite of everything. To find a dear niece…my own sister's child…I cannot tell you what it means to me."

"Ma'am, you will come to stay with us after we are married?" Sebastian did not look at Prudence as he spoke.

"You are to be married? I guessed as much. My dears, I wish you happy." She took Prudence in her arms. "I shall expect an invitation to your wedding."

She was smiling as she waved them off.

"Prudence, you are very quiet!" Sebastian's hand was gripping her own. "No more arguments?"

"Arguments, sir? Why should I argue with you?" Her face with its secret eyes and slow-curving smile was turned away from him.

"Oh, I thought you might find some reason…the choice of church…or our honeymoon destination…"

"I haven't said I'll marry you," she said demurely.

"Come here, you tantalising creature, or I'll box your ears."

He kissed her then and for a time the world was lost in the wonder of their love. She was breathless when he released her, only to press his lips against the fluttering pulse inside her wrist. His mouth was warm against her skin and she felt a delicious tingle of excitement.

With a sigh she rested her head against his shoulder.

"I didn't think you'd noticed me," she confessed. "Not in that way, I mean…"

"What! Do you think me blind? How could I fail to notice you? After all, you tried to kill me when we first met."

"I was dressed as a boy," she reminded him happily.

"You didn't deceive me for an instant. I think I must have loved you from the start. But, Prudence, you won't do that again, I hope?"

"Try to kill you, my lord? Not unless I have good reason…such as another woman…" She laughed up at him, confident of his love.

"You need have no fear of that. You are all that I desire. No other woman in the world possesses your courage, your spirit, and your strength of character."

"I thought you wanted to box my ears," she teased.

"I may yet do so," he said fondly. "You know exactly what I mean. There is to be no more dressing up in breeches."

"They were useful," she mused with a wicked look.

"And each time you wore them you managed to get into trouble. From now on, I intend to wear the breeches in our household. And another thing, Prudence, I will not have you addressing me either as 'sir', or 'my lord'. My name is Sebastian. Do you understand me?"

"Yes, Sebastian." She laid a loving hand against his

cheek. "You are so dear to me," she whispered. "I ran away because I could not bear to be so close to you and yet so far. I thought I must betray myself…"

"You hid your feelings well." He was laughing down at her. "Sometimes I despaired of winning you. You can be the prickliest, most exasperating creature in the world."

"And yet you love me?" she said in wonder.

"Can you doubt it?"

"No, I don't doubt it," she said slowly. "You asked me to be your wife before you knew that I was…"

"Respectable?" he offered helpfully.

"Well, yes."

"You are mistaken. I don't consider you in the least respectable…after all, you tried to join the navy…that is most unsuitable for a woman." His eyes were twinkling as he looked at her.

"I did not!" she cried indignantly. "I was hit on the head…"

"Ah, yes! How is your head? We seem to have forgotten your injuries." He reached up to touch the bruise.

"I can't feel it any more."

"Good!" He ruffled her hair with the old familiar gesture. "I can't take you back to Hallwood with a lump upon your head. My mother will fear the worst. When I left the house she was most insistent that I should not beat you senseless."

"I thought you might very well do so…that is…if you ever found me."

"There was no doubt that I should find you, even without Dan's help. I knew that all I had to do was to make enquiries as to a recent fracas in the town. Trouble follows you like honey bees to a hive, my love."

"You should not make game of me," she reproached

him. "You seem always to be laughing at the things I do."

"Would you have me frown at you? My darling, you have had little happiness in your life. From now on I want to see you laugh yourself. My only wish is to protect you from all misery. I wish you could believe me."

"I do!" When she looked up at him her heart was in her eyes.

"Then kiss me, sweet." He pressed his mouth into the hollow of her neck, seeking, demanding in an urgency of passion.

Prudence bent her head and found his lips.

"Sebastian, I love you," she said softly.

As his mouth came down on hers the past was washed away. Now all that mattered was the future.

* * * * *

Modern Romance™
...seduction and
passion guaranteed

Tender Romance™
...love affairs that
last a lifetime

Sensual Romance™
...sassy, sexy and
seductive

Blaze Romance™
...the temperature's
rising

Medical Romance™
...medical drama on
the pulse

Historical Romance™
...rich, vivid and
passionate

27 new titles every month.

*With all kinds of Romance for
every kind of mood...*

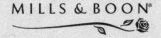

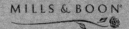

The **Elizabethan** *Collection*

Two historic tales of love, treason and betrayal...

Hot-blooded desire...cold-blooded treason...

Two dramatic tales set in the passionate times of Elizabeth I

Paula Marshall & Marie-Louise Hall

ONLY £5.99

On sale 20th December 2002

Available at most branches of WH Smith, Tesco, Martins, Borders, Eason, Sainsbury's and all good paperback bookshops.

1202/24/MB59

MILLS & BOON

Helen Brooks

Lynne Graham

Kim Lawrence

BUSINESS
Affairs

Three brand-new stories about falling for the boss

Available from 17th January 2003

*Available at most branches of WH Smith,
Tesco, Martins, Borders, Eason, Sainsbury's
and all good paperback bookshops.*

0203/24/MB62

Don't miss *Book Six* of this BRAND-NEW 12 book collection 'Bachelor Auction'.

Who says money can't buy love?

On sale 7th February